The Polish Woman

Also by Eva Mekler

FICTION

Sunrise Shows Late

NONFICTION

Bringing Up a Moral Child (Co-author)

Contemporary Scenes for Student Actors

The Actor's Scenebook

The Actor's Scenebook, Volume II

The New Generation of Acting Teachers

Masters of the Stage:
British Acting Teachers Talk About Their Craft

The Polish Woman

A Novel

Eva Mekler

BRIDGE WORKS PUBLISHING
BRIDGEHAMPTON, NEW YORK

Published by Bridge Works Publishing Company,
Bridgehampton New York

Distributed in the United States by National Book Network, Lanham,
Maryland. For descriptions of this and other Bridge Works books,
visit the National Book Network Web site at www.nbnbooks.com

FIRST EDITION

The characters and events in this book are fictitious. Any similarity to actual
persons, living or dead, is coincidental and not intended by the author.

Library of Congress Cataloging-in-Publication Data
Mekler, Eva.
The Polish woman : a novel / by Eva Mekler. — 1st ed.
p. cm.
ISBN-13: 978-1-882593-99-6 (alk. paper)
ISBN-10: 1-882593-99-5 (alk. paper)
1. Poles — New York (State) — New York — Fiction.   2. Jewish women
— Fictioin.   3. Holocaust survivors — Fiction.   4. Inheritance succession
— Fiction.   5. Jews — Identity — Fiction.   6. Jewish fiction.
I. Title.
PS3563.E423P65   2007
813'.54 — dc22   2006034130

2 4 6 8 10 9 7 5 3 1

The paper used in this publication meets the minimum requirements of American
National Standard for Information Sciences— Permanence of
Paper for Printed Library Materials ASNI/NISO Z39.48 — 1992.

Manufactured in the United States of America

For Michael and Julia

Acknowledgments

Many people helped bring this book to life. I am deeply grateful to Nancy Weber and Joshua Karton, and to Mark Alpert, Johanna Fiedler, Steve Goldstone, Dave King, Melissa Knox, Louise Farmer-Smith, Nancy Kline, Susan Malus, and Betsy Mangan.

Special thanks to my agent, Al Zuckerman, and to Claire.

Part I

Part I

Chapter 1

It had been raining since early morning. Karolina Staszek sniffed the animal scent of damp wool from winter coats and jackets that filled the overheated subway car and felt her eyes begin to itch. She pulled off a glove and rubbed her lids hard. The train was half-empty at this mid-morning hour, and most of the passengers looked half asleep. Across the aisle, a droopy-eyed student, probably on his way to classes at a Manhattan college, buried his chin in his scarf and stared at a textbook balanced on his knees. Next to him, a broad-shouldered man in workman's boots with a metal lunch box propped on his lap slumped in his seat, dozing.

Karolina herself had not slept well the night before. She'd not slept well in weeks really, moving through her days groggy and distracted as if her mind and body inhabited separate universes. Everything had changed since she'd seen Jake Landau's picture and obituary in the newspaper; now, the thought of presenting his nephew, Philip, with her extraordinary story made her nervous.

She pulled out her compact and inspected her face again. Today, the tiny crow's feet fanning out from the corners of her eyes made her look older than twenty-nine and she rubbed at the lines, worried that her pale, drawn face gave the impression she was insincere. She snapped shut her compact and tossed it back in her shoulder bag. It was pointless to worry. She needed to concentrate on how best to explain herself. Where should she begin? With her childhood memories? When she first had an inkling that something was wrong? Or last month when she saw Jake Landau's obituary? Did it really matter since she knew she was likely to spill out her thoughts and feelings as they presented themselves? Noah Landau believed she was telling the truth about her relationship to his Uncle Jake. So why not Philip? But Noah had been infatuated with her since the day she came to work for him and she suspected he'd believe anything she told him. Noah had cautioned her that Philip, Jake's other nephew, might be hard to persuade. He told her Philip was smart, quick-witted and hard working — he'd graduated at the top of his class in law school — but he could also be arrogant and strong-willed, a lawyer with a lawyer's cynical turn of mind, Noah had added, not without a trace of dislike for this cousin.

Karolina was suddenly afraid. What if Philip Landau didn't believe her? What if in her eagerness to convince him that she was telling the truth, she became confused and her English failed her, and he ended up thinking she was a fraud? Perhaps she should put off seeing him. Her life was so uncertain, so unstable. She could lose her job and then she'd be even more dependent on Jim, just when their affair was beginning to fade.

No, it was too late to back out. Delaying her meeting with Philip Landau might make Noah think she was an unprincipled schemer.

The train slowly made its way across the Williamsburg Bridge to Manhattan. Karolina gazed out the rain-splattered window at the East River and thought of Warsaw and how mist hovered over the Vistula in just such weather. Her mind wandered back to dark winter mornings, to the feel of a heavy blanket tucked around her shoulders, and her father beside her in the wagon, driving her to school down the frozen, hard-packed road. Thinking of home and how loved she'd felt when her parents were alive, filled her with deep pleasure; still, she knew that whatever comfort she derived from envisioning Warsaw or Lubartow or Lublin would inevitably turn painful. Happy memories always exact a price.

Paper rustled at her side. An elderly man in a heavy tweed overcoat had snapped open a newspaper with the headlines: PROTESTERS GATHER IN NEWARK FOR ANTI-WAR RALLY AS U.S. PLANES POUND HANOI. Every day the tabloids screamed of anti-Vietnam marches and race riots in the largest typeface the front page could accommodate. Nineteen-sixty-seven was drawing to a close and it seemed to Karolina that America was coming apart. A few months ago, blacks in Detroit tried to burn down their city. Last month, young men publicly destroyed their draft cards in an act of defiance that in Poland would have sent them to jail for the rest of their lives. Karolina marveled at the audaciousness of Americans. How far could the police be pushed, she wondered, before they started shooting everyone in sight?

She recalled a Saturday the previous May, when Jim managed to steal away from his family for a few hours. In the six months since he'd brought her to the States on an art grant, they'd been rendezvousing weekly at his friend's midtown apartment. But the place was not available on weekends, so this time they had met in front of the fountain in Central Park. They'd been unaware that an anti-Vietnam rally had taken place in another part of the park until protesters straggled by, some still holding up their homemade signs, like school children showing off their art work. The group moved slowly down the path, looking wearily content and giving off an air of quiet camaraderie. She and Jim stopped to watch, and as the marchers moved past her, she saw on their faces a sincerity of purpose and conviction that moved her deeply. These were people who knew who they were and where they belonged. Had she ever felt this sure of her place in the world?

Mounted police had appeared on a nearby rise. Their faces, half-hidden by helmets, gave them an anonymous, sinister presence. Jim pulled her onto a grassy knoll, far enough away to be safe, close enough to witness any incident. The officers hovered a moment, then tapped their spurs, and in what seemed like an instant, they were bearing down on the marchers, herding them, pushing them toward the park exit where they had been heading all along. People scrambled out of the way. Some fell to the ground and dropped their signs; others rolled onto the grass, then righted themselves and fled. Within a few minutes, everyone had dispersed. The police brought their horses to a standstill and surveying the scene with silent disdain, slowly, deliberately trampled on the abandoned posters, crushing the cardboard and splintering the wood, giving any protestors still looking on one last reminder of who was in charge, one last indignity to remember.

Tears welled up in Karolina and she had leaned into Jim's shoulder and wept. No weapons had been drawn that day and no one had been badly hurt, yet the almost-violence, the humiliation of that afternoon stayed with her like the shadow of a physical pain. She had cried, long after Jim had gone home to his wife, long after she had returned to her apartment alone. She cried until she no longer knew if she were crying for herself, for Jim, for their dying affair or for her ever-diminishing faith in the possibility of peace. There would always be hatred and violence in the world. The human race seemed addicted to it.

Now, the train was speeding past the 51st Street platform and with a stab of panic she realized she had missed her stop. She'd have to transfer to a downtown local or get off at the next station and walk the ten blocks back to Landau's law office on West 49th Street. A half-hour earlier it had been raining hard in Brooklyn; even if it had cleared up now, the air would still be biting cold.

Before leaving Williamsburg, she'd called Landau and Gottlieb and asked the secretary if Mr. Landau would be in his office all morning. Yes, his secretary said, and when she told Karolina she needed an appointment, Karolina thanked her and hung up. She didn't know why she wanted to arrive unannounced, but she trusted that using Noah's name would get her seen.

Karolina stood up and clasped her coat collar to her neck. Nothing she'd told herself had calmed her, and now she was feeling damp and feverish with anxiety. She adjusted her scarf more securely around her head and waited for the door to open. Yes, she would walk. The sting of cold air on her face would feel good. It would clear her mind, it would rejuvenate her, it would give her time to gather up her courage before she confronted Jake's nephew, Philip Landau.

The day the Polish woman came into Philip Landau's life he arrived early at the office intending to tell Simon he wanted to end their partnership. He busied himself all morning rechecking the details of an upcoming traffic accident trial and now it was approaching noon and he still hadn't made the short walk down the hall to face Simon. Normally, he had no trouble shelving qualms once he'd made up his mind. Not that he hadn't given a lot of thought to making the break — he'd been gearing up for a big life change since the end of his marriage two years earlier — yet each time he pictured Simon, he put it off. His partner would be hurt and angry — all the emotions he himself would feel if he were left stranded just as business was starting to pick up.

He gazed across the room at the photo Ellen had taken of him and Simon at a Knicks' game the year before. They'd just signed on a malpractice suit they were sure would land them a sizable settlement and they stood in the Garden's back row with their arms slung around each other's shoulders, grinning deliriously into the camera. Those were good times. He and Ellen had been seeing each other for about a month. They talked law passionately. Made love passionately.

Philip gave his hair a quick, rough rake and let out an exasperated sigh. Was it loyalty to Simon or just plain guilt? Probably both. Simon counted on him for friendship, for legal advice, even for tips on handling the difficult women he was addicted to, and although Philip felt flattered, he might have enjoyed the hero-worship if their partnership had brought them more success. They'd been friends since law school and cocky enough to believe that, with Philip's trial skills and Simon's boyish charm, they could slave a few years, make a reputation as big-time litigators, then move on to the work they'd dreamt about — Philip back to civil rights and constitutional law, Simon ready to storm into his banker father's corporate world having proved he could make a six-figure salary on his own.

It hadn't worked out that way. After eight years of practicing law in the world of backroom deals and politicos in judges' robes, all they'd acquired was a bad case of cynicism and a client list of small-time litigation and negligence suits that barely covered expenses. Simon might think it okay to be taking home a few hundred a week, but Philip had come to the end of a long, dismal road. He hadn't gone to law school to become a businessman, a Hessian, a hit-man-for-hire. He was tired of living in a state of suspended misery, tired of dragging himself to work to face the assortment of house closings and landlord-tenant squabbles that littered his desk. Last month, when his Uncle Jake died and left him $300,000, he felt he'd been handed a reprieve. Jake's money could buy him time to find his way back into civil rights. *And* put Alice in private school. *And* pay his ex-wife her alimony on time.

During the year they'd been dating, Ellen had seen his unhappiness up close and had started needling him. A committed Legal Aid attorney, she was eager for him to stop chasing money and do something "relevant" — her favorite word and one that made him wince. "You're deluding yourself if you believe you'll just walk away from a lucrative practice once you have one," she told him, and although Philip had his own ideas about what motivated most of the do-gooders she worked with, he suspected she was right.

So last night he'd called Abe Drottman.

Gearing up the courage to make the call wasn't easy. He hated asking for favors, not because he feared being indebted, but out of personal shame at needing anything from anyone. There were other firms he could check out, but if he were going to risk his small income for a position that might earn him even less, it would have to be with the best. Which Abe was. His old professor had marched with King in Selma and Montgomery, and over the last decade had become a star defender of high-profile civil rights cases. Philip had been one of his favorite students at Columbia and they'd kept in touch during Philip's brief tenure at the ACLU. When he left to go into personal injury law, Abe cut him loose, relegating him, Philip supposed, to the rank of ambulance chaser. Philip rarely paid attention to what people thought of him; still, Abe's silence cut him.

After agonizing over what he'd say, Philip told himself he'd sound like a fool if he was anything but his usual blunt self, and since he wasn't sure that Abe would even take his call, he decided to try him at home. When Abe got on the line, Philip told him straight out what he wanted. Abe went silent for a long moment and Philip braced himself for a royal snub. Then, in a voice that said he'd been waiting for Philip to come to his senses, Abe asked if he was willing to work on a civil rights violation case.

"The American Jewish Congress is representing a Jew who was refused accommodations at an Atlanta hotel and I've assembled a top-notch team for the case. We're working *pro bono* for the organization, but I can give you a small salary. And who knows? Maybe you could learn something," Abe added in his customary sardonic drone. "Maybe you can even be of help," he threw in with a mollifying laugh. "I'll be in midtown around one tomorrow. I can fill you in. Interested?"

Philip was stunned. "Sure, I'd like to hear more," he said, managing a cool, professional tone, yet when he replaced the receiver his

8

hand trembled. He flopped down on the couch, then sprang up a moment later and began pacing around the living room, trying to sort out his thoughts. He'd just been offered a chance to work with one of the best legal minds in the country! And on a Jewish case! What could be better? A hero, a Jewish hero. Or about to be. Odd, he thought, that this should come to mind.

Now, Philip gazed out his office window at the rainy, mist-bound spires of St. Patrick's Cathedral, leaned back in his chair and felt a spike of exhilaration, something he rarely permitted himself. He'd take Simon to lunch somewhere quiet. He'd explain. He'd reassure him that he'd always be there for him, always be available for consults, still be his buddy. Simon would understand. He'd get over it. He'd have to.

He was about to dial Simon's extension when he heard a rustle and, looking up, found Dorothy standing at the door, smoothing back the gray hairs that were always drifting down from her bun.

"There's a woman outside to see you," Dorothy said, rolling her eyes toward the waiting room. "She doesn't have an appointment."

"Know who she is?"

"She said your cousin Noah sent her. She has an accent."

They exchanged knowing looks. His family was always sending him feisty widows eager to sue some Miami Hotel for a lumpy mattress or their landlord for a chipped lobby tile. But every once in a while European immigrants like his father or camp survivors like his Uncle Jake showed up with stories that tore at his heart — only they could talk away half the day if he let them. So he and Dorothy had a little rescue plan going: If he wanted more time with the person, he'd buzz and tell her; if not, she'd come in after fifteen minutes and gravely inform him that his next appointment was waiting.

"Okay, send her in."

The woman stood in the doorway for a moment, a tall, lean figure in a black vinyl raincoat and high-heeled leather boots, untying a silky mustard-yellow scarf she wore on her head. She looked somewhere in her late twenties and more handsome than pretty, with a broad, high-cheekboned face, widely spaced blue eyes, and a fringe of light brown hair hanging in damp strands across her forehead. Her vinyl coat still glistened with raindrops. As Philip rose to greet her, he remembered his father mentioning that Noah had hired a Polish

9

nanny to take care of his three-year-old daughter. "A Polish *shiksa* no less," his father had added bitterly, "to bring up a Jewish child."

"Excuse me, please," the woman said politely. Her voice was high-pitched, but pleasant, her accent decidedly Slavic. As she moved into the office, her stiff coat crinkled and Philip couldn't decide if she was trying to look like Audrey Hepburn or one of those Warhol Chelsea girls who seemed to turn up on every magazine cover these days.

"This is a surprise," Philip said, taking in her sharp, almost day-glo blue eyes. "Usually my family never sends me anyone under sixty."

She looked confused, then smiled tentatively, exposing a row of small, perfectly shaped teeth. "Thank you for seeing me. Noah sent me. I am nanny to his little girl, Amanda."

"I know."

"Ah, he told you I was coming?"

"No. I figured it out."

She gave him a quizzical look, then put out her hand and gave his a quick, firm shake. "Staszek. Karolina Staszek."

"Please. Take a seat." Without taking his eyes off her, he tented his hands and rolled over the possibilities. Noah had sent him a green card problem. Or maybe this woman had found herself a hippie willing to marry her just to make a statement against The Establishment and now she needed someone to finalize the papers. Any lawyer could handle this, but Philip was the only lawyer in the family and the price was right. True, she was appealing in an earthy, European way, but suddenly she seemed like too much work. He glanced at his watch. It was after noon. He should call somewhere nice and make reservations for lunch.

She caught his glance and half-stood. "You are busy now."

"I've only got a few minutes," Philip said, "but go ahead."

"No, no, I must tell you whole story and there is not enough time now." Tilting her head to the side, she considered him briefly, then lowered her eyes. "But I can come back," she said. "Is this okay?"

Her odd mixture of candor and coyness struck him as flirtatious, a package he wasn't used to. And those eyes. He relaxed in his chair. "Give me a minute. Let me see if I can postpone my appointment."

Relief flooded her face. She perched herself on the edge of the chair and placed her hands over the black shoulder bag she'd propped on her lap. "Thank you."

He picked up the phone and buzzed Dorothy. She answered immediately.

"Do I need to bail you out?"

"No, just tell my appointment I'll be a little late."

"Not a typical family friend, I gather."

"Not at all." He hung up. "Please," he said, nodding. "Go ahead."

"Thank you. I am grateful." In the short silence that followed, he pulled out a pack of Lucky Strikes and a small box of wooden matches from his desk drawer, then looked at her. "You permit?" she asked, looking up. When he nodded, she accepted the cigarette and lit it. "I have been nervous all morning about coming here because I must tell you my story is strange. It is strange because I myself am not sure how much is true. That is why I come to you for help. I thought I was ready to tell this, but. . . ." She let out a nervous laugh, dismissing her silliness. "I come here from Poland one year ago. I won grant to study sculpture in United States."

"Oh? I thought it was hard to get a visa from a Communist country."

"Yes, but since Gomulka is president we have new freedom for artists. Sadly, now I hear from friends in Warsaw these things change." A small frown appeared on her forehead as she struggled to collect her thoughts. "When my grant was finished I wanted to stay in your country, so I asked director of Polish-American Foundation, Mr. Jim Lubetski, for job in his office and he gives me job. My Polish friends warned me I would be unhappy in America, knowing no one in art, but I thought to myself, I am unhappy in Poland, so what is difference? A few weeks ago, I left —"

"I wish I could help you, but immigration law is not my area," Philip interrupted.

"This is not a worry. I have papers." She gazed somberly at the floor a moment. "I wanted to leave Foundation job . . . for personal reasons and then —" She lifted her shoulders in a helpless shrug. "What to do? I thought maybe I could work for New York Arts Council your Mayor Lindsay set up, but with my poor English, this was not possible. People told me artists here work in restaurants, but

11

for me children are more interesting than serving coffee, no? Even when I was student in Lublin, I like to work in nursery."

"Lublin? Did Noah tell you our family is originally from there?" Philip said, warming to her. "*Ja rozmawiam po polsku,*" he said, giving the "*r*" his best trill.

She let out a delighted laugh. "*Naprawdę mówisz po polsku.*"

Philip stopped, startled by the unfamiliar pitch and melody of Polish without a Yiddish accent. "No, not fluently, but I understand a lot. My father and his brothers spoke it to each other when I was a kid." What he didn't tell her was that the Landaus had no love for Poles and only spoke Polish when they fell to reminiscing about their life before the war. It was at times like these, when his uncles communicated in the language of their youth, that Philip caught a glimpse of the light-hearted young man his grouch of a father must have been — which was maybe why he, Philip, still had a fondness for the language.

"Oh, there is much to tell," she said, waving her arm dramatically. "But I have to say this in correct order. I feel I am not so crazy when I speak it to someone else." She tossed back her hair, exposing a strong chin and long neck, and squinted through a cloud of rising smoke.

"When I was still at Foundation a person in office showed me . . . what is the word for notice of person who has died?"

"Obituary?"

"Yes, obituary in newspaper. My friend said, look, this person was born in Lublin like you. I read in newspaper this Jewish man, Jake Landau, was in Maidenek concentration camp and his first wife and daughter died in war. When I saw his picture I felt strange shiver as if something I once knew touched me. And the name, Landau, I say, I know this name. But how can this be? All morning I stare at his picture, trying to find in myself what was so familiar. Then I see his funeral is in place near Foundation office so I go." She shifted uncomfortably in her chair and began to fuss with her collar. "There were many people sitting in chapel who spoke kindly of this man. I stand in back, waiting to hear something, I do not know what, that would explain why I came here. Then a little girl ran down the aisle, crying. She bumps into me and I pet her head, and speak softly to calm her. A woman came to take her, but child was crying so hard I follow them to lobby and make a puppet from my scarf to amuse her. The little one stopped and the woman thanked me for my help. Later, when people were leaving, this woman — it is Noah's wife, Linda — comes to me and asks how I know her family. I was embarrassed to say — it sounds crazy, no? — so I make up story that I walked by and became curious because of big crowd. Linda complimented me, saying I was very good with children and I say this is because I have experience in nursery in Poland. I am working now, I tell her, but want to find job with children. She is pleased and says she needs a nanny for her Amanda. We talk a little more and I give her Foundation telephone number, saying she must check with director Jim Lubetski to know that I am good, responsible person."

Here she stopped abruptly, as if something had suddenly occurred to her. "I saw you leave with a woman, an older woman who is crying. I notice because you are handsome man." She delivered this piece of information matter-of-factly, simply as an observation. Philip was surprised by her frankness, then gave her a wry half-smile she seemed not to notice.

"When I went for interview, I tell Linda I am Catholic, but she said this is not important in America." She crushed out her cigarette in the ashtray and stared at it a moment. "Excuse me for speaking so much," she said with a soft sigh. "You are kind to listen. Everyone has been kind to me, Noah and Linda — and now you."

Philip sat back, curiously moved by the play of emotions on Karolina's face. He must have shown it because she put her hand on his desk and leaned in confidentially.

"Two days ago I see picture of Jake Landau in Noah's album, picture from Lublin when he was young man. He is Noah's uncle, *tak*? And your uncle, too?"

Philip nodded. "Jake was my father's brother. He came to the States after the war."

"I recognized his face," she said, her voice dropping to a half-whisper. "I think this man hide me on farm to save me from Germans. I think . . . he is my father."

A curious silence filled the room. Philip considered how to respond to this ridiculous statement, then let out a laugh. Talk about 1940's melodrama! A gray afternoon, a strange woman in a raincoat — the only thing missing was a fedora on his head and Private Investigator etched in gold letters on his front door. Just the kind of thing he used to joke about with his law school buddies when they sat around schmoozing at the West End Bar.

She was watching him carefully now. "I think you were not expecting this," she said with a guarded smile. "I was not, either."

"Look, I'm sure you've made a mistake," he said kindly. "If my uncle hid his child — and, frankly, I never heard anything about that — he would have done everything he could to find her. Unless, of course, he knew for certain she was dead."

She shook her head tragically. "He would not find me. My parents — the people who raised me — move from our farm to distant village when the Germans left Lublin. I think they are afraid someone will come back for me. I believe your uncle put me in hiding just before he was deported. I have calculated dates, Mr. Landau. I was four years old. This is why I do not remember."

Philip studied her anxious waiting face. Jewish? No way. From her square jaw line to her milky complexion and blue eyes, she was a *shiksa*, a Polish *shiksa* at that, just like his father said. Suddenly, her soft, rambling tone and theatrical gestures, her distracted stare, no longer seemed intriguing, but erratic. It crossed his mind that he had a psycho in his office. "Look, I'm sorry . . ."

She leaned in closer, her voice urgent now. "Listen, please! I have many ways to explain why I believe this. When I was child I have dreams of riding in automobile with a man I do not know. But our village had only horse carts and wagons. I do not see a car until I am ten. Whenever I ask to my mother about my dreams, she crosses herself and looks away. I accepted this because she was superstitious person. My father . . . I was close to him, but he did not speak often." She shook her head solemnly. "It is hard for you to understand such a person, Mr. Landau; you have modern ideas in America. He was poor farmer. He did not have the words. Then I forget about these dreams, but . . . things come back."

Her smooth, mesmerizing voice and the open sincerity in her face pulled at him, but he caught himself and drew back. A wave of unease spread. This woman could have followed Linda to Park East Chapels. She could have cased out his family and finagled her way into Noah's home. And here she was, trying to claim Jake's money.

He started to rise, ready to shuffle her out, but she stopped him with a trembling hand.

"No, please. I must tell you everything. Many times I dream of big doll house and fancy toys and women I could not know, women in lace collars with dark hair who held me on their lap. Their hands were white and soft, not like hands of women who dig radishes." She looked up at some distant memory. "When I said these things to my father, he put finger to my lips and I knew he would not speak of them. When I saw the picture of your uncle, I recognized him. He is the man in car who brought me to farm." She took a long breath. "And the most important thing you should know —"

"You know my uncle was a rich man," Philip said, angry now. "He left a big estate."

Karolina looked startled. "He had a business, I know, I read that —"

"Jake had no children. He left his money to his widow and Noah and me."

Her eyes grew wide.

"It's a lot of money," he said. "You had to know. I'm sure Noah and Linda talked about it."

"Oh, no, never!"

"You told Noah about this, right? Why didn't he call to say you were coming?"

"He said you are lawyer, you can help. I want to find out for sure if this man is my father. And I want to know the rest of my family. It would explain many things that have troubled me." She gripped the front of her raincoat, her knuckles a white ridge against the black vinyl. "This is difficult for me, Mr. Landau. I was raised Catholic. My family did not like Jews — my village did not. My friends, if they knew I was Jewish . . ."

"Is that supposed to win me over?" he threw in.

She shook her head, not listening. "I did not expect this."

"Did you expect me to believe your parents took you from a Jew and never said anything about it?"

"Never a word." She stood and gazed at him as if she suddenly remembered he was there. "Please excuse me . . . I did not know this . . . The money makes everything different." The woman pulled open the door and rushed past a puzzled Dorothy into the outer lobby.

Dorothy called to him over her shoulder. "She left her umbrella."

Philip watched the woman disappear into an elevator, then picked up the phone and dialed Noah.

"What were you thinking?" he said when his cousin got on.

"So, you saw her." Noah sounded breathless. His secretary had caught him on the way out.

"Yeah, I saw her. She's quite a crazy," Philip said. "Just what were you trying to do to me?"

"Wait a minute. I sent her so you could hear her story, so you could help her —"

"Help her how? Find a psychiatrist?"

"Are you saying you don't believe her?"

Was it possible that cautious, level-headed Noah had bought this far-fetched story? "Noah, the woman's insane. How could you let her into your home —"

"Didn't she tell you what happened to her, what she knows?"

"In great detail. And when I mentioned Jake's money, she ran out."

Noah released an exasperated breath. "Oh, God, I really messed this up. I should have called first. Karolina didn't know about the money."

"Come on, Noah, she works in your house. She had to know. You and Linda must have talked about his estate. The woman probably overheard —"

"No! Just listen a second. Karolina came to me two days ago. She was holding our photo album, pointing to an old picture of Jake. God, she looked like she'd seen a ghost. Then she told Linda and me the whole story."

Noah's wife was a plain stick of a woman, responsible and listless, the kind of person who treated fun like an assignment. "I can see why you fell for her. She's a looker and a very good talker — like any con artist."

"No —"

"Hold on a second, will you? I want you to hear what this sounds like. A woman we don't know turns up at Jake's funeral, worms her way into your home, then claims she's Jake's true heir. Is that what you want me to believe?"

"I told you she didn't know anything about the money. And she's not *claiming* anything. That's the point. She just wants to find out for sure if Jake's her father. That's why I sent her to you. I was sure you'd want to help." Noah had turned on his cool, professional voice, the one he thought made him sound reasonable and wise. "What exactly don't you believe?"

"The question is why should I believe any of it?"

"What about the names?"

"Names?"

"Didn't she tell you?"

"Tell me what?"

"She knew the names of Jake's wife and daughter."

Philip went into double-time, scouring his mind. He couldn't remember ever having heard the names of Jake's first wife and daughter. They'd died in the concentration camp along with Jake's sisters and parents. His uncle never talked about them or anything from the past. The Landaus always treated him like a damaged survivor and steered clear of war talk when he was around.

"How do you know she's right?" Philip said. "No one ever mentioned them. It was always 'Jake's first wife, Jake's first family, Jake's life before the big H.' "

Noah's breathing turned raspy. "I'm really sorry about this. I should have . . . Listen. I went to Chase yesterday with Jake's accountant to clean out Jake's safety deposit box. We found his wife's and child's German ID cards stuffed in with a slew of other documents, including Jake's birth certificate and the yellow star he must have worn in the camp. That's why I sent Karolina to you right away. When she showed me Jake's photo, she told me she remembered the names Chava and Rachel. She was right. Those were the names on the ID cards."

Chapter 2

Karolina's meeting with Philip Landau so unnerved her that by the time she arrived at work that afternoon, all she could manage was a perfunctory nod at Linda Landau before disappearing into Amanda's room to take charge of the child. Linda, who was running late for her afternoon job at Columbia Library Arts, barely noticed, and scooping up her coat and knit hat, called to Karolina from the vestibule, saying she'd left cheese and apple slices in the fridge for snack time, and if they went out, Amanda's new snow suit was hanging in the front closet. Then she was out the door, leaving Karolina sitting on the bed, staring at the lapful of toy animals that the child had gathered for their daily game of On the Farm.

Karolina moved through the rest of the afternoon simmering with anger. Even bathing Amanda didn't distract her, and the child played serenely with her water toys while Karolina sat on the edge of the tub, staring at the pink bathroom tiles, rerunning her disastrous meeting with the lawyer cousin. Why was the man so suspicious of her? Hadn't she given him enough information to take her seriously? She'd hoped to see Noah that evening to tell him what had happened, but he was working late, and desperate to get home and sort out the day in peace, she left as soon as Linda returned, skipped art class and headed for Brooklyn.

At six o'clock the subway platform was jammed. Karolina leaned against a post, hugging her raincoat to her body. Was it the cold from the cement platform seeping through her boots or her fury at Philip Landau that made her tremble so? The crowd around her continued to thicken with strangers. This was her first winter in America, and she felt miserably homesick. How she longed to be on familiar streets, to understand what people were saying without needing to unscramble meaning, to have a simple exchange and know that her words were right.

She took in a lungful of cold air and burrowed her chin into her coat collar. To think that Noah had sent her to that man! "Philip's a good lawyer," he'd said. "If he agrees to help, he'll know where to look." And what had he done? He'd leaned back in his chair, narrowed his sharp black eyes and practically accused her of lying. And for money! She, who'd chosen an artist's life, knowing she'd never earn more than enough for a small flat in the factory section of Warsaw and one or two good skirts a year. Even if she'd been a success in Warsaw, she'd never have a fraction of what these Americans had. The past July, when Jim's wife and sons had been on Fire Island for the summer, he'd taken her to his apartment for the first time since they'd started their affair. She'd moved, awestruck, through the sprawling rooms overlooking Central Park, touching the silky couches and heavy draperies, and gazed with amazement at the two small Monet pastels and the original Lautrec prints hanging on the walls. She remembered especially a beautifully sculpted female figure sitting on his library shelf and recalled how she rubbed her fingers together, imagining the smooth texture of newly sanded stone and wondering where in New York she could get top-grade marble, not the pitted, veined variety she'd used in Poland. Then, in the kitchen, she'd been assaulted by shelves of appliances she hadn't known existed: a yogurt maker, a gadget for opening cans, a blender for making drinks — even an electric knife. How extraordinary! It probably took longer to learn how to use these utensils than make the food.

She drifted toward a less crowded spot on the platform, stomping her numb feet. Her thoughts began to race. The obituary had noted that Jake Landau came to the States in 1946. In only twenty years he'd become a rich man — at least that's what his nephew had said. *If* she was his daughter, she could be entitled to some of his money. No, she wouldn't let herself think about that. If she even hinted at money, they'd all think she was a fraud — Linda, Noah, their whole family — and more than anything she needed them to help her unravel all the vague, half-remembered incidents, the two strange names that had rattled around in her head for as long as she could remember. She was sure she'd never heard the names spoken in

19

her home or anywhere else, yet they seemed a part of her. She just *knew* them — or *had* them. She squeezed her eyes shut. When? When was she first aware of them? When did they first come to her?

Karolina wakes to the crunch of her father's boots on the snow surrounding their farmhouse. She throws off her quilt and rolls over in her narrow bed. Chava. Rachel. *She's spent a restless night tangled in vague yet familiar dreams she can only hang on to for a few fluid moments after waking. All that's left now are the names. Karolina sighs, then looks out the frosty window into the yard. It snowed again last night, then the temperature dropped. A scuffle from the kitchen. Her mother, putting wood in the stove.* Chava. Rachel. *They're not Polish names, yet they don't seem strange at all; she knows instinctively they belong to last night's dreams and to other dreams before that, and it's this history inside her that makes her feel she's known the names as long as she's known her own.*

Karolina quickly gets out of bed and stiffens against the November cold, then wiggles into her dress, puts on her school apron and wool leggings, slips her feet into her rubber boots and runs into the kitchen. Kicia stretches languidly, wipes his face with his paw, then jumps noiselessly from the bed and follows. Her mother is standing over the stove, warming milk for groats. Karolina rushes to the table and sits down while her mother places the bowl on the table, then turns to stoke the fire. The kitchen is warm. Gray morning light seeps through the flowered curtains.

She eats quickly, warming her cheeks in the steam rising from the hot cereal. Rachel. Chava. *She stops, blinks and drops her spoon.*

"What's the matter, kochana*?" her mother asks, laying a hand on her shoulder. "Did you have bad dreams again?"*

She doesn't answer. She begins knocking her feet rhythmically against her chair, and bends down to scratch Kicia's chin while he half closes his dreamy eyes.

"Well?" says her mother, her eyes sharp with concern.

Karolina shakes her head. No matter what she says, her mother will get upset and mutter a prayer against the evil eye or spit out the side of her mouth. Why does she want to know Karolina's dreams when they frighten her so? Karolina runs her finger around the rim of the bowl to scoop up the last sticky grains of cereal, grabs her coat and book bag from the peg and heads for the door.

Outside, the morning fog has lifted as far as the forest that borders the farm, and the leafless trees are still shrouded in morning mist. Her father hitches up the horse while the animal stomps and snorts steamy clouds in the cold air. He lifts her onto the wagon seat, then gets on himself and with a quick flick of the reins, the horse moves forward. The six mile drive to school will be hard going in the snow.

Chava. Rachel. *Karolina opens her mouth to speak, then catches herself. The last time she tried to tell him about the people who haunt her dreams he stomped off to the barn. It was unlike him to act this way and she promised herself never to bring it up again. Now, sitting next to him in the cold dawn she can't stop herself.*

"Tatush," she begins. "Do we know people named Rachel and Chava?"

His breath shoots out in short jets of steam.

"Do we?"

He shakes his head.

"I must have heard them before . . ."

"Don't speak of it again." He snaps the reins hard. The cart speeds up and she's thrown against the wooden backrest.

Karolina burrows into her seat. Her tatush *rarely gets angry and she doesn't like to see his face crease with displeasure. She closes her eyes and lets the cart rock her over the newly fallen snow.*

All that day in school Karolina feels confused and preoccupied. Images come and go: A shaft of light flooding the hay loft; brown eyes widening with fear; the sound of snarling dogs.

"Karolina, are you asleep?" Pani Danuda shouts and the other children stare, surprised that she, who is rarely scolded, is spoken to this way. Karolina feels her cheeks grow hot and she drops her head. It's growing dark outside. Only a half-hour more and her father will be waiting outside to take her home.

Pani Danuda turns back to the blackboard. "Take out your writing tablets. Copy these."

Karolina stares at the board. The words blur. Rachel. Chava. *She feels her teacher's skirt brush against her shoulder, then a stick comes down hard against the side of her hand. She cries out, clutching her fingers.*

"Now do I have your attention?" Pani Danuda says. "You've been dreaming all day. Stop it."

Her eyes sting with tears. She puts her hand to her mouth and sucks her bruised fingers.

"Keep your eyes on the blackboard," her teacher continues, and walks toward the front of the room.

Thinking back, Karolina imagined that her teacher's small, sharp rap had sealed off a part of herself and that was the day a parallel life took root inside her. During the years that followed, the names would simply present themselves at different times, grasped without being said, understood without being heard, just as they had that morning when she lay in bed, waiting for her father to hitch up the wagon and drive through the freshly fallen snow to her small, wooden school-house on the outskirts of Lublin.

The subway pulled in and Karolina let the crowd on the plat-form jostle her into the car. People pressed against her and the air in-side thickened with the smell of sweat. Clutching the subway strap, she closed her eyes against the rhythmic clanging of the metal wheels and thought of the man who raised her, locked away in his sad life; of her other father, the one she would never know, and the woman who'd given birth to her. The newspaper said Jake's first wife had died during the war, she assumed in a concentration camp. She pic-tured her real mother crammed into a chamber, terrified by the gas hissing through the ceiling vents, and saw, a naked child, clinging to the woman's thigh, breathing in the sour stench of fear, of vomit and defecation filling the misty room as the women clawed at the sealed doors. Oh, the horrible irony of it! To think that a simple quirk of fate, a small tear in the sequence of time could have transmuted a Jewish child intended for the ovens into a Polish farm girl now living in America — with the relatives of her Jewish family! Impossible!

When she looked up they were going over the bridge toward Greenpoint. Behind her an expanse of black water stretched under the wintry gray sky toward the lights of Manhattan. Someone slid open a window and frosty air filled the car. She would not let Philip Landau intimidate her. She knew what she knew. Tomorrow she'd make sure to stay late and wait for Noah to find out if the cousins had spoken.

Chapter 3

For a moment after he hung up with Noah, Philip was so stunned he didn't know what to feel. The idea that Jake's daughter had survived the war was nothing short of a miracle; that his uncle might have lived out his life believing his child was dead struck him as unspeakably tragic. But could it be true? The more he thought about it, the more alarmed he became. If Noah backed this woman, which he sounded committed to doing, she could persuade a judge to look into her claim — which meant the court would lock up his $300,000 in escrow. Without the cushion of Jake's inheritance, giving up his practice to work for Drottman was going to be risky. Maybe too risky. He felt a flash of shame to be thinking about money at a time like this; still, why should he believe a stranger who'd barged into his office out of nowhere? What exactly had she presented him as proof? That she'd been hidden on a Polish farm but had no memory of it? That she had dreams of dollhouses and dark haired women with "white hands?" That she'd found herself attending the funeral of a man she didn't know because something about an obituary photograph gave her a "strange shiver?" And to top it all off, she'd come to the conclusion she was this stranger's daughter only after he was no longer alive to corroborate her story. All of it was at best coincidental. All of it, it seemed to him, was preposterous.

Yet she'd known the names of Jake's wife and child. No matter. Once he looked into it he was sure he'd find an explanation. Still, Philip's practical side told him it would be wiser to hang on with Simon until the Polish woman's story played itself out. He might be able to squeeze out a few hours for Abe's case on weekends when Alice was with her mother. Yet, even as ideas took shape in his mind, he knew he was kidding himself. Abe would never agree to his working part-time on a case like this and, if he stayed where he was, he ran a real risk of slipping back into the frantic, money-driven rut he wanted to ditch. He'd end up seeing even less of his daughter than he had over the past few years, end up neglecting Ellen even more, continue to neglect his parents who'd feel neglected even if he saw them twice a day. He was turning thirty-four next month. He'd already racked up too many bad choices: drifting into marriage because he'd felt too guilty to back out after three years of dating, then leaving the ACLU to try to make real money when Alice was on the way. No, he wasn't going to back out now. If Jake's money got held up, if he started leaking money faster than it was coming in from Abe, well, he'd just have to find a way to scrounge up more work.

Philip rubbed his eyes with the heel of his hands, remembering that Simon would be joining him to celebrate Ellen's birthday that night. He was tempted to put off making the break so the evening wouldn't be spoiled, but before he could talk himself out of it, he picked up the phone and buzzed his partner.

At Joe and Rose's Chop House on Third Avenue, Philip waited until their beers arrived before he told Simon his plans. "I won't be moving out for another month, not till after the first of the year," he wound up, "but of course I'll pay my share of the rent and Dorothy's salary until you can make other arrangements or find someone to replace me."

Simon stared down at the foam in his glass, thin-lipped and silent. "I can't say I'm surprised," Simon said, in a clipped tone that said he was. Philip muttered that he felt really terrible about the whole thing, which he did, and left it at that. Simon, a well-bred Westchester Jew, said he felt the same way, and they ate their steak sandwiches in silence, finished their drinks, then headed back to the office, vanishing into their respective spaces as soon as they walked through the door.

Abe Drottman didn't show up till 6:00 P.M.

He'd called Philip after lunch to say he'd be late for his two o'clock appointment, but four hours was a bit much, even for the man who held the world's record for never starting a class on time.

Dorothy showed Drottman in with a curt nod. She gave the

24

man's hundred-year-old overcoat and battered attaché case a quick glance, then flashed Philip a look of disapproval before pulling shut the door.

Drottman slumped onto the couch and pulled his fingers through his mop of shaggy gray hair. White stains marked the sides of his wing tips where they'd gotten soaked by the rain.

"Leonard Dills at the NAACP has filed a law suit on behalf of two Negroes who were refused accommodations at the Groveside Hotel in Atlanta," Drottman began in the bored tone that signaled he was in a hurry. Which he always was. "Dills got word that the American Jewish Congress is representing another potential plaintiff, a Harry Leibner from New York, who was turned away by the same hotel."

"When?"

"Last September. He booked a room at the Groveside and when he arrived later the same day, a clerk summoned the hotel manager who informed Leibner they had no room for him."

Anger seeped through Philip, warming the space behind his eyes. Three years after the Civil Rights Act and the bastards were still at it: No Negroes. No Jews. He glanced at Alice smiling back at him from the photograph on his desk and an image erupted. He's standing at a check-in counter holding Alice's hand when a pimply-faced clerk with a Dogpatch twang asks him to sign the register. The guy sees the name 'Landau', eyes his curly, black hair and olive complexion, and turns them away. Philip sees himself lunge across the counter, grab a fistful of the kid's shirt and pull him forward so hard he can feel bony chest ribs crack beneath his hand.

He pinched the corners of his eyes hard, waiting for his pulse to slow. Drottman's voice filtered back.

"Dills asked the American Jewish Congress if they want in on the law suit. They said yes and called me," Drottman said.

"Why do you think Dills is interested in adding a Jew to the case?" Philip asked.

"The Black Panthers have been shooting off their mouths to the press about Hebes and Kikes. Dills thinks adding a Jewish plaintiff to an NAACP case is a good way to signal his position without making a formal statement against the separatist brothers."

Which seemed like a very good idea. Philip was fed up with being called a Jewish Honky by the black power people. Some of his old friends at the ACLU might not mind being kicked in the teeth for being born white — or was it for not being black? — but he did. He'd marched, he'd demonstrated, he'd voted. His parents were Eastern European Jews; his grandparents had lived through pogroms; his uncle had survived the Holocaust. No one was going to tell him they'd cornered the market on racial discrimination or lecture him on persecution. That blacks needed to sound off after two hundred years of injustice was understandable; that they needed to slap around people who were helping them fight racism was not.

"I'm told Leibner is having second thoughts about being a plaintiff," Drottman said. "I'll want you to interview him. He was in one of those death camps, in Poland, I think. You'll know how to talk to him. My people will start working with the NAACP lawyers who are about to depose the hotel staff. We plan to use a notice to produce documents to get all the reservations and receipts back three years to January 1964. Christmas is coming up so we probably won't need you in Atlanta till after the first of the year. There's no way to know how long it'll take. The case could be big."

Philip felt a rush of excitement. If Abe said big, he meant monumental.

Drottman eyed him soberly. "So? Still with us?"

Philip couldn't restrain a euphoric laugh. "As I live and breathe."

Chapter 4

From the moment Philip met up with Simon at the Café Brittany, he could tell dinner was going to be a bust. Simon wore a small, tight smile, and the overly solicitous way he helped his new, neurotic girlfriend and Ellen seat themselves signaled that Philip was in for a tense evening.

In between the strained small talk, Simon lapsed into long-faced silences while his girlfriend tried to compensate by working double time to appear perky and merry. For Ellen's sake, Philip kept his tone light and ignored the gloom directed at him from across the table.

It was Ellen herself who came to the rescue. She knew about Philip's talk with Simon and picked up the slack with amusing riffs on her new Legal Aid boss whose Alabama drawl sounded so much like George Wallace everyone in the office freaked out whenever he opened his mouth. Philip had given her a brief rundown on the Polish woman on the ride to the restaurant and although Ellen was dying of curiosity, she knew better than to bring up the subject.

Ellen's story had brought a reluctant grin to Simon's sulky face. He glanced around the table, then leaned back in his chair and stared into his glass of wine. Everyone fell quiet as if they were awaiting a verdict.

Simon shifted uncomfortably. Finally, he raised -his glass to Philip. "Just promise you'll never show up as my opposing counsel."

Relieved, Philip held up his own glass and met Simon's gaze in a silent toast of thanks. The fear that they'd part on unpleasant terms had hovered over him most of the afternoon and it occurred to him that it wasn't only guilt he'd been feeling, but sadness as well. Simon had a sunny nature, a generous spirit and a predisposition to enjoy life — qualities Philip knew he himself lacked — and he felt a sudden pang of nostalgia as if their relationship were already a thing of the past. Simon, the bearer of good news, made it a point to start off most days trying to cheer him up. Over a cup of coffee and a wedge of Schraft's pecan cake he'd lean on Dorothy's desk, relating tidbits from The Wall Street Journal or the late news about how the housing market was on an upswing and they'd be doing ten closings a day before they knew it. Sometimes it would be news flashes about the bright future of litigators in manufacturing cases, an area they'd been trying hard to develop. From the beginning, Philip knew Simon was trying to pre-empt his increasingly black moods, and although Simon's relentless optimism occasionally irked Philip, he appreciated his partner's good intentions.

The rest of the evening, though not the kind of joyous celebration Philip would have wanted to mark his new beginning, was pleasant enough and Ellen seemed genuinely pleased. His Boeuf Bourguignon was cooked to perfection and having Ellen at his side made him feel good. She was a knockout in a black silk dress and dangling earrings, and after her first glass of champagne, the freckles scattered across her small, upturned nose turned a sweet, cinnamon-red. With her arm draped around his chair, she gazed out at the flower-filled restaurant, relaxed and happy. When everyone had finished their cherries jubilee and miniature meringues, the waiter slipped a bill onto the table and before anyone could budge, Philip grabbed the check, raised his arm like a traffic cop and tossed down his personal credit card.

The four of them drove through the falling snow in silence. At 67th Street, Simon and his girlfriend climbed out and the cab headed down Park Avenue toward Philip's apartment. Quiet settled inside the car. Philip took hold of Ellen's hand and lay back on the headrest. She gave him a reassuring kiss on the cheek, then lay her head on his shoulder.

"Are you worried about that Polish woman?" Ellen asked.

"A bit."

"You think she's a crazy?"

"Crazy enough to want Jake's inheritance."

She sat up, all lawyer now. "Is that what this is about, money?"

"Don't know. Could be."

"What does Noah think?"

"He's the one who sent her. We're meeting for lunch tomorrow. I'll know more then."

"But he believes her, right?"

"Apparently."

Ellen bowed her head in thought, sending her glossy auburn hair sliding over her forehead. "Let me give Larry Fine a call. He's an expert in estate law."

"Good idea."

The edges of Ellen's mouth creased in disgust. The afternoon rain had turned to snow and the streets were white and deserted. "God, those Poles" she muttered. "My parents get apoplectic every time they're mentioned." Her father had come to the States in the 1920s, but like Philip, she had European relatives who'd been killed by the Nazis. "You know, after you told me about that woman, I kept thinking about a friend of my parents who came here after the war. He said the Poles kept right on killing the Jews even after the Germans left." She shook her head sadly. "Imagine that."

That was the problem. He could imagine only too well.

He put her hand to his lips, wanting suddenly to warm himself against her, to lose himself in the simple pleasure of making love. But Ellen wasn't big on midweek sleep-overs. She liked to keep to her schedule, to be up by six and sit in her sunny Brooklyn Heights dining room, drinking her Viennese blend while she sifted through her papers preparing for her workday. He decided to chance it. He gave her neck an exploratory nuzzle and breathed in the flowery Diorissimo perfume he'd given her on the way up. She pulled away with a doleful smile. "Call me right after you see Noah," she said, a small yawn escaping from her mouth.

"Sure," he said more snappishly than he intended, and turning away, gave her hand a perfunctory pat.

When they pulled up in front of his building, Philip told the driver to head for the Brooklyn Bridge and got out. He stood at the curb a moment, watching the car disappear into the night, then looked down East 38th Street. Falling snow glistened under the streetlights and collected in creamy mounds along the steps in front of the neighboring townhouses. He hauled himself up the stairs to the second floor, shook the snow from his overcoat and entered. He felt ready to sleep for a week.

Philip undressed quickly and crawled under the quilt. Twenty minutes later he was still tossing. Something about the Polish woman gnawed at him. The word *goyish* came to mind, but with a twist. It occurred to him her particular form of Polish goyishness had kicked up all the bad Pole stories he'd heard growing up. When he pictured her theatrical gestures and how she'd blushed with humiliation when he'd hinted she was there for the inheritance, he realized the money wasn't all of it. Somehow, he'd absorbed his tribe's distrust of the people they'd lived with for centuries, and he hadn't been aware of it until a Pole was sitting across from him, trying to convince him they were related.

Why this should surprise him, he didn't know. He had a thousand memories of his parents warning him never to forget what the Germans did, what the Slovaks did, the Croats, the Hungarians, the Lithuanians; never forget that no one helped even though they knew what was happening to the Jews, when they could have done something, *should* have for the sake of simple humanity. Not one country in the whole world, they harped, not one leader, not even our hallowed President Roosevelt tried to stop it. Never forget the vile, unspeakable tortures, the grisly experiments, the lines of naked people waiting to fall into graves they themselves had been forced to dig; never forget that farmers, townspeople, even professors watched starving slave laborers herded past them and did nothing, *nothing*. And narrowing their eyes in a particularly hard way, never forget that the Poles, who'd been neighbors, school friends, teachers, had abused the Jews, cursed them, killed them with relish even when they didn't have to. The Poles were the worst, they'd declared over and over, with the pain and bitterness of personal betrayal, *the worst*. Sometimes, during these tirades, Philip listened stunned as much by the scope of his parents' knowledge as by the horrors they depicted. He was six years old when America went to war and for four long years he'd sat on the living room floor, eyes glued to the luminous radio dials and listened to his parents' nightly translation of the news into a personalized broadcast on the fate of the Jews. How, in God's name, could they ever imagine that he'd forget?

He tossed fitfully, then pounded his pillow into a ball. As he began to drift, an image came to mind of a medieval Madonna, her face mottled by ancient layers of paint, her cheeks streaked with green and yellow tears. Philip recalled the picture from an article in *Time*, describing the yearly pilgrimage devout Poles made to the town of Czestechowa where it was said this painting, known as the Black Madonna, had once cried real tears. He remembered, too, a photo of Polish peasants lined up outside the church waiting for a glimpse of the portrait and thought Karolina's parents must have looked like them. Now, floating between sleep and waking, Philip saw again their crude, exultant faces and he was filled with loathing at their stubborn faith, at their belief in a merciful God.

The next day, when Philip showed up at the luncheonette near Noah's West 33rd Street office, his cousin was already seated in a booth, staring blankly at the room. At thirty-two, Noah still had that glazed, unfocused look of a kid who'd just gotten up from a nap. Still, under his *zhlubby*, little-boy exterior, Noah was a plugger. Which was how he'd made it to vice president at Schwartz and Solomon Accounting.

The restaurant was jammed and overheated, the clatter of dishes and cutlery drowning out what sounded like a new Beatles song coming over the sound system. Philip hated cheap lunch-hour places, but Noah had suggested it, and since it was clear from their phone conversation that they were at opposite ends of this Polish woman issue, he wasn't going to antagonize him right off the bat. Of course, Noah was right that the woman's claim had to be pursued, but he'd make it clear he wouldn't accept her wild story without solid proof.

"Sorry I'm late," Philip said, making his way through a group squeezing past him to the register.

"I got hungry, so I ordered."

Philip slid into the booth. "Good."

"Alice okay?" Noah asked.

"Terrific. She played a bumblebee in a dance recital last month. She had the loudest buzz in the group."

The waitress set down a turkey club in front of Noah and shoved a metal bowl of brine-flecked pickles and green tomatoes into the center of the table. Philip and Noah reached for the bowl at the same time, knocked hands, then sat back and laughed. As kids, they'd make a contest out of who could swipe the most pickles and always ended up fighting and stinking so badly of garlic their parents had to wash them down before letting them back in the dining room. Philip had a go at being Noah's buddy in high school, something both families pushed hard for, but wasn't sorry when his nerdy cousin opted for Midwood High's math team over cruising for girls along Flatbush Avenue. Noah had grown into an old-fashioned square who still used Brylcreem and, Philip could see, still went to his father's barber in Brooklyn for a trim.

"So, tell me what you know about this Karolina Staszek," Philip said, making a show of perusing the menu.

"She started working for us last month, when Linda went back to work. We liked her right away, but of course we checked her references. We got one from a Jim Lubetski who heads some kind of Polish-American Art foundation. Seems he brought her here on a grant. We also got a letter from her landlord in Greenpoint." Noah's owlish eyes perked up behind his black-framed glasses, his way of registering satisfaction. "They both said great things."

The waitress was back with her pad open and pencil poised. Philip ordered a tuna salad on rye toast, then turned to Noah.

"I got the impression she was glad to leave Poland," Noah said.

"Who can blame her? It's not exactly the land of opportunity."

"No, it was something about her life there. She once told me she never felt like she belonged. Now I understand why."

Philip looked up, alert. Noah wasn't the kind of warm and fuzzy guy who inspired personal conversation. "You two talk?"

"A little, but it's not so much what she says. It's just a feeling about her." He turned thoughtful for a moment. "She seems so . . . sad."

"Oh, yeah?"

"I have the impression she always felt — oh, I don't know — alone, I guess, and now she suddenly has a family."

"You've led a sheltered existence," Philip joked. "You're just not used to European women, is all. Too many Brooklyn princesses in your past."

Noah's mouth tightened into a thin line. "Not Linda, of course,"

Philip added, "but you gotta admit, Brooklyn isn't famous for its sophisticates." He remembered a few Susans and Barbaras Noah had brought along to holiday dinners, plain, bookish girls who looked like they'd rather be home studying for their SATs. A couple of years back, Noah had married a skinny, sober-eyed, blonde librarian from Long Island, a kind of Jewish Twiggy. She kept Noah on a short leash. Which he seemed to like. But maybe the sexy Polish nanny had changed all that.

The waitress plopped down Philip's sandwich. He lifted a slice of rye, inspected the tuna and took a bite. "So what story did she give you?"

"Look, it's not impossible that somehow she planned all this," Noah said, color rising in his face, "but it doesn't make sense that she could know the names of two people who've been dead for over twenty years, names nobody else knew."

"Okay. Point taken. Why don't you start by telling me about her background. What's she told you about herself?"

"She's an artist, a sculptor. She studied in Poland and said she worked for a bookbinder in Warsaw. She was in a few group shows, that's how she met the American. He saw some of her pieces and brought her here on a grant."

"Did it ever occur to you that people who work with books know how to look up things? They have access to libraries, to government files. The whole thing could be a scam. Maybe she's part of a Polish ring claiming to be Jewish so they can get inheritances. She might have come across a record of Jake and his family in an archive in Lublin." Philip felt superior coming up with this explanation, and its possibilities grew as he spoke. "Let's say they research the records of people who died in the Holocaust, locate their relatives in the States and pose as long-lost relations — sisters, children — who were given away to Poles as babies. She could have followed Linda to the funeral home as a way to meet her."

"She's been here almost a year. Why wouldn't she have made direct contact with Uncle Jake before?"

"Because Jake would have asked questions she couldn't answer. Maybe she was waiting to get more info on the family before she took him on. Maybe she waited too long."

Noah shook his head with exaggerated pity. "That's what they

33

taught you in law school, right? To come up with absurd reasons just so you can prove your case."

"No, cousin, they taught me to think of alternative possibilities — just in case I came across that *rare* entity called a dishonest person."

"You've got it wrong," Noah said loudly, then stole an embarrassed look around before lowering his voice. "She's not like that. I know. I've watched her." He flushed, then looked down at his half eaten sandwich.

She's hooked him, Philip thought, lock, stock and inheritance. Little Noah is sleeping with the nanny and she's conned him good. "So how does Linda feel about all this?"

"She likes her — a lot," Noah said. "Karolina's nice to have around. Sometimes I think Linda gets a little jealous."

"Of you and Karolina?"

"Of course not! Of Karolina and Amanda. But that's only natural when other people take care of your children." Noah squinted over Philip's shoulder as though something in the distance had suddenly caught his attention. "I don't know, there's something about Karolina that's hard to put into words."

Philip knew what he meant. The Polish woman had the aura of a wounded spirit, someone who looked young and seemed old. It was a cultural style he'd noticed in the few Eastern European women he'd met. They had a veneer of animation that barely disguised a world weariness, a disillusionment with life. And he had to admit the whole package was seductive.

"Did you ever talk about Jake in front of her?" Philip asked.

"Come on, how do you expect me to remember everything I've said while she was in the room? And what difference would it make? I didn't know their names."

They both fell silent. "So where do you want to go with this?" Philip finally asked.

Noah had been squeezing his sandwich and now mayo was dripping onto his plate. He seemed a little befuddled, unlike his usual tightly held-together self. "You're the lawyer. That's why I sent her to you. There must be documents somewhere, Polish records, birth certificates, something to establish her origin. She said she wanted to be 100% sure herself."

"Whoa, wait just a sec. Shouldn't *she* be the one to do the proving?"

"What about the names? Isn't that enough to start taking her seriously?"

"Is it?" He rattled the ice in his coke, then eased into his in front-of-the-jury voice. "Look, I'm not trying to be hardnosed about this, but we can't just swallow this story whole. You're absolutely sure she didn't hear the names from you?"

"I didn't *know* them, Phil. And if I did, why would I tell her?" Noah was now glaring at him full out. "Just what *is* your problem with this woman? Or is it Jake's money you're so worried about?"

Noah knew about his business problems, knew he was banking on Jake's bequest; still, he wasn't going to get any sympathy. His cousin had always been jealous of what he'd once called Philip's charmed life. While Noah was holed up at home studying his ass off to get good grades, Philip played basketball and ran around with girls, then ended up with a full scholarship to Columbia. He'd worked hard to overlook Noah's resentment in the interest of family. He wasn't about to let himself be baited now.

"First, we need to do whatever we can to get at the truth of her claim," Philip said calmly. "And that's going to take time."

"That's okay. Just help her get started." He leaned in, his long, sallow face suddenly vivid with feeling. "What if she's really Jake's daughter?"

"Jake's dead and I wonder how happy Rosalind will be watching a child that's not hers get money that's supposed to go to her — and to us."

"Come on, Phil, we've got an obligation here. Just *talk* with her again. Imagine what it would have meant to Jake?"

Philip tried to imagine what it would feel like to lose his child, but the thought was too horrible even for a fleeting fantasy. He pictured a sleepy Alice curled against his chest and his heart took a flip. Jake must have spent his life tormented by memories like that.

"Okay," Philip said. "Give me her address. I want to see how she lives. It'll be easier to get to know her that way."

Noah pulled a small notebook from his jacket pocket and quickly leafed through the pages.

"What time does she leave your house?"

"Around 5:30. Earlier on Tuesdays and Thursdays when she goes to art classes."

Philip copied down the address and phone number. "Any boyfriends?"

"I don't know. Linda says she never talks about her personal life. Karolina once mentioned she doesn't like the Poles she meets in Greenpoint, but there's an older guy who calls sometimes." Noah fixed him with an indignant look. "Look, if you openly accuse her of lying, you'll make it extremely awkward for her to work for us."

"You think your new, rich cousin will want to stay on as your nanny?"

Noah lifted his glasses and rubbed his blurry eyes. "I guess not."

No, he couldn't be sleeping with her. Such a bore couldn't interest a good-looking woman — unless, of course, she was using him.

Philip opened his agenda and leafed through the pages. "I'll see her tomorrow. Try to find out if she's going straight home and give me a call in the morning. I promise not to come on like gangbusters. I'll just poke around a little to make sure we're getting a straight story."

They ate in silence for a while. Philip knew he was playing it hard. He'd spent a grand total of twenty minutes with the woman before he'd written her off; still, he always went with his gut reactions until he had enough reason not to.

"What if it's true she was given to Poles, but she's got the wrong family?" Noah asked. "We could help her find out."

"Sounds like you've grown very fond of her."

Noah studied a piece of lettuce on his plate, then wiped his fingers on the napkin. He straightened his tie without looking up. "Let's get the check, okay?"

Chapter 5

Karolina yanked off her wet boots, gave her icy toes a quick rub and snuggled into the couch. She was not ready for winter. Autumn in New York had surprised her with days that lingered warm and golden long into October, and then the weather turned suddenly cold with an abruptness that was new to her. Taking her glass of tea from the side table, she lowered her face to the rising steam, thinking how much she missed her walks through Central Park. When she still worked at the Foundation, she and Jim would stroll down paths lined with trees in dazzling shades of rust and yellow and red. They had time then before slipping away to the east side apartment of Jim's friend from Chicago. Except for weekends, they had the place all to themselves. Once the weather changed, they stayed behind at the office until all the staff left, then rushed through the winter dusk to make love before Jim went home to his family. That was last month. Since she left the Foundation, they'd been meeting once a week and on the rare Saturday when his sons weren't playing basketball or football or whatever it was that American boys played on weekends. The boys needed him, Jim had said, his eyes turning sad for her benefit. His wife was not a disciplinarian and they were doing poorly in school. Karolina hadn't questioned his sudden interest in the sons. By now they both knew their relationship was fading and neither of them had the courage to face it.

There was a knock at the door. Karolina roused herself and padded across the living room in her stocking feet.

Mrs. Domanski stood in her usual quilted housecoat and slippers. Her yellow hair, already in curlers for the night, gleamed like rows of tiny corn. Everything about the landlady was square — her face, her boxy frame, even her hands were as wide as the man's.

Mrs. Domanski ceremoniously held up a glass casserole and spoke in Polish. "*Kurczeta!* I made some for dinner. Here. For you." Her perfectly round bright blue eyes roamed Karolina's face for a moment. "You don't look well, dear. My husband was just saying you've grown so thin, you've become too American. . . ."

"Oh, I'm fine, thank you." She stepped aside so her landlady could look into the living room. Mrs. Domanski liked to peer over her shoulder for signs of male life in the apartment, then remembering herself, she'd look away abruptly as though no one would notice if she were quick about it. Karolina had decided long ago to make snooping easy for her.

The landlady was the cousin of Zosha Mazurek, the mother of Karolina's old school friend. Before Karolina left Poland, Zosha had written the Domanskis for help in finding Karolina an apartment. As it turned out, the Domanskis were looking to rent out the ground floor of their Greenpoint row house, and when Karolina showed up at their door, they decided instantly that a *gymnasium*-educated Polish woman with a green card and no children would make an excellent tenant. Of course, they expected she'd marry soon, for at twenty-nine she really was too old to be fussy. They'd tried to broker a match with Tadeusz, a neighbor's son who helped out in the Domanskis' deli, and the couple was openly disappointed when he stopped coming around. Karolina was not. Lanky, sullen Tadeusz had little to recommend him. Like the other Polish men Karolina had met in Greenpoint, he was a simple, good-hearted soul whose conversation consisted of short exchanges about the rising cost of food and the latest soccer match.

Karolina regarded the layer of grease coagulating on top of the *kurczeta*. "You're very kind, really, but I'm not so hungry tonight. I'll save it for tomorrow when I go to dinner with friends." There were no dinner plans, but she wouldn't dream of hurting the woman's feelings. She'd learned long ago never to argue with family, even make-believe family, about food. Better to take the cutlets, toss them out later and return a clean dish. That way everyone would be happy.

"But there's so little," Mrs. Domanski cried, shaking her head tragically. "I'll bring you some more."

"No, no, I'll cut the chicken into pieces and we'll eat them as appetizers. The Americans love it. They call it finger food." Taking hold of the still-warm casserole, Karolina carried it to the kitchen alcove, switched on the fluorescent lights and waited a moment while the room vibrated an avocado green. She felt a pang of nostalgia for the simple white stucco and rough hewn tile of her Warsaw kitchen, the ancient porcelain sink permanently stained by countless dinners of all the families before her. At home, everything was marked by the past; here, rooms crumbled not from use, it seemed, but from the flimsiness of plasterboard and imitation wood paneling that Greenpoint Poles tacked up everywhere.

She set the food on the matching green Formica counter and returned to the living room. "I was just running out for a quick sandwich. I want to catch your husband before he closes the shop."

"Don't worry. He's open late on bingo nights." Mrs. Domanski surveyed the room critically, reached into the pocket of her housecoat and pulled out a long rope of imitation pine needles covered with tinsel. "There is no Christmas in here," she boomed with tyrannical jolliness and lumbered toward the bookcases.

Amused, Karolina folded her arms across her chest and watched Mrs. Domanski deftly arrange the plastic strips into loops and hang them along the edge of the bookshelves. She had to admit that she'd grown fond of the woman's affectionate bullying. With the Domanskis, she didn't feel quite so much the orphan, a feeling that had overtaken her during the past year.

"Better, *tak?*"

The room with its rickety, foam stuffed couch and mismatched club chairs did, in fact, look cheerier. "You're right. Much better."

Mrs. Domanski slipped into the kitchen, took the *kurczeta* from the counter, shoved it onto the bottom rack of the refrigerator, then took a moment to peer in. "Empty," she said, pointing an accusatory finger at the shelves. "I'm making *kotlety* tomorrow and I'll bring you some. No, don't argue with me. They keep for days. Eat them when you want. And tell my husband to give you a bag of the dried mushrooms that just arrived. So good!" she sang out, throwing kisses in the air. "But you don't cook, do you? Then take a few cans of sauerkraut and some of that good ham that comes in packages."

"Good idea. Can I bring you back something?"

Mrs. Domanski slapped her wide hips. "Don't I already get enough to eat?"

Once her landlady had gone, Karolina took up her boots and tried to wriggle in her feet, but the clammy leather resisted, and she fell back against the couch exhausted. When she had arrived this evening, her first impulse was to call Jim for advice, but she knew he'd insist on finding her a lawyer and she wasn't ready to make the Landaus her enemy. There was no one else she could call. Except for Valerie from the Art Students' League, she'd not made friends here. But then, she'd always been a loner, preferring solitude to the small talk most people needed to get through before they revealed anything interesting about themselves.

She sat, hunched in her coat, staring vacantly at the shabby, impersonal room she'd never made her own, and saw with sudden clarity that she'd always lived like this, unwilling to leave her mark, unable to anchor herself to the present. She'd hoped that coming to America would jolt her out of the peculiar dislocation she'd felt all her life, but instead, she'd hovered again, waiting for a future with Jim to take shape, waiting for she knew not what. Then, a face in the newspaper had startled her from her lethargy and now she had no choice but to find an answer. Tomorrow, she'd start investigating on her own. She'd send off letters to the archives in Warsaw and Lublin; she'd comb whatever records had survived the war for date discrepancies, name changes, anything that might yield a clue to her past. It could take months for information to make its way back across the Atlantic; if nothing turned up, she'd ask Jim to lend her money for a ticket to Lublin and track down people in her village who might have known her family. Someone somewhere had to know about her past.

A spasm of hunger erupted. She should eat something or she'd wake up ravenous and spend a feverish night trying to sort through the thoughts wildly flapping around in her head.

The phone rang.

"Yes?"

"It's Philip Landau."

She sat forward, clutching the phone. "Mr. Landau!"

"Listen, I spoke with Noah yesterday. He told me what you two talked about."

"Oh, I am so glad to hear from you! Please excuse me for leaving so quickly, but when you spoke of your uncle's money —"

"Can we meet ?"

"Yes, yes, of course. When?"

"I dropped off some legal papers in Brooklyn. Noah gave me your address. I could be there in twenty minutes."

"Here?"

"It's hard to talk at the office. We'll have more time at your place." He paused. "Is that a problem?"

She panned the room frantically as if he were already standing there, assessing her home. Of course, he wanted to see how she lived, what kind of person she was. This was understandable.

"I was going out to buy something to eat, but I will be quick. Twenty minutes is good. Please come."

"Okay. See you then."

"Wait! Do you know Greenpoint? I live on Driggs Street, a small —"

"I'll find it," he said and hung up.

She replaced the receiver, shivering with excitement. If he was coming so late he probably had no appointments afterward. There would be time to sit and talk. She could explain herself. He would hear her out.

She snatched up her boots, and with a few determined twists managed to pull them on. She glanced at her watch. Seven thirty. He'd probably had dinner already, but she should have something to offer him, a beer perhaps or a pot of coffee. And cookies. She'd pick some up at the deli. Thank God he was giving her another chance! Winding her scarf around her neck, she checked herself in the hallway mirror, wondering if she should change into something more presentable than her work clothes. But there was no time. She grabbed her purse and charged out the door into the cold night.

Chapter 6

Under the dim light from the street lamps, Philip could make out stocky men in heavy plaid jackets and women in fur-trimmed boots and headscarves pouring out the side door of the flagstone church on Dyer Avenue. Ten minutes had passed since he'd called Karolina from the phone booth on the corner. He had ten left to kill before he could show up at her door. That morning, after Noah told him she was going straight home from work, Philip had the impulse to appear at her door unannounced, but decided that would come across as too belligerent. He wanted her relaxed, cooperative. He'd call first, then give her as little time as possible to prepare for him. He'd start out casual; once he gauged her reaction, he'd know what to do.

He cracked open the car window and scraps of Polish drifted in. Studying the group huddled at the church, he was struck by how old-world they seemed: the women cheek-kissed and pressed each other close; the men looked solemn-faced, nodding silently before heading down the side streets. Their European habits were so familiar, so like his own family, yet there was a grimness about the people, a beaten-down quality that he hadn't expected. Most of the stores along the avenue were shuttered tight. Facing him was a Polish travel agency, a hair salon called Snip Snip, and a fabric store with its steel gate down. The only light came from a deli across the street with salamis and what looked like animal parts hanging in the window. Pork, probably. Poles loved pork, the knuckles, the bellies, even the heads. His parents always averted their eyes when they passed places like these, and when his father was in a particularly lousy mood, he'd mumble *kurwa trafe* and spit on the ground. Philip laughed to himself. How pleased Meyer would be to have him carry on the tradition.

He got out of the car and looked around. He'd never been to the Polish section of Brooklyn and was surprised there wasn't a speck of paper or rubbish anywhere. Glass storefronts gleamed under the lamplights. Even the garbage cans lined up in front of the apartment houses looked scoured. Poor, but neat, and very clean, he thought, which explained why those of his mother's friends who could afford cleaning ladies always looked for Polish women to hire.

He was about to cross to the deli to ask directions to Driggs Street when he saw Karolina through the store window. He recognized the raincoat first. She leaned across the counter, handing money to a man, then came out, hugging a brown paper bag to her chest. So she *had* gone out for food. Stepping into the shadow of a tree, he watched her move down the avenue in easy, loose-limbed strides, gliding along with her coat billowing out behind her. He stayed put for a few moments, then followed her down a side street of two-story, asphalt-shingled row houses with red and white Christmas lights strung across awnings and looped through metal handrails. She stopped in front of a building with a blinking reindeer stationed in the front yard, rummaged in her purse for her key, then went in. Philip hung back. Better not knock now or it would look like he'd been following her. At the corner he spotted the lights of a luncheonette and headed toward it. The young man behind the counter with a flat face and vacant eyes silently handed Philip the Marlboros he asked for, took his money, then went back to his newspaper without so much as a word. Ten minutes had passed. He headed back to her house.

"Come in," Karolina said, stepping away from the door. She smiled up at the swarthy face and dark eyes, the burnished cheeks and black, windblown hair that fell across Philip Landau's forehead. She remembered a tall man, but in his camel coat and chestnut muffler he seemed to tower over her. As he moved into the apartment, he brought in the smell of fresh, cold air.

Philip stood with his hands in his pockets, waiting. When she extended hers, he shook it and gave her a small smile.

"I am so pleased you have come," she said, ushering him in. "I

43

knew when you spoke to Noah he will tell you all the words that —
how do you say? — stick to my throat because I am afraid to speak."

"Well, I'm here to talk."

"Give me your coat," she said eagerly. He handed it to her and
she tossed it over her own on the living room chair. "Sit, please."

Philip ignored her and rubbing his hands together, turned away
to survey the apartment. She was conscious of a coolness in his manner as he ran his eyes over her bookcases decked with Christmas decorations, then the few knickknacks she'd brought from home, three
corn-husk dolls dressed in Polish costumes, her marble figures from
art school, and the nesting dolls the Hankowskis had given her on
her twelfth birthday. Humble objects, yes, but they would tell him
who she was. He glanced around the living room, then stopped
abruptly when he saw the wooden crucifix mounted on the wall.

"So," she said too brightly. "I just came back. I have beer, but if
you like, I can make coffee. I buy *Chruściki*, good Polish cookies."

"No, nothing, thanks," he said absently. "But you said you were
hungry, so go ahead."

She moved into the safety of the kitchen, wondering if she
should make a pot of coffee anyway. It might make the mood more
congenial. "You are sure I cannot offer something? I have much food.
My landlady left chicken cutlets." She peeked out of the alcove. He'd
taken one of her Polish novels from the coffee table and was leafing
through it as though it were a magazine. For a moment she wondered if he was going to turn it over and shake it.

"I can see this is not what you want," she said. "You have come
to talk and I am delaying you." Quickly, she unwrapped the cheese
sandwich she'd bought at the deli, grabbed paper napkins off the
counter, took a plate from the cupboard and marched back to the
table. As she came into the room, she felt him take in her body and
wished she'd changed into something more stylish than her shapeless
skirt and cardigan. His eyes on her were suddenly brazen, apprecia-
tive, and feeling awkward, she tugged discreetly at her sweater to
straighten it.

"Come," she said and gave the back of the chair an exaggerated
motherly pat. "You have nothing to fear. No, it is I who am nervous
after our meeting. We did not have good beginning."

At last he seemed to relax and, meeting her eyes, let out a

resonant, ironic laugh. Sliding onto the chair, he unbuttoned his jacket and leaned toward her. He wore a pale blue shirt with a button-down collar that reminded her of an American in Warsaw who'd once come to Marek's shop, looking for first editions of Sienkiewicz's *Quo Vadis*. He'd worn such a shirt and even though the man was middle-aged and graying, something about tiny buttons holding down a small collar made him look young. Americans had a talent for looking youthful. Her people seemed worn and used up before they reached forty.

"So," Philip said, easing his elbows onto the table. "Tell me about yourself."

"Oh, how can I begin? These weeks since I saw your uncle's picture, I cannot tell you how it has changed my life. Like a big stone has come loose from my heart," she said, putting her hand to her chest. "You know, Mr. Landau, for a long time I feel something is wrong, that I have not been . . . my true self. Now I think, I have found my family and I will know them." She stopped to search his face for a resemblance to the man whose picture had so disturbed her, but no, there was nothing in his smooth jaw line and deep set eyes that looked like Jake Landau. "I talk too much," she said with a laugh, "but I am excited to speak with you."

"Good. There's a lot we need to clear up. How did you first hear about Jake?"

"In the newspaper."

"I mean in Poland."

"Oh, I never heard about him before. I only remember little pieces, but when I see your uncle's photograph . . ." Again, she felt the surge of release she'd experienced the first time she saw Jake's picture.

"You could have overheard your parents talking about him when you were growing up."

"Oh, no. I would remember such a thing."

"Maybe they did business with him before the war and his name was mentioned."

"Yes, this could be. What did he do in Lublin?"

"Don't you know?"

"No, only that he has construction company here. He has the same in Lublin?"

"Why Lublin? You said your closest village was Lubartow."

"Yes, our farm was a few kilometers from Lubartow . . . But I told you this when we met in your office —"

"— tell me again."

Her pulse began to race. "Please, you go too fast . . ." He was spitting questions at her before she could answer, trying to catch her in a lie. They were already in a courtroom. She put down her sandwich, agitated. "You are suspicious of me. Why?"

He shook his head dismissively. "That's neither here nor there."

"I do not know this expression. What does it mean?"

"My feelings have nothing to do with it. What matters is verifying your claim."

"Yes, this is how I feel! I cannot trust my memories alone. You are a lawyer. That is why I came to you. You spoke with Noah. Now you know what I know, but still you are angry."

"Angry? No, not exactly."

"Then why do you speak to me like I am criminal?"

His considered her coldly, his eyes narrowing into a hard glint. "I don't have to tell you that the Poles treated my people very badly during the war. You know what I'm talking about. You yourself told me you'd have a hard time today if people knew you were a Jew. Why should I trust you before I know more?"

There it was, the old hatreds resurfacing! She'd sensed it the minute he saw the crucifix. "You are wrong, Mr. Landau." She threw up her hands in dismay. "Not all Poles were bad to Jews. Some helped."

"Not enough.

"The people who raised me did. I am living proof."

"Not yet."

"But there are many stories like mine," she said hotly. "Surely you have read about children who were hidden by Poles, by Belgians — even Germans. It is known."

"Those children aren't claiming inheritances, are they?"

"I have not said one word about inheritance! Only *you* speak of money."

He opened his eyes wide, mocking her. "Can I take that to mean you're only interested in being known as Jake's daughter and don't want anything else?"

She'd wanted him to be frank, but still he was tactless and rude, and now he was infuriating her. "At last you are honest. Good! I will tell you — how do you say? — straight. When I left your office I did think about inheritance. But this is normal, no? I am not brainwashed by Communists. Money is money. It helps in life, but for me truth is most important. You should feel the same way, yet you are already judging me."

"Whoa!" he said, holding up his hand. "I didn't say that. Any lawyer will tell you there are other ways a person could have gotten the information you have."

"What information? Noah did not say if my memories mean anything or who are the names I remember."

"He didn't know at the time."

She waited for more, but still no response. "You know something now?"

"Yes," he said and fell silent.

She lifted her hands in supplication. "I have told you all that I know," she pleaded. "I know nothing more. If you do not tell me, I must ask Noah tomorrow."

Philip rubbed the back of his neck thoughtfully, as if considering. "Jake never spoke of his wife and child. A few days ago Noah found documents in Jake's safe confirming their names. They're the ones you mentioned."

Karolina felt the blood leave her face. "My God!" she whispered, and before she knew what was happening, she found herself standing weak-kneed alongside the table. So it was true! There was proof, solid proof! She grew dizzy, trying to find a focus for the images bombarding her, for the chaotic procession of thoughts in her head. She walked unsteadily to the cabinet, grabbed a bottle and two water glasses, then slowly made her way back to the table and poured the alcohol with trembling hands. She took a long sip, then gazed at the filmy particles floating to the bottom of the homemade vodka Mr. Domanski had given her. "Thank you! You do not know what a great gift you give me. To finally hear something that can prove . . ." She turned the glass around in her hand, watching the liquor coat the sides of the tumbler, flooding with memories of her *tatush*, remembering how he would stare into his glass when he drank, his pale blue eyes deep with thought. She sat a long time, filling with a buoyancy as though she were floating in her chair.

47

"My *tatush* was good man," she blurted out at last. "He would be happy that I finally know, so I will drink to him." She took another swig to loosen the knot of tears gathering at the back of her throat.

"I will tell you about my *tatush*," she continued, needing to talk now, even to this stranger, to spill out the thoughts that seemed to roll over her unbidden. "He was big drinker, but he never drank in our house . . . no, never . . . because he did not wish his family to see him drunk. There were many men like this in our village, Mr. Landau. They were like club. Every Saturday night they meet at tavern in Lubartow, and every Sunday morning you see . . . saw them in church, pale and sleepy and sorry. Only a few times did he take vodka in front of us . . . only when he needed to tell something difficult." Her dear, kind father. How she longed to hold his calloused hands in her own, to rest her cheek against his shoulder, to relieve him of the terrible secret he had carried for so long. "When he died two years ago, I went to close our house and found his bottle behind stove. I was surprised it was only half full. My mother was dead for a year, but even though there was no one to stop him, my *tatush* did not touch drink in our house." She ran her fingers along the side of the bottle, then drew a sharp line across its middle. "I could actually count the times he drank at home.

"I remember one day in early spring, just after the war. I was seven and my *tatush* came into the house and I saw a terrible fear in him. He took out his bottle and told us we must leave the farm. I do . . . did not understand why. Farmers do not leave animals unless there is great danger. Years later when I asked him about this time of abandoning, he told me a big story that a potato disease in our region destroyed crops and that was why we left. But now I understand differently. The Jews were coming back to Poland. We moved because he was afraid someone would find me and take me away from him.

"We went to live with relatives in Koromov, a village about two hundred kilometers from Lubartow. It was not a good time for us. Away from the farm my parents were silent with each other. They never spoke about why we left.

"I did not go to school. I stayed in the house with my cousin who was younger and when I became bored, my *tatush* taught me to carve and I learned to make many things: animals, barn, house, all from wood. This is when I began to love sculpting.

"We returned to the farm a year later and I was so happy when I saw the bales of hay in the barn loft . . ." Her voice rose with excitement at the memory. "I threw myself on them and become covered in straw and pigeon droppings. I remember how angry my mother was because it was still winter and she must wash me before I catch a sickness. She was always afraid of something. That night our neighbors came and my father's friend, Darius Hankowski, told us that when we were gone a stranger came to look for us. I remember my mother was not happy at the news, that she paced the kitchen, biting her lips.

"Sometime later that year — I don't remember exactly — we were in Lubartow and when a skinny man in dirty clothes walked past us, my *tatush* became white like ghost. He stopped and squeezed my hand until he was gone. My *tatush* was so big — both my hands fit into one of his — I wondered why he was afraid of this stranger. This was in 1945. I see now why he was frightened."

Philip raised his eyebrows in question. "Are you saying it was Jake?"

She shook her head. "No, he would recognize us. Time passed. My parents must believe Jake is dead. Life became normal again, but later that year I . . . started having dreams."

Philip was toying with the vodka bottle now, tipping the neck back and forth with his long, tapered fingers. He looked up for a moment and she thought she detected a hint of sympathy in his gaze. She tried to catch his eye, but he ignored her, and worked the bottle, churning up the particles each time they floated to the bottom.

"When I recognize your uncle's photograph in newspaper and then in album, I guessed the names must be mine and my mother's, but I could not know for sure. Until now."

Karolina became aware of the clock ticking in the next room and her own low, heated breathing. She felt weary; still, she couldn't restrain a tired smile. "It is amazing, no?"

Philip didn't answer. Instead, he rose abruptly, thrust his hands in his pockets and began to pace. He paced with a swagger, his shoulders steady, swiveling his hips in the kind of walk she'd seen on athletes and teenage boys. Twice he stopped and looked as if he were about to speak, then tightened his lips and continued pacing.

Finally, he slid back onto the chair. He stared at her so long she

49

wanted to turn away, but she forced herself to meet his eyes. "I believe that you believe this," he said solemnly. "Still, we'll need solid proof. You understand what I mean by that?"

"Evidence?"

"Exactly."

"Of course! Tell me what must I do."

"Is there anyone in New York who knew you in Poland?"

"No, I don't think so."

"Then there'll be documents to gather, dates to check to see if they agree with what you and I already know."

"Yes! I was thinking I must do this! And you will help?"

He nodded.

"Oh, I am so glad! Yesterday I was sad you did not believe and today. . . . Thank you."

His eyes slid away. He seemed agitated again. He put his hands on his thighs and pushed himself up abruptly. "I've got to go," he said and moved toward the living room. Why was he leaving? What had she said?

"But we have much to discuss —"

"— you look exhausted. This is enough for tonight."

"Yes, of course. It is late. We will speak again. I would like to better know the family — your uncle, your father." She smiled shyly. "After all, you could be my cousin."

Philip gave her a half smile in return and grabbed his coat. "Maybe so."

She hurried after him and watched with mounting anxiety as he slipped his coat on. Words began to tumble from her. "I can write letters to officials in Poland. I will start tomorrow!"

"Fine."

She grabbed his arm. "Wait! The names you found. Tell me . . . which one was the daughter?"

"Chava."

"Chava." *She* was *Chava*. Her first name. The one she was born with. She repeated the name, echoing the harsh "ch" and short "a." "This is Jewish name?"

"Yes."

"What does it mean?"

"I think it's Hebrew for Eve — the first woman."

She felt suddenly giddy. "Chava," she whispered to herself and heard the door click shut behind Philip Landau.

The night felt painfully cold. It was only nine, yet the street was deserted. Philip rooted in his coat pocket for his cigarettes, lit one and shook himself to clear his head. The woman had unnerved him. Somewhere in the middle of her story he'd been seized with an almost physical sensation that she was telling the truth. No one could fake the feelings he'd seen slip across her face, the emotion in her voice. She seemed guileless, a strange mixture of strength and vulnerability he hadn't encountered before. Watching her, he felt almost convinced, but now, away from her clear, luminous eyes, away from her musky scent, he couldn't let go of the nagging sensation that he was being conned.

The church on Dyer Avenue was shut tight. A crèche stood in the front yard and the spotlights planted in the snow cast a ghostly glow over the scene. He studied the life-size statues of the holy family painted in vulgar shades of turquoise and felt a familiar tension in his shoulders. As a kid he and his friends habitually crossed the street when they spotted Christmas decorations or crosses, as though their God would strike them dead if he caught them standing too close to the competition. Philip stood a moment, marveling at the baby Jesus. Someone had actually dressed him in a tiny knit sweater. He took a last, harsh drag on his cigarette and ground it into the snow-covered sidewalk.

By the time he got home, it was almost 10. After a hot shower, he carried Ellen's leftover lasagna to the couch and sat down to eat. He'd been feeling so good, so up since his meeting with Drottman. The only thing preventing his life from being all around terrific was money, which, thanks to Jake, was going to cure itself. Or so he'd thought. Was it the money that made him suspect the Polish woman? He wished it were. He could deal with that. But there was something about her that was eating at him, something connected in his mind with her complete and utter goyishness.

In the distance the metallic scraping of a snowplow pricked a memory. Philip is ten years old. The war's been over for more than a year and his Uncle Jake has just arrived from a displaced persons camp in Germany. His mother and Aunt Bertha, having cooked a feast in celebration, brush the crumbs from the linen tablecloth and scrape the plates clean while the brothers — Philip's father, Meyer, and Noah's father, Izzy — talk with Jake. Philip has left Noah crouched over a Monopoly board on the living room floor and wandered in to listen to the men talk about their Lublin boyhood. They remind each other of the pranks they pulled on the *lerner* who taught at their *cheder*, about visiting their cousins in Yelna, a nearby village so small they'd referred to it as a *dorf*, about the speckled eggs and *kaise*, the dried squares of pot cheese they used to bring home and a *hein*, a chicken for *shabbos* — usually so scrawny, Meyer snickers, it barely filled a child's stomach. Their sisters, Luba and Hinda, have crushes on boys in the *dorf* and always come along *oiskepitz* in their nicest clothes. Philip leans against his father's shoulder and listens, loving the sound of these words and the pleasure he senses the men take in them. But then, at the mention of the dead sisters, Jake's face falls vacant. Meyer and Izzy avert their eyes. After a moment, Jake speaks: "Remember Kasimir, the dairy man on the road to Yelna?" "Yes," says Izzy, relieved that the silence is broken. Meyer chimes in: "He was a good *goy*. He never overcharged us." Jake ignores them and continues in a hollow voice: "When I came back from Maidenek, I stopped by to see him. I thought maybe he could tell me who was left. My head was shaved. I weighed eighty pounds, but he recognized me. He took one look and said, 'What! You're still alive?' and shut the door in my face. Can you imagine a neighbor did such a thing?" Philip's stomach knots in anger. He tugs at his uncle's shirtsleeve. "Why didn't you punch him in the face?" he shouts. "Why didn't you go back and shoot him," he yells, jabbing the air with his little boy fists. Jake lays a bony hand on Philip's shoulder, takes a sad breath and looks away.

The revenge fantasies started soon after that night. Philip would lie in bed, picturing himself as John Wayne, riddling a Nazi with a machine gun, or shooting some thick-necked Pole in the mouth and watching with satisfaction as the man's face exploded in a blur of blood and bone. Philip's father and uncles would stand by, grim-faced but appeased. He was their pain-easer, their pride, their avenging angel and the fury he felt at the injustice done to them, to all Jews, filled him with an enormous sense of power. He'd hoarded this anger since childhood and kept it in reserve like a secret reservoir of strength he knew would always be there, quietly waiting inside him.

Philip wandered over to the window to gaze out at the deserted street. Below, a car engine whined, struggling to free its ice-packed wheels. If Karolina was Jake's child, she had been very young when he'd given her away. She'd been brought up Catholic. She probably attended the church he had passed, the one with the statues out front. Even if she is Chava Landau, she's a Pole now — one with a crucifix hanging on her living room wall.

After Philip left, Karolina switched off the table lamp and stretched out on the sofa. She felt achy, as she did after a day of hammering stone. When her eyes adjusted to the dim light coming in from the street, she gathered her afghan around her shoulders and searched out the crucifix. It had belonged to her mother's mother and always hung on the wall near the tiled stove that had been the center of their home. The day they left for Koromov, her mother had carefully rolled the crucifix in a clean towel and tucked it into a carpetbag, and she'd rehung it as soon as they'd returned to the farm. After her father's death, Karolina had taken it with her to Warsaw and propped it on her dresser near a window so she could see it first thing in the morning. It was old and made of ash, a difficult wood to carve, but even in the dark living room she could make out the articulated lines of Christ's hair and the tiny thorns encircling His head. She loved this crucifix not only because it was beautifully crafted, not only because it reminded her of childhood, but also because the mixture of sadness and euphoria in Christ's face seemed to lie at the heart of her feelings for her religion. Life was full of suffering, He seemed to say, but believe in me and I will quiet your heart. Believe in me and you will find peace. Peace. Comfort. She'd known so little.

She burrowed into the corner of the couch and let her thoughts drift. When she'd told Philip about leaving the farm, she'd been conscious of holding back, as though reining in the images was the only way she could make sense of them in his presence. Now, the memories roiled up inside her and she let them find their own logic.

*   *   *

53

She hears her father hurrying toward the house. Something in his heavy footsteps catches her attention. She drops the doll she's dressing and goes into the kitchen.

Her mother stands near the stove facing the front door. Her face is creased with worry. "Janek?" she asks. Her tatush sets down the milk can in the doorway, pulls off his kapelusz and runs his fingers through his sand-colored hair. His cheeks are flushed as if he's been running.

"Janek!" her mother pleads when she sees him take down the vodka from behind the stove. He grabs a glass, tosses back a drink, and closes his eyes. Her mother tries to seize the bottle, but he holds it down on the table by its neck.

"One more!" He drinks again, then shoves the bottle to the other end of the table. "Maria, we are leaving."

Her mother glances quickly at Karolina, then back to her husband. She puts a finger to her lips. "When?" she whispers.

"As soon as you pack. Take only a few things. We don't have time." He opens his arms to Karolina and she climbs onto his lap. She smells the cow feed on his rough woolen jacket. She senses she mustn't ask questions, but she's frightened by the sound of his voice. "Tatush," she cries, burying her face in the warmth of his neck. "No!"

"Shush, shush," her mother murmurs, running her hand across Karolina's forehead. Then she reaches inside her pocket for her rosary and begins to weep.

"Go pack your things, then come and help your mother." Her tatush sets her down and gives her a small nudge. "Fast," he says, and she runs to her room with panic rising inside her.

The sun is setting by the time they start loading the wagon. Her parents barely speak while they gather their things, moving silently through the house, filling bags and boxes with clothes, piling dishes and pots into egg crates. The precious down quilts are carefully folded into clean flour sacks and left for last. Earlier, Karolina heard muttering in the kitchen, but could only make out a few words. ". . .say moved long ago . . ." her father said. ". . .no children. . . . Darius knows where, but he will never tell." Then her mother's tearful whisper, ". . .they would have found out, anyway . . ."

After Karolina stuffs her dolls and wooden toys into her own small sack, she stands in the kitchen and watches. No one asks for her help and she can feel them avoiding her. Stepping outside into the cool spring air, she

pulls her sack behind her and sits down on the stone steps to wait. The for-
est in the east looks smoky in the failing light. Birds flock to nearby trees in
excited chirping. Her parents gather the chickens into a wire cage and tie
the cow to the back of the cart. The pigs are to be left behind. They've been
promised to a neighbor, her father says, in return for looking after the farm
while they're gone.

By the time they finish loading, night has set in. She sits between her
parents on the wagon with a shawl draped across her knees. The nights are
still chilly and she smells wood smoke blowing from the Hankowski's house.
Everything is silent. Only when they've been on the road for long minutes
does she turn around to look. The moon has risen and floods of silver-gray
light filter through the trees onto the house. Karolina wedges herself deeper
between her mother and father, grips her doll's arm, then turns again and,
with terrible sadness, watches her house recede into the distance until it is
only a ghostly shadow against the blue-black of the night sky.

It was snowing again. She thought of winter streets in Lubartow and
the muffled clip clop of hooves on soft, snow-covered country roads.
Her limbs grew heavy and she felt herself sinking. Bunching a velvet
cushion beneath her head, she rolled onto her side and suddenly
Philip's face floated up. It occurred to her that she'd confused him
and he had fled. He didn't want to believe her. Yet he did. She could
feel it. She wished that he were here now so she could tell him all
that she remembered, all that was coming back, and he'd see, as she
did, that the pieces were finally coming together.

Chapter 7

"I want sleep, Kiki," Amanda cooed, sucking noisily on her thumb.

Karolina dislodged the child's finger and threaded the small arm through the flannel pajama sleeve. "Soon, my *kociatko*, soon."

Amanda always got sleepy around five, just when Linda and Noah were due home and would want time with her. Lifting her into her arms, Karolina kissed her neck, then her ear, then the tip of her diminutive nose. Ah, the wonderful, fragrant scent of a child's warm skin. She took an almost shameful delight in holding Amanda, loving the peace that overcame her each time she rubbed her face against the velvety cheeks. Children. How she loved the sincerity of their joy, the completeness with which they let themselves be loved.

Karolina would be thirty the next year. How long would she have to wait to start a family? A familiar longing took hold. During her first year in Warsaw she'd fallen in love with a painter, and shortly after they broke up she discovered she was pregnant. For weeks she moved through her life in a half-daze, tormenting herself with the idea of having the child. She began to study the few women in her group who lived with artists and had their children. She watched them at art exhibits and premieres, hovering in corners with screaming babies or bored, over-tired toddlers while their lovers gathered in groups, planning openings in remote cities without a second thought to the families they'd leave behind for months at a time. After a while the men showed up with younger, fresh-faced mistresses at their sides, women who stayed late at cafés, smoked endless cigarettes and distractedly picked pieces of tobacco from their carefully lipsticked mouths while their lovers talked about camera techniques and the French acrylics they'd bought on the black market. Karolina had an abortion, but for months afterwards she awoke with a heavy heart. Now, there were moments when she held Amanda's small hand in her own or lifted the delicately boned body in her arms that the hollow ache she associated with killing her child returned to pain her again.

Amanda wiggled, and hoisting her higher onto her shoulder, Karolina began to hum a lullaby. It was an old song, ancient she supposed, one that had lulled Polish children to sleep for generations. It struck her as ironic that a Jewish child would one day remember this lullaby with nostalgia. What would Philip think if he saw her now? He'd be angry, she supposed. His comments about Poles betraying Jews during the war had stung her and even though he'd said he'd help, she was worried. He'd left abruptly and not entirely convinced, it seemed to her. All day she'd waited with a kind of breathlessness for him to call, but the day had faded to evening and she hadn't heard from him.

The front door banged shut. Amanda squirmed to be let down. "Daddy home," she said, stretching out her small hands toward the dining room.

Noah was standing at the table, his lanky frame hunched over containers of Chinese takeout. Amanda ran to her father and buried her face in his lap while Karolina stationed herself in the doorway.

"Honey bun," Noah murmured, hugging Amanda to his chest. Averting his eyes, he motioned for Karolina to sit.

There had been an awkwardness between them since that night several weeks ago when Noah had tried to kiss her. She'd seen it coming, of course: the side-long glances, the lingering looks when he thought she wasn't watching, his flush and abrupt turning away when their eyes met. One evening when Linda worked late, Karolina had stepped from Amanda's room to find him waiting in the hallway. He'd given her a questioning look, then leaned forward and kissed her. She'd felt such longing on his mouth, such craving from this gentle, timid man that she'd been tempted to make love to him right there in the hallway. Instead, she shook her head at his pleading brown eyes and gave his cheek an affectionate rub before disappearing into the kitchen. Since then Noah had been reserved in her presence, not, she suspected, because he was hurt by her rejection, but because he was afraid she might leave.

"Philip told me you met last night," Noah said, scooping slices of beef onto his plate.

Karolina rushed to the table. "You spoke?"

He nodded. "Look, I'm sorry about the ID cards. It would have been awkward if I told you before Philip."

"He is still suspicious, yes?"

Noah smoothed out an imaginary crease in Amanda's pajama top. "I don't care. He's not the only one in the family this concerns." The harshness in his voice surprised her. Noah always spoke of people in a neutral, but well-meaning tone. Obviously the cousins weren't friends.

"I think you do not like Philip," she said.

"He's doing okay. There's no reason for him to be so . . . ungenerous."

"You speak of money?"

"Yes."

"Please understand it is not —"

"You don't have to convince me. Listen, I called someone in immigration for advice. He said getting information from Poland could take a long time. There's a lot of red tape involved."

"Yes, I know," Karolina laughed, relieved that he was willing to stand by her. "Red tape is communist invention. That is why they call tape *red.*"

There was a rustle behind them. Linda was standing at the door, pulling off her knit cap. She smoothed down her long blonde hair, then rubbed her nose, still red from the cold. She was in her usual mini skirt and ribbed sweater. Grown women dressing like little girls looked foolish to Karolina, but it was the new American fashion. Even the mothers in the playground wore coats so short their thighs turned red and chafed in the cold weather.

"What's so funny?" Linda asked. She sidled up to the table and ate a few spoonfuls of chicken and broccoli from a container.

"Just comparing bureaucracies," Noah said. "Actually, we were talking about Philip."

"Oh? Did they meet? What did he say?"

"It sounds like they're going forward."

"Good. I'm glad he's taking this seriously." She studied her drowsy child curled against Noah's chest. "What, sweetheart? Sleepy already?"

Amanda half opened her eyes and gave her mother a big yawn.

"No nap again?" she asked, lifting Amanda into her arms.

Karolina threw up her hands. "I tried, truly. First hot bath, then rubbing back, like you say, but she would not sleep."

"I never get to spend time with her anymore."

"I have told you Polish cure for this problem —"

"Oh, no," Linda laughed. "Honey laced with vodka is not, in my opinion, appropriate for a three-year-old."

"You think I am barbarian with old-fashioned European ways," Karolina teased, "but to go against children's nature, you must take strong actions."

"I may take stronger actions than that," Linda muttered. Balancing Amanda on her knee, she pulled off her calf-high, burgundy suede boots. "Her whole childhood is flying by while I waste my life on card catalogues. I need more time at home." She gave Noah's hand a meaningful pat. "For all our sakes."

Panic shot through Karolina. Linda thought she was leading Noah on and wanted her out! She might even believe they were sleeping together. She'd been so careful not to encourage Noah, praying that direct looks at the right time would bring him to his senses. She'd been a fool to think Linda wouldn't notice.

"Your working was never my idea," he muttered.

"I've already mentioned it to personnel. They can get someone from Columbia Library Arts to do an internship till they find a permanent replacement for me." Linda stared solemnly into her husband's eyes. "I thought I should let Karolina know I'm thinking about it, so she can keep her ears open for another job."

"Read me, Kiki, read me!" Amanda broke in with a wail, rubbing her sleep-swollen eyes with little fists.

"Shush, my *kociatko*, your mama will read."

Linda handed the child to Noah with a small, impatient toss of her head. "Why don't you put her to bed so Karolina and I can talk."

Noah glanced anxiously from his wife to Karolina, then lifted

Amanda and together they moved down the hallway to the nursery. When the door closed, Linda pushed herself away from the table and crossed her thin, stockinged legs.

"This is getting complicated, isn't it?" Linda said, "now that the whole family's involved." Her pale face creased with worry. She was no longer the shy, warm-hearted woman Karolina remembered from their first meeting. They'd been friends of a sort — Karolina used to arrive at the apartment a few minutes early so they could share a pot of coffee before Linda set off to work. That was before Noah started stammering every time Karolina walked into a room.

"You must not leave your work. I will look for other job."

Linda moved a morsel of chicken around her plate. "No, it is better this way. Maybe you should tell Noah, you know, that you agree it's best to work elsewhere."

"I want you to know there is nothing between us."

Tears filled Linda's eyes. "I know."

"I did not mean for anything to happen."

"But it has," Linda said.

"I am so sorry —"

"I don't want anyone to be sorrier . . ." She ran the back of her hand across her eyes and took a long breath. "So call your friend. Maybe he can help."

Linda knew she had a lover, but not that he was a married man with children, and now Karolina was grateful she'd never shared the details. "Yes, I will call him."

There seemed nothing left to say. Linda spread her long, thin hands out on the table and stared at them with unfocused eyes. Karolina gazed out at the living room. The functional, nondescript beige couch, the bland matching chairs suddenly struck her as incredibly lonely and she turned with sinking heart toward the darkness looming beyond the tall windows. No art classes tonight, no meeting with Jim. She would go directly back to Greenpoint alone.

Linda touched her sleeve tentatively. "It's as though you've lived someone else's life. Do you have any idea why your parents never told you?"

Her throat tightened. "Perhaps because they were afraid I would blame them. I can only guess."

"Your parents are both dead, aren't they?"

Karolina nodded.

Linda gave her arm a consoling pat and shook her head. "Then you'll probably always have more questions than answers."

Karolina turned onto Dyer Avenue and made her way down the icy street toward St. Stanislaus. The moon was full, a fat white disc floating in the night sky. The church stayed open till ten, long after bingo ended and most of her neighbors were in bed. But Greenpoint was a safe area and the old priest left the doors unlocked until he himself was ready to retire.

She pushed open the tall, carved doors and stepped into the church vestibule. Votive candles sent a dim light climbing up the nave. Crossing herself, she slid to her knees and gave herself to the silent, almost palpable comfort she'd known since childhood. When she was young, church had been a magical place where she whispered her secrets to the little boy who was lucky enough to be God's Son. As she grew older, so did Jesus, but it was the Son, not the Father, that she often prayed to. He remained, in the heart of her imagination, a grown man with a child's innocence and she trusted that the purity of His knowledge inside her would always lead her back to what was true. She folded her hands on the railing and bowed her head. "Holy Mary, mother of God . . ." she began and waited for the familiar closeness to descend. Nothing. She clasped her hands tighter. ". . .Pray for us sinners now and in the hour of our death." Linda's words echoed back. *You've lived someone else's life.* No, she wanted to shout back, she was still Polish, still Catholic, still her father's daughter. Her *tatush* had given her the best life he knew. And her unhappy mother? By the time she died, Karolina had long given up trying to understand her remoteness. As a child, she'd been loving, but later, as Karolina approached her teen years, they'd barely spoken. The house had fallen into silence then, her mother slipping more and more into fear and sadness, her father spending more time in town with his drinking friends. Perhaps her mother's distance was purposeful. Perhaps it was her father's idea to keep Karolina, and her mother had resented raising a Jewish child? Perhaps. Perhaps. Linda was right. She would never know.

"Hail Mary, full of grace, the Lord is with thee, . . ." Somewhere at the edge of her memory a picture was forming. Her classmates were standing in the field adjacent to their school, looking down at uprooted stones they'd found, strange stones engraved with Hebrew letters. They made jeering comments that all the *Zhidi* were dead, burned up by the Germans. She remembered the contempt she'd felt for the people who wrote in squiggles and was glad, like the others, that the Jews were gone. I am like those stones now, Karolina thought. I have been turned over and underneath I am marked with a foreign alphabet.

She heard a soft jangle. The priest moved through the altar, his keys falling against the folds of his cassock as he gathered the chalice and plates. Karolina clenched her hands and listened to the sound of her breathing echo in the cold air of the church. She was still a mystery to herself, her life still a blur. Secretly, she'd hoped that a new country would jolt her, that away from the haunted stones of her home, the veil of estrangement that had hung over her would miraculously fall away. Jim would save her, would be the one who would illuminate the dark landscape in which she moved. She hadn't known how much her love for him was a need to recreate herself, that she'd been mistaken to entrust her life to another.

When she opened her eyes again, the glare from the altar candles hurt and she blinked to dispel the pain. Everything *was* different now, but not at all as she'd hoped. One cousin was still suspicious of her; the other seemed ready to jeopardize his marriage *for* her. Noah was her only ally and now his wife had banished her from their home. She pressed her hands to her lids and stood up. She would take care of herself, she thought, briskly turning up the aisle, and she would do it alone if she had to.

Chapter 8

Traffic across the Brooklyn Bridge was still light at 3:30 and Philip made it to Bensonhurst in under half an hour. Turning down 18th Avenue, he caught sight of Harry Kantrowitz bundled up in a black overcoat and thick gloves salting the walkway in front of his dairy store. Philip loved the bricks of butter and scallion cream cheese wrapped in glossy paper his mother brought home from Kantrowitz's, and when he had time, he'd double park and run in for a few slabs to take back to Manhattan. Waiting for the light to change, he glanced past Harry through the steamy shop window. Except for Mrs. Kantrowitz, sitting glumly on her stool next to the cash register, the store was empty. Kantrowitz's Dairy was the last family-owned grocery on the avenue. The Daitch supermarket that had opened a few years back had siphoned off customers from the local merchants and Harry, like Philip's father, was just hanging on until he could retire. Both men belonged to a group of Bensonhurst Jews who migrated south each winter to spend a month sitting on benches in Miami's Dorchester Park instead of the benches in front of their Brooklyn homes. When Meyer retired, Philip would have to make a once-a-year appearance in Florida — which would be okay if he could tie them in with Alice's school vacations. He could take her to the ocean, to see alligators and herons in the Everglades, and the dolphins at Sea World. And she'd get to spend time with her grandparents. His ex-wife never got used to the shouting matches that passed for conversation in the Landau house, and after their split, Philip threw himself into drumming up work and could only manage a few Saturday drop-ins on his parents. Alice would sprawl on the floor with the paper dolls and coloring books his mother always had waiting, and Dora seemed happy just to stroke her granddaughter's head while Philip and his father ate their smoked fish and bagels. Too much time had gone by. His daughter would grow up without any feeling for her European family, without a connection to her roots. He was not going to let that happen.

Philip turned down 68th Street and found a spot near the house. Roughly half the two-story, red brick row houses on the street were covered in Christmas lights — the only thing that distinguished Catholic from Jewish homes. The neighborhood was a relatively harmonious mixture of working class, family-rooted Italians and Jews. Everyone sent their children to the local public schools and mixed-faith friendships were tolerated until high school or as soon as a girl started wearing a bra — whichever came first. Philip's parents kept quiet when he played stoop-ball with Salvatore Puglesi who lived down the block, and Philip suspected his father knew he spent Saturday afternoons making out with his Italian girlfriends in the balcony of Loews' 86th Street. And why not, Meyer would have said, if his son was getting something from the *shiksas* that a marriageable Jewish girl would never dream of giving? But had Philip so much as mentioned Angela or Veronica in his parents' presence, they would have gone berserk.

Philip's father had shoveled a narrow path through the snow and Philip walked cautiously from the curb to the low, wrought-iron gate that enclosed his parents' tiny front yard, then maneuvered himself up the stoop to the front door, cursing each slippery, frozen step. Every winter he begged his father to hire a neighbor's son to do the work, but Meyer always blew him off, even after Philip warned his father he'd have a serious lawsuit on his hands if someone fell. He wasn't sure if it was saving money or saving face that kept his sixty-five-year-old father with angina shoveling away, but every winter the pathway got narrower and narrower.

His father opened the door before Philip could knock. "This is some story, no?" Meyer said, his voice raspy with agitation.

Philip hung his coat in the front closet and put a reassuring hand on his father's shoulder. "Isn't it, though?"

His mother came out of the kitchen, kissed him on the cheek and gave him one of her aggrieved looks before slipping back to her domain. She spent most mornings helping out in their furniture store, and when she came home after lunch, she changed into her regulation house dress and rubber-soled slippers and started washing down the plastic chair covers and linoleum floor as though an army of kids lived there. Dinner got earlier every year. Philip could smell onions frying in the kitchen.

Philip squeezed past the oversized mahogany coffee table to the sagging brocade couch while Meyer lowered his bulky frame onto his beloved Castro recliner. This morning, when Philip called, his father had been so upset by the news of the Polish woman that he'd closed the store early and hurried home to wait for him. It was just 4:00 P.M. and he'd already changed into his cracked leather slippers and brown Perry Como cardigan.

"You see what life is?" Meyer said. "A man dies and a month later his child shows up."

"Maybe."

Meyer eyed him. "It's not true?"

"I don't know, Dad. Too soon to tell."

"You haven't told Rosalind yet, right?"

"No."

"Maybe you should wait until you know for sure what's what with this woman?"

"Jake and Rosalind were married for twenty years! He must have talked to her about his child. And if he didn't, somebody's got to tell her the news. This woman isn't going to disappear. Didn't Jake *ever* say anything about hiding his kid?"

Meyer stared out from under scruffy brows. "No."

Jake's death had hit his father hard and he could feel Meyer grow tense in anticipation of their conversation. Talking about the loss would make him angry — the only way Meyer knew to deal with pain. But there was no way around it. "How come you don't know more about what happened?"

"You're mad at me for not knowing?" Meyer's voice rose an octave. "You know Jake wasn't a talker."

"I'm not mad. I'm just asking. It seems strange."

"How could I know anything? Jake was still a bachelor when me and Izzy left for the States."

"When was that?"

"In 1933. He moved to Rovno right after to apprentice with a leather tooler. That's where he met his wife."

"So you didn't know her?"

"No, they came back to Lublin just before the Germans marched in. By then, me and Izzy were gone six years."

"He must have talked to you about his family when he first came to the States."

"Sure he did. He said they were dead. All I know is what your Aunt Hinda wrote and that wasn't much. Nobody got letters after 1939." Meyer's face took on that hollowed-out look he got whenever the war was mentioned. No matter how crabby, how short-fused or unreasonable Meyer got, Philip always buckled under his father's grief.

"That's when they all got caught — your aunts, your grandparents. Ah, if they'd stayed in Rovno under the Soviets, who knows, maybe they could have escaped to the Russian zone." Meyer rubbed his chest and grimaced. " Maybe someone would have survived."

"I need to know exactly what Hinda wrote," Philip said.

"I think Jake married in '35."

"You *think* or that's what she wrote?"

"She wrote. They had a little girl, I guess about a year later."

"You *guess?*"

Meyer threw up his hand impatiently.

"Dad, I need you to be precise."

"Hinda wrote that for *sure*, so you can calm down." He stared over Philip's shoulder at some distant memory. "I can tell you Jake's wife must have been from a poor family because Hinda wasn't happy about the marriage. She wrote the wife was *prost*, you know, coarse. Hinda always gave herself airs as if our family was rich or something." He let out a short laugh. "Okay, your grandfather had a leather business, but we weren't fancy people. Your aunts — may they rest in peace — always treated Jake like he was a little gentleman. They kept forgetting they lived over a store."

Philip tried not to look glazed. Meyer's attitude toward his dead relatives had always been defensive. The more faults he could find in them, the less guilty he felt that he'd survived — as if they'd brought tragedy on themselves with their uppity attitude.

"Boy, were they disappointed when Jake ended up a laborer — excuse me, a *craftsman*, Hinda called it. Craftsman, schmaftsman, he still worked with his hands. And tell me please what's so wrong with that?" He fell into a brooding silence. Then: "Remember when Jake first came over and he stayed with us? Didn't I give him work in the store? Didn't I lend him money? And why not? How many brothers does a person have?"

Philip pictured the gaunt, bent man with the empty eyes who sat at their table while everyone crowded around him, hammering him with questions and falling all over themselves to feed him. At night that first week, Philip lay in his room with his door ajar, listening to his father and uncle talk. Except for the names of the towns, Philip couldn't make out much of what they were saying, but he sensed the anguish in their voices. Jake spoke in a husky murmur, barely audible except when he barked out *todt, todt* like a chant in the dark after Meyer asked if anyone had survived. Then, for the second time in his life, Philip heard his father cry. The first had been six months earlier, in June '45 when he got the letter that Jake was alive.

"I'll tell you the truth," Meyer said, "when I first saw him, I couldn't believe it. A stranger he was, my own brother, who used to be the funniest one in the family, always a *kuntzler* with a little joke. *Ja*, the war did it to him," he nodded, pumping the folds under his chin. "Even later, when he got rich, he never had *nachis*." Meyer swabbed his nose, grunted softly, then stole a glance at Philip. "You're suspicious, aren't you? That's why you're pestering me."

"I'm not pestering you, Dad. I just can't believe no one in this *whole* family ever talked about Jake's daughter!"

"Believe it! You remember how Jake got when anyone mentioned the camps. He just stared like he wasn't here. All he said was the daughter was dead. I was afraid I'd give him a heart attack if I asked anything." Meyer's cheeks began to tremble. "I miss him, Philly. I could never say it, but I loved him . . . my own brother . . ."

Philip edged to the corner of the couch and put his arm around his father. They sat together, Meyer with his head down, Philip, kneading his shoulder until Meyer motioned him to stop.

"Dad," he whispered. "I can't stay. I've got to get to Rosalind's before the Brooklyn-Queens Expressway jams up."

"You come here almost never and when I try to talk, you're

rushing out," Meyer growled. "No wonder you don't know anything."

It was useless to point out he'd been working his ass off. He was his father's only pleasure. He could never visit enough or call enough, never make up for his suffering, imaginary or real.

"I just don't get it," Philip ventured. "If Jake did give his daughter to Poles, why wouldn't he have told you?"

"He once said something about being a coward. Maybe he thought if he'd kept her with him . . . I don't know, maybe he could have saved her." He sounded hoarse. He'd given up smoking years before but his voice had never lost its scratchy edge. "People have all kinds of crazy ideas. Who knows? He never talked about the old country. He got married, he got rich, he got a new life and that was that."

Shadows deepened in the living room corners. Philip gazed out the window to the sycamore tree that grew in the patch of earth behind the house that passed for a back yard. In the springtime, when Philip was a kid, his father would bring up a card table and folding chairs from the basement and they'd eat dinner in the sun. He didn't do that anymore. He said it was too much trouble. These days, anything that might bring a little pleasure was too much trouble.

Meyer switched on the ceramic shepherdess lamp next to his chair and squinted into the new brightness. "You know your grandparents went to Treblinka. You heard of Treblinka?" he asked for the hundredth time.

"Dad —"

"Jake said *Kaddish* for all of them on Yom Kippur, so he must have thought the daughter was dead. Ah, remember when your mother lit *yortzeit* candles for the family? Every year we had to put them on a higher shelf because you were so wild, such a little *gonif* and we were afraid you'd burn the house down. Nobody could tell you anything." He let out a sudden laugh. "You'll never guess who came into the store this morning. Rosa Mandel! She was shouting like a crazy woman that she heard about you from her cousin who said you were a big lawyer. 'I knew he'd be a *macher*,' she screamed. Ha! And that *yenta* was always yelling for you to get off the stoop."

Short, squat Rosa, with hair the color of lead, lived next door and spent most of her waking life perched on her bench guarding the block. Throughout high school, Philip had scandalized her with his tight chinos and Presley pompadour, and the time she'd seen him with one of his Italian girl friends, the ones with dyed black hair and frosted lips, she'd put her hand to her heart and looked faint. If he caught her narrowing her eyes at him, he'd sashay over and tease her with a big hug, then watch with amusement as she grew pink-faced and flustered before shooing him away. Later, when Philip made captain of the basketball team and won a Merit Scholarship, she confided to Dora Landau that she'd always known he'd be a somebody. For that, his mother forgave Rosa everything.

Philip got up and began to pace. It was getting late. "Let's get a timetable going. When was Jake deported?"

"In '42. To Maidenek."

"You're sure?

"I'm sure."

He reasoned that anyone would have kept a child until the very last minute. If Jake did find someone to hide his daughter, it would have been before the Germans finally shipped all the Jews in the Lublin ghetto to concentration camps. According to the identity card, Chava Landau was six at the time, old enough to remember.

"How'd Jake's first wife die?"

"How? By the Nazis, of course, like your aunts, like your grandparents, like everybody else."

"When?"

"I don't know."

His mother was suddenly standing in the entrance to the dining room, holding a long serving fork in her hand.

"I made you a plate," Dora said.

"No thanks, Mom."

"Pot roast."

He shook his head.

"Look at you," she said, pointing the utensil at him as if he didn't know who he was. "Always so skinny."

"I know where to come if I want fattening up."

She padded into the living room and sat on the ottoman next to the couch, holding the fork upright. A few bits of meat glistened on the tines.

"Philly, darling, what's with this *meshugenah* story? Jake dies and leaves you money, and a week later he's got a daughter?"

"It happens," Meyer said. "Just a couple of years ago there was a big article in the Forward that a woman tracked down a niece who was given to Poles during the war."

Dora dismissed him with a wave of her hand. "*Tatenu*," she whispered to Philip as though he were an inept child. "I'm worried."

"Of course you are, Mom." Philip gave her cheek a playful pinch. "That's your profession."

"You know what I mean," she said, pushing his hand away. "You're not rich *yet*, you know, and that alimony you pay . . ." She shook her head tragically. She'd never liked his ex-wife, always called her a cold fish. But divorce, especially if there was a child, was unthinkable to Dora, who would rather her son had stuck out a bad marriage than see him fail at anything, even love.

"In other words, your mother is afraid you won't get the money Jake's left you."

"Of course he'll get it! His uncle wanted him to have it." Dora's plump face turned blotchy. "You gave Jake the money to start his business and when he begged you to go in with him, all of a sudden you were too scared to risk — what? A broken-down furniture store on Bay Parkway? Now what have you got to leave your son?"

Philip toyed with the lid of the porcelain candy box on the coffee table and waited for them to play it out. He'd learned years ago that it was useless to interfere.

They'd end their lives at each other's throats and there was nothing he could do about it.

"I bet Ellen has something to say about this," Dora said, sweeping aside the wisps of gray hair that had fallen onto her forehead. "She's upset, right?"

"Don't start, Mom."

"Excuse me for mentioning anything. You're only my son."

"I don't know how Ellen feels," he said, giving his stock answer.

When he'd told Ellen about his meeting with the Polish woman, she'd gone over all the legal angles like the professional she was, then let the subject slip away. Which didn't surprise him. Ellen kept her distance when it came to his family. It wasn't her family, she'd say, and although they agreed they weren't ready for marriage, Ellen had too much pride to let on how she felt. There were times, though, especially when they made love, when Philip sensed she wanted him to overwhelm her, to make her open up in spite of herself. But he held back, reluctant to force from her what he wasn't ready to give himself.

Dora turned to her husband with a blistering look. "You could do your son a favor, Meyer."

"What, what favor?"

"You could say Jake told you he *knew* for sure his daughter was dead. Who would question you, huh?"

"He never said that!" Meyer bellowed.

"Why did he light candles and say *Kaddish* if he didn't think so?"

"Just because he *thought* she was dead doesn't mean she was!"

"You know why your father would let this woman take your money?" Dora said, rubbing her eyes with the back of her hand. "Because he wants everyone should sweat for every penny like he did. God forbid anyone, even his son, should have it too easy. I've kept quiet for years, but not anymore. It's your money. You shouldn't let anyone take it from you."

"Dora, you've said enough!"

"Sure, sure, enough," she mumbled and shuffled back into the kitchen. Philip heard pots clanging.

A rope of pain uncoiled in his stomach. His mother was right. Meyer was congenitally suspicious and if he so much as entertained the Polish woman's claim, it was because it rankled him that Philip would have money without slaving for it. Even on the day he'd announced his scholarship to Columbia, he'd caught a quiver of resentment flash across his father's face. Without struggling to make a living, Philip would forget his working class roots — like Jake — and he'd no longer respect his father — like Jake. Being loved by children wasn't that important to Meyer and his European cronies. But respect? That was a must.

He didn't have the heart for this kind of talk, he didn't have the strength.

He was about to make his escape when he noticed the family album out on the dining room table. He picked up the tattered Naugahyde book and flipped past the first section with pictures of his mother's parents taken in Russia just before the pogrom that drove them to America. When he was a kid, he called them the "brown people" because their dark hair and stern sepia faces made them look like American Indians stuffed into European clothing. He leafed ahead to the Lublin section and stopped at a photo taken just before Meyer and Izzy left for America. The brothers and sisters had gathered in the dusty courtyard of their house for a farewell shot. Hinda and Luba stood at either end with their arms around their brothers' shoulders, smiling into the sun. They had short curly hair cut in waves that dipped on their foreheads and their flowered dresses were long-sleeved with a touch of lace at the collars. Jake was in the center wearing a fedora rakishly tilted to one side, grinning at the camera with a mischievous expression Philip had never seen in all the years he'd known his uncle. Who was this man who'd smiled and laughed and joked, who'd married a young woman and carried his child in his arms?

Thinking back, Philip found it curious that Jake, who'd suffered the most of the three Landau brothers, had been the generous one. He'd had an uncanny knack for figuring out what Philip and Noah wanted and always brought something along when he visited: Tinker Toys, Etch-A-Sketch kits, Howdy Doody holsters. The year the Dodgers won the World Series, Jake gave them baseball cards of Duke Snyder and Peewee Reese, gifts Philip was sure Rosalind picked out, since Jake, like most Europeans, didn't know a thing about American sports. The year before, when Alice turned five, Jake gave her a gold Star of David and an Israel bond worth five hundred dollars. He'd presented these gifts, muttering it was nothing, nothing, while Philip pumped his hand in thanks. His parents couldn't afford this kind of extravagance, yet even though Meyer resented Jake's money, he never begrudged his brother's generosity — not then. After all, Jake was *childless,* Dora would whisper when Jake was out of earshot. What greater tragedy could befall a Jew?

Philip ran his hand across the cracked binding and closed the album with a heavy heart. Meyer eyed the book, then dropped his head.

He's been looking through it, Philip thought, that's why it wasn't in its usual place.

Meyer leaned against the back of his chair. The pockets under his eyes were swollen. Since his angina had been diagnosed, he'd turned into an old man. "Something about this woman doesn't smell right to you, heh?"

Philip nodded.

"So? What do you want me to do?"

"Do?"

"You want I should say . . . what your mother said?"

His poor father; if he couldn't get respect, he'd settle for gratitude, even if it meant lying .

"No, Dad, don't."

"How are you going to find out for sure?"

"The usual way: hard work."

Meyer heaved himself out of his chair with a sigh. "It's getting late. The BQE is bad at this hour. Better take the Belt."

"Don't fight with Mom about this, okay? It'll work out, I promise."

Meyer waved him off.

Philip was at the front closet. "I want to stop by with Alice next week. Ask Mom if it's okay."

"Why? You think we have important appointments somewhere?" Meyer's broad face broke into a soft grin. "That little *momza*, I bet she's grown a foot. I'll tell your mother to make the pineapple kugel the little one likes so much."

"I'll let you know tomorrow which night is good. I'll probably have to work late so I couldn't get here till later than you like to eat, but at least we can spend a little time."

"New customers?"

"Yeah, and I'm doing some volunteer working for the AJC. "

"Yes? What kind?"

"A public accommodations violation down in Atlanta."

"Tell me in plain English."

"A hotel that won't rent rooms to Jews."

Meyer shoved his hands in his pants pockets and glared at the floor. There were brown spots on his forehead Philip had never noticed before. "You see?" Meyer said, bitterly. "You turn your back for one minute and the *goyim* are ready with their knives.

Chapter 9

There was a moment during Philip's drive to Great Neck when it hit him that Jake's death was the first in his immediate family. He pictured the young Jake smiling out at him from his father's album and was seized with a profound sense of loss for this uncle and for all the relatives who, somewhere in the not too distant future, would start dying of heart disease or cancer or fade into senility. He hadn't realized how much his meager sense of Judaism depended on these European Jews; except for a couple of commonplace words, he didn't understand any Yiddish or Hebrew or even the significance of most of the holidays, since he'd refused lessons beyond what he needed to chant his Bar Mitzvah. Once everyone was gone, what Jewishness would be left? The prayer shawl his father kept in a worn velvet bag and only took down on the high holidays? Nostalgia for the smell of kasha and frying onions? The memory of Jake's tattooed forearm peeking out from his shirt-sleeve? This sense of loss was new, and Philip felt overwhelmed by the tug of his roots, something he'd resisted since childhood, since he was ten years old and first saw those blue numbers crudely etched into his uncle's flesh. Of course, he'd known what the numbers meant — they'd all been bombarded with newsreels of stick-figure survivors holding up emaciated arms for GI camera crews — but the man who came to live in Philip's house from a ravaged Europe was *his uncle*, and he'd been branded like a steer, like a goddamn animal by another human being. When he first saw the tattoo, Philip's heart had thudded wildly in his child's chest, and from that day on a barrier had sprung up between him and the people who'd let themselves be humiliated and tortured and finally slaughtered. Even when he was older and understood the impossibility of resisting the Nazis, so great was his initial revulsion to those blurred numbers that the barrier remained impenetrable. Now, this Polish woman's claim suddenly made him feel hugely Jewish, Jewish with a vengeance. The thought that a Pole might be trying to deceive a Jew again, stripping one of his money even in death enraged him. This was America, dammit! No more sheep!

Philip stared at the glistening highway before him. It was snowing again, a light feathery snow that swirled menacingly out of the darkness into his headlights. When he'd phoned his Aunt Rosalind that morning she'd sounded strangely distant, and he realized only one month had gone by since Jake's heart attack. He dreaded telling her about the Polish woman. His aunt's childlessness had been the tragedy of her life, and now, after losing Jake, she might be about to inherit a child who wasn't hers and probably not even her husband's, but who was going to demand a birthright and put her through hell to get it.

He pulled into the circular driveway of Rosalind's two-story Tudor house. The top floor was dark and a faint light came from the living room. He cut the engine and sat staring at the house through a haze of falling snow.

The Landaus were a small family; his mother's immigrant parents had died before he was born and her only brother had moved to Chicago as a young man and never returned. Most get-togethers took place in Jake and Rosalind's large Long Island house. Visiting them was like going to a fancy restaurant with fine linens and crystal water goblets, only the food was too American for Dora and Noah's mother, Bertha, both of whom insisted on bringing along their homemade *real* kreplach, *real* flanken, *real* babka, which Rosalind accepted graciously.

"Come in, come in." Rosalind stepped aside to let Philip brush snow from his overcoat, her round dark eyes sparkling with delight as she took him in. A torn black mourning ribbon hung from the pocket of her beige silk blouse. When she stood on her tiptoes to kiss him, her stiff beehive brushed against his cheek. The house was, as always, immaculate. Tasseled pillows lined up on the white couch. Porcelain *tshatshkes* filled the glass shelves — a "regular museum," Dora always called it. Rosalind had covered the dining room table with one of her elaborately embroidered tablecloths, the only European touch in her otherwise modern American home of beige-toned furniture and wall-to-wall carpeting. She'd laid out a cake dusted with powdered sugar and placed a silver coffee urn on a lace doily next to it.

Rosalind had lost weight. Her slacks were loose around the hips and she looked diminished in her buttoned-up blouse. Even her shoulders seemed to have shrunk.

"I haven't felt like going out yet," she said. "But it's nice to have people over." She cut into the cake and was about to put a slice on his plate when she glanced at the grandfather clock against the wall. "Will this ruin your appetite? Are you having dinner with Ellen later?" She gave him an impish grin that reminded him of the first time Jake brought her to meet the family. She'd had a booming laugh then and an eagerness to please, and everyone liked her right away. She'll be great for Jake, they'd said, she'll put a little life into him. Rosalind's parents, second generation Jews who owned a stationery shop in Flatbush, were against her marrying the greenhorn who worked in his brother's furniture store, but, as Dora put it, the *alte maidl*, the old maid of thirty-eight, had fallen for the European whose quiet manner she took as a sign of character. Over the years Jake's gravity had drained much of Rosalind's liveliness and left her with a benign cheerfulness that made her seem more simple than happy. Now, a moment's coyness had turned her into the lively aunt who'd always been his favorite.

"Ellen's got a Legal Aid thing tonight," Philip said. "I'll grab a bite later. Tell me how've you been getting along."

She shook her head stoically. "Oh, you know. I went to my bridge group last night. The women are really so good to me, but then everyone goes home. I left all the lights on so it wouldn't feel so empty when I came back, but that made it worse. We never did that when Jake was alive." Her eyes brimmed. "He wasn't old, Philly, only sixty-three. He had many years yet."

Philip took her hand. "Roz . . . what do you know about Jake's wife and child?"

She looked startled. "They died in the war. I know everyone was surprised I mentioned them in the obituary, but I wanted to . . . out of respect."

"Do you have any idea why nobody ever talked about them?"

"Your uncle put it all behind him when he stepped off the boat."

She leaned back with a sigh. "I only found out about them after we married. I wasn't getting pregnant so we went to a specialist. The first time we met with the doctor, he asked Jake if he had, to his knowledge, ever fathered a child. Would you believe Jake looked straight at him and said 'Yes.' I couldn't say a word, I was so shocked and hurt that he'd keep such a thing secret from me! After, he told me he'd been married and had a daughter. When the tests came back, it turned out it was my fault we couldn't have children."

"Did he tell you their names?"

"The wife was Rachel, the child Chava. She was named after somebody's grandmother, I think. Noah told me he found the cards in the bank box."

Philip was suddenly up, trying to string together the right words. There was no way he could make this easy. He put his hands on her shoulders. Gray roots were visible where she parted her blonde hair. Sweet Rosalind had always seemed more youthful, more energetic than his mother. Tonight she looked older than sixty.

"You're upset, Philip. What is it?"

"A woman showed up claiming to be Jake's daughter."

Rosalind gasped and put her hand to her mouth. He could see her chest heave beneath her blouse.

"Noah and Linda have a Polish nanny. She claims Jake hid her with Poles during the war. She says she recognized Jake from the obituary and a picture in Noah's album."

While Rosalind sat transfixed, Philip paced the room, describing how the Polish woman had showed up in his office three days earlier. He told her about their meeting the night before and how certain things she'd said made sense while others, like meeting Linda at the funeral home, seemed too contrived to be a coincidence.

A film of sweat covered Rosalind's face. She pulled a tissue from her blouse cuff and dabbed at her forehead. "My God! Jake never said anything. Have you asked your father about this? What does he say?"

"He's heard about children who were given to Poles, so he thinks maybe."

"And your mother?"

"You know my mother, always the cynic. But that's because she's worried about me." He gave his neck a quick rub. He wasn't going to talk with her about Jake's money.

"And Izzy? Bertha? What do they think about this?"

"Noah probably told his parents, but I haven't talked to them yet."

She threw up her hands in astonishment. "I can't believe this! Jake's daughter alive! Is it possible?"

"Yes, it's possible, but the question is, is it true? Try to remember what else Jake told you. Does anything come to mind?"

"Nothing, nothing . . . he looked for the daughter, that much I know, so he must have hoped. Right after we married, he got lots of official-looking letters from Polish agencies. He told me they were his birth certificate and other papers he needed for legal reasons, but later, after the specialist, I realized, no, he's searching for his girl even though he said she was dead." Rosalind fingered the black mourning ribbon thoughtfully. "For a long time I thought he was sad because we couldn't have children. But it was just the opposite. He didn't want any. That's why he married me, because he thought I was too old." Philip reached for her hand again, but she stopped him. "It's all right, Phil. I know he loved me. But he didn't want another child. He went along with the fertility treatments because of me. Later, he said he was relieved it didn't happen. He didn't want to risk losing another child. The foolish man thought if he didn't talk about it, he could keep it a secret, even from himself." She took a moment to catch her breath. "Tell me what she looks like," Rosalind asked suddenly. "Does she look like Jake?"

Philip thought of Karolina and for some reason it wasn't her face that came to mind, but the thick, luxurious hair she wore swept up in heavy folds on top of her head. The hair was a mass of golden brown waves and he recalled the way a few loose strands hugged the curve of her neck. Then he pictured the blue eyes, the high cheekbones and her narrow, slightly turned-up nose. No, she didn't look like the young Jake or the old one or anyone else in the family. But neither did he for that matter. His hair was black, his complexion tawny. People usually took him for Italian or Spanish, but not Jewish — until they heard Landau. Both his parents were fair-skinned and his mother's eyes were a deep blue — *shiksa* eyes, his father called them, like the Polish woman's. "She doesn't look like him particularly, but I can't judge."

Rosalind sat up with a start. "Wait! There's a picture! I found it in Jake's wallet. He must have carried it around for years."

She hurried to the breakfront, pulled open a drawer and began leafing through a stack of papers. "Here," she said. "Look at this."

She handed him a small black and white photograph about two inches square. It was badly tattered along the edges and crisscrossed by deep cracks patched on the back with yellowing scotch tape. The photo was faded and worn to white in places where it had rubbed against the leather wallet; still, he could make out a little girl about two years old propped on a woman's lap, clutching a rattle in her fist. Only the woman's arms and hands were visible, and there was a wedding band on the ring finger of her left hand. The child wore a crocheted hat with a pompom, a dress, thick leggings and tightly laced leather-soled shoes. The picture was blurred, as though it had been shot through a cloud of smoke, but he could make out round eyes, a small upturned nose, and the faint outline of a rosebud mouth. The cheeks were plump, the ankles and wrists pudgy. Generic child. Anybody's child. He tossed the picture aside.

Rosalind's anxious eyes were glued on him. "Well? Could it be?"

"I don't know. It's impossible to tell if the eyes are light or dark, and only a few strands of hair are sticking out."

"What about the nose, the shape of the face?"

Philip lifted his shoulders in a helpless shrug. "It doesn't matter, anyway. Children's looks change as they grow."

Rosalind hunched over the photo, scrutinizing the small faded square, then hugged herself and began to rock. Tears streamed down her face. "Look how white it is, how many times he rubbed it! All those years he carried this with him and I didn't know," she moaned, letting her head fall to her chest. " Oh, my poor, poor Jake."

Philip took her in his arms. After a moment, she pulled away and made a little worried noise while she wiped her cheeks with her damp handkerchief. "She says she's Chava?"

"Yes."

"When can I meet her?"

"You don't have to — until we know more. And maybe never, if we find out she's lying."

"Do you think so?"

"I just don't know. She's got nothing concrete, just vague memories. She could have found those names in a registry in Poland and tracked Jake to the States. It's not hard to do, if you know where to look."

Rosalind shook her head in sad disbelief. "What a thing to make up."

"People get creative when money's at stake."

"But you said you spent the evening with her. You must have an impression of the kind of person is she."

"It doesn't matter what I think," he said. "I'm planning to go to the American Jewish Joint Distribution Committee. They've got deportation rosters in their archives. I'll start looking through them. If a Chava Landau is listed, it means she was shipped to a camp. Then I think it's unlikely this woman is Jake's daughter. But even if Chava wasn't deported, she could have died some other way. The burden of proof is on this woman. I'm sure her attorney —"

"What! She has an attorney already?"

"I don't think so, but she'll probably want to get one."

Rosalind stretched her arms out on the table and began adjusting her rings. "What's her name?" she said, staring at the back of her hands.

"Karolina Staszek."

"Does she have a place to stay?"

"She rents an apartment in Greenpoint."

"Oh, I thought, maybe if she was living with Noah and Linda, I could give her a room here . . ." Rosalind blushed. "I'd like to meet her, anyway."

"There's no reason to get you involved yet. We have a lot to clear up first."

Her face crumbled with pain. "I loved your uncle," she said, gripping Philip's hand. "Oh, I know your parents thought he was cold to me. That's how it looked from the outside . . . but we were close. He used to cry in my arms." She swallowed back tears. "If this is his child . . ."

"Let's wait and see how this turns out before you open yourself up for disappointment."

"Maybe you're right. Maybe I'm too eager." She looked past him into the darkness beyond the picture window. The pane was opaque with mist. "I hate this time of night," she said and gathered a few crumbs into a pile near her plate.

Chapter 10

Philip woke early on Saturday hungry for Alice and determined to purge Simon, Karolina, even Abe Drottman, from his mind. He hadn't spent a full day with his daughter in months, and lately, when they spoke on the phone, he heard a note of sadness in her voice. Alice had a fierce intelligence, yet was a contemplative child, a muller by nature, and because she never showed resentment or anger, it was hard for him to gauge how she felt. He swore he'd make today fun from start to finish and there'd be more like it. Dorothy had already done the research for him. TWA ran two daily flights between Atlanta and New York. Once Drottman's case got under way, he'd be able to fly home for weekends with Alice.

He drove to Brooklyn Heights to pick up his daughter, then swung by State Street for Ellen. Crossing the bridge on the way back, Philip gazed at the New York City skyline spread out before him. After a week of sleeting rain and snow, a brilliant December sun fell in silver strips across the East River, and here and there sea gulls circled small, white-crested waves. Brimming with pleasure, he belted out a medley of half-remembered show tunes in a falsetto that kept Alice and Ellen doubled over with laughter.

Ellen had begged off the day's entertainment; she wanted to stay at his apartment and cook dinner while she caught up on her briefs. She said hacking onions and crushing tomatoes helped stir up the right amount of indignation she needed to get through her Legal Aid cases. Alice's best friend was going to join them for a movie but had come down with strep throat, so the rest of the day belonged to Philip and his daughter — which suited him just fine.

First, they went to a matinee of *Snow White*. Alice sat transfixed with one hand clutching his and the other hidden in a giant-size bag of popcorn, and squealed only once when the wart-faced witch made her apple pitch. Afterwards, they cruised the Christmas windows at Lord and Taylor, then headed back to his apartment for Ellen's spaghetti and meatballs. The evening ended with Ebinger's Black-Out Cake swimming in mounds of fresh cream that Philip whipped up himself.

That night Philip was ten pages into *Eloise* before Alice's eyes began to droop. He was tiptoeing out when he heard a rustle. He lowered himself onto the edge of her bed and tucked the covers tightly across her shoulders. The room felt chilly. First thing Monday he'd ask Dorothy where to find heavy curtains to cut down on the drafts from the leaky casement windows. And maybe a flannel nightgown and a pair of fuzzy animal slippers while she was there. Rabbits. Alice loved rabbits.

Alice wiggled free, sat up and took hold of his hand, then eased her doll onto the pillow. It hadn't left her side since Philip had surprised her with it that morning.

"Daddy?" she said, blinking into the dimly lit room.

"Yes, my love."

"Why did Snow White eat the apple?"

Why indeed? "Because it was red and shiny and she couldn't help herself."

"I could," Alice said, jutting out her chin. "Unless I was very, very hungry."

"That's reassuring," he laughed.

Alice tucked her legs under, readying herself for a chat. She'd always been afraid of the dark and her imaginary fears usually kicked up real ones. Bedtime was the preferred time for getting them off her chest.

"Mommy has a new friend," Alice said solemnly.

"Ah."

"He's not as nice as you."

"That goes without saying."

She thought a moment. "He's short."

"I'm glad you told me. I'll have him arrested right away."

She frowned, wanting to be taken seriously. "And he doesn't let me watch TV."

"Hmmm, why is that?" he said carefully.

"He says it's not good for me."

His ex had developed a penchant for wormy, school-teacher types who ate dinner at 6:00 every night and always paid their bills on time. And disapproved of candy. (Philip had found a box of "natural" raisins in Alice's coat pocket.) But that's what his former wife seemed to need now — an antidote to him. When they'd separated, she'd blamed him for the bust up of the marriage: he was reckless, temperamental and never around, and the compulsive way he pursued his work had given her a taste of the future, one she didn't want. Afterwards, Philip had been surprised at how relieved he'd felt, as if he'd just lost a hundred pounds he didn't know he'd been carrying around. She had stopped figuring in his life months before. They hardly made love by then; they didn't even kiss with real affection. A year before she officially ended their marriage, while he was in Peoria interviewing pesticide researchers for a negligence suit, he'd realized that days had gone by without once thinking of her. They just moved through their lives together, she with her lesson plans, he with his briefs. They shared a space — when he was in it — and a child. Now, he ran through the conversation he'd have with her about the boyfriend who had the nerve to boss his kid around. He guessed it wouldn't be hard to convince her to make the boyfriend lighten up. She was as worried as he about Alice's compliant nature. Alice didn't need more limits. She needed more whimsy in her life. She needed more of *him*.

"Should I stay with you until you fall asleep?" he asked, muzzling her neck.

She nodded and slid under the covers. "I miss you, Daddy," she whispered.

Philip felt something fracture in his chest. This was the first time she'd told him how she felt, and although there was no reproach in her voice, he ached with remorse. He'd been a failure as a father *and* a husband. Even as a lawyer. He lay down next to the child and gently smoothed back a honey curl from her forehead, then traced the gentle slope of her nose. Her skin was incredibly fine, her complexion a shade of alabaster she'd inherited from his wife's side. "I miss you too," he murmured, swearing he'd spend more time with his little girl. He'd make absolutely sure to get to Brooklyn a few days a week to have dinner with her. He'd arrange for Alice to sleep at his place more often and find a way to bring her to school in the morning. He didn't give a damn if her mother objected. Never again did he want to hear his child say that she missed him.

Strains of Dylan's "Maggie's Farm" drifted in from the living room. Philip switched on the porcelain cat lamp Meyer had given him and turned the dimmer to low.

"Did you have a fun bath?"

She nodded, too vigorously, he thought, then lay still.

Ellen had volunteered to bathe her after dinner, and while Philip cleared away the dishes, he'd heard her take a stab at conversation. Even though Alice had met Ellen before, she'd answered in that overly polite tone she used with strangers. Ellen wasn't used to children. She didn't have the patience to get down on the floor to cut out paper dolls or play Candyland. She was trying hard, he knew, but Alice's combination of braininess and childishness confused her. But there'd be plenty more weekends for Ellen to get used to Alice. He'd talk to her, give her tips. Ellen would loosen up. All she needed was time.

He sat until Alice's grip loosened and her breathing turned regular, then slipped out and gently closed the door behind him.

Ellen looked up from the papers she'd spread out on the dining room table. Her portable files sat on the floor nearby. "How's she doing?"

"All right. Just fell asleep."

She glanced at the kitchen clock. "God, it's almost midnight. Does she always stay up this late?"

"It's a treat. Her mother's a tyrant about bedtime and she's not used to this apartment."

"Or me." She sighed. "I try, believe me I do. But it takes a while for kids to get used to new people, right?"

"Of course."

She came into the living room, sat down in a chair opposite him and propped her legs onto his lap. She looked tired. Her auburn hair had drooped out of its flip. Philip pulled off her socks and began to massage her arches.

"I've been thinking about Noah and the Polish woman," she said, her eyes turning dreamy as he kneaded her feet. "What a story.

Here's this quiet guy, no great shakes in the looks department, totally insecure with women, and for the last month he's had this hot babe in his house."

"She's not exactly a hot babe."

"She's good looking, right?"

"Attractive enough."

"In what way? Womanly? Femme fatale? One of those 'I want to be alone' types?"

He grinned wickedly. "All of the above."

"Oh, really?" she said with raised eyebrows. Philip gave her toes a playful yank.

"Okay, let's say Noah's really gone on her." Ellen shifted in her chair, rolling up the cuffs of the man-tailored shirt she always wore around the apartment. Philip could tell she was starting to cook. "So, now he's obsessed with this mystery woman, this European exotic, and when he finds the ID cards, he tells her the names so she can get a slice of Jake's estate in exchange for a promise that they'll run off together. Then he'll have his portion of Jake's money *and* The Woman He Loves. But — and here's the beauty of it — they can never turn each other in. They're stuck together forever." She tossed back her hair with a laugh. "What do you think? I see a cross between Barbara Stanwyck and Simone Signoret."

Ellen liked to turn Hollywood late at night, especially when she got over-tired. Normally, Philip played along until they had a routine going that sent them into hysterics, then straight to bed. He wanted to make love, but he was wiped out. In between trying to close out his active cases and endless Atlanta updates from Drottman's office, he hadn't made it home before midnight all week, and when he crawled into bed, thoughts of the Polish woman swirled up, seriously cutting into his sleep. He closed his burning eyes and sat quietly for a moment, listening to Dylan's soft twang.

"There's always the possibility that she is who she says she is," Ellen said.

"Yes, there is that."

"Did she say outright she wanted money?"

"She said things like 'Money is money. It helps in life, but I am wanting to discover the truth,' " Philip said, trying on a Polish accent. "I'm not finished with her yet." He sat up, sending Ellen's feet

85

sliding onto the carpet, then checked himself, surprised he needed to exaggerate his distrust of the Polish woman, as if confessing his ambivalence would make him unfaithful to Ellen.

She let her mouth fall half-open in that seductive grin she couldn't contain whenever he talked tough. "Hey, is that all I get?" she said, nodding at her feet.

"Yep. It's time for a little tit-for-tat." He pulled off his crew neck. "Come here and manhandle me." She climbed behind him and straddled his hips. "I finally got through to Larry Fine today," she said, working on his shoulders. "I explained about Jake's will. Without more details he can't be sure, but if the woman does go to court, he says all monies will be put in escrow until the case is settled."

"Shit!"

"A lot depends on the wording of the will."

"Like?"

"Any statement that implies Jake *would* have left his money to a child if he had one."

"I know there was the standard 'In the event I die without issue' clause," he said, "but that's all."

Jake's will had been drawn up years earlier to protect any children he might have with Rosalind, but legally it would include biological offspring from other marriages. With that insertion, even illegitimate children could petition the court.

"That could be enough for a judge to admit her claim," Ellen said. "I'll need more before I call Larry again, like dates of birth, where she grew up, went to school — like that."

"I've got an appointment on Monday with a Mr. Weinstein at the Joint Archives. He's going to get me started looking through the concentration camp deportation lists. I'll call Larry myself when I know more."

The last thing he was looking forward to was pouring over lists of Jews who'd been slaughtered by the Germans, but it was the only sensible way to begin. All his life he'd tried to sidestep such horrific stuff. Now he'd have his nose rubbed in it.

Ellen slipped onto his lap and gave him a long, sleepy-eyed gaze. Last year, when he'd bumped into her at 110 Centre Street, she'd stopped him dead: the little go-getter he knew in high school was sporting a navy suit and pumps, and had a portfolio tucked under her arm as though she were born with it there. The tight pony-tail was now a bob, the scrawny body tight and curvy. She looked like a sexy Sandra Dee and he was a goner. Ellen was classier than the women he was used to, including his ex-wife, and he was more than a little surprised when she showed an interest in him. It didn't take him long to figure out that the girl who'd gone off to Brandeis in cashmere sweaters and Pendleton skirts, and dated tennis-playing Jews who tooled about Larchmont in MGs, was turned on by his diamond-in-the-rough style — something she thought she'd left behind when she fled Brooklyn for a New England college. She'd never admit it, of course, even to herself, and he wasn't about to point out that the very qualities she was drawn to were the ones that got him in the most trouble.

She started unbuttoning her shirt. "Do you think she's asleep?" she whispered, gazing at him with molten eyes.

He pulled her to him and slowly caressed her breasts until with a throaty laugh, she stood up and disappeared into the bathroom. A moment later, he heard water running. Ellen liked a bath before sex. Philip stretched his achy arms over his head, then knocked the cushions off the couch and began unfolding the hide-a-way bed. Sex would do him good.

Chapter 11

Karolina rushed down the steps of the Art Students' League, anxious to get over to the East Side. Jim had called that morning, saying he wanted to meet early because he had to have dinner with his sons that evening. *Had to*, he'd said, not *wanted to,* as though he expected her to believe that he didn't adore his children, that they were merely an obligation and she was his only real pleasure. He'd turned careful with her since she'd told him about the ID cards because, she sensed, the possibility of an inheritance troubled him. He liked having her dependent on him; if she had money, she might need him less. It was fine for her to live in Greenpoint where she was unlikely to meet men of interest, fine for her to work as a nanny so he could play patron to her struggling artist. The thought angered her, yet she knew she'd let it happen. She clasped her collar tightly around her neck, shivering at the thought of seeing him. She had to end the affair, had to.

She was hurrying across 57th Street when she heard her name called and, turning, saw Val, a friend from the League, hurrying toward her, her long, patch-work suede coat flapping in the evening wind. The streets were slushy from the light drizzle that had been falling most of the afternoon and by the time Val reached her the hems of her bell-bottom jeans were soaked.

"Got time for a bite?" Val asked, releasing her shaggy mane of black hair from under her coat collar. Val was a delightful fright with half-ponytails held up by beaded clips and multi-colored rubber bands. Her face was smooth and round, her eyes almond-shaped, like a gypsy's. And she usually dressed like one. They'd met in drawing class four months earlier and when they were both free, took a light dinner together at Wolf's Coffee Shop on Seventh. The hamburgers were mediocre, but Karolina loved the creamy cheesecakes that reminded her of home.

"No, I must hurry to East Side," Karolina said. "But come. It will be a pleasure if you walk with me."

"Going to your boyfriend's place?" Val teased.

"No, Val, my *lover*."

Val gave her a bashful grin and lit a cigarette. Americans were so shy about the word "lover." Even promiscuous, marijuana-smoking Val seemed to find it too bold. When she wanted to sound blasé, she used childish expressions like "your old man" or "your main squeeze."

They linked arms and made their way toward Fifth Avenue. "No parties tonight?" Karolina asked. "No dancing? You go home?"

"Unfortunately," Val pouted. "I asked the new model — his name's Roy, by the way — if he wanted to come for a drink, but he said no." She let out a dreamy sigh and rolled her eyes. "What a bod!"

The "bod" who'd posed for their drawing class that evening was a muscular blonde with long, hard limbs and a wide chest. Val had spent most of the class chewing on her thumbnail, staring at his genitals.

"Val, darling, you are too modern for me. Where is your Jerry tonight?"

"Working at the Armory. His 'Happening' opens on Saturday and he has to stay late." She turned abruptly, sending her hoop earrings jingling. "Say you'll come! It'll be fun."

Karolina knew Val thought of her as worldly and wise, an "artiste" from a world uncorrupted by bourgeois values, and was dying to show her off to her friends. But moving through a room crowded with twenty-year-olds looking for someone to spend the night with wouldn't be fun. Karolina had hated it in Warsaw. She'd hate it in New York.

"You know this is not — how do you say? — my cup of tea — which is strange expression, no?" she said with amusement, "Since Americans drink coffee." Val's art, a mixture of Pop and Dada in psychedelic colors wasn't Karolina's cup of tea either, but at least the girl was making an effort to learn the basics of drawing.

"Then how do you expect to meet new men?"

"Must I?"

"Yes, you must, since it's obvious your old man doesn't make you happy."

Val's blunt way of cutting to basics was hard to dismiss. Which was what had attracted Karolina to her in the first place.

"You are right," Karolina said. "And one day I will."

"If I'm right, why not on Saturday?"

"Because I am one-man-at-a-time woman."

One-man-at-a-time woman. Karolina liked this expression because it seemed to capture her relationships with men. By nature, she'd always been sensual and passionate, but even though her first sexual urges were strong, she'd been too afraid that God would punish her to give in to them. During her last year at *gymnasium,* her art teacher showed her a book on the works of Rodin and Camille Claudel. Karolina, who'd never seen anything so beautiful, so skillfully executed, became infatuated with the two artists' work and their tempestuous love affair. The notion that there were people who felt free to live lives driven by their passion for art and each other — and without guilt! — seemed, to her seventeen-year-old romantic soul, the utmost happiness. Then came Warsaw and art school, and talented, educated people, free thinkers who shunned the church's prohibitions without necessarily turning away from God. Although many of them slid in and out of each other's beds too easily to suit her, once away from the petty minds and emotional stinginess of rural Poland, she felt within herself the growing certainty that physical love was an inherent extension of emotional love. When she fell in love with André, sex seemed natural. A few years later she met Gregorie and felt the same way. Even now, in this adulterous relationship with Jim she felt no shame, knowing she was not responsible for his unhappy marriage. She'd loved them all, but one at a time. Of course there were people who would say her belief was a justification for sexual permissiveness. Still, she felt instinctively that her God could not be so small as to condemn her for an act that was a part of His design.

Karolina quickly glanced at her watch. Six fifteen. "Come," she said to Val, picking up her pace. "I will walk with you to train before I go downtown."

They threaded their way through the crowds of shoppers. The streets had been quiet when she'd walked down from Noah's flat on

West 82nd Street to the Art Students League. Now, people poured out of office buildings, heading for the brightly lit stores along Fifth Avenue.

At the entrance to the IRT, Val rummaged through her canvas portfolio for a subway token. "Are you signing up for Robertson's class again?"

"Yes, I am enjoying very much." Karolina hadn't taken a drawing class for several years and was delighted to discover she could still capture the curve of a muscle or the contours of a face. Drawing freed her up for her morning sculpture classes, made her eager to take up her chisel, as though she had easier access to all the unseen miraculous folds and twists of the human body. She wouldn't dream of giving it up.

"Me, too." Val clasped the front of her coat closed and hoisted up her bag. "You should dump the guy, you know."

Tears sprang into Karolina's eyes. English could be so cruel. Dump, like garbage, like Mrs. Domanski's leftovers. Is this what she was going to do? Is that why her stomach had churned throughout class, why her hands had trembled when she buttoned her coat?

Val stared down at her shoes. "I'm sorry. It's just that I like you and it's hard to see you in a funk."

"You are right, as usual. But I will be all right."

Val kissed her on both cheeks, European style. "I'll see ya next week." And she turned and disappeared down the subway steps, her hair bobbing behind her.

Karolina walked east along 57th to Fifth. The avenue was sparkling with Christmas lights. People hurried past her with purpose, their hats pulled low on their foreheads, jets of frosty air streaming from their mouths. Before turning south and heading toward the apartment on 46th Street, she stopped a moment in front of an antique furniture store called La Vieille Russie to admire a cherry wood chest of drawers. The piece was beautifully detailed with gracefully carved legs, filigreed brass pulls, and perfectly joined corners. A skilled craftsman had built this to last a lifetime. She'd love to replace the flimsy pine dresser the Domanskis had given her, but this chest would be outrageously expensive. Strange, to be wanting such things. She'd never owned more than could fit into two boxes, and the men she'd lived with — first André, then Gregorie — had studios with

91

mattresses on the floor and faded French movie posters tacked to the walls. Which was fine at the time. It was more than fine; it was young, it was fashionable — neither of which she was any longer. Now, she wanted permanence, stability, a love to grow with. She breathed in a lungful of cold, sharp air. She wanted a chest of drawers that would last a lifetime.

As usual Jim had arrived ahead of her and was already half-finished with his scotch and water. Sitting on the couch arm, he pulled loose the knot of his tie and gave her a slow, tender grin, just as he had the first time she saw him at a gallery in Warsaw. She turned away, always a little unsettled by the frankness in his face, then slipped off her coat and paused, the hanger suspended from her hand. Had she really loved this man, or merely needed to? She gave her head a little shake of self-reproach. No, she wouldn't let herself turn bitter and belittle what they'd had. Cynicism was just a cheap way to make their parting less painful. She hung up her coat, the lone garment in the closet, then went into the kitchen.

She returned to the living room, swinging the beer bottle by its neck. Jim was sitting on the couch with his feet on the coffee table. She sat down beside him, gently touched his cheek, then leaned into his outstretched arm and stared into the golden light that filled the room. The next hour stretched out before her. They would sip their drinks quietly, mutter a few words about the bad weather or how their week had gone. Then he'd take her by the hand and lead her into the bedroom. The important talk would come later — if there was time before he rushed home for dinner. Nothing was allowed to interfere with the sex. After a year of these meetings, this was the one thing neither of them had tired of because, she suspected, her increasing remoteness fed Jim's passion. The more pessimistic and moody she became, the more he wanted her. The last few times they were together, the sex had been slower, more demanding, as though he could force the unhappiness out of her body with his own. Even despair had its uses, she thought.

A stack of gift boxes sat on the floor near the door. Presents for the sons, Karolina thought, expensive presents tied with huge gold and plaid ribbons that would get tossed out with the wrapping paper. Jim was generous by nature, extravagant — he liked to surprise her with perfumes and lace underwear, womanly gifts he thought she'd want, though she never really did — but even her poor Greenpoint neighbors seemed crazy this time of year, racing around with packages overflowing in their arms. Christmas in Poland was not about shopping, but maybe that was because there was so little to buy. She touched her neck absently, remembering the tiny gold cross she'd received from her parents for Confirmation but lost during her first year in art school, and the doll's bed her father had carved from a single piece of pine. Those gifts came wrapped in simple brown paper, not tied with the kind of fancy ribbons women back home only wore in their hair. Suddenly, everything about the room annoyed her: the ugly Danish-modern couch, the dull brown corduroy armchairs, and worst of all, the curtainless windows, the yellowing shades that gave the apartment a lonely, unused feeling. A disposable dwelling. Anyone could walk away from it in a minute.

"Karolina," he whispered into the curve of her neck.

She pulled away to take in the lean, craggy face that had meant so much to her. How handsome he was, still athletic, still muscular; yet it was his green eyes she'd first noticed when he'd introduced himself at the art show. Her sculpture interested him, he'd said, clearly interested in her as well, and could he talk to her about his grant program for Eastern European artists? Maybe they could discuss it over dinner? His teasing grin, the knowing glint in his eyes, his elegant manner had all delighted her, and when she'd answered in her halting English, his smile had been so open, so American, that she'd accepted.

Sometime during that first week of dinners and sightseeing they spent the night together. She was delighted by the silly jokes he tried in his Americanized Polish and then, when she rocked with laughter, how he kissed the top of her hands and told her he'd never known anyone so womanly. When he offered her a grant to study in the U.S., she accepted at once. She knew he was married — he had not hidden that from her — and when he'd explained that his was a loveless marriage and he and his wife stayed together for the sake of the children, she believed him. Her career seemed to be going nowhere. Beyond the occasional art show, she couldn't drum up interest in her work, and she'd been estranged from Gregorie for months before he'd left to work on a film in Lodz.

Their first six months in America had been thrilling. Jim was clever, charming, at ease in the world, a cultured, educated man with a refined sensibility. And he loved her. She could see it in his eyes each time he looked at her, each time she entered a room. Regardless of her moods, he took such unabashed pleasure in her that she began to fall in love, and the more she loved him, the more convinced she became that she too could glide through life as if she deserved all the wonderful things it had to offer. Still, the sense of dislocation that had plagued her all her life lingered. His love was an overlay, a veneer. *A lie.* What she'd fallen in love with was Jim's talent for happiness — and the woman she saw reflected in his eyes, the woman she *might* be.

In the distance she heard the soft hum of traffic. She pressed her face against Jim's cheek, overwhelmed by all that was about to end. He cupped her breast and found her mouth, then he took her hand and led her into the bedroom.

Later, when she awoke, Jim was sitting on the edge of the bed tying his shoe laces. A fine mist from his shower filled the darkened bedroom. She glanced at the clock: 7:30. He was right on schedule. The street was quieter now, only the occasional crunch of tires on the hardened snow.

"You've been looking pale, *kochana*," he said. His family had come to America from Proznan when he was a baby and he spoke Polish in the soft hissing dialect of the north.

"Oh, I'm fine." She propped herself up on her elbow and watched him. It was his nature to be happy. It wouldn't take him long to find another woman. She was glad she felt no anger, no jealousy. It would make parting easier.

"What happened with the Landaus?" he asked.

"Linda is leaving her work. She asked me to find a new job."

"I knew it would get messy once you told them."

"No, they are kind. It is the cousin, the lawyer I told you about. I think he does not trust me."

"I can't say I blame him. He's got a lot to lose."

"It will not be good if the cousins go against each other."

He stood to buckle his belt. "Then come back and work for me until we find you something else."

She knew he didn't mean it. When her grant ended, he'd

drummed up a part-time clerical position for her at the Foundation. But the staff had grown suspicious of their relationship and when she told Jim she was leaving to take care of Amanda, she'd sensed his relief. She'd been ready to go, desperate to get away from his phone conversations with the wife, from the twin sons in baseball uniforms staring back at her from the photographs that cluttered his desk, from the constant reminders that she was a mistress.

"You know this is not possible," she said.

"Should I call around then? I could ask Jerzy Morath if he can find you something at the consulate or maybe part-time work at the embassy."

"Yes, I will need to make money."

"You know I'll help you out."

"I will not take money from you."

Jim adjusted his shirt collar, then carefully centered his tie. They'd had this conversation before.

"Tell me what the lawyer said."

"He questioned me, very hard, very unpleasantly, really, before he told me about the documents." She watched him gather his wallet and change from the night table. His movements looked unhurried, but practiced. He would not be late.

"It's his job to be tough. As I said, he's got a lot to lose."

"No, he is suspicious because I am Polish. He said he did not trust Poles because they were bad to his people."

Jim switched on the bedside lamp and turned to the dresser mirror to smooth down his sideburns. "Sure, I can imagine. My father always called them lousy *Zhidi* in that not-so-charming peasant style he brought with him from the old country. I had to go to college before I found out Jews were human. I, on the other hand —" He threw her a rakish grin and came to the side of the bed. "I am charmed by the prospect that you are a Jewess." He turned over her hands and kissed her wrists. "That explains why I'm bewitched by you."

She fell back on the pillow, annoyed, pulling the blanket around her bare shoulders. "Just because I grew up in Poland does not mean I am prejudiced."

Jim watched her from under his brows. "Didn't you tell me you had a boyfriend who turned out to be Jewish and you stopped seeing him?"

"That is not the reason I broke with André!"

"*I* didn't say that. *You* said it ended because you were uncomfortable with him. That was the word you used."

She stared at him in disbelief.

"Then why did it end with André?"

She blinked into the room. "There are many reasons, but they are always the same one."

"Which is?"

"You stop loving."

Jim put his hands on his hips, bowed his head, and waited, as though he knew what was coming.

"I wish to end this," she heard herself say.

He lowered himself into the small cane-backed chair next to the night table. "I know it's hard on you, but I can't hurt the children." His voice was dry and pleading.

"It is not because of the children. We must part."

The chair creaked. Jim picked up his suit jacket and sighed. "I have to go."

"Of course. You must not be late."

He walked to the side of the bed. "I'll call you in a few days. We'll talk about it then."

"It is over, Jim."

He reached out and touched her hair. "*Kochana* . . ."

She twisted away so he wouldn't see the tears starting. Before she could speak, he went into the living room. He'd grown used to the routine they'd established over the past few weeks: she'd pick a fight, he'd wait a few days to let her settle down, then they'd meet as though nothing had happened. Only now there would be no more meetings. She heard the rustle of his overcoat, then the sound of the door clicking shut.

Karolina switched off the lamp, fell back on her pillow and flung her arm across her forehead. Circles of light from the lamppost glowed through the translucent shade and she stared so intently at the luminescent rings they seemed to shimmer. André. The last time she had seen him she was in a studio at school, finishing a clay torso for an exhibition. It was late and she was giving the piece a final sanding when André tip-toed in and left a box of books and toiletries she'd forgotten to take when she'd moved out of his apartment. She pretended not to see him and kept working until he slipped out. Then, in a moment of shame at her cowardice, she ran after him. Outside a light snow had begun to fall. She stood on the corner, hugging herself against the cold and watched him hurry down the dimly lit street. Each time he rushed past a street lamp a halo of amber light fell on his tawny head. Dear André. She'd hardly thought of him during the past five years, but since she'd seen Jake's picture, he'd come to mind often.

Had she really told Jim that André made her uncomfortable? She couldn't imagine. She didn't have strong feelings about Jews, yet Jim had misinterpreted what she'd said. When she moved to Warsaw, she learned that a handful of Jews remained in the city, but they were assimilated, as Polish as she was, and she had not given it any thought. She'd not met any — except for André, and that had been a surprise.

She'd gone to his parents' apartment for dinner and they were standing in the kitchen, warm with the smell of roasting potatoes and garlic. His mother rolled up her sleeves to rinse her hands in the sink and Karolina saw a long, deep scar on her elbow. André caught her glance and told her that his mother had been injured while interned at Piontki, a German munitions factory near her home town of Radom. A guard had cut her with his bayonet to show the other inmates what happened to slow workers. Karolina nodded in sympathy. She knew people in Lublin who'd survived slave labor camps, she said; in fact, her father's closest friend had been sent to Auschwitz. "But we are Jewish," André said. His mother threw him a sharp look and changed the subject. Karolina stared at the floor, embarrassed. For the rest of the afternoon André wore a sullen, accusing expression, as though the scene had been her fault.

Shortly after that, she began to watch him, as though his confession had somehow changed the way the light fell across his face. During quiet moments, while he painted or lay in bed reading, she searched his face, thinking, yes, she could see it now, his eyes were too almond-shaped, his chin too round, to be Slavic. They began to drift apart. He was too young, she told herself, too moody and introverted, qualities she had mistaken for depth of character. And he was a bad painter, a Kandinsky imitator who would never find his own style. For a while he ignored her coolness, then became increasingly morose. To Karolina, the affair seemed over because it had run its course, and anyway, she was already taking an interest in her Graphics teacher. It wasn't until that last night, watching him disappear down the snowy street that she felt guilty. Had she left him because he was a Jew?

Had she absorbed her people's hatred?

She sat up suddenly and shivered. She remembered she'd broken with André shortly before Easter, then gone to visit her parents for the holidays. When she arrived, some impulse she couldn't name seized her and she told them bluntly that she had a Jewish boyfriend. Her mother frowned, crossed herself and left the room; her father remained seated at the kitchen table, but said nothing. Karolina remembered being enraged, but toward whom? Herself, her parents, André? After a few moments, her father rose and went to the barn, leaving her alone in the kitchen. Why had she needled them? What had she wanted from her parents? The opportunity to defend André so she could convince herself she wasn't anti-Semitic? To pry from her family something that had silently hovered between them all her life? But they hadn't taken the bait. No one had spoken of Jews. Instead, she sat at the table, alone, listening to the emptiness in the house, waiting for her fury to pass before she rose and walked to the barn to help her father spread feed for the horse.

Karolina tiptoed across the bare floor to the window, pulled up the shade and pressed her feverish cheeks against the frosty panes. What had she really felt for André? She didn't know, but like all her attempts to recover the past, she became, in her thoughts *less* abel to recapture her time-blurred memories.

Uncomfortable, she whispered and let the word roll around in her mouth. Jim was right. Uncomfortable was exactly what she'd meant, even if she hadn't said the word.

Chapter 12

The reception area of the American Jewish Joint Distribution Committee looked more like a warehouse than an international relief agency. Boxes of manila files and papers filled three-quarters of the room, and ledgers yellow with age lay strewn across an ancient leather couch. The walls, a faded institutional green, were cluttered with grainy photos of World War II survivors crammed on crowded ship decks. When Philip approached the stocky middle-aged woman behind the desk, she lifted her bifocals from her nose and buzzed the switchboard. "Mr. Weinstein will be right out," she said in a monotone and returned to her crossword puzzle.

A moment later a small man in his late sixties came shuffling down the hallway. He wore a black vest and bow tie, baggy trousers and rubber-soled shoes, and as he drew nearer, Philip saw he had on a *yarmulke*. The man stopped and eyed Philip's wet raincoat. "Hang it up or you'll soak everything," he barked in the general direction of the coat rack. "Then follow me."

Philip did as he was told. He'd grown up with men like this, men who scolded and nagged and bullied, and in the end slapped you on the back and beamed with pride if you could out-yell and out-argue them. He followed Weinstein past deserted offices with open cartons piled on top of dusty oak desks, amazed that this mess of a place was the main archive for the most important relief agency of World War II.

Weinstein led him into a room with metal tables, wooden file cabinets and a couple of old-fashioned hand-cranked adding machines on pedestals. Two microfilm machines sat on stands in corners.

"You're the one interested in Poland, yes? There have been a lot of you since the Eichmann trials. Twenty years since the war ended and suddenly everybody wants to know. It's about time, believe you me." Weinstein waved at the cartons on a nearby table. "I took out what we had on Poland." He peered over the tops of his bifocals at Philip. "That's what you said on the phone, yes?"

"Yes."

"That stack there, that has the Joint's survivor lists, the other comes from the International Red Cross."

Philip stared at the boxes and raked his hand through his hair. This could take months. "Look, I'd better narrow this down. I'm looking for the names of two people who died during the war."

"Then just work with the Red Cross. They got the records of people the Germans put on transports. The lists are divided by camp and they're alphabetical." Weinstein began inspecting the reels. "You said the people you're looking for were deported to the camps, yes?"

"I'm not sure."

Weinstein gave him a long, hard look. "Listen, *boychik*, maybe first you should tell me what you *do* know so I can save you a few years work, eh?"

"Okay," Philip said, holding up his hand apologetically. "I'm looking for a mother and daughter. Their ID cards were stamped March 1941."

"From where?"

"Lublin."

Weinstein touched an ink-stained finger to his nose and thought. "The Lublin ghetto was formed in '41, but they didn't start deporting until April '42. Most Jews from that city got sent to Belzec." He began rummaging through the microfilm again.

"Belzec?"

"Of course you never heard of it. It was a small place, but they did a good job killing, believe you me." He picked out a reel and stepped up to a machine. "Belzec was one of the first extermination camps. Very primitive compared to what came later, but the Germans had to do the best they could on short notice." He slipped the film onto a spool and began to thread it. "While they were building the camps that you *did* hear about, the Germans got the clever idea they could gas Jews by hooking up mobile vans to trucks and pumping in exhaust fumes. Of course it was slow, but it was a beginning." He flipped a switch and a soft hum filled the room. Behind him the screen began to glow.

"Belzec was only for extermination, so if you find your people listed here, it's almost certain they're dead," Weinstein said. "If they're not on the list, they could have been shipped somewhere else."

"I know one family member who was sent to a camp called Maidenek," Philip said.

"Okay. Let's see. Jews were sent to Maidenek in the winter of 1942 after the Lublin ghetto was liquidated," Weinstein said. "We have those lists too, but don't get too excited. A name on a list doesn't mean a person survived and it doesn't mean they didn't. The Germans only kept records of people they put on the transports, not the ones they killed." He pulled open a file drawer marked "M" and removed boxes of microfilm.

"So how do you confirm a death?"

"Sometimes word of mouth is the only way. If you're lucky, you come across somebody who knew somebody who saw that person go to the gas chambers or get shot or whatnot. And they're usually right."

"Word of mouth!"

Weinstein gave him a half-smile. "A lawyer, yes?"

Philip stared at the half-dozen boxes labeled Belzec and Maidenek strewn across the table. "Isn't there any way to narrow this down?"

"Could be. How old were these people?"

Noah had told him Chava's ID card listed her date of birth as 1936; the mother, Rachel, was born in 1914. Philip made a quick calculation. "If they were deported in 1942, the mother would have been twenty-eight, the child six."

"If the child's on the Belzec list, she's dead for sure," Weinstein said. "If she's on the Maidenek list, she's probably dead too. Children couldn't work, so it was cheaper to kill them right away."

Philip continued to stare grimly at the humming screen of the microfilm machine. Despite all the films he'd seen, all the stories he'd heard there was always more horror to add to the pile.

"What about hiding? Could you smuggle a child out of the ghetto? Into the country, say, to live with Poles?"

"For money, it was possible. The ghetto in Lublin wasn't strictly closed like the ones in Warsaw and Vilna. You could move around a little. Jews from other towns came to Lublin because they heard there wasn't such a food shortage. But the overcrowding was terrible. No, in Lublin you had the privilege of dying from typhus before you starved to death."

"And the children the Poles hid. What happened to them?" Philip asked.

"Not many survived. Most were handed over to the Germans. It didn't take much to tempt the Polacks; a kilo of sugar per Jew was the going price. Sugar was scarce during the war and you know how people like a little something sweet after dinner."

Weinstein continued to check the labels on the microfilm as though he were perusing breakfast cereals. An archivist of mass murder, Philip thought grimly, the custodian of a morgue.

Philip loosened his tie and ran a finger around his damp shirt collar. "How about afterwards? Did many Poles keep Jewish children?"

"It happens. Last year there was a story about a woman who found her niece after twenty years. The girl was brought up by Poles and was living in Cracow with her Polish husband and child. Nobody knows a thing about her past. Then the aunt comes along and says, you're Jewish and your real parents died in the camps and what's more, these people who raised you are anti-Semites and criminals. So what do you think this girl does? She picks up herself and her baby, leaves Poland and moves to the States to live with the aunt, just like that." He gave Philip a smirk. "Tell me, Mr. Lawyer, did she need to know this? Can she have a normal life after such an experience?" Weinstein paused to scrutinize him. "You're looking for this kind of person?"

"Maybe. I don't know."

"So where do you want to start?"

If Chava turned up on the Belzec reel, that would be the end of it.

Weinstein picked out the box, placed it next to the machine and gave the screen a quick pat. "Listen, *boychik*, you better get started." He handed Philip a spool. "So, did they teach you how to use this in law school or do I have to do it for you?"

Philip mounted the Belzec reel dated March 12, 1942, and catalogued one of the first deportations. He scrolled past the leader tape and a map of Eastern Poland appeared on the screen. A broken black line, like railroad tracks, connected Lublin and its surrounding towns — Zamosc, Lubartow, Piaski, Trawniki — to a swastika labelled Belzec. Lubartow! Karolina had mentioned that she grew up there. Each town had a number under it, indicating how many people had been shipped to Belzec. Sixteen hundred had been rounded up in Lublin that day alone!

He scrolled up. Names printed in old-fashioned type flew by, some with pencil lines drawn through them — probably people who'd died in the boxcars and would bypass the gas vans for direct shipment to the crematoria. A life wiped out with a line. He fast-forwarded. When he got to the beginning of the L's, he slowed down and searched for Landau.

Five reels later Philip had still found nothing. He sat back exhausted and rubbed his burning eyes. For two hours he had looked at entire lives reduced to a single line: a name, a date of birth and an occupation. Anger kicked in and he started to feel better. Rage took the sting out of his wounds. Always had. He got up and began to pace the narrow space between the table and the machines, then stopped to stare at the word *Judentransport* on top of the page. He'd stay until they closed the fucking place, if he had to. Grabbing another reel, he scrolled to the K's. *Kantrowitz, Pesach; Kyrzinsky, Yankel; Lamsovkys, Avram; Landau, Benjamin.* Philip's heart constricted. It was Jake's father — his own grandfather! Under Benjamin he found *Reisel* — his grandmother. Both on the same transport. To Belzec. His grandparents, there, on a death list. No pictures of them had survived, but the names summoned up the faces he'd envisioned since childhood — part Meyer, part Izzy, part Jake — and part himself. Furiously, he spun the microfilm forward and back to check if any names were out of order. He'd found no errors in alphabetization on previous lists, but he had to be sure. No Rachel or Luba or Hinda. No Chava. Maybe this transport was only for older people. He scanned the column of birth dates and found several from the mid-to-late 1930s. So children *had* been on this train. Then why not Chava? He jotted down the frame numbers with his family's names and quickly rewound. With a trembling hand, he reached for a Maidenek spool and threaded it.

The first Maidenek reel was dated October 1942, eight months after the Belzec transport. Philip scrolled directly to the L's. He adjusted the focus and names floated up at him: Liebowitz, Avram; Lemsberg, Perl; Landau, Jakob. Jake! He put a shaking finger under the name and slid it across the screen to the next column: *b.10/3/06,* then to the last column: *occupation, lederarbitier.* Probably German for leather worker. Hinda was listed beneath her brother and then Luba. But no more Landaus. Images flashed: Luba's and Hinda's flowered dresses, lying like empty bodies in a pile; stacks of dusty, battered shoes and mounds of gold teeth, like pirate booty; he pictured himself, kneeling beside piles of shorn hair, digging for the aunts' dark, wavy locks, so like his own. Sweat began to bead on his forehead. He put his face in his hands and waited till his heart slowed. God, what humans did to each other! He fast-forwarded to the end of the L's. Again no Chava or Rachel. All the camps in Poland had been in full swing by then. They could have been deported to any one of them. It seemed unlikely that a child would be separated from her mother at this stage in the process. It could be that Jake and his wife hid Chava in the Lublin ghetto before they were deported, but it would be hard for a six-year-old to survive on her own. *Six years old.* Didn't Karolina say she was *four* when she'd been brought to the farm? At her apartment, she'd told him she was *seven* when her family moved to Koromov in 1945. Chava was born in 1936 — which would make her *six* in 1942 and *nine* after the war. There was a two-year discrepancy in Karolina's version, a two-year difference in their ages.

He clicked off the machine and leaned heavily against the back of the chair. For the first time that day he felt his shoulders loosen. The Polish woman had gotten it wrong; still, the age discrepancy was such a damning blunder, he wondered what she could have been thinking. If she'd found family records, she would have known Chava's correct birth date — unless she'd assumed the documents had been destroyed in the war, and since Jake was dead, she'd counted on no one knowing the exact birth date. If she was a scam artist, she was a bad one.

When Philip walked into Weinstein's office, the man was hunched over a large directory, munching Saltines from a box on his desk. Philip handed him a form to photocopy the Belzec and Maidenek lists. Once he confronted Karolina with the age discrepancies she'd probably drop the whole thing; still, he'd keep backup documents of the other deportations just in case.

Weinstein swept aside the crumbs on the paper with the back of his hand. "You found what you need?"

"Not exactly," Philip said.

"I didn't think you would," he said, returning to his book. "It's better to go directly to the Polish agencies for help."

"You could have told me this before I spent three hours . . ."

"Ah, but this way you got a little education." Weinstein removed his glasses and massaged the red creases on the bridge of his nose. "Anyone who sees those lists is not going to forget so quickly."

Before Philip could snap back that his parents had already done a good job in that department, Weinstein pointed at a listing for the Polish-American Committee on WW II Survivors. "Here. Get in touch with these people. They'll tell you how to search for hidden children." Weinstein held up his hand. "Don't say anything. I've worked here long enough to know that's what you're looking for."

"The birth dates the Germans stamped on the identity cards were accurate, right?" Philip asked.

"Oh, yes. The Germans got them from city records and synagogue lists. Very good record keepers, those Germans."

"How do I get a copy of a Polish birth certificate?"

"Lublin again?"

"Yes."

"Born before the war?"

"Yes."

"Try the Warsaw Registry first. They'll tell you where else." He pulled out a directory from the pile on his desk, wet his finger and leafed through it.

Philip copied the addresses onto a piece of paper, then tucked it into his jacket pocket.

"Come back if you need anything else." Weinstein gave him a humorless smile. "Always happy to help."

Back in his office, Philip considered calling Noah to tell him about the hole in Karolina's story, then decided his cousin might let it slip and give her time to concoct an explanation. He dialed Noah's home number. It was after two. Unless Karolina was out with Amanda, she should be there.

She picked up on the third ring.

"Hello?"

"Hello, it's Philip Landau."

"Oh, I am so glad," Karolina burst out. "I have been wanting to speak again."

"I did some research today. That's why I'm calling." Philip was conscious of speaking slowly and as though she had trouble understanding English — which was stupid. She was quick and sensitive to nuance. When they'd spoken at her house, he could tell she'd grasped everything he'd said — and a lot he hadn't.

"Research?" she asked.

"At the Jewish archives. They have lists of Polish Jews who were deported to concentration camps."

"Deported? I do not understand."

"I'll explain when I see you."

"You have found something?"

"Maybe."

He heard a soft release of air, then quiet.

"It's better if we talk face to face," he said.

"Yes! Good. After you left I remembered — oh, how do you say — memories came back." In the silence that followed, he imagined her pursing her lips in that European way she had when she searched for words. "Maybe they will mean something. Maybe they will help."

Philip recalled she'd said she had a green card. And of course there'd be a passport. He'd ask to see them first and go on from there. If she was lying, somewhere along the way she'd make a mistake and he'd catch her.

"How about tomorrow night?" he said.

"Yes, this is good."

"I'll come by your place. Seven, okay?"

"Yes."

Chapter 13

"Look, Kiki, I make smoke," Amanda said, squeezing clumps of clay in her little fists. She held up the spaghetti-like strands for Karolina to admire, then pulled the coils from between her knuckles and stuffed them into the chimney where one by one they flopped over like wet noodles and slid down the pitched roof of her doll house. Her face dissolved in tears.

"Do not cry, my *kociątko*," Karolina said, patting the small back. "I will help, you will see."

Amanda watched with fierce concentration as Karolina gathered up the clay pieces, rolled them into thick coils, then secured them to the chimney. She was a spirited child and could easily bring up a tantrum if she had to wait. Still, Karolina adored her commanding, take-charge manner so common in American children. Polish children were watchful and obedient; instead of getting frustrated, they'd sit quietly and wait while she demonstrated a brush stroke or a modeling technique.

The TV went on in the living room. A moment later, Noah appeared at the door.

Amanda ran to him and gave him a quick hug, then charged back to her doll house and began rearranging the miniature furniture. Karolina felt a pang of longing. She'd run to her *tatush* like this, so proud of the farm animals he'd taught her to whittle, so eager to share her joy with him. He'd not been an affectionate man — a kiss on her Saint's Day, a brief ruffle of her hair before she went to bed was all he could give — but it had been enough. She had been loved.

Noah seated himself on the edge of the bed, lifted a koala bear from Amanda's pile of stuffed animals and began to pick at its matted nylon fur. He always started off bashful when he was with Karolina, as if he needed reassurance she was willing to talk with him.

"I spoke to Linda last night," he finally said. "We agreed you should take your time."

Karolina busied herself gathering the leftover clay strewn across the carpet and began resealing it in cellophane. "No, I make much trouble for you."

"No, you don't."

"I think it is better I leave. I have already looked." The day before, she'd stopped into several Madison Avenue art galleries to inquire about a receptionist job. One gallery owner, a well-dressed man with a small, neat beard and a cultivated manner, asked if she knew how to catalogue art and when she'd told him she did, he took down her phone number and promised to call if something came up. Encouraged, she'd made up her mind to look at other galleries further north on Lexington Avenue. No more nanny jobs. No more children she'd grow to love and have to leave.

Noah sighed. "I don't want you to . . . rush it. If you feel you have to get other work, okay. But take your time."

She propped herself against the bedpost and listened to Amanda whisper to her dolls. She was using her bossy voice to scold them for spilling milk which she, herself, had done the day before — only no one had scolded her for it. The sun was setting over Riverside Drive, flooding the room in a warm haze. Karolina gazed into the gentle light and let the softness of the air soothe her. "It is groovy here, no?"

Noah let out a short laugh.

"I am not using word correctly?"

"Yes, yes — in a way. Where did you hear it?"

"People in park."

"With long hair and dirty clothes?"

"I know it is hippie word," she tossed back with mock defiance. "But I like it. It is like music." She closed her eyes and puckered her lips. "Groovy. Murmur. Flower children," she said, elongating the vowels. Showing off new expressions was her little vanity. It thrilled her when she understood English without needing to translate in her head, and if the words were pretty, she liked to use them.

"I have remarked — is that correct word? — that you are not

sympathetic with hippie people," she said. "You do not like it when they make strikes against the war."

Noah motioned toward the living room where a TV newscaster was describing a demonstration in Detroit. "Hippies protest. Only workers strike."

"In Poland, these groups are together."

"Not here. Here workers side with the government. They're in favor of protecting Vietnam."

"Protecting?" she asked, surprised. "This is strange thing to say. No, I do not agree with you about this war. These people are right to make *protests*." Maybe the demonstrators were naive as she'd once heard Noah say. She believed as much herself on days when she was feeling particularly hopeless about the future; still, she liked that young people flouted rules and exposed lies, that someone challenged the smug, self-righteous establishment. She knew what it was like to live in a country with too many rules and too much fear.

"Don't you believe we should fight communism?" he asked. "You, of all people?"

"Oh, so you think this is about fighting communism."

He hesitated a moment, then smiled sheepishly. "Well, maybe not entirely . . ."

Now the TV commentator was talking about a march led by Martin Luther King. Noah was sympathetic toward the civil rights movement, but unhappy with King's open stand against Vietnam.

"And Dr. King? You will say he is Communist because he is against this war?"

He shrugged. "That's different."

Karolina waited for more, but Noah wasn't really interested. Political discussions were a way for him to spend time with her even when Linda was down the hall. When she first came to work for the Landaus, he'd seemed only vaguely aware of politics. It was only after Karolina mentioned that she found most Americans weren't interested in politics that he made a show of favoring both Johnson's civil rights legislation *and* his hard line on Vietnam. She was sure he believed it, especially once he heard himself say so, but she never saw him read anything but the financial news, and the living room shelves were filled with accounting manuals and paperback novels that looked left over from college days.

"You never told me your impression of Philip after you met with him," Noah said, directing his attention to one of Amanda's frilly pillows.

Karolina swung around. "You spoke?"

"No, not since our lunch last week."

"He finally called today," she told him. "We have appointment. He is coming to my flat tonight."

Noah's eyes were alert behind his black framed glasses. "Again? Why?"

"He went to Jewish archives," she continued. "He would not say what he found."

"I'll call and find out what he's up to."

"No, please! He does not trust me. If you speak to him, he will think — how do you say? — I am putting you against him."

Noah gave her a small nod of understanding, then slid closer and put a consoling hand on her shoulder. "Listen, Karolina. He's not going to be easy no matter what he found. Jake had strong feelings about the Poles. Philip and I heard a lot about it growing up."

"He has already told me this. You feel this way, too?"

"No, of course not, but I want you to understand this could be difficult for the family until they're sure of you."

Exactly what did he want her to understand? That her Polish parents were criminals? That she was required, in order to gain membership in their Jewish clan, to hate them? She shrugged Noah's hand from her shoulder and twisted away.

"I am victim in this, too! I am one who has lost *all* parents."

During the past weeks she'd tortured herself imagining what might have happened if she'd met Jake. She pictured herself extending her hand to him, saw them exchange a few words, smile into each other's eyes, register each other's presence. She'd rerun the scene, hoping with repetition it would take on the texture of reality, and she could make herself believe that she'd actually met this man she believed was her father. God, to think she'd been so close to knowing him. If he hadn't died, if fate hadn't taken him from her, he might have recognized her. A vision rose before her: a car screeching away, crushing deep black tracks into the fresh snow, a shadowy figure looking back at her. No, a father couldn't forget his child's face.

"Tell me about him," she whispered.

"I guess you could say . . . he was a quiet man."

"Was he happy in his life?"

Noah shook his head. "He seemed outside things, like he was listening in on other people's lives."

Sweet, kind Noah meant only to help her and she wanted so much for him, here, now, to understand what her past had been. "You are right," she said with feeling. "There was hate in my home. My mother used to cross herself when she heard the word Jew. In church they said Jews deserved punishment because they killed Christ. And I . . . I did not think this was wrong; no, it was normal for me!" She felt her eyes mist. "Now these things come back and I am shamed."

He touched her shoulder and she leaned in to reach for a tissue from the box on Amanda's dresser.

A moment later, Noah stood up and slipped his hands into his pockets. He cleared his throat. "I spoke with the family. They'd like to meet you at the Chanukah party Linda and I are having next week."

"Yes, this is good." She blew her noise. "But I am nervous."

"Don't be. Once they've heard what you have to say, I think they'll get over any uneasiness."

Amanda was at his side. She put her mommy doll on his knee and made kissing sounds as she walked it up his leg until it came to rest on his lap. He heaved her up into his arms. "Okay, sweets. Time for your bath."

The child rubbed her eyes, dewy with sleep. "Bye, bye, Kiki," she said, waving her doll as her father carried her down the hallway.

Outside a flutter of honking echoed down the street. Karolina went to the window and watched traffic snaking up the highway toward the George Washington Bridge. In the distance, cable lights glittered. She heard the low rumble of bath water and then Amanda's laughter.

The party was next week.

All the Landaus would be there and she would have to face them.

She'd met Noah's parents only once, during her first week of work, when they'd come over for dinner. They'd politely introduced

111

themselves, then hovered around the child, coolly exchanging opinions with Karolina on how clever Amanda was. At the time, their aloofness seemed natural since she was only the nanny, but how would they treat her now? Philip had been evasive on the phone; if he'd found anything positive, he would have sounded more encouraging. He must have spoken with Noah's parents by now and with Jake's wife. Perhaps he had warned them against her. She hugged herself tight to ease the mounting fear. Oh, God, it seemed impossible! She, a Catholic and a Pole who still carried a trace of distaste toward Jews, how could she explain that she was one of them?

Chapter 14

On Monday Philip received a cardboard box labeled "Chianti." He ripped away the duct tape and when he saw the files inside he knew it was from Abe Drottman. That Abe would store depositions for an important civil rights suit in an old wine carton didn't surprise him. A few years back he found himself walking past the run-down commercial building on West 39th Street where Drottman had his offices and, on impulse, decided to drop in just to remind Abe of his existence. Abe wasn't there, but when he looked around, the chaos was of such epic proportions that he could have been standing in the Lost Mail archives of the post office. Stacks of papers and files lay scattered on the floor, on window ledges and chairs. The place stank of cigar smoke and half-empty coffee cups, and the ancient, scarred oak desks with their goose-necked lamps seemed out of another century. He and Simon had furnished their office with budget furniture from the Door Store that gave it a simple, unpretentious look. Dorothy, with her order loving soul, kept the office neat and dust-free. Picturing working in Drottman's place depressed Philip, but when he reminded himself of Abe's brilliant legal arguments and the superb clarity of his reasoning, he decided the chaos would be a small price to pay.

Philip leafed through the documents. Dill's lawyers at the NAACP had deposed check-in personnel, bellhops, maids, kitchen staff and waiters at the Groveside Hotel and, according to their statements, no one had been instructed not to rent rooms to Jews or Negroes and they had overheard no statements to that effect. The NAACP had already lined up fifteen plaintiffs who claimed they'd been denied accommodations over the past three years. But even though the American Jewish Congress had sent a mailing to its membership asking anyone who'd been refused rooms at the Groveside or anywhere else to step forward, to date no one had responded. Until they could locate more Jews, Harry Leibner was it, and Drottman had warned Philip that the man was getting cold feet.

Dorothy had set up Leibner's appointment for 2:00 P.M., but he was already waiting in the reception area at 1:30 when Philip returned from lunch. Leibner, a small elegant man with a narrow creased face and thinning silver hair, wore a tailored suit with a red silk handkerchief tucked into his breast pocket and carried himself like a man accustomed to wearing fine clothes. After politely introducing himself, he followed Philip into his office, sat down on the couch opposite the desk, carefully crossed his legs and waited while Philip gave him a rundown of the Groveside case.

"We need you to be a plantiff in this case," Philip wound up. "The management of the Groveside was breaking the law. As of January 1964, no one in this country is allowed to refuse public accommodations to anyone because of race, creed or religion."

Leibner's face remained impassive. "I told Drottman I want to know more before I agree. How do you expect to proceed with this case?"

The man's German accent surprised Philip until he remembered Leibner's file said he'd been attending university in Berlin when Hitler came to power and ousted the Jews. His wealthy Hamburg father had owned textile factories before the Nazis confiscated the business and shipped Leibner and his entire family to Buchenwald, then on to Auschwitz. He was the only survivor. After the war, Leibner started up what had turned into a successful garment business. The man was a big contributor to numerous charities and a respected member of the New York Jewish community. His cooperation in the Groveside suit would get a lot of attention in the Jewish press.

"First, we make a motion to intervene you as a plaintiff. Then the lawyers would continue to get information from the defendants through discovery. The hotel would probably want to depose you. The case will most likely go to trial and you would have to testify about what happened to you that day," Philip said.

"Will they be punished?" Leibner interrupted.

Philip stopped pacing. He knew what was coming. "Yes."

"How?"

"It depends."

"On what?"

"On the judge," Philip said. Leibner obviously wanted to hear something commensurate to the offence against him.

"I'm interested in punishment."

"We're also interested in sending a message to the southern states."

A band of red rose from Leibner's collar. "Messages are not my business."

Philip rubbed his forehead, willing himself to stay calm. He'd been around old-world Jews and survivors long enough to know they needed time to spew out their rage before they could think clearly enough to hear you. His father usually let loose with a string of Polish curses before he could talk about the war, and Uncle Izzy turned a thousand colors and chewed on his lower lip. Jake, the only one who'd actually been in a camp, had turned red and silent, as if he were afraid to test the depth of his hatred.

Philip pulled up a chair next to Leibner and sat down. Their knees were almost touching. "I know how you feel. I have family who were in the camps, but the larger legal issues are important. We need you to help us out,"

"Let me explain, Mr. Landau," Leibner said, articulating the words like a schoolteacher. "My wife and son were with me when the man at the hotel said there was no room for us. This shame, in front of my family, this after I showed him my reservation confirmation..." He paused, stone-faced, and clasped his hands on his lap. "The man was smiling at me. I remember that smile from the camps, like I was an animal, like a dog who didn't deserve ... Tell me, please, why I should humiliate myself in court, why I should have to do this in America?"

Philip was glad Drottman couldn't hear this. Abe had less patience than he did — which wasn't saying much — and wasn't good at handling reluctant witnesses. Abe might be brilliant in front of a jury, but he had no sympathy for human foolishness or pride if it stood in the way of the law. Which was why he'd sent Leibner to see him, Philip, son of European Jews, nephew of a survivor.

"Because in America you can," Philip said. "Because unless people like you take action, it will happen again."

"I'll tell you something," Leibner said bitterly. "After the war I wasn't disillusioned like the other survivors. I thought, here things will be different. I read the newspapers. I was happy for the *shvartsers* when they got their rights because it would be good for the Jews too. I was wrong. If people can break the law now, after the protests, after the state troopers, the dogs, the water hoses — after the Supreme Court! — they will break it again." He gave Philip a stark, knowing look. "And they will do more."

"I promise you there will be punishment," Philip said.

"But not enough . . ."

"You and I know there will never be enough. Look, this case is a trial run, so to speak. The hotel management is testing the law. If an establishment like the Groveside is found in violation, it will make it harder for others."

"How?"

"If the court finds that the hotel discriminated, which it will, it will order an injunction restraining the hotel from refusing to admit Negroes or Jews. If the hotel owners don't comply, they'll be held in contempt. After that, the court will order the hotel to file a report of compliance periodically to show which Negroes or Jews had registered as guests at the hotel and which had been turned away. They'll be forced to rent to everyone; if not, we could close down the place."

Leibner was now directing his gaze at the floor. For one awful moment, Philip had the feeling his only plaintiff was about to bolt. "It was humiliating," he whispered.

"We can't make the *goyim* like us. We can only keep them from hurting us."

Leibner blinked, then falling back with heavy sigh, gazed vacantly at the afternoon sunlight that fell in bright streaks across the carpet. After a moment, he closed his tired eyes. "All right," he said, squeezing the bridge of his nose. "So what's next?"

"You won't be sorry," Philip said, giving Leibner's arm a gentle squeeze. He grabbed a pencil and legal pad from his desk. "We start at the beginning. Where were you when you called the hotel to book a room?"

Chapter 15

Karolina gave Philip a curt little bow of the head, smiled tightly, and stepped away from the door to let him in. When she gestured for him to enter, he noticed that her hands shook, and feeling confident that he wouldn't have a hard time cracking her story, he pulled off his scarf, slipped out of his coat and handed them over with a casual nod. She moved quickly into the living room where she dropped his things over a chair.

Tonight she was wearing a pink cardigan set and a black skirt made of some kind of clingy knit fabric that set off her figure. The skirt was long and sexy-tight, like the kind Italian girls wore when he was in high school. He noted that she'd prettied herself with a flowered scarf she'd knotted around her neck. Near the alcove, he spotted the table set with plates and what looked like a plum cake resting on a paper doily. A cake. For him. Here he'd been gearing up for a cross-examination and it looked as though she'd arranged an intimate rendezvous to soften him up for the next installment of her saga. Now that she knew he'd been digging into files at the Joint, maybe she'd decided on a last-ditch seduction and was waiting to assess his mood before she came on to him.

He turned and casually surveyed the room, taking in the mixture of cheap modern furniture and brightly embroidered pillows in what he thought of as standard folk patterns. Everything was neat: Polish books lay stacked on a coffee table and the couch cushions had been plumped. Had she straightened up for him or did the place always look unlived in? Last time, the room had been too dim for him to notice.

She stood at his side a moment, playing with the top button of her sweater. "Come," she said, extending her arm toward the table. "We will talk." He nodded, and she was about to lower herself onto a chair when her hand flew to her mouth in surprise. "I have forgot coffee!" she said and was up again. "You would like?"

"Sure."

She disappeared into the kitchen alcove. Philip followed and leaned in to study her while she pried open a can of Savarin. She worked the opener with strong, capable hands, then scooped the coffee into the top of a percolator. When she bent over the counter, he took in her full, rounded hips and the deep curve at her waist. There was a sensuousness about her, a kind of looseness, even in the way strands of hair crept out of her French twist. She gave her sweater an absent tug at the waistband to straighten it, but the fabric gathered up again exposing an inch of pink slip beneath.

Back in the living room, he saw that the bedroom door was ajar, and while she filled the pot with water, he walked over and looked in. A pale yellow chenille bedspread. A glass-shaded lamp on a small, wooden night table. In the corner, a sheer, white nightgown lay flung across a chair, and terry-cloth slippers, also in white, rested on the hooked rug next to her bed. No picture of a bleeding Christ. No haloed saints; still, the room had the feel of a nun's cell.

"In Poland, coffee is like gold," she called above the running water. "We find it only on black market." It seemed to him she was straining to sound cheerful, as if he were a buddy who'd dropped in for a chat. "But here, I have only to walk to grocery and poof, so many. So I take one with pretty label. I hope it is good."

He drifted over to the bookcase to get a better look at the marble figures displayed on the shelves and picked up a female torso, a kind of Venus de Milo without a head. The piece was detailed, lifelike, beautiful. "You made these?" he asked, running his finger slowly across a hint of drapery carved around the hips.

"When I was in school." She'd stepped into the alcove. A dishrag hung from her hand.

"They're good."

"You like art?"

"This kind."

"Ah." She leaned against the frame of the alcove, smiling. Her eyes were amazingly blue. "And what kind is this?"

"Realistic, I guess," he said.

"Yes, I too like what is true to eye."

Philip smiled, impressed by the way her bare-boned English got to the heart of things. She'd make a sympathetic witness. If he had to go to court he might have a tough fight.

He chose another statue and traced the curved rib cage on a male figure. He could almost picture the muscles beneath. He wondered how many lovers she'd had and if she studied their bodies while she lay beside them on the rumpled bed sheets. "You still work at it?" he asked, inwardly enjoying his private association.

"Yes, at the Landau's. I am working on very important American theme by Mr. Disney called The Seven Dwarfs." She grinned like a kid, and as her face relaxed, he was struck again by how good-looking she was. She wore no makeup that he could tell, yet her complexion was creamy white with streaks of pale pink across her high cheek bones. Her nose was thin and graceful, her mouth fleshy. Voluptuous, yes, but classy, like those European actresses in the Antonioni films Ellen dragged him to.

He replaced the statue and brushed his hands together. Enough chitchat. He unbuttoned his jacket and sat down to business.

She cut into the cake, but when he held up his hand, she moved the slice to her plate and stared at it for a long moment. "I have been thinking of you since your call yesterday," she began. "I am sure now."

"Of?"

"Who I am." Her eyes filled with humor. "I know I am sounding dramatic," she said with a wave of the hand, "But I have no more doubt. After you left, memories came back."

"Like?"

"Something when I was little. When Jake brought me to farm."

"You remember him taking you there?"

"No, seeing him leave."

"So you recalled his face?"

"I think so. It did not come clearly. He was moving away . . . in the back of a black car, a big one. When I saw his picture at Noah's, it was same."

"Do you remember where he took you from, where you'd been living?"

"The memories do not come like this. They are only flashes. I

119

was child." She watched him for a moment. "You do not believe me."

Her matter-of-fact tone caught him off-guard. She was taking the lead again. He waited a beat. "What's your date of birth?"

"June 20, 1938."

"Chava's identity card says she was born on April 30, 1936. That makes you two years younger."

Karolina's eyes grew wide and puzzled. "How can that be?"

He'd expected some sign of panic at being caught in a lie, but she just seemed perplexed. Then to his amazement, she burst out in astonished laughter. "Oh, so many things make sense now! I see why I was always the tallest in class, why — how do you say — I developed early. So I am over thirty. Oh, this is not good news."

He waited.

"Don't you see?" she rushed on with excitement. "My parents must have given my school wrong birth date because they were afraid someone would come back to claim me."

"Don't you need a birth certificate to start school?"

"In Poland? After the war? Everything was in chaos. The Russians were taking over and everyone was . . ." She gestured wildly with her arms. ". . . mad. Many people were without papers. If my parents told school they had no birth certificate, no one would make fuss. You Americans, you are so trusting! You think because you make laws, people will obey, but in Poland it is easy to forge papers, to overlook laws. For a little money, you can get anything."

"Come on, everyone has papers of some kind —"

"This is not true! I once asked my mother why there were no pictures of me as a baby, no documents, and she gave me same reason I give you now — the war, always the war." She shook her head from side to side, marveling at her own thoughts. "Now I understand everything. There were no papers because I was born into another family — your family."

"You're Catholic. That means you were baptized."

"Of course . . ." She stopped, stricken. "But not if I am Chava."

"That's easy enough to check. Just write the church to see if papers exist for a Karolina Staszek."

"Good. I did not think of this. I will write." Her mouth opened in surprise. "But our church was badly bombed before the Russians came. I do not know what was destroyed."

"Don't you need a priest to be baptized?"

"Yes —"

"Then contact him."

She shook her head sadly. "*If* I was baptized, it was by the old priest of our church when I was baby. And he died a few years after war ended. The one who made my confirmation was new to parish."

Philip threw up his hands in frustration. Talking to her was like pouring water through a sieve. "So, you're telling me you got a passport without documented proof of age."

"Yes! When I received grant I sent ministry my art school records, which came from my high school in Lublin. And that must have come from my elementary school."

"That's a convenient explanation . . ."

"But true! And I am not the only one. Much was destroyed."

"Take a minute to listen to yourself. No records. No people who knew you." Philip paused to drive the point home. "Would *you* believe you?"

"But these feelings are too strong in me!"

"Okay," he said, drawing his hand across his face. "Why don't we start by looking at your passport?"

To his surprise, she rose instantly and went into her bedroom. He heard drawers opening and when she returned, she crouched next to him. "See!" she said, eagerly opening her passport. "I am not lying."

The date of birth read June 20, 1938. The photo inside showed her with her hair down around her shoulders, looking out at the camera with a suppressed smile, as though she had a secret that made her happy. She'd had hopes. He could see it in her face. Of what? Money? Love? He remembered Noah's comment about the American who'd sponsored her. Whatever it was, it hadn't turned out the way she'd planned or she wouldn't be living alone in this shabby section of Brooklyn. He flipped through the rest of the passport, checking for other immigration stamps, but except for the U.S. seal of debarkation, the pages were empty.

"If your parents forged your papers, why would they make you two years younger and risk you looking older than your stated age? Why not one year? Why not just change the month?"

"Maybe they didn't know how old I was when I came to them," she said. "It was wartime. I think Jake must bring me in secret and in

121

great hurry. I do not think anyone in such a situation will stop to chat."

It seemed to him that a parent would remember to cover such contingencies if his child's life was at stake. "You know, we can clear this up right away. Every country has registries. All you have to do is see if birth records exist under your name."

She rose and slid into her chair. She looked tired now. Faint blue patches ringed her eyes. "Yes, but I must tell you, Mr. Landau, I fear we will find nothing. All of Warsaw burned. When I first came to the city there were so many broken buildings. Even now in 1967 much is not rebuilt."

Philip had grown increasingly irritated. Now he was fed up. This woman was more aggravating than Leibner. First thing tomorrow he'd write the agencies Weinstein suggested. He should have done it right after his bout with the microfilm. "I'll send out inquires tomorrow. If documents come back with the same birth date as the one on your passport, then you'll have to conclude that you're the daughter of Polish farmers."

"Do you want me to write them in Polish?" she asked. "I think it will help."

"Sure." Meyer read Polish. He'd check the content. Dorothy would send out the inquiries on office stationery. A legal letter could speed things up.

"And if there are no records?"

He lifted his hands and shrugged.

Fury gathered in her face. She slapped the table with her hand, rattling his empty plate. "For me these things are too coincidental *not* to be true! I have a lifetime of memories now explained."

Philip was oddly moved by this outburst and had a sudden urge to protect her from herself, to take her hand and tell her to stop deluding herself, stop grasping at facile explanations. But the smell of burnt coffee filled the room and Karolina was up, dashing to the stove. She reappeared, holding her hands open in a helpless gesture. "I am better with tea."

All her explanations, though theoretically possible, added up to a string of absurdly improbable coincidences. Arguing had only given her a chance to solidify her arguments. He pushed himself away from the table. It was useless to continue. "Never mind about the coffee."

There was a soft knock at the door. When Karolina opened it, a heavy-set woman in a flowered housecoat spoke to her urgently in Polish, then looked over at Philip.

"My landlady, Mrs. Domanski." Karolina motioned to the woman. "This is Philip Landau."

"I will not disturb," she said.

"It's okay. I was just leaving."

The woman whispered something to Karolina, then disappeared down the hall.

"The walls are thin. She is not used to the noise." She gave him a self-deprecating frown. "Or the smell of burning coffee."

He went to get his coat while Karolina leaned against the doorframe, frowning as if he were a kid who needed reprimanding. "You did not say what you found at archives."

"Nothing. But seeing the lists reminded me that your and Chava's birth dates are different."

"You were looking for Chava's name on deportation list, yes? And if you found it, you would believe she is dead."

She was way ahead of him. There was no reason not to tell her the truth. "Right. I didn't find it. But that doesn't mean she didn't die some other way."

She watched him now with cold determination. "Noah and Linda are having Chanukah party next week," she said tersely. "For me to meet family."

"You might want to hold off on that until we have something more solid."

"I will go."

"Fine. If that's the way you want it, I'll be there."

She nodded curtly and swept past him, trailing a faint, earthy aroma like dried flowers. When she passed him the scarf he'd forgotten on the chair, their hands touched and she hesitated. She looked hurt and helpless now, and hearing the sound of her low, rapid breath, he wanted to comfort her. He pulled away abruptly and headed down the narrow hallway to the street door. Before he grasped the knob, the evening came spinning back: the spunkiness of her convictions, the intensity of her emotions, his feeling that she believed what she said. He swung around, looking for something to say that might ease the tension, but her back was already to him, her

123

hand on the door to her apartment. Just before she pulled it shut, she paused and gave her sweater the same tug to straighten it, like a child trying to regain her dignity. Later, when Philip tried to assemble his images of that encounter to pinpoint the exact moment when his feelings toward Karolina began to change, it was this small gesture — that innocent tug at the back of the sweater, that unconscious fixing that wouldn't keep — that would come to mind first.

Chapter 16

Her landlady must have been watching from the window because she was at Karolina's door the minute Philip was gone. Karolina braved a smile and let her in, then retreated to the kitchen and fell against the counter with her head in her hands. The suspicious, condescending bastard! The *skurwysyn!* She grabbed the percolator, dumped the blackened coffee grounds into the trash can, then gave the pot a sharp twist with a sponge. How Philip Landau infuriated her!

"I hope it's not too late," Mrs. Domanski called from the living room.

The kitchen clock read 8:45. Her landlady had a few minutes to nose around before her favorite TV shows. As soon as the woman left, Karolina would start drafting letters. He'd see that he hadn't intimidated her. She took a few deep breaths to steady herself, then marched into the living room.

Mrs. Domanski was already seated at the table. "Ah, where did you get this?" she asked, pointing to the cake.

"A bakery near the Landaus' flat."

"You brought it all the way from Manhattan for the friend who was here, *tak?* I can't blame you. A nice-looking man."

Yes, Philip was handsome, and when he'd turned his sultry eyes on her before leaving, her heart had lurched like a schoolgirl's. He was probably used to getting his way with American women, even if he had no charm. He was barely polite. She burned with anger. He'd eyed her flat like a policeman. He'd looked at her as if she'd been brought up on charges.

125

"His name is Landau, you said. A relative of the people you work for?"

"Yes."

"He looks like an Arab, not a Jew." She cut a piece of cake and slid it onto her plate. "But they are a related people. Dark."

Karolina shifted uncomfortably. "Don't forget to take a piece for your husband."

"Thank you. Umm, all butter." She smiled out of the side of her mouth. "A special cake for a special person."

"*Just* an acquaintance. He's checking on a legal question, making sure my green card is in order."

She glanced at the empty plates. "But he didn't eat anything!"

Karolina shrugged and lit a cigarette.

"What do you hear from Tadeuz?" Mrs. Domanski asked, pressing her fork down on the crumbs

"I don't."

"I know he likes you." She gave Karolina's cheek a pat. "When Zosha wrote about you, I thought I was getting a farm girl for a tenant. Then you show up — an art student from Warsaw! And so *atrakcyjna*, too." She glanced at her watch. "Maybe one more small piece?"

Karolina cut another wedge.

"Well, I'm glad you're meeting people. You should go to the Polaski Club. They have dances on Fridays."

Karolina smoked silently, thinking about the letters she'd write. She'd compose them in Polish and attach English versions. Her English spelling was poor, but if he needed better copies, his secretary could correct them. Tomorrow morning, on the way to work, she'd drop them off at Landau's office.

"The fruit is not the same here," the landlady said sadly. "This is good, but the plums lack a certain sweetness. Remember Armianska Square? Ah, blackberries! They were my favorite. I used to wait for market days just for the berries. If you didn't get there early, the heat ruined the fruit." She gazed into her plate and sighed. "Here the food tastes dead."

Karolina stopped abruptly, her cigarette suspended in her hand. Mrs. Domanski was from Lublin. She'd come to America *after* the war. She might know something about her family. She might have heard rumors.

"You knew my parents, didn't you," Karolina asked, attempting a casual tone.

"Oh, not well. They used to come to Zosha's store for nails and metal parts, but not often. You lived too far from town. It's your neighbors, the Hankowskis, that I remember. I heard the wife lost an arm during the war, *tak*? "

"That's her. My family was close with them. I thought you might be able to give me some information."

"What kind?"

"Did you ever hear of Poles hiding Jewish children during the war?" she blurted out.

Mrs. Domanski eyes widened in disbelief. "Hide *Zhidi*? My God, do you know what the Germans did if they caught you?" She took out a pack of Winstons and lit one. Her husband was asthmatic and she never smoked in her apartment — another reason she liked to visit Karolina. "The people you work for are accusing you of something, is that it?" Mrs. Domanski screwed up her eyes. "Jews say terrible things about us here. Just go and ask them if they would have helped *us*, go ahead. We suffered just like them — more! — but nobody talks about that." She gave her body an indignant twist and re-settled herself in the chair.

"I was just curious," Karolina murmured.

"Did the Hankowskis hide someone? Is that why you ask?"

"No, no, someone mentioned a story they heard, that's all, and I wondered if it could be true." Stupid to be so blunt. If Mrs. Domanski found out she was Jewish, she'd turn into a different person in the woman's eyes. But there had to be someone who'd known her family during the war. She searched her memory for people who might know about her past. Maybe her mother's cousin or her daughter, Pola? The Staszeks had stayed with them in Koromov for a year after the war.

"Do you remember the Jewish ghetto in town?" Karolina asked, rolling the tip of her cigarette along the rim of the ashtray.

"Of course. We had to walk past it every day. The Germans wanted us to see what they would do if we didn't cooperate. Terrible!

127

Those *Zhidi* were dying like flies." She gave Karolina a grim stare. "The Landaus had relatives there, is that it?"

Yes, she wanted to shout, *me*. But she nodded calmly and continued. "When did the Germans start deporting Jews? Do you remember?"

"In April of 1942. I remember because there was a blizzard the day of the first roundup and I was in Zosha's store, picking up firewood her husband had found. Can you imagine? Snow at Easter time! We heard the Jews screaming in the square when they were carted off."

April '42. Philip said the identity card listed her born in October 1936. If he was right, she would have been almost six when she was brought to the farm, old enough to remember. But she didn't. Why? She raked her memory of the streets of Lublin, its stone houses and its copper-colored eaves, and glimpsed, in the distance, a child, hurrying down a winding alleyway. She closed her eyes and strained for clarity. Someone was holding her hand, but when Karolina looked up to see who, the sudden movement dislodged the vision. She returned to find Mrs. Domanski watching her with her hard, nut-brown eyes. "Let me tell you something," she snapped. "Just because a Jew speaks Polish doesn't mean he'll be your friend. Even in America, you can't trust them. They are the same as they were back home, only here they don't cross the street when they see a Christian."

The woman's eyes turned moist and her cheeks began to tremble. She'd lost her sister and first husband in a slave labor camp and now talk of the war was disturbing her. Karolina touched her hand. "I'm sorry I upset you. It's just that . . ." She scrambled for a story. "I've been feeling homesick lately and thinking about the old days on the farm. There was a cousin of the Hankowskis who used to visit in summer. We played together as children." She opened her eyes wide in earnestness. "I was wondering if you or Zosha knew what became of her. We were very close."

Mrs. Domanski's face brightened. "There was a man who used to work in Zosha's store. He worked for the Hankowskis during the war, then went to help out Zosha. He might know."

"On the farm? During the war?"

"Yes, a poor fellow, all alone." She tapped her forehead meaningfully. "Not so smart, as I remember, but a strong worker. He probably gave Darius Hankowski a hand with the animals and got a little food in return." She paused, thoughtful. "Darius suffered in a German camp — and Zofia lost her arm. You see! You should tell the Landaus that the Jews were not the only ones."

Darius, dear Darius, with his crooked smile and long, sunhardened face. When he came into her house, he always announced himself by slapping his cap across his knee, sending a cloud of grainy dust into the air. It was a habit that annoyed her mother, although she could never stay angry at him for long. By the time he died, a few years before her father, Darius looked like an old man. The endless drudgery of farm life had crushed his heart in the end. He'd deserved his Saturday night drunks, he and her father. Her *tatush* most certainly would have told Darius about her. He *couldn't* keep something so important from his closest friend. And that man who worked on the Hankowski farm would know something about her, no? A child couldn't just appear from nowhere without people noticing.

"What's the man's name? Is he still alive?" Karolina asked.

"That was more than twenty years ago. I can write, but I'm sure he doesn't work there anymore. You remember how bad business has been since the Soviets . . ."

"Don't trouble yourself. I'll write Zosha. I'm ashamed I never thanked her for putting me in touch with you." Another letter she'd send off tonight.

Karolina cut a generous slice of cake for Mrs. Domanski's husband, a thin, quiet man who never had much to say, but who gave her a toothy smile whenever she walked into his deli. It struck her that she never thought of him by his own name, Pawel, but simply as Mrs. Domanski's husband.

The landlady lumbered toward the door. "It really isn't bad for American cake, you know."

Karolina tucked the sheet of wax paper over the rim of the plate. Now was not the time to tell her that Lichtman's, the store near the Landaus' where she'd bought the dessert, was a Jewish bakery.

Chapter 17

"Hello, hello," Izzy Landau said, trundling over to Karolina's side. He made a small coughing sound to clear his throat, took her hand and shook it vigorously. Noah's father was a short man with a large head and a mop of thick salt and pepper hair neatly combed down at the sides. He tried a smile, but it came out looking more like a grimace. "Who would have thought such a thing could happen . . ." He trailed off, then glanced at his wife, a small, gray-haired woman with soft hazel eyes who stood beside him, nervously fingering the neckline of her angora sweater. He urged her toward Karolina with a little prod. "This is Noah's mother, Bertha."

The woman reddened and rolled her eyes, then gave her husband a mock jab with her elbow.

"How silly!" he said, slapping his forehead. "We already met when we were here last month."

They were uneasy in her presence, but Karolina had expected that. She grinned, trying to hide her own awkwardness, then extended her hand and gave Bertha's a firm shake.

"Nice to meet you," Bertha said, flushing with embarrassment. "I mean to meet you again."

"Yes, it is good to see you." Karolina searched Izzy's face for some hint of herself in the man who could be her uncle, but no, there was nothing in his slanted eyes or round jawline that resembled her. He watched her carefully, clearly wondering the same thing and they stood this way, bashfully eyeing each other for a moment.

"So . . . Noah told you I am from Lublin, yes? But did he tell you his mother came from Chelm," Izzy laughed. "The famous village of fools?"

"Of course I know of Chelm. But why fools?"

"From the Sholem Aleichem stories," Izzy explained. "The famous Jewish writer? Even in New York people know his stories."

"No . . . I do not . . ."

Silence. Izzy stared into his glass of ginger ale. What felt like minutes passed. Another cough. "So, I hear you grew up near Lublin."

"Yes, our farm was half-way between there and Zamosc."

"Zamosc," Izzy said softly, rolling the word around in his mouth like a piece of candy. "I once had a friend from Zamosc who apprenticed with me in the leather trade. Maybe you knew the family Friedman?"

Karolina had often gone with her father to Zamosc when he needed a plow or wagon spokes from a blacksmith there. As she remembered, there were no Jews left in the village and no sign that there ever had been. "My parents might have known, but I do not remember."

"And the cafe on ulica Prowska in Lublin?" Izzy's face lit up with eagerness, sending his bushy eyebrows higher up his creased forehead. "It had a big red and white striped awning. The owner used to put empty coffee sacks in the window for decoration, but he only served tea. Me and Meyer, we used to go there after Bund meetings. We were all Socialist then."

Karolina shook her head regretfully and studied her drink again. How nice it would be to share a memory with this man, this possible uncle.

"But you still have market day, yes?"

"Yes, of course," she said. "The wagons still come in from the country."

"They held it on Friday mornings so we could get everything before *shabbos*."

Market day in Lublin had been on Monday while Karolina was growing up. She remembered distinctly because her father picked her up early from school to help with the shopping, and still shaky from his weekend drunks, would fall asleep with the reins in his hands.

She usually ended up driving the cart while her father dozed with his head on her shoulder, and would only wake him once their farm was in sight, before her mother saw him and scolded them both. But she had given Noah's father enough disappointment. "Yes, it is still on Friday."

Noah stepped up to the circle. He looked particularly bookish in his gray pullover and dark pants, like a professor overseeing a school party. "Karolina has been wonderful with Amanda," he said, holding out his glass of punch toward her. "I don't know what we'll do without her." His father looked puzzled. "Karolina's an artist, a sculptor. She's looking for a gallery job. It'll be better suited to her interests."

Her heart warmed with gratitude. Noah was trying so hard to win them over to her side. A few days ago, she'd overheard him on the phone telling Izzy he had startling news, trying to persuade them with his own eagerness that he was impressed with her. The last time his parents visited, Karolina had noticed how they deferred to him, how timid and respectful they were, trailing him with shining eyes when he spoke, and leaning in to listen to everything he said. America had been good to them. They were proud of their successful son. If he trusted her, they would try to, no matter what other people thought.

"You must be hungry," Noah said. "Linda bought some appetizers from Zabar's on Broadway. Go, take Mom and eat something."

With a sigh of relief, Izzy ushered Bertha toward a side table where they helped themselves to chunks of smoked fish and slices of seeded rye bread. Karolina watched him assemble a sandwich and devour it in two bites while Bertha daintily spread a napkin on her lap and nibbled on a piece of fish. When she noticed her husband stuffing himself, she gestured for him to slow down as she quickly stole a glance across the room.

"Do I look nervous?" Karolina whispered to Noah who hovered protectively at her side.

"Yes," Noah whispered back. "But don't worry. You knew the names. That clinched it for them."

"Clinched?"

"Settled it."

"They are not worried about — my reasons?"

"I'm not, so they're not."

"And Linda?"

"You know Linda. She wants to do what's right."

Linda, who'd been arranging small wooden *dreidels* on the linen cloth, looked up, and motioned for Noah to return to his parents. She'd cleared the living room of Amanda's toys and stacked her library journals and Noah's tax manuals behind the sectional couch. She'd been cooking furiously all morning and although her chicken casserole and potato pancakes were ready, she busied herself rearranging the radish roses and cucumber slices into neat rows. She moved from platter to platter with her mouth set in a determined line, as if willing the afternoon to go well.

Clutching her drink, Karolina drifted over to the bank of windows that overlooked the glittering Hudson. A ship was slowly making its way up the choppy river past a cluster of houses nestled against the Jersey cliffs. She absently smoothed down her black wool dress, then took a swallow of her foamy rum punch. All morning she'd agonized over what to wear before settling on this long-sleeved sheath Jim had bought her for their first evening out in New York. It was the nicest garment she owned. She eyed Linda's fashionable, pale green mini dress and white stockings, then Bertha in a navy and white striped angora sweater and matching A-line skirt, and felt like the only immigrant in the room. Karolina looked ready for a funeral, or worse, like a foreigner who didn't know how Americans dressed for Chanukah, or how Jews celebrated the holiday for that matter. Was there a special ceremony to mark the last day? Did they light another candle in the candelabra Linda had set in the middle of the table or maybe put on skull caps and recite a final prayer? What did it mean to be a Jew beside being born one, she wondered? She should have been more prepared. She should have looked up the holiday in a book.

The doorbell rang. Murmured greetings floated in from the hallway, then Noah was approaching with a couple she guessed were his uncle and aunt.

"Uncle Meyer and Aunt Dora," Noah announced.

A short, barrel-chested man with thick shoulders and a fleshy neck clasped his hands behind his back and bowed stiffly. His wife's face was long and pinched, the kind that always looked worried. Her bright blue eyes took in Karolina from head to toe, then she gave her

133

a quick nod. Philip's parents. Of course they would be skeptical.

"Where's Philip?" Noah asked Meyer. "Didn't he come with you?"

"He's getting Rosalind in Great Neck," Meyer said. "You know what the expressway is like." He panned the room. "And where's my Alice? I thought she was here."

"She's with Amanda down the hall at the Feiners'. We'll see the children later," Noah replied.

Linda put her arms around Dora's shoulders. "Everything's out on the table. Have something while we wait."

"Who can eat at a time like this?" Meyer boldly assessed Karolina. His brown eyes were deep-set and small like his brother's, but without Izzy's good-natured gleam. "At least tell us when these . . . memories started."

"A long time ago really . . ." She threw a glance at Noah. "But the picture in the newspaper *clinched* it."

Noah covered his mouth with his glass to hide his grin.

The doorbell sounded again. "They're here," Linda called from the buffet table, and everyone turned toward the hallway.

Philip was standing at the entrance to the living room with a small, blond woman in a fur coat and matching hat. Jake's wife. Everyone gathered around them, and Philip hugged them each in greeting. His cheeks were still red from the cold, and again Karolina noticed how dark he was, as though he had a suntan all year round. He gazed around the living room and when he found her eyes, he gave her a curt nod before turning to help his aunt remove her coat. They hadn't spoken since his last visit. When she'd dropped off the letters she'd written to Poland, his secretary had said that he was out.

Rosalind Landau stood next to her nephew, twisting the gold bangles on her wrist while her family chatted with her. When she caught sight of Karolina, she stood very still and regarded her mutely. The others hung back while the woman slowly crossed the floor.

"So," Rosalind said. Her tearful eyes roamed Karolina's face. "What can I say? If you are as nervous as I am . . ." A small smile quivered into place and she held out her ringed hand. Karolina clasped it in her own.

"I am very glad to know you," Karolina said simply, instantly liking the warm, open face.

"Philip has told me, of course, but we are all anxious to hear from you." Again, she searched Karolina's eyes and, as if suddenly remembering there were other people in the room, she turned to them. "Yes, there's a lot to talk about."

"But first there's lunch," Linda announced from the table.

An hour later Noah steered Karolina to the ottoman he'd hauled in from his bedroom, while the rest of the family arranged themselves around her on the L-shaped couch and dining room chairs. Everyone had made strained small talk while they hurried through lunch and although she'd tried to eat, Karolina's stomach had churned so badly, she'd simply moved her fork around the plate until the meal was over. Philip had been congenial, if a bit aloof. He'd asked about her art classes and looked amused when she'd described the disheveled art students at the League who liked to talk about the drugs they took and haggle over which variety of marijuana gave them the best high. At one point, Izzy surprised her by venturing a few words in Polish. "They don't come to the tongue so quickly anymore," he'd apologized. "Mostly we speak Yiddish at home."

Now the family was ready for her story. Noah handed her a whiskey, then withdrew to the back of the room to sit on a folding chair next to Linda. Karolina gazed into the sepia-colored liquid, took a sip and began.

She told them of her childhood on the farm, of the secret glances and whispering that had passed between her parents while she was growing up, of the nagging sensation she'd always had that something was hidden, unsaid. She described her dreams and the peculiar names she'd carried inside her for years, and how, when she spoke the names aloud, there was nothing more forbidden, nothing she could do that upset her parents more.

She explained how her family left their farm after the war and didn't return for a year. There seemed to be no reason for this move; in fact, it was hard for her father to find work and her mother hated being dependent on the cousins with whom they were staying. They'd moved from their farm, Karolina now believed, because they feared Jake would come looking for her.

She could feel them waiting, scouring her with their eyes. She paused to take a long sip of whiskey, then continued.

135

She'd been terribly shaken when she saw Jake's picture in the obituary, she told them, because the moment she recognized him the puzzle had started to fall into place. Memories came back nearly every day now, as if seeing Jake's face had pried open a hidden door. "I know you are still wondering how this can be, how my parents could have done such a thing. I cannot blame you. You have suffered much . . . and I am a reminder of the old life that is gone — and in such a terrible way. Only now I begin to understand this kind of pain."

"You will never know!" Meyer called out suddenly. Philip hushed him and put a comforting arm around his father who fell back against the couch, his face tight with indignation.

The anguish in his voice touched her. "You are right, of course, Mr. Landau. I should not compare. But," she said heavily, "no matter what the crime, the people who raised me loved me. They saved me. Do not judge them too harshly because I myself am struggling not to. Please . . . forgive me if I cannot express myself well. There is much in my heart I wish to say, but I do not have the words."

Here she stopped, her body hot with all that was unsaid and feeling, in the glare of their attention, the full impact of the events that had befallen her. I am in exile from my country, she *could* say, from my people, from myself. And I fear I will never belong to either Poles or Jews.

After a few moments, Meyer looked around the room with astonishment. "That's all? You don't remember anything else?"

"Since Jake's picture, I remember things every day. "

"So? Tell us. You haven't said much yet."

"Just the other day I remembered coming to the farm in a car, a big black car."

Izzy turned toward the others, flailing his arms in excitement. "Jake bought a car just after we left for America," he shouted out. "Luba wrote he bought a used Russian car in Rovno, a black one."

"No one else had a black car in Poland?" Meyer muttered with contempt. "And what of Jake's first wife? A child remembers a mother, no?"

Since she'd first seen Jake's photo, Karolina had tried to summon an image, a feeling, a scrap of memory that might belong to this woman, but nothing came. She bent forward, aching to know. "No, but I want to! What was she like ?"

Meyer looked up with exaggerated surprise. "We should tell you? Don't you know?"

"All . . . all I remember is women with lace — or how do you say, crocheted collars?"

Philip's head shot up. He swung around to face Noah. "Do you have any pictures of Luba and Hinda?"

"No, just one of Jake when he was in the DP camp and a couple from his wedding. Why?"

Philip shook his head dismissively, then put his elbows on his knees, leaned forward and watched her.

"We were poor people," Meyer continued. "We didn't have fancy clothes with lace."

"Not even on holidays?" Izzy questioned. "When we went to *shul*? Didn't Mama wear something when she *benched lecht* on *shabbos*?"

"That was a shawl, not a collar," Meyer shot back. "And she put it over her head."

"Hinda and Luba had a few nice dresses. Maybe . . ." Izzy turned to his wife as if she might know simply because she was a woman.

Hungry to hear more, Karolina blurted out: "Where did they live? A house? A flat? Maybe something more will come if you tell me."

Meyer sat up with a huff. "A child can't just appear from nowhere without someone becoming suspicious. How did the Poles explain you?"

"I do not know, I do not know . . ." she said, rubbing her burning eyes. Points of blue light exploded in the blackness behind her lids. The room around her grew distant. A word took shape. *Yelna.* Something floated up from the edge of her memory, something more felt than seen. A barn. A dog. A child running across a yard in muddied shoes.

"Yelna," Karolina whispered to herself, turning the word over as though it would reveal itself once she gave it sound. "I remember this name. There was a dog. Yelna?"

An intense silence filled the room. When Karolina looked up, the air was shimmering with bright sunlight. She smoothed her damp hair from her forehead and waited. Bertha blew her nose. Rosalind's lips trembled. Dora averted her eyes and clasped Meyer's arm. And Philip, who had been sitting with his head bent over his clasped hands, looked as if he were seeing her for the first time.

"*Gott in himmel*," Izzy muttered to himself. "Uncle Yossel lived in Yelna! That was the name of his *dorf*! He lived there in a wooden house. He kept a vegetable garden behind it. And he had an old dog, the lame one that lived in the barn . . ."

"The place where the cousins lived . . ." Bertha gasped.

"Remember, Noah?" Izzy said. "I once told you about it. You, too, Philip, how when we were boys . . ." He grabbed his brother by the arm. "Meyer, we went there in the summer to get away from the heat! Luba and Hinda, too. It was only 30 kilometers from Lublin. Jake probably went there with the wife and child before the Germans came." Izzy's eyes grew round with astonishment. "How could she know this?"

"Yes, yes, Jake mentioned this once," Rosalind said, working the handkerchief in her hands. "I remember."

"Maybe she got this information from records in Lublin!" Dora shouted at the others.

Rosalind waved her hand. "I've heard this theory already," she said. "How could anyone connect the names of people who died twenty years ago with my Jake? It's ridiculous. And Yelna? Would records say that Jake's uncle lived there? And that the uncle had pets?" Her face filled with amazement. "Oh, this is too much! Everything I have heard this past week, what I am hearing now . . . I believe it's possible. This woman *could* be Jake's child."

"This is not proof." Dora lifted her chin with dignity. "And I will say what no one else has the courage to say. This woman wants money — my son's money — and your son's too," she said to Bertha who was squeezing her hands in her lap, looking embarrassed. "You are a mother. How can you believe such a tale!"

Karolina leapt from the ottoman. Tears of humiliation welled up. "I am *not* lying," she said, looking wildly around the room. "I did not know about money!" She stumbled slightly, anxious to leave, mortified by the accusations and the vulgar, shameless display of greed.

"Please stay!" Rosalind jumped in. "I have something to say. You know I am not a superstitious woman, but a few nights ago . . . How can I say this? I dreamed Jake came to me." A murmur rose from the group. She raised a hand to silence them. "I know, I know, but this is important. He was standing by the side of my bed in those striped pants from the camps, but he looked just like the day he died. He had a baby blanket in his hand and when he lifted the little rag for me to see, his face was so pained. I woke up with such a heavy heart." She shook her head and sighed. "I thought to myself, he's blaming me for not giving him children. But why should he do this; he was the one who didn't want any. So he must have come for another reason. He didn't speak in the dream, but his face told me his child was alive."

No one moved. Meyer closed his eyes and put his hand on his chest. "Listen to me, Rosalind. You are not a good judge of this."

"I can judge what it means to be *executor* of my husband's estate."

Noah stood up from the back of the room. "I don't know why Philip's convinced his parents that this is some cockamamie scheme cooked up in Poland."

Philip shook his head with annoyance. "I came here like everyone else to find out the truth." A few wavy strands of hair fell across his brow that he brushed aside. "This is new to me, too."

Meyer shrugged. "So? What now?"

"I would like to get to know Karolina," Rosalind said.

"So this is how you will decide?" Meyer grumbled. "Over coffee and a danish?"

Rosalind's mouth began to tremble. "I'm sorry this is upsetting everyone so much. I can guess why. But you have to admit, Meyer, that there is enough here to make us wonder, no?"

A calming certainty had settled over Karolina. As long as they suspected she was lying, as long as there wasn't some proof besides her personal recollections, they — and she — would always be plagued with doubt.

She stepped into the center of the room. "Please stop," she called out with feeling. "I also need to know truth. Until then, I do not talk of money."

Meyer looked as if he wanted to speak, but Philip stopped him with a silencing hand, then nodded for her to continue.

"So what do you think we should do?" Rosalind asked.

"I think we must find people who knew me," Karolina said.

"People from Lublin or Zamosc — or Yelna. You are right, Mr. Landau," she said to Meyer. "A child cannot appear from nowhere without someone noticing."

Philip rose from his chair, put his hands in his pockets and began to pace. "Did Jake have friends here in the U.S. from before the war?" he asked Rosalind.

"He knew a few Polish Jews," she said, "but no one from Lublin."

"Would he have confided in any of them, told them about his past?"

"Why, if he didn't even tell me?" she said.

"And Uncle Yossel?" Philip asked.

"Dead!" Meyer said before Rosalind could answer. "All of them."

"There must be people still living who knew Karolina's parents," Noah said. "We should track them down."

"Is that possible from here?" Rosalind asked. "Wouldn't this have to be done from Poland?"

"Yes, I have been thinking same thing," Karolina said.

"Someone from the family, someone who lived there should go," Rosalind said to her brothers-in-law.

"I will never put my feet in that country again!" Meyer cried out.

"Oh, I couldn't . . ." Izzy said.

"What about Noah or Philip?" Rosalind asked. "They know enough about the family history. They would be good at looking things up. And Karolina could help with the language."

Linda stared at Noah with apprehension. "I don't think I can leave right now," Noah muttered.

Philip seemed not to be listening. He continued pacing, as though a thousand thoughts raced through him. "I might be able to get away for a week," he said finally, running his thumb across his lips.

He'd been walking in a small circle near the couch, looking agitated, distracted; still, Karolina sensed he was enjoying the confusion that spread through the room. She could see it in the way he moved his shoulders, in the way his eyes shone with command when he stopped to survey the tense faces of his family. He seemed more intrigued than anything else.

"Could you, Phil?" Rosalind asked. Philip nodded. "Oh, that would be wonderful! Do you agree with this, Karolina?" But before she could answer Rosalind added: "I'll pay, of course — for both of you. It's only right."

Karolina's head swam. She was going back to Poland! She gazed past the Landaus and felt herself drift from the room. Her mind raced to the streets of Lublin, past the shops that lined the town square, the stores where her parents had bought food and farm supplies, straining for names to connect to the faces she had known as a child. She would track people down! She would make them tell her what they knew! She'd write her cousin Pola. And that man Mrs. Domanski had mentioned, Josef, who worked on Darius Hankowski's farm during the war. She would scour the archives. She would find him. "Yes, of course I will go."

Just then the front door flew open and Amanda bolted in with a thin, blonde girl of five or six trailing behind her. The child had a serious face and intelligent light brown eyes, and when she spotted Philip she ran and grabbed his hand, then gazed, somewhat alarmed, at the adults crowding around her.

Karolina scooped up Amanda and kissed the small, rosy face.

"Lucy gave me two bags," Amanda said, proudly holding up a mesh bag full of empty gold wrappers. "I ate them."

Karolina put her hand to her chest with feigned shock. "A whole bag, *kochana?*"

Alice, who'd been eyeing Karolina, took a few tentative steps toward her. "My Daddy gave me Mindy," she said, lifting up the doll for inspection. Alice was fair, but had her father's sharp jaw and slender nose. Unlike Philip, her movements were calm and deliberate, unusual in so young a child. "She has lace panties that go all the way down and her shoes . . ." Alice expertly undid a mother-of-pearl button and released the black-patent leather strap. "They come off like this, see."

"This is wonderful doll," Karolina marveled, and Alice bobbed her head in agreement.

Philip kept a protective hand on Alice's head while he looked

141

on. There was an easy closeness between father and daughter that surprised Karolina. What an odd man. One moment hard and contentious, the next tender, almost needy. Unpredictable, she decided. *Temperamental,* just as Noah had once described him when he was trying to be tactful. Spending a week with him would be difficult. She could never be sure if he'd come along to help or to monitor.

The children's entrance had broken the tension and the families eased back into their customary selves. Karolina carried Amanda to the edge of the living room to watch the Landaus talk in the abbreviated, banal language of people who had put up with each other for years. Studying them from a distance, she saw that despite their tailored clothes and good shoes, they still looked like country Poles. Meyer and Izzy were thick-necked, barrel-chested men with square jaws and big hands; Bertha and Dora, broad-hipped with wide foreheads and deep-set eyes, were just like middle-aged women back home. They used their hands freely and spoke with an emotional inflection she knew well. Either of these women would look natural walking down a country road, carrying a crate of eggs; she could picture the men at home behind a bakery counter or vegetable stand in Lubartow. What had she expected?

What *could* she expect since she knew nothing about Jews except the superstitions passed down to her by peasants? She'd anticipated something less familiar, she supposed, something *more* Jewish, whatever that meant. Yet these people seemed terribly, reassuringly familiar.

She positioned herself near the window so she could listen in on the conversation. Meyer was complaining that Mayor Lindsay was wasting their tax money on a Jazz Mobile; Izzy, who'd collared Philip at the table, was warning him that the Egyptians were massing at the border again and Israel would soon have another war on its hands. Philip seemed to be paying attention, but as soon as he caught her eye, he nodded at her as though they shared a secret understanding.

Later, when everyone was milling around the hallway closet, Philip came up behind her and took her elbow.

"Noah's parents are driving Rosalind home. I'm heading to Brooklyn to drop off Alice. I can give you a lift to Greenpoint afterwards. I'd like to talk," he added confidentially.

She felt uneasy. This man confused her. Halfway through the

Landaus' interrogation, she'd sensed a shift in him, and when she'd chanced a look in his direction, his gaze had been questioning, even a bit puzzled, and without the poorly concealed hostility she'd come to expect.

Before she could ask what more he wanted from her, Rosalind stepped up to them and rested a gloved hand on Karolina's shoulder. "It's been quite a day," she muttered with a tired smile. "We'll speak, yes? Philip will give me your number." She touched her nephew's cheek. "You'll drive her home, dear? It's cold to wait for a subway."

"Looks like we've been given orders," Philip said, taking Karolina's coat from her hands and holding it out like a matador's cape for her to slip on.

Night had fallen. The street lamps were on. Karolina walked alongside Philip and Alice, her head bent against the icy wind that blew up from the river. At the corner, Philip crouched to adjust Alice's coat collar and tighten the flaps of her fuzzy white hat. When they reached his car, he quickly swept the candy wrappers from the front seat, helped Alice in, then opened the rear door for Karolina. The back seat was covered with files and loose documents. Crumpled paper lunch bags littered the floor. A man with little time, she thought, a man who ate on the run, yet he'd offered to go to Poland with her.

While they waited for the engine to warm up, Alice scrambled around in her seat and faced Karolina with luminous, watchful eyes. "Do you go to Amanda's house every day?" Alice asked.

"Not weekends, but yes, all other days."

Alice tilted her head, considering. "You live in Brooklyn?"

"Yes."

"Will you visit me, too?"

"I'm sure I will see you again at Amanda's house," Karolina said, playfully touching the tip of Alice's nose. Alice seemed to accept this answer with equanimity and sat back down. Karolina had spent half an hour sitting on the floor in Amanda's room, helping Alice dress and undress her doll while Amanda sifted through the toy box for her wooden farm animals. Alice had played silently, but with concentration, and although she hadn't smiled much, Karolina could feel her quiet pleasure.

Philip dropped Alice off at a four-story house on a quiet

residential street, then drove down Atlantic Avenue toward the Brooklyn-Queens Expressway. The view from the expressway was breathtaking. A crystal-clear night, glittering skyscrapers to the left, a slice of moon pinned against the night sky to the right. The temperature had dropped. Karolina could feel the cold night air pressing against the car windows. It was probably snowing in Warsaw.

Lights from the oncoming cars washed over Philip's face. She studied his brooding profile, looking for some sign of what he was feeling, but his mouth was set in a determined line while he concentrated on the road. She settled back, feeling like a spiteful child, reluctant to say anything to put him at ease.

"There could be visa problems," Philip said suddenly.

"Problems?"

"Leaving the U.S. shouldn't be hard. Getting back in might. Communist countries are tricky, as you know."

Dread washed over her. What if she couldn't get out of Poland? She hadn't realized until this moment how much she wanted to stay here, in New York, in America. The thought of her sad, impoverished country wrung her heart, but she had no future there. The Soviets would bleed the country dry before letting Poles succeed in anything but growing potatoes, and if she was Chava Landau, how would she ever feel at home again? A Jew in Poland? Just remembering the look on Mrs. Domanski's face when she spoke about the Landaus made her churn with indignation and shame.

"You have a green card, right?" Philip asked, as though reading her thoughts. "Then you'll probably be okay. I'll have my secretary call the consulate on Monday for the necessary documents. Let's hope everyone hasn't disappeared for the holidays."

"Christmas is big day for Poles," she said. "I am sure many are at home."

"Well, we'll do what we can."

A light was burning in the Domanski kitchen when they pulled in front of her apartment. Philip cut the engine and turned toward her. He scrutinized her face for a moment and when she didn't speak, turned shyly away. "They were tough on you," he said.

"Like you."

She caught the shadow of his grin.

"You said you wished to speak with me," she said.

144

He nodded. "You were pretty convincing."

"You are saying you have changed your mind?"

"I've been a bastard, I know, but this whole story has been a big surprise." His eyes shone like black silk in the darkened car. "I'll take a look at my schedule and let you know about possible dates. Can you get away?"

She nodded. "Linda is leaving her job next week."

Philip slipped his arm across the back of the seat. "Have you thought about who to contact in Lublin?"

"Yes, I have already written letter." Then: "You are busy man," she challenged. "Why do you take time for this?"

"For Jake. The man spent his life mourning his child. It's what he would have wanted." There was tenderness in his gaze. "And because you surprised me."

He answered so swiftly, so sincerely that for a moment she was silent. Then the darkness inside the car enclosed her like a confessional. "Oh, this is too much!" she said, her head falling back against the seat. "How am I to make sense of what you say?"

"I know. It's a confusing business."

"No! This is not a business."

"Just an expression," he said. His voice was thick with apology. "We'll be spending time together. I hope we can be friends." He took her hand and gently encircled her wrist with his strong fingers. "I'd like that."

She gazed at the palm beneath hers, sure that one sign from her and he would gather her in his arms. A flutter rose at the base of her throat. Some instinct — self-preservation, pride, she couldn't tell which — held her back. This turnaround was too quick. He was a clever man. If she gave in to her sexual attraction, he was capable of using it against her. See, he would say, look what a schemer she is, seducing me for Jake's money.

"I have always been a friend," Karolina said and quickly slid out of the car. At her front door she groped in her handbag for her keys, then stole a glimpse back. In the dim light from the street lamps, she could make out his watchful face still turned toward her.

Chapter 18

Karolina was scooping breaded chicken slices onto Amanda's dish when the phone rang.

"Hello, *kochana*." Jim had given her a week to cool down. Now, his voice had its usual post-fight cheerfulness. Karolina waited for the knocking in her chest to subside, then wedged the phone between her shoulder and ear, and placed the Beatrix Potter dish before Amanda.

"Yes, Jim. It is you."

"I have all evening," he said. "I'll meet you when you get off. No classes tonight, right? So it's six?"

The familiarity of his voice momentarily filled her with the urge to tell him everything. During their year together, she'd grown accustomed to relying on him for comfort. Whenever she despaired of her future, he would take her in his arms and, smoothing back her hair, whisper reassurances that everything would be fine. He enjoyed playing the wise older man, and even though she knew he wouldn't offer help that might take her away from him, she needed the consolation of being comforted by someone who loved her. Now, she felt ill with the certainty that she wouldn't see him again.

"No," she said. "I cannot come."

"What time, then?"

He'd force her to tell him bluntly, cruelly, before he'd let go.

"No time. It is over. We are over."

"There's a new French restaurant on Eighth Avenue," he said. "We could grab a bite before we go back to the apartment."

She gazed with amazement into the air. Jim's ability to ignore what he didn't want to hear was astounding. She yanked a terry bib from the refrigerator hook and roughly fastened it around Amanda's neck. The child twisted sharply, then looked up in surprise.

"We've been through this before," Jim said.

"And now it is finished, *koniec.*"

Amanda cautiously bit into the piece of chicken, keeping her eyes on Karolina's face.

"Why must you be so dramatic?" he said.

"I have nothing more to say." If she didn't hang up soon, she'd burst into tears in front of the child.

"Look, how about we go to St. Thomas over Christmas? You've never been to the Islands. A whole week, just the two of us. What more do you want me to do?"

"I want you to do nothing because I will not see you again. I am sorry. Good-bye, Jim."

She hung up, then braced herself against the counter. Her heart felt lined with lead. Amanda continued to stare, the bewilderment in her face turning to fear. "No cry, Kiki," she scolded. "Eat," she said, holding out her fork like a peace offering.

Karolina bit into the floppy ribbon of chicken. "Umm, delicious," she said, swallowing a sob. Jim would call again, and she knew that she would have to tell him again and again, until he understood. *Koniec.*

Chapter 19

"It is so kind of you to send taxi," Karolina said, squeezing Rosalind's thin hands. She followed the woman into her living room and made herself comfortable on a white brocade couch while Rosalind lowered herself onto the nearby matching chair. In the quiet of her own home, Rosalind looked different from the week before. The softness of her features seemed more kind than docile.

"It's hard to get here without a car." Rosalind fussed with the perfect crease in her beige slacks. "I won't keep you late. I know you have to be at Noah's early."

At the top of the staircase leading to a second floor, Karolina could make out brass sconces and champagne-colored walls trimmed in elaborate molding. She knew that Jake was rich, but she'd not expected a mansion. "You have beautiful house," she said.

"It doesn't look lived in." Rosalind blinked out at the room. "When we first bought it, I thought we would entertain a lot, but Jake wanted a quiet home. It's too big for one person." She paused. "It was too big for two."

The phone rang and Rosalind rose, disappearing down a long hallway covered in thick carpeting.

The room was filled with gleaming glass shelves and porcelain knickknacks. A plush, wheat-colored carpet covered the floor and matching velvet draperies hid the view of evergreen shrubs and shade trees she'd noticed when she arrived. No, this room was not lived in. It was a monument to professional decorating.

Rosalind's voice drifted toward her from a back room. "Yes, she just arrived." Then there was muffled whispering.

A moment later, Rosalind returned, carrying a crystal decanter.

She poured brandy into a small, gold-rimmed glass she'd set on the coffee table in front of Karolina. She'd not put one out for herself. "That was Philip," she said.

Karolina gave her a neutral nod.

"Noah told me you had trouble with him. I'm sorry."

She sipped the sweet orange-flavored liqueur, trying to decide how truthful she should be. "Philip is difficult man. But I think you are wise woman and know this."

"Yes, of course, but . . ." She shrugged apologetically. "You mustn't blame him entirely. He's a lot like Jake and Meyer. He doesn't trust easily."

"Then who should I blame if people are not nice?" she said, then stopped herself. "Excuse me. You have been kind with your feelings. I hope not to insult."

"No, no, I don't want to make excuses." Rosalind touched her forehead. "How can I put it? Until Philip met you, I don't think he realized what he'd inherited from his family."

Karolina was about to protest that this was no longer an issue, when Rosalind's hand flew up in alarm. "Oh, I don't mean money!" She let out a little sigh to calm herself. "Polish Jews who lived through the war . . . well, they're suspicious people. Jake was like that, naturally, and so is Philip's father. Even harmless Izzy is bitter. You know what happened to the Jews in Europe. How could the survivors not be angry? Philip's always had this anger inside him. You just made him realize how much he hated the people who did nothing . . . while six million died. That's why he gave you a hard time."

Did Rosalind expect her to be comforted by this explanation? Should *she*, Karolina, take responsibility for Philip Landau's hatred of Poles because she'd been brought up as one? She had only been a child during the time of the concentration camps. *She* was not to blame. Clearly, Rosalind was the kind of person who tried to make everyone happy. She was too good-natured to suspect her relatives of greed. Karolina decided not to debate the issue. It was not in her best interest.

"I came here wanting to please you and now I am rude about your family. Forgive me."

"No, no, it's only natural. This is an extraordinary situation. Everybody's upset." Rosalind took a moment to adjust the rings on her hands. "Please believe that Philip wouldn't take time to go with you to Poland if he didn't think you were honest. He wants to do what's right. Let's forget this now. I asked you here to get to know you better. Noah tells me you've had an interesting life. He said you're an artist."

"I was sculptor," she said. "But I did not make a career."

"It's a difficult profession anywhere, I should think."

"Yes, difficult." Karolina glanced at the painting on the opposite wall: an orange and mauve sunset, a ridge of deep-blue mountains, an Indian canoeing across a gray lake. In oils. Even from a distance the brush strokes looked stiff and amateurish. How much did people pay for such an ugly painting? Yet, why should she care if it gave Rosalind pleasure? She was rich enough to buy whatever she wanted.

"You must believe I know nothing of money when I first speak with Noah," Karolina said.

"He told me."

"I did not know the names were on ID cards until Philip came to my flat."

Rosalind nodded.

"I want to explain —"

"And now you have," Rosalind said with a wave of her hand. "Dear, I didn't ask you here to interrogate you."

"We both know this is examination. I am stranger and you want to judge me. It is only natural."

"You're right, of course, and brave to say so. My family thinks I have no sense, but I don't think I'm such a bad judge of character." She looked at Karolina pensively. "Tell me why you left Poland."

"I saw what my future was. I did not like it."

"And what was that?"

Karolina took a sip of her liqueur, then lifted out her cigarette pack. "You permit?" she asked. Rosalind nodded and Karolina lit one, then took a deep puff and collected her thoughts. She sensed she would be understood. "When I finished school I began to show my work. At first the critics are kind. Oh, I know Americans think we are backward country, but this is only because Communists make stupid mistakes in economy. Artistic life in Eastern Europe is very active, very alive. When Gomulka became leader in Poland, he gave people freedom and suddenly it was like a great flowering after a long struggle. There was so much new work. You have heard of Grotowski's theater?"

Rosalind shook her head apologetically.

"But you know Roman Polanski from the Lvov film school, yes? 'Knife in the Water' was showing here last year."

Rosalind shook her head again.

"You should see these things. I think you will appreciate." Karolina tossed her head to disperse a plume of rising smoke. "But — there is always a but, no? — it turned out bad for me. You see, my pieces are . . . representational. And I work in stone, which is unusual. My friends always say that I chose this material because my father kept stones in his pockets to touch when he became nervous." She smiled to herself. "But I do not agree with their analysis."

"Sculpting is an unusual choice, isn't it?"

Karolina found it amusing that most people thought sculpting had stopped with Michelangelo. She'd often laughed about it with her art school friends. "For me it is very satisfying. It is hard work, a kind of labor, to break down stone, to tame it. You are tired and dirty and there is dust on face and in hair, even in shoes like you have come out of a mine. But from all this smashing and pounding, you have a beautiful thing, and if you are good, you have touched something true. It is ironic to make something delicate by breaking stone, no? And after, touching what you have made —" She cupped her hands. "It is like body hunger that has become . . . satisfied."

Rosalind's gaze was kind and encouraging. She nodded for Karolina to continue.

"In the end I was told I have skill, but not imagination. My work, they said, was conventional and romantic." She still remembered the vacant smiles and stiff nods she'd received on her three small pieces, "Variations on a theme by Rodin," at her last group exhibit. She had thought of the pieces as a kind of anti-Kiss commentary on the Rodin sculpture she'd adored as an adolescent and had come to resent with the fury of a disillusioned romantic. Her pieces depicted a male and female nude desperately trying to embrace, but in each piece moving further and further away from each other until, in the third sculpture, their fingers barely touched. For two years she'd worked with a frenzy and passion she'd never known before and, in the end, she thought they were her best work. After the opening, a friend had taken her aside and gently suggested she try another medium. Marble is so difficult, she said tactfully. Perhaps clay or even papier-mâché will open you to a fresh approach. Karolina had been so hurt she'd barely spoken to this friend after that and soon found herself drifting away from the art crowd she'd known since she first came to Warsaw.

"Art has to be political to please," Karolina continued. "Soon anything is art only if it is . . . defiant." She brandished her hands in the air, as though she could wipe away the hurt of that opening night. "Empty canvas is art; a marble ball tied in middle with black string is art. Glue nails and rope together and people praise it as sculpture about repression. My friends loved the angry life they were living more than their work. And it is a false life. I cannot respect this. I stopped working for a while, then it became harder to return. When the chance came, it was not so difficult to leave."

"And now?"

"I take classes, that is all. But I see from your newspapers that art world is the same in New York. Perhaps I should tie myself naked to a hammer and sickle . . ."

"So you came here because you felt you didn't fit in."

The comment jolted Karolina. This woman had a talent for digging out the fundamentals. "Yes, and because I met an American who offered a job. And because I thought I loved him." She waited for Rosalind's reaction, but she remained respectfully silent, watching her with her calm hazel eyes. "It does . . . did not work out," Karolina added.

"I'm sorry."

"No, it is time to make an end. When I think back, it is normal that I always felt different . . . apart. I am uncomfortable with myself for as long as I can remember. I thought learning about my past would give me peace, but I still question the truth of my memories and still feel — how do you say — abandoned, like an outsider, as if my life has been but . . . a vapor." Karolina's gaze drifted toward the picture window where frosty triangles had formed in the corner of the panes. Rosalind made it easy to talk, yet once the words were out she felt the old heaviness creep in.

"Jake was a lot like that," Rosalind murmured. She picked up a white leather photo album from the coffee table, slid in next to

152

Karolina and opened the book. "But never mind about that now. Come, let me show you something."

The first few pictures were of Rosalind and Jake's wedding. There was Jake in a dark suit, still gaunt with the look of a newly arrived refugee, and Rosalind at his side, her hair swept up and crowned with a bride's tiara. She beamed back at the camera while Jake held her elbow with a cautious smile on his face — the same face she'd seen in the newspaper almost two months ago.

Next came Philip and Noah as boys, gathered for a formal family picture, both looking surprisingly the same as today. They were about ten years old with long skinny necks that rose from loose shirt collars and little-boys' hair obediently slicked back from their faces. Standing behind them were their parents, young and slim, and looking happy.

Rosalind ran her hand across the photographs. She came to a photo of Philip sitting at a table with his arm around a young woman.

"That's Philip's girlfriend, Ellen. She's a lawyer. Just think, when I was young it was an accomplishment just to know typing and shorthand. Oh, I wasn't independent the way women are now, but I had a good job. I traveled, you know, and I always had nice clothes. I even had a few boyfriends before Jake." Rosalind shook her head, marveling. "Imagine. A lawyer! When will she find time to take care of children?"

This Ellen had a small, oval face with a pointed chin and shining eyes. She was dark, like Philip, and probably in her late twenties, yet her face seemed adolescent in its untroubled smoothness. So American. Karolina had expected any woman of Philip's to be older, at least more sophisticated looking than this *girl*, as Rosalind called her. Philip held a whiskey glass and stared at the camera as if he had been interrupted in the middle of a thought. As usual, he looked slightly irritated and darkly handsome.

"They are planning to marry?" Karolina asked before Rosalind could turn the page.

"Who knows? Nobody's in a rush these days. Everybody talks about *finding* themselves first." Her voice began to tremble. "I don't think I was ever lost. I knew I wanted a family. This wasn't to be, but Jake and I managed to make a life. We found our way together. Being without him is very hard. When he died, I lost my only real job."

A few pages on Rosalind and Jake appeared in front of the Eiffel Tower, at the railing of a ship, in front of a stone monument carved with Hebrew letters. Then came photos of Amanda in a swim suit and matching bonnet, sitting on Linda's lap at the edge of the ocean, and one of Philip balancing Alice on his shoulders. He wore a sweatshirt and a baseball cap, and grinned broadly as he clasped the child's hands for support. Rosalind flipped to another page and here was Alice again, sitting on a couch next to a thin woman with a lean face and straight, shoulder-length hair parted down the middle. The mother's child, no doubt, Philip's ex-wife. The woman looked more mature than the girlfriend and less appealing. A bit stern in the eyes, Karolina thought.

Toward the back of the album Rosalind stopped at a sepia photo of two women sitting on a tufted sofa. Karolina stared into their earnest faces. She studied their dark, glossy hair, so much like Philip's, and their flat, almost Oriental, faces. Their eyes — slanted, shrouded in shadow — drew her closer. Something at the edge of her memory floated up, hovered an instant, then vanished.

"Do you recognize them?"

"No."

Rosalind looked sad. "I was so hoping you would. They're Jake's sisters, Hinda and Luba. Jake's child lived with them after his wife died."

"Jake told you this?"

She nodded. "Over the years I put little things together. He told me his wife was killed while they were still in the ghetto. She went out after dark for some reason — he was never clear why, because there was a strict curfew for Jews. The Germans shot her. Jake wasn't there at the time. From then on, he and his daughter must have lived with the rest of the family, his sisters and their parents, I think."

"But you did not say this last Sunday."

"I wanted to see how much you would remember by yourself."

So this was a test. And she was failing it. Karolina leaned in to study the photo, hoping that some spark of recognition, some detail would spring up and dispel all doubt for both of them. Nothing. "No. I do not know them."

"Jake must have relived the night of his wife's shooting a thousand times," Rosalind said. "I think he believed if he'd been there, he *would* have kept her from going out and she might have survived, as he did. Then the poor man tried to save his child and she died, or so he believed. In his mind, he failed them both. Of course, it wasn't his fault — but this is what people hold inside themselves." She closed the book slowly and let her hand linger on the cover. "The aunts' pictures didn't mean anything to you, yet you remembered their names. And Yelna? Where could that have come from?"

"I do not know. It is a mystery."

Rosalind sank back on the couch cushion and the two women sat in silence bathed in the soft yellow light from the table lamps. The house was still. No traffic sounds, no crunching snow.

"It's getting late," Rosalind said, rousing herself, "and we haven't even discussed your trip. I spoke to a travel agent about flights to Warsaw, but we can't book anything until the consulate approves both your visas. This turns out to be harder than I thought. Philip's already had some problems." She paused to align the crystal candy dishes on the glass coffee table. "Some official said it could be difficult for him to get a visa because he's Jewish, so Philip called a friend in the mayor's office who pulled some strings. When Philip called back, the official at the Polish consulate said there was a surcharge for faster service — in cash. We paid it."

Karolina felt her face redden. "The Polish consulate is not the Polish people."

"I didn't mean that . . ."

She put her glass down on the table with a clatter. "Are there no dishonest people in America?"

"Don't be upset, dear. I just thought you should know."

Yes, of course. She was stupid to get angry. Rosalind was right; she should know what would be waiting if she claimed to be a Jew.

"I'm told it won't be hard to book hotels in Warsaw," Rosalind continued, "but you'll probably need to spend most of your time in Lublin near your farm. Who knows if there are decent places to stay."

"Of course there are."

"Jake never talked much about Lublin. I guess I always pictured a *shtetl*."

Karolina threw up her arms in a gesture of impatience. "Lublin is not such a place. It is big city with beautiful, ancient castles and churches. People come from far to visit. There are many places to stay."

"Then why don't I just give you the name of the travel agent. You'll do better than I. Find a place that will be comfortable."

Karolina's anger subsided and left her feeling ashamed once more of her bad behavior. "Please excuse, but I cannot bear when I hear you sound like rest of family." Rosalind's shoulders sagged. Her eyes misted and she turned away. "Tell me why you do this," Karolina said, taking her hand.

"I've been thinking a lot about Jake," Rosalind said, adjusting her gold bracelets. "That's natural, isn't it? I never understood him very well, just that I was never enough." She squinted into the distance as though her eyes pained her. "Maybe now I can make it up."

Part II

Chapter 20

At 9:00 P.M. when the pilot shut off the seat belt sign, Karolina was still staring out the window into the darkness.

"You're okay?" Philip asked, knowing she wasn't. She'd looked tense and drawn since they'd hooked up at the check-in counter of LOT, the Polish airline.

Karolina nodded.

"No, you're not."

She threw him a startled look, then returned to study her reflection in the blackened window. "I am frightened," she murmured. "What if we find nothing? Oh, I do not expect you to answer," she added, her back still toward him. "But thank you. I am glad you are now friend to me."

Philip wanted to take her hand or touch her shoulder, wanted to show he understood what she was going through. But her stiff, remote tone warned him not to. They'd spoken several times over the past two weeks, yet even after he'd assured her he was going to Poland to help, she'd still sounded cool and distant, even a little punishing, he thought.

Karolina pulled down the window shade, settled back and closed her eyes. Light from the overhead spot spilled across her face. She wore no makeup except a smudge of lipstick so pale it made her mouth look naked, and when Philip stole a look at her, he felt something soft and sore in his gut. In the three weeks since the Chanukah party, he hadn't stopped thinking about her, hadn't stopped asking himself why the hell he was leaving New York to hunt down records buried in a quagmire of Communist bureaucracy in some remote Polish village, hadn't stopped wondering if he'd pushed aside doubts about her honesty just so he could be with her. Yet, each time he'd been tempted to cancel the trip, he'd recall the way she sat in Noah's apartment, hugging herself, one slender leg snaked around the other, gazing feverishly across the living room. How he'd felt her hesitate for a moment before pulling her hand from his when they sat in the car in front of her apartment. And each image had kicked up a sharp rush of adrenaline. It seemed as though accepting her truthfulness had loosened a strange and powerful attraction he'd been stockpiling since the first time they'd met. He'd never felt this way before. He'd kept his passion for his work, for Alice, yet always held a part of himself aloof from the women in his life. Even as he'd walked down the aisle toward his future wife, he'd harbored a nagging suspicion that he was making a mistake. He loved Ellen, yet when he thought of her, she triggered no craving, no rush of longing. She was smart and fun, a good buddy he enjoyed having sex with. And that had seemed enough.

Eight hours of plane time lay ahead. Wearily, Philip pulled a stack of papers from his briefcase and fanned them across his tray. When he'd told Drottman he was leaving the country for a week, Abe hadn't asked why, just messengered over copies of transcripts of the depositions the AJC had filed with the Atlanta District Court, assuming Philip would want to be kept up to date on the case wherever he was. Philip tried to concentrate, but each time Karolina shifted, he became even more aware of her presence. He couldn't think of what to say to ease the tension. There wasn't much left to discuss, anyway. Their itinerary was set: first stop, the Warsaw Registry, then on to Lublin to look for people who'd known her family. She'd said she'd written to the mother of a friend in Lublin who might be helpful, but hadn't gotten a response.

An hour later a food cart rolled down the aisle and they were each handed steaming metal trays. Karolina stared groggy-eyed at the small mound of gray potatoes and mahogany-colored meat patties. "I am not hungry," she said, nudging the food aside.

"Pretty sorry looking, I know, but it's a long flight." He hated the patronizing tone that came out of his mouth, but she made him feel as tongue-tied and sulky as a rejected kid. Which he was, given the way she'd fled the car after his clumsy come-on.

She shrugged her desultory European shrug and curled against the armrest. A few moments later her breathing settled into a rhythmic hum.

Philip downed his tasteless dinner, emptied a miniature bottle of Jack Daniel's into his cup and took stock of the other passengers, most of whom had finished their dinner and settled back with the blank stare of people bracing themselves for boredom. They were a stout, middle-aged bunch with graying hair and ill-fitting clothes. The men were thick and pasty, the women lumpy in flowered dresses and old-people's cardigans. Even the way they sat with their hands folded on their laps looked foreign.

From the moment he boarded the plane, Philip felt as if he'd stepped into a different world. Everything, from the grimy upholstered seats to the frayed cuffs on the uniforms of the LOT stewardesses, reeked of poverty and strangeness. The three women servicing the cabin were good-looking in a typically Slavic way, with high cheek bones, blonde hair and blue eyes, but they watched him with a hostile attention that made him feel like he'd dropped from another planet. And all of them — the passengers and the crew — had the resigned look of people for whom living was serious business. Well, what did he expect? The singing proletariat, extolling the joys of the Communist state?

Karolina slept for most of the trip while Philip drifted through snatches of suspended time. He roused himself just as they were beginning their descent and found her pressing her face against the window. The plane dropped lower and he could make out slate-colored rooftops and stone church spires. In the distance he was surprised to see a modern skyline, then recalled that Warsaw had been leveled by the Germans during the war. Over the past few weeks, he'd grown excited at the prospect of seeing the old world his family came from; now he wondered what, if anything, would be left of the Jewish quarter. Dorothy had been unable to locate any guide books for him, and the cheap black and white brochures sent him by the Polish consulate contained nothing but descriptions of government buildings and hymns of praise to the glories of the Soviet rebuilding programs.

At passport control, they had their visas stamped by a baby-faced soldier in a military trench coat with a rifle slung over his shoulder, looking as if he'd stepped out of a World War II newsreel.

161

Once in baggage claim, Philip tried translating a few signs, but couldn't get his mouth around the strings of c's and z's. Listening was easier: if he paid close attention to the conversations around him, the words resolved into meaning — which relieved him. The nuances might escape him, but he'd be able to fill in the blanks.

Karolina watched workmen haul in baggage from the runway area. "You wish to begin immediately, yes?" she said sharply, scanning for their suitcases. "We will go to archives after the hotel."

"Good. Let's."

His new Samsonite carrier appeared, then her navy cloth suitcase. As he went to lift them, a porter in dirty white overalls jumped out of nowhere, grabbed their luggage and dragged them outside the terminal. Karolina slipped the man an American dollar and he broke into a broad grin, exposing a row of tobacco-stained teeth, then shoved ahead of the people waiting for taxis and frantically motioned for Karolina and Philip to hurry. Philip patted the cash he carried in the hidden pocket of his overcoat. She'd instructed him to bring American money as well as Polish. "Zloty do not get things done," she'd said. "Dollars do."

The taxi sped through stony streets lined with soot-coated houses, most with cracked stoops and rotting window frames, and if it wasn't for the occasional lace curtain and empty flower pot, Philip would swear the buildings were abandoned. Workmen in green overalls emptied buckets of soapy water onto the sidewalks and pushed long brooms across the sparkling wet pavement. They looked tired and glum, but it was only 6:00 A.M., too soon to pass judgment on a country he felt primed to dislike.

She'd booked them rooms in The Europejeski Hotel, an imposing, classic building, although somewhat decayed, with a carved stone facade and shabby lobby. At the front desk, a pretty young woman in a blue jacket with the hotel insignia embroidered on the lapel carefully copied their passport numbers into a ledger. She gave Philip a coy, appraising look and said she hoped he'd enjoy his stay. He was so grateful he understood her that he thanked her in Polish and made a little bow before taking the set of rusty keys she held out to him.

They took a small caged elevator to the second floor. Karolina kept her back to him, angling her body to avoid contact in the cramped space. She stepped out first and walked ahead of him down the hallway. "I will meet you in lobby at noon," she said, stopping in front of his door. "Then we go to archives to ask for birth certificates."

Philip had gone into overdrive and was itching to start. "Why not now?"

"No. The wait will be long. Rest first." And without waiting for a reply, she marched down the hallway to her room, one hand clutching her suitcase, the other holding the strap of her shoulder bag like an officer who'd discharged her orders. In New York, she'd struck him as someone struggling to keep up her courage and this gave her a fragile dignity that had touched him. On her own turf, she had an air of self-possession, of confidence. Another surprise. One he liked.

The room had the grim feel of a low-budget motel but was large enough to hold a double bed, a massive armoire and an upholstered chair. White lace curtains in need of laundering hung from tall windows that opened onto a courtyard of leafless trees. He dropped his bags and stretched out on the bed, wondering if Karolina was sleeping or just thinking, like him. She was probably too tense for a nap. One week wasn't much time to comb records and track down people, especially if they ran into dead ends. He rolled over, and the next thing he knew, the phone was ringing and his travel clock read 11:30 A.M.

Chapter 21

When Philip entered the lobby, Karolina was already seated on a tufted red velvet settee, reading a Polish newspaper. She'd changed from her cardigan into a silky, turquoise-colored blouse that shimmered when she moved. With her raincoat draped over her shoulders and a flowered scarf wound round her neck, she looked right at home and, for the first time since leaving New York, relaxed.

"Anything new?" he asked, nodding at the paper.

"Auf..." she said, exhaling with a little pout. "As always. America is evil capitalist. Soviets are saviors. The wise Gomulka will improve food situation with help from our great Russian patrons." She snapped shut the newspaper, then looked him up and down. "You look better now."

"So do you." Her skin shone buffed-clean, her blue eyes clear.

She tossed back her hair as though making the point and regarded him silently. "So, you are anxious to begin, yes?" Slipping her arms through her coat sleeves, she bowed dramatically toward the hotel's revolving front door. "Come," she said. "Warsaw awaits us."

The air outside was biting cold. Philip turned up the collar of his overcoat. Surrounding him were streets lined with pre-war, small stone houses, thickly shuttered, each with tiny window balconies. The buildings were only two and three stories high, leaving a broad expanse of cloudless blue sky.

Many of the streets they passed had mounds of concrete and bricks piled along the edge of the sidewalk. When he asked why, Karolina raised her shoulders with exaggerated weariness. "Soviet progress. It is more than twenty years since Warsaw is destroyed and still not built again."

The shops that lined both sides of the street were jammed with carved saints and crucifixes, and Philip wondered if Poland's entire economy rested on the sale of religious paraphernalia. He pictured his father and uncles walking past places like this and saw them slipping off their *yarmulkes* and hunching their shoulders to make themselves inconspicuous. Did they avoid the Christian part of their town? Did they cross the street when they saw a church, as he had when he was a kid?

In the weeks before his departure, he'd thought more about his family's past. Over the years his father's childhood stories had turned increasingly contradictory, so that one moment Meyer would be reminiscing about the beauty of the Polish forests and the next ranting against the *cholerah goyim* who liked to beat up Yeshiva boys on Christmas Eve. The last time he'd visited his parents, his father had slipped him the address of the Landau leather shop in Lublin. "Look for the house," Meyer had said, his eyes tearing. "You should see where your family comes from." On impulse Philip had asked if he'd consider coming along, but his father had turned white with disbelief. "What's to see? The whole country's a cemetery."

They turned down ulica Piwna. *Ulica*, he said to himself, trying out the word with the soft hissing "cee" he remembered his father used. *Ulica*, he repeated out loud, testing the sounds.

"Good," Karolina said. "Soon you will speak like native."

Philip broke into a grin. "Yeah?"

"No," she said, without breaking her stride. "But I wish to encourage."

Encouraged nonetheless, he sounded out the street names printed on the buildings. She looked amused by his efforts and when he got to words like *sześć* and *dziewięć*, the Polish names for numbers he'd heard but never seen written out, she laughed and stepped in close to show him how to purse his lips to make the correct sound. He repeated the words slowly while gazing into her face. What kind of lover would she be? Hot, he guessed. She was sensual. He'd seen it in the way her hands lingered on Amanda's hair, in the way she stroked the silk scarf around her neck, and he could feel it now, in the uninhibited way she ran her finger tips across his mouth. She caught his look and turned away, but not before he saw a hint of pink spread across her cheeks.

Ten minutes later, they were standing in front of a four-story modern building. The sign on the flat concrete façade read Warsaw Registry. Inside, the decor was generic civil service, circa 1930, with floors, walls and benches in dark brown wood and worn counters smudged with ink stains. A pale-faced, young clerk in a pilled wool vest approached them, exchanged some words with Karolina, then handed her forms and disappeared among shelves bulging with yellowing manila folders. Karolina filled out the papers and sat down on a bench.

"How long do you expect this to take?"

"Longer than you like," she said, leaning back and closing her eyes.

He put his elbows on his knees, hunched over and waited. He'd not expected her chilliness to last. A week of this was going to be murder.

A few clerks slumped at their desks, pretending to work; others trudged between rows of tall shelves as though counting the minutes till closing time. When he glanced at Karolina, she was hugging herself tightly and her forehead was deeply furrowed, as though she was bracing herself for a blow. This had to be a tense time for her, but she'd made it clear she didn't want any comfort from him.

Forty-five minutes went by and he was still watching two stony-faced clerks push papers across their desks. "Jesus! Are we going to sit here all day?"

"Americans have no patience," she said without opening her eyes.

A few minutes later a clerk beckoned them to the counter. He looked to be in his thirties and wore frameless wire-rimmed glasses like John Lennon's.

"I'm sorry, no birth certificates for a Chava Landau and Karolina Staszek exist in our archives," the man said. "Lublin records were originally housed in our building on Plac Pilsudskiego, which was destroyed during the war."

Karolina turned away with a long, frustrated sigh.

Philip was incensed. "I sent a letter two weeks ago. Why did you keep us waiting so long to learn this?" His Polish came out broken and clumsy, but he was too infuriated to care.

"We don't work during Christmas," the clerk said stiffly. "You should inquire at the Lublin Registry when you get there."

Philip shot a look from the clerk to Karolina. How did he know their travel plans? Was this routine in a Communist country or were they being tailed because he was a Jew?

Karolina muttered something to the clerk, then led an exasperated Philip outside.

"You told them where we were going?" he asked, unable to restrain himself.

"Of course. You cannot travel in Poland without telling authorities. They check at every station . . ."

"So I have to keep looking over my shoulder all the time?"

"Why bother? They do not hide their spying."

"That's it for Warsaw then," he muttered. "Nothing more on our schedule and we've got half a day left." Before leaving New York, he'd checked with Weinstein about additional records from the camps liberated by the Soviets, thinking that Chava's name might appear on a transport list to Treblinka, Chelmno, Sorbibor or any one of the countless smaller camps the Germans had erected all over Poland. But Weinstein said the Russians still kept classified whatever they'd found and despite pressure from international organizations, refused to share information. So the Warsaw Registry was their only source until they got to Lublin.

"I want to see the old Jewish quarter," Philip said. "Is there anything left?"

She shook her head. "No. Destroyed by Germans. But you should see more of Warsaw. You will not have time on way back."

"Sure you won't mind being my guide?"

"Of course not," she said sternly. "I will not abandon you."

They wandered across Plac Zamkowy and down several narrow back streets until they arrived on a long thoroughfare. Karolina pointed out the seventeenth-century Royal Castle, once the seat of Polish nobility that sat on the hill overlooking the city, then took him past baroque churches with ornate spires and elaborate stonework dotted with cherubs. Pausing in front of the Grand Opera embellished with Greek sculptures, she began to extol the brilliance of the craftsmanship that had been a hallmark of the city's cultural life. Even though the buildings were more *ungepatchket,* more ostentatious than he liked, Philip couldn't help being impressed. He mumbled something to that effect, and Karolina launched into a passionate speech about the high culture that had flourished in Poland before the war.

"Americans are not interested in Poland," she concluded as though this were a foregone conclusion. "Why should they be? When our artists and intellectuals leave, they go to Paris or Prague and live with respect as émigrés. Only our poor go to America where they become refugees — which Americans make sound like dirty word."

"Then let me take this opportunity to apologize for my countrymen's ignorance."

She gave him a hard look. "You are mocking me."

"In a way. But, I'm not sure anything I say in any language will be right."

"Practice. It will come." She plunged her hands into her trench coat pockets and walked on.

Pedestrians hurried past them in old-fashioned coats and large fur trimmed hats that hid their eyes, and every once in a while a young woman in a short skirt and high boots passed by and if it wasn't for the kerchief on her head, he'd swear she was American.

A few streets down they came upon groups of people lined up in front of a bakery and a butcher shop, clutching rope bags and baskets, and stamping their feet to keep warm.

Karolina swept her hand over the scene with contempt. "More Soviet progress. We could be rich country, but Russians tear everything away from us, even our bread." Suddenly, the air filled with chimes and people rushed for the churches, which seemed to be on every street.

"Polish people go to church often," Karolina informed him when she saw him staring at the crowds. "Before work, after work, all the time."

The wind turned gusty. She squinted up at the darkening sky. "I know this weather. "Come," she said, pulling him across the street. "It is going to rain."

He followed her into a restaurant steamy with the smell of fried food. The tables were covered in red-checkered tablecloths, and a few customers sat hunched over beer mugs and glasses of tea, smoking cigarettes and chatting softly. The burly man behind the counter motioned them toward an empty table near the window.

"Enough for today," she said, shaking out her scarf. "You are tired. So am I. We have long train ride tomorrow. We eat now and go to sleep early."

He looked down at the stained tablecloth and empty soda bottle filled with plastic flowers. "Here?" Philip asked. He'd had vague hopes of finding a good restaurant later in the evening for something special, maybe even ordering a bottle of French wine, if there was one. They'd relax. They'd talk. They'd stop taunting each other. *This* place had about as much atmosphere as a truck stop diner.

Two claps of thunder boomed in quick succession, then the sky exploded with rain. She looked at the street through the splattered windows. "I lived a few streets from here," she said wistfully. "I came here often when I was in art school. The food is good."

The street outside was narrow and cobblestoned, and curved gracefully toward a flagstone church at the corner. Past the misted panes Philip made out windy alleyways that reminded him of Paris. He pictured an artist's studio with high ceilings and arched windows in one of the gabled houses. There'd be an unmade bed in the middle of a bare room, rumpled sheets, her sheer nightgown dangling from the headboard.

"At last something makes you smile," she said.

"I like this part of town."

"You have been to Europe?"

"England and Paris after I graduated from college."

"You took your *Wanderjahr* at the wrong time."

"What's that? German?"

"Yes. A common expression. It means a year to — how do you say?" — she brandished her hand in the air while she spoke, enjoying her own theatricality — "to roam, to be free, to be young before one begins one's studies."

"It was only a summer."

"Ah, Americans, always in a hurry."

The rain turned into a gentle, rhythmic patter against the window panes. Suddenly the restaurant felt cozy, intimate.

She slung her arm across the back of her chair, ran her fingers through her damp hair and regarded him with interest. Her face had softened. Maybe she'd grown tired of one-upping him. Maybe she was ready to call a truce. He unbuttoned his jacket and settled back, waiting to see where this new mood would take her.

"So, you liked Paris?"

"Very much. It'll be great to take Alice when she's older."

"She will appreciate. She has what we call an old soul."

"The old part worries me."

"Do not worry. I know children. She is happy inside."

"I hope so. It's hard to tell. I don't get to see her as much as I'd like."

Karolina picked up a miniature spoon from the tiny glass salt cellar and ran it slowly across the grains. "She does not live with you?"

"No, with her mother."

"You are divorced."

"Yes."

"Life without children is sad. I think this is why Polish people do not divorce, even though Soviets permit."

"I thought it was because they were Catholic."

She considered this. "Yes, you are right. I try too much to show my people in good light."

He couldn't resist. "You should try harder."

"Why should you not think well of them?" she said, coloring. "They are people like any other. Ah, you see! Our conversation always becomes angry. We will be together for many days. We *must* stop this."

"Okay, I promise I'll behave." Philip folded his hands like an obedient child, hoping to elicit a laugh. "Pick a topic and watch how good I'll be."

"No, no, you speak of something." Flinging her hand up like an orchestra conductor, she plucked a word from the air. "Work. Tell me of your work. You charm clients and make big success?"

"Charm? I'm sure you've noticed that isn't my strong point."

"I have," she replied with a small smile. "But I am too polite to mention."

Philip threw back his head and laughed. "And you?" he asked, wanting to keep the mood personal. "Tell me what makes you smile."

"Little," she said dryly. "But you have noticed this, I think."

"I was afraid it was just because of me."

She was playing with the salt again, scooping up tiny spoonfuls and letting them spill back into the bowl. "Let us have a drink," she said abruptly. She called out to the man at the counter in a commanding tone and suddenly her transformation seemed complete, as though the sounds and rhythms of Polish had drawn out her real self, and there she sat, self-assured, even a bit imperious. He thought of Ellen and how well he knew her — and who she would be. He had only to look at their married friends to see what was waiting for him: the move to a bigger apartment, weekly Knicks games with his male friends, occasional Broadway musicals with other couples. Finally, the daily commute from the house on the Island — the whole package. He'd never let himself think that far ahead before, never let himself ask if that was the life he wanted.

The waiter brought over two shot glasses and a unlabeled bottle, and poured them each a drink. He asked if they were ready to order and without consulting Philip or the menu, she did.

Karolina held up her glass in a toast, then downed the drink. "Mazovian vodka," she said, flushing as though the alcohol had already made her tipsy. "Very special, very good. But be careful. It is easy to drink too much."

"And how much is *too much* in this country?" Philip asked.

"The important question is how much is *enough*," she laughed. "No, I should not make jokes with you."

"Why not? Aren't we friends?"

"I must behave like responsible person or you will not trust me again."

"You're making me feel like a member of the KBG. I didn't come along to spy on you."

"I know. You have come for Jake. And because you like me." She paused to stare at the glass cupped in her hand. "You are attractive man. I do not wish to complicate."

A jolt of pleasure passed through him.

"It is a nervous time for me," she went on, toying with her drink. "Vodka helps, but it can make much trouble."

Philip decided the opportunity was golden. He took her chin

and lifted her face to his. "I'll keep an eye on you," he murmured.

"Please," she said, removing his hand and sitting back. "We will be together for many days. Do not speak of this again."

"Are you sure that's what you want?"

"It is."

His instincts said stay with it, keep talking, give me a chance to show you how *un*complicated my feelings are. But her face had taken on that practiced blankness that made him feel graceless and blundering. They sat in strained silence until their food arrived.

She dove into her meal and ate without lifting her head. Philip inspected his *perogis* and fried meat turnovers, and after a few cautious stabs, he cut into his food. There was a moment when the smell of kasha drifting from a nearby table conjured memories of childhood and it struck him that Polish food was, essentially, Jewish food. If he closed his eyes, he'd think he was in Katz's Deli on Delancey Street.

They wove their way back to the Europejeski through the wet streets and thickening dusk. The streets were quieter; the crowds had thinned out. Only a few cars drove by. She walked beside him with her head thrown back as though she enjoyed the cold air on her face and in a moment of courage, Philip tried to slip his arm through hers. But she gently moved aside without breaking her stride.

By the time they reached the hotel, Philip felt glazed with fatigue. At the elevator door, they made arrangements for the morning and turning wearily toward their respective rooms, they took awkward leave of each other.

Chapter 22

The travel alarm went off at eight. Still drifting in a jumble of dreams, Philip lay motionless in a pool of pale sunlight streaming through the thin curtains. He closed his eyes and languidly let a dreamy image unfold: Karolina nuzzles against his shoulder while the plane drones through the darkness over a sleeping Europe. She smells earthy and warm and he sees the desire in her eyes. He reaches out to run the back of his hand against her mouth and is jolted awake by the feel of coarse linen against his knuckles. A hotel room in Warsaw — alone. Karolina was down the hall. Kneading his pillow into a ball, he stared at the window until his grogginess began to ebb.

He was slipping on his navy pullover when there was a knock at the door. Karolina stood in the hallway in her raincoat.

She rushed past him, into the room. "I spoke with my cousin, Pola, the one we stay with in Koromov after the war." Tossing her purse onto the floor, she let herself fall heavily into the chair near the window. "I thought she came to my farm when I was child, but she says no, she met me for first time when we stayed in her house." She gazed at the courtyard below, lost in thought. "But I remember playing with someone, running and playing . . . I tell Pola to ask her parents if they knew anything, but they live now in Silesia. She will call to them. At least this saves a trip to that miserable little town. I am not surprised Pola still lives in Koromov. She probably looks fifty by now, although she is younger than me." She gave a despairing shrug and dropped her head in her hands. "I was hoping she could tell us something. . . ."

Of course, she'd been banking on her cousin having information about her whereabouts during the war. This disappointment had thrown her into a panic.

"Think for a minute. If Pola knew anything, is there a reason she'd want to keep it secret?"

"No."

"What did she say when you explained why you were asking?"

Karolina looked away. "She was not enthusiastic."

"I don't understand. Explain."

"She told me my parents are . . . were not sympathetic to Jews and would not hide one. She wanted to know why I think I am one."

"Did you tell her?"

"Yes."

"And?"

"She said living with Jews in America has made me crazy." Karolina scowled at him as if he were to blame. "I am only telling you because you want to know." Then she threw herself against the chair and waved her hand impatiently. "Pola talks like that because she is peasant."

"You mean Poles are so disgusted at the thought you could be a Jew that they wouldn't admit to it if it were true?"

"At least you will not have to worry that anyone lies for me," she snapped and turned back to the window with a dismissive turn of her shoulders. "Do not blame me for other people's faults. I do this too much myself."

Her face, in profile, was tense with indignation. He tried to imagine how he'd feel if he were in her place. Maybe if he found out he was really black he'd understand; being a Jew in this stinking country was a lot like being a Negro in Mississippi. He pictured Warsaw's crumbling buildings and dilapidated streets, the long lines in front of food stores and he couldn't help feeling a twinge of satisfaction. Let the fuckers suffer. They'd certainly earned it.

"And your landlady's cousin in Lublin?" he asked. "Did you get in touch with her?"

"No one answered when I called Zosha's store, but I have address," she said, touching her purse. "We will visit her tomorrow."

"What about the Lublin Registry?"

She threw up her hands again. "They tell me everything before 1944 is destroyed."

"And your church? Did they have anything?"

"A woman at St. Bartolomeo will speak with Father Tomasz about my baptism papers. He knows me. He made my confirmation."

The church papers could be crucial. They would verify Karolina's age. And the priest might know more about the family. How much he'd be willing to help a Jew was another story.

"Where's the church?" Philip asked.

"About 20 kilometers from Lublin."

"We'll go there right from the train."

"It is too soon. You have seen for yourself that nothing moves quickly here."

"I'm willing to bet everyone in your village knew about your phone call the minute the churchwoman hung up."

She rose and shook herself. "You are right, of course. We will go to the church first." She looked at her watch, then heaved a great sigh at the faded floral wallpaper. "Oh, I cannot bear these walls another minute! I wish to visit a friend while there is time. You can come if you like."

Chapter 23

By the time Philip and Karolina stepped onto ulica Chopina the bright sky had turned a uniform white. He followed her along a different route back to the Plac Zamkowy, down tight alleyways that snaked for several streets before emptying into another square filled with *Antikwatry*, secondhand bookstores.

She stopped in front of a gift shop filled with toys and scarves, and gilded ceramic ashtrays stamped "Warszawa."

"Something for the children, yes?" she said and led him inside. A middle-aged woman wearing a man's cardigan over a brown wool dress greeted them from behind a counter. Karolina pointed to a shelf of dolls in peasant dresses and the two women began chatting.

"I am bargaining," Karolina whispered to him over her shoulder. "We are past Christmas. Dolls are not so expensive now, but shopkeeper gives high price because she sees you are foreigner." She narrowed her eyes slyly. "She will lower price, you will see."

Philip looked down at himself, smiling. "Is it that obvious?"

She gave him a look that said he must be crazy. The woman set down a wooden cart and horse, explaining that the toys were handmade by artisans in the Tatra Mountains. Karolina examined the miniature farmer seated on the cart. "I know Amanda will like this, but tell me what you think. For Alice, too?"

"Not her kind of thing," Philip said and wondered what besides dolls was. Since the divorce, he'd lost two years of watching Alice grow, missed the day she read her first word, the afternoon she found her balance and rode her two-wheeler alone. That wasn't going to happen again. He scanned the shop for something special, then wandered over to a display of nesting eggs like the set he'd seen in Karolina's apartment. They were made of papier-mâché and painted to look like a pair of winged fairies holding wands. He opened the largest, then the next, imagining the delight on Alice's face when she saw how perfectly they cradled into each other. God, he'd buy her something every day just to see that look.

"What do you think?" Philip said, setting the eggs on the counter.

"Yes, this is good," Karolina said, "but you must put something in last egg, something special to eat. It is Polish custom."

"Okay. Name it."

"Chocolates." She glanced quickly at her watch. "But we will wait and find shop in Lublin."

"A good one, though. The best one."

"So American," Karolina quipped.

The storekeeper wrapped their gifts in brown paper, packed them in a used shopping bag with a homemade twine handle and handed Philip the packages.

They walked through a few winding streets when, without explanation, Karolina stopped in front of a bookstore and entered. The shop smelled like a new pair of shoes. Shelves were stacked with torn books, rolls of paper stock and scraps of green, cordovan and brown leather. A bald, heavyset man in his late sixties stepped out from behind a curtain and when Karolina turned around, he broke into a huge grin and sang out her name. She rushed into his arms and kissed him on both cheeks.

"This is Marck Tarkowski," she said to Philip. The man wore a dark brown suit shiny with age and a black wool scarf around his neck. He bowed with a "*Dzień dobry*," then hustled them into a back room crowded with sheaves of paper and rolls of thick twine. Marek offered chairs, sweeping a pile of books and Soviet magazines from a small table. A journal cover caught Philip's eye: A young man with long hair and a bandanna held up a burning American flag while a line of U.S. soldiers looked on. Naturally, the Soviets were having a field day with America's troubles in Vietnam.

"*Proszę*," Marek said, urging them to sit.

"Marek is my dear, dear friend," Karolina said. "I worked for him before I left for America." Marek's eyes glowed with affection, and he held her hands and kissed them while she talked. She spoke in English though it was clear from Marek's benign smile that he understood nothing. "He was good to many of us from art school. Like a patron," she said proudly.

Two unframed paintings hung on the opposite wall, work by Marek's artists, no doubt. Both were day-glo soup cans in that comic-book style Philip remembered from a Warhol exhibit he and Ellen had gone to the previous year. The pictures seemed crude compared to Warhol's photographic detail, but it amused him that even in a country where there wasn't enough to eat and little of anything to buy, an artist's first impulse was to copy America's lead and celebrate consumerism.

Marek bowed his head and listened as Karolina explained the reason for her visit. When she finished, he spoke in the deep, raspy voice of a heavy smoker.

"It's a bad time," he said in Polish. "Gomulka has let the politicos purge Jews from government positions. You see, it's the same old story: the Jews are too pro-Soviet, they say, or too anti-Soviet, and since the Israelis have won this war against Egypt, the Soviet ally, it means the Jews here have changed their allegiances and can no longer be trusted. No one is going to help an American Jew who comes around to snoop."

Karolina's face paled. "Is it that bad?"

Marek ran his large, swollen hands across his face and nodded somberly. "Didn't you hear about André? His parents lost their government jobs because they are Jewish and they all moved to Cracow to look for other work. He stopped by to see me a few months ago. He's given up painting; he's a designer now with a theater company. The family is desperate to go to America." Something seemed to occur to him. "What do you think?" he said, inclining his head toward Philip. "Maybe your friend here can sponsor them?"

"Is he serious?" he whispered in English.

"Yes, he is," Karolina said. "He thinks Jews always want to help each other. Most Poles believe there is — how do you say? — a brotherhood among Jews."

"Conspiracy is the word you're looking for, right?"

She held him with a dark look. "No, this is not what I mean." He was starting to feel like a fool with his running commentary on the state of Polish anti-Semitism. He'd better keep the rancor down or he'd find himself sifting through archives without her.

"So? What is your answer?" she said.

Philip folded his arms across his chest and summoned his wryest delivery. "Tell Marek my reputation in the States would only hurt your friends' chances of getting in."

Karolina seemed puzzled for a moment, then laughed. When she finished translating, Marek, too, let out a husky, good-natured laugh, then slipped a cigarette from a pack labeled Caro, broke off the filter, and lit it. "Ah, America is the hope of the world," he said. "If only they didn't make this terrible war."

"Tell me," Karolina said, turning to Philip with a challenging air. "You believe like Noah this Vietnam war is about communism?"

Whenever Philip ran into foreigners in New York, they attacked him for everything from hosing down Civil Rights marchers to JFK's assassination. Now, Vietnam was giving them another reason to taunt him. Yes, he was against the war, but this wasn't the time or place to explain that he felt too old for hippie politics and too cynical for the conventional brand.

"Let's just say this is a war we can't win," he said, praying she'd let the topic go.

Karolina fell silent, lost in thought. He was glad she hadn't picked up the ambiguity of his comment. "We envy your young people. They grow up with the privilege of freedom and now they have the courage to test it. I wish to tell you . . ." She stopped to search for a word. ". . .that it encourages Polish people to see Americans resisting their government when it becomes oppressive and imperialistic."

Oppressive. Imperialistic. Back home he would have fled anyone who talked this high-minded lingo, yet here, in a country where foreigners were routinely tailed, the words sounded different.

"Just this morning I read in paper Communists make new laws forbidding certain books. Imagine! Forbidding books, like the Nazis! You will see, people will make demonstration in streets and government will call in Soviet troops." She punctuated the air, sending up little ringlets of cigarette smoke. "Then Poles will fight and maybe die for what you believe are normal things. Maybe this is naïve, but we must all resist government when it is . . ." Here she squinted at the ceiling, then shook her head in frustration. ". . .bad."

Philip sat back and watched, more intrigued by her impassioned outburst than her argument.

Marek had had enough of the sidelines. He leaned over and whispered in her ear. Amusement filled her face.

"What did he say?" Philip asked.

She pursed her mouth in a way he thought of as particularly French. "Oh, he would like to show you my work."

Marek padded to the far side of the room and picked up a two-foot-high sculpture half hidden by books. He brought it to the table and placed it gingerly in front of Philip.

"Karolina make," he beamed.

The statue was of a couple standing with their feet embedded in stone so that they seemed to be growing out of a single block of marble. The woman leaned into the man with her hands on his shoulders and her forehead resting against his lips while he held her tightly, one arm around her waist, the other cupping the back of her head the way you'd hold a baby. Her face was calm, yet she looked inconsolable. The man gazed over her shoulder into the distance. His body was lithe, youthful, but had the solidity, the weight, the *feel* of physical resignation. There was no comfort in this embrace, only shared hopelessness.

Philip slid his hand across the polished marble and let his fingers trace the woman's small, triangular face, her full mouth, her upturned breasts. He pressed his open palm against the torsos to touch the place where their bodies fused and felt the disturbing solitude she had captured in stone.

"Beautiful," Philip murmured, and heard how inadequate, how trite the word sounded.

She looked over her work appraisingly. "Thank you. It is my best."

"This is wonderful. Do you still sculpt?"

She shrugged. "A little, in classes. Oh, I will go back one day. I must." She made a sweeping motion toward the statue. "You see, in my work I have always been drawn to what is personal . . . human," she said, giving him a wry smile. "I save my politics for the café — or Marek's store."

Marek slapped Philip on the knee and motioned toward the statue with a proud grin. "Good, yes?" he said in English.

"Very good," Philip said. "*Piękne*," he repeated in Polish.

Karolina rose and hugged Marek tightly. She would try to stop by again, she told him, before she left Poland. "Come, American," she said, taking Philip's arm. "We do not have much time."

Outside, Karolina hurried toward the end of the street where a line of taxis idled, spewing diesel fumes into the air. "There is something I wish to show you." In a few minutes they were moving through a neighborhood of cement apartment houses. The taxi circled a wide expanse of dead grass between two buildings and let them out near a playground where children pumped on swings and chased each other around an ancient, rickety slide. Two old women in head shawls and fur-lined boots looked on from nearby benches. One tossed seeds at the flock of pigeons cooing at her feet.

Karolina walked to the side of a building and stopped in front of a tarnished bronze plaque set in a boulder. It was dated April 23, 1943. All Philip could make out was "Mila 18." He recognized the address from the Uris book that had been popular several years earlier. She'd taken him to the site of the Warsaw Ghetto.

"What does it say?"

"'Here . . . in this place, brave Polish citizens gave their lives to fight the Germans.'"

His throat thickened. "No mention of Jews?"

"No. The city was mostly destroyed during the last months of the war. When this was rebuilt, no one thought to . . ." She stopped, her breath still misting the air. "No, I cannot defend Poles in this." She gazed up the street toward one of the apartment blocks. "I once lived nearby with a friend, the one who is now in Cracow. I passed this every day. There have been moments during the last weeks when I imagined myself here with the Jews . . ."

They were surrounded by modern, prefab apartment houses already cracked and water-stained. In this place, he thought with anguish, right here hundreds of thousands of Jews had lived and worked and died — without a single sign to commemorate them!

Everything Jewish had been swept away. The area was free of Jews. Or would the Poles, like the Germans, say *clean* of Jews?

"I wanted to see it again," she said. "All is different now."

"Is it?" The words stung the air before he could stop them.

Her face gathered color. "Will you be happy if I hate Poles? Will that make me more Jew?"

Yes, he thought, enjoying the relief he felt just saying *yes* in his head. *Yes*, he thought again, twisting the word to sweeten the anger he felt. These fucking Poles couldn't even give *dead* Jews credit for their suffering.

"When I see sign, I do not feel hate," she said. "Only sadness for what happened, sadness for them, sadness for me."

"Sadness?" He repeated, mulling over the word, trying to make it sound right.

"If you knew Polish well I would say *rozpaczy*, which means regret and pain and many other things all at once. It is very complicated word, very Slavic, because sadness is complicated thing. Maybe in your world life is simple, nothing is complicated . . . there is only black and white." She yanked at her belt and headed back to the taxi. "But you do not really understand my language."

No, I don't, he thought. He stamped his feet against the cold, suddenly disgusted with himself, with both Jews and Gentiles and everything they hated about each other.

Back in the lobby of the Europejeski, the receptionist signaled Karolina and handed her a piece of paper. Karolina glanced at it, then gripped Philip's arm with alarm. "They have called from St. Bartolomeo," she said, breathlessly. "They have found baptism papers."

Chapter 24

The taxi Karolina had arranged to take them to the church of St. Bartolomeo was waiting outside the Lublin station. The driver nodded perfunctorily, put the car in gear, and gunned the accelerator. Traffic was light; they passed a few cars heading toward Lublin, but once they turned off the main highway onto the road to Lubartow, horse carts filled with lumber and potato sacks appeared.

Philip had been somber and irritable since leaving Warsaw and they'd said little to each other during the two-hour train ride. Karolina knew he'd been pained by the omission of any reference to the Jewish ghetto on the plaque at Mila 18 and, although she was sympathetic, she'd decided to let him ride out his mood by himself. Friction seemed always on the verge of flaring up between them and she was tired of apologizing for her country, for her culture, for its past. She had her own worries. Since Marek's account of the present Jewish situation, she'd grown fearful of what might be waiting for her.

Now, as Karolina pondered the countryside from the taxi window, she couldn't help feeling that something was wrong. It was always snowing in the winter of her childhood and this bleak, snow-less vista felt odd. The landscape of her memory was filled with high, white drifts and weighted tree limbs that drooped like ghostly talons along the sides of the deep-rutted roads. Poland was the crunch of wagon wheels and the unexpected explosion of snow bursting from the eaves of the house, the crack of ice under her feet, the sound of animals snorting in the cold morning air. As a child, she'd loved racing across white embankments, delighted to be free of the smoky kerosene lamps and stove heat of the house. Once — she must have been seven or eight — she'd found a compass under a boulder behind the barn and holding the cracked leather case in her mittened hand, gazed with fascination at the floating black-tipped arrow under the glass. But the red swastika embossed on the cover had made her heart constrict with fear and she'd hidden the instrument in a far corner under her bed, knowing it was an evil, forbidden thing her parents would take from her. Somewhere across the years she'd forgotten the compass, then lost it. She thought how fitting it was that the memory of a Nazi compass should come back now. Where was she heading? What more was buried beneath the old snows?

When the taxi pulled up in front of St. Bartolomeo she told the driver to wait alongside the stand of pine trees near the entrance. She didn't know how long they'd be, she added, but he was not to worry. They'd pay him for his time in dollars. He turned off the engine and sat back, giving her a wide smile before tipping his *kapelusz* over his brow.

The small stone church with its pitched roof and modest stained-glass windows looked as austere as ever; still Karolina could never come here without remembering the close, safe feel of the pews and the pungent smell of polish that floated up from the wooden rails. She peeked round the side and caught sight of the familiar grouping of shrubbery next to the back door. Nothing had changed.

She hurried up the steps of the church and swept through the narrow corridors of St. Bartolomeo with Philip trailing behind. She knocked rapidly on the heavy wooden door to the priest's study and when she heard his muffled voice reply, she pushed it open. Father Tomasz sat at his mahogany desk, examining a ledger. He stood up stiffly as they entered.

"I was told you would be coming," he said. He eyed Philip coolly, then extended his hand toward Karolina, who kissed it and swiftly slid onto the upholstered bench alongside his desk. She felt a moment's anxiety about Philip's grasp of Polish; if she had to stop and translate every word, the priest would become suspicious.

"I'm in town for a short while," she said. "Thank you for seeing me."

The priest was gray-haired now, and thick about the face and shoulders. A line of red flesh bulged where his clerical collar pressed into his neck. What had once been an elegant profile was now weighted with jowls. When he first came to St. Bartolomeo, Karolina and her friends had thrilled over the gravely handsome young priest with the melancholy face. She remembered how she lay awake at night, dreaming up transgressions so she could spend more time in the confessional with the mysterious voice, and how her heart thudded wildly when his tapered fingers slipped the Eucharist into her mouth. But he'd not been popular with the farmers in his parish, only with the women young enough to mistake good looks for character.

"You are looking well," Father Tomasz said in his melodic voice.

"Thank you, Father." Karolina considered his morose face. "So are you."

Father Tomasz smoothed down the front of his cassock where the buttons strained against his torso. "A little larger than last time, no?" he laughed. "So, you're here on a visit or to stay?"

"A visit. With my friend."

The priest nodded to Philip. "A little vacation to show him Poland?"

"*Tak*," Philip said, sitting forward. Karolina was suddenly glad he was there. He was quick and shrewd. Even if he didn't catch everything that was said, he would sense what was going on.

"America agrees with you, then?"

She nodded brusquely. The priest still had the look of someone who judged every answer and found it wanting.

"The last time I saw you, you were seventeen. I was told you had won entrance to art school in Warsaw. Your parents must have been proud."

It was a measure of Father Tomasz's disconnection from the farmers in his parish that led him to believe they would be pleased to have an artist in the family. Her parents never understood what sculpting had to do with living, and till the day they died never mentioned Warsaw except to question her about the price of vegetables in the city.

Philip panned the room, inspecting the Eucharist plates and chalices displayed on a low chest next to the fireplace. He shifted impatiently beside her.

"My friend is from New York. Landau. *Pan* Philip Landau."

She knew the priest expected more, but she didn't want him on his guard. It was enough that Landau was a Jewish name.

Father Tomasz blinked. His gaze hovered between them for a moment. "Landau?"

Philip asked. "You know it?" His accent was thick and his grammar poor, but the few short sentences he'd ventured in the hotel were to the point, and this simplicity gave him a commanding air.

"There were many Landaus in Lublin before the war," the priest said. "It's a Jewish name." He cleared his throat. "So, you've come for the baptism papers?"

"Yes," she said. "I called from Warsaw . . ."

"May I ask why?"

"I'm applying for citizenship in America. There's some uncertainty about my date of birth."

Father Tomasz looked surprised. "Why would there be uncertainty?"

"My birth certificate was destroyed during the war. I was told baptism papers would be acceptable as official proof."

"Well, the date is right here." He removed a paper from a file and pointed to the date on the bottom. "June 20, 1938."

The priest handed her a paper with the heading "Testimonium nativitatis et baptismi." Karolina scanned the document, her heart heavy with disappointment. The birth date didn't match Chava Landau's; it wasn't even the same year. Yet what had she expected? If her parents wanted to hide her identity, of course they'd give a false date. Still, she'd hoped. The notation on the corner of the page caught her eye. "But this says 'Official Church duplicate'," she said, her voice rising, "issued in 1945 when I was seven years old!" She looked to the priest with alarm. "Where is the original?"

He took the paper from her and examined it. "Probably destroyed during the war."

"Then how can you be sure when or if a baptism took place?"

Father Tomasz stared back at her, astonished. "Of course it's correct. Why would anyone lie about such a thing?"

"Ask him what proof the church requires before it can issue duplicate baptism papers," Philip said. She repeated the question in Polish.

"Usually a birth certificate is enough," Father Tomasz replied.

"And if there is not one?" Philip asked.

"It's customary to require two witnesses who can testify they were present at the baptism. Legal verification was needed for all sorts of things," the priest said. "You know how fond the Russians are of documents."

There were four signatures at the bottom of the paper: her parents and Darius and Zofia Hankowski. The Hankowskis were her parents' best friends; if she'd been in hiding, they would have known. They would have lied. Karolina pictured the four of them huddled together in front of a church magistrate, crudely scrawling out their names on the official-looking paper. They were unused to writing and would have worried that their signatures would somehow reveal their treachery. She could see them exchanging glances. She could see the fear in their eyes.

She showed Philip the paper. "We must make record of this," she whispered in English.

He shook his head. "This isn't evidential."

"I told you my parents probably lied to get false papers." She pointed to the notation at the bottom. "Look! A duplicate. This means only proof of my birth as Karolina Staszek rests on the testimony of my parents and their best friends. The Hankowskis would lie also."

Philip shot a glance at the priest who was scrutinizing them over tented hands. "Didn't he just say duplicates were common after the war? Or did I misunderstand?" Philip sounded regretful. "Legally, this doesn't mean much."

Karolina knew intuitively that he was right about the legality of her situation. But with every new step they made and every dubious clue they uncovered, she was more convinced than ever that the circumstantial events of her past were far too coincidental not to be true.

The door to the study groaned open and an old woman in galoshes and a black head shawl entered, carrying a tray with teacups and a plate of sugar-coated cookies. Basia Zambrowski had lived in the church for as long as Karolina could remember, and she recalled seeing the woman move through the back rooms with a bowl of mashed potatoes cradled in her arm, as though she needed to eat all day long just to keep her frail body functioning. Karolina knew little about Basia except that she was an orphan and that Father Demetrius, the previous priest, had taken her in at a young age. For years, Basia had roamed the church's warren of small rooms — cleaning, cooking, tending to the needs of the clergy in this remote parish of peasant farmers. Most of her life had been slavishly devoted to Father Demetrius; what was left would be used up by his successor, Father Tomasz.

"Basia wants to impress the guests from America," the priest said, nudging a cookie toward Karolina. When she shook her head, he leaned back reluctantly and tugged at the straining buttons of his cassock. Basia ceremoniously poured tea from the metal urn, tossed in several lumps of sugar and stirred slowly before handing him the cup.

"It's nice to see you, *Pani*," Karolina said.

The woman adjusted the gray hairs escaping from under her head scarf and made a little curtsey. "Same here. Tea?"

"No, thank you." As Karolina watched the woman sweep a few crumbs from the linen tray liner, it occurred to her that Basia had lived in the church through two world wars. She probably knew more about the lives of the local people than anyone else in Lubartow.

"May I ask you a few questions about Father Demetrius?"

Basia stole a look at Father Tomasz. He nodded. "A saint, a saint," she whispered, wiping her face with a corner of her apron. "He was famous for his kindness. Ask anyone. You know he took me in, don't you? I was only fourteen," she said, rushing to get out the words before anyone could interrupt her. "My parents — God rest their souls — left me with nothing, not a *zloty*, not a crumb —"

"I'm sure Karolina is aware of Father Demetrius's virtues," Father Tomasz said.

"Tell me," Karolina asked gently, "do you know if I was baptized by Father Demetrius?"

"I would think so. Everyone in our parish was."

"What year?"

Basia screwed up her filmy eyes. "Can't you do the reckoning? The year you were born, of course. Do you remember, Father?"

"It was before my time," he said, without looking up from his ledger.

"But the paper must say, no?" the old woman asked. "*Pani* Rujetski spent the whole day crawling around the storage room looking for it. What a storm we had last week! Water leaked over everything. We had to put up the rain buckets all over the place."

"Let me talk," Philip interrupted in English. Basia glanced at him as though she was suddenly aware of his presence. He rose, slipped his hands in his pockets and leaned against the low chest. "My family is from around here," he said, enunciating carefully. "Perhaps you knew them."

"Really?" Basia said. "Did they attend church here?"

"No. We are Jewish."

"Oh."

"The family Landau."

The woman's eyes shifted momentarily, then she shot a glance at Father Tomasz who became rigid in his chair.

Karolina drew in a sharp breath. "You knew them?"

"I've heard the name," Basia said.

"Where? When?"

"There were Landaus with a leather store in Lublin, no? I seem to remember some went to America." She looked at Philip from under hooded lids. "Are you related?"

"You did business with them?" Karolina cut in.

"Me? What would I need leather for? Father Demetrius did. Oh, no, it's not what you think. He was not a vain man. He was very sick with his arthritis. Why, he could hardly walk the last years. He needed special boots just so he could stand for Mass and I remember the Landaus sold him kidskin, you know, the kind you line with felt. There was a shoemaker on ulica Lublianka who made them up with rubber inserts —"

"But you knew the Landaus," Philip interrupted, towering over her. "You met them, *tak?*"

Basia paused for a fraction of a second. "I . . . no . . . one of them came here one night —" She blinked several times, trying to find a place for her eyes.

Karolina was on her feet now, standing next to Philip, crowding the woman, no longer caring how threatening she sounded. "Who came? When?"

The woman turned uneasily to Father Tomasz who sat in tense

silence with his hands spread on top of his book. "The son, I think," she said.

Jake! She was talking about Jake. "You said he came at night. Why at night?"

"I don't know, *Pani* Staszek, my memory, you know . . . I may be mistaken . . . I don't really remember," Basia said. "Probably on business." She began fussing with the cuffs of her blouse. "Father, it's time for Vespers."

"Business? At night?" Karolina said.

"Did this Landau visit you during the war?" Philip demanded.

Basia backed away. "Excuse me, please. I have much to do. The vestry is still flooded. We have to mop —"

"This is important! Tell me!" Karolina pleaded. "Was it during the war?"

But Basia had already opened the door. "Father Demetrius was a good man," she muttered. "Good, even to Jews," she added and left.

The room suddenly smelled of damp chimney ashes. "Father . . ." Karolina said, straining to think. "Father . . . I have reason to believe the Landaus were my real parents and hid me on the farm during the war."

He looked incredulous. "What makes you say such a thing?"

"I can't go into it now."

"Is that why you're here?" he asked with disdain. "This *Zhid* wants to help you reclaim the Landau property?"

Zhid! The priest had spit out the word with an ugly, wrenching twist of his mouth that made her stomach pitch. "Will you please tell me what you know?" she cried.

"Me? I know nothing. I came to Lubartow directly from seminary in 1945." The priest carefully squared the edges of the papers on his desk. "What happened before then is not my business."

"*Not* your business that I may have been hidden, that I may have been kept from my real family?"

"*Rumors* are not my business."

Philip leaned over the priest's desk. Father Tomasz froze. "Why don't you tell us about it?" Philip said, holding his finger down on the priest's book. "Or would you like to talk to our lawyer?"

The priest kept his eyes fixed on Philip's hand. He hesitated, then cleared his throat. "There were many rumors that people hid Jews for money, and turned them over to the Germans. All the stories come to nothing, but they always make Poles look bad. The Russians make sure of that." His voice grew strident. "Did you hear about the Jaleks who owned a bakery on the ulica Nowy?" he said to Karolina. "I was told the Germans found a Jew hiding in their basement and hanged the whole family, including the children, right in the middle of Pulsudski Square. People said the Jaleks didn't know anything about the man until the Germans found him — but the Germans executed them anyway." He held her with his pale gray eyes. "There were other brave Poles who risked their lives to help Jews and afterwards were accused of being collaborators, of handing them over —"

"Why are you telling me this?" Karolina yelled. "You *do* know about my parents!"

The cups on the tray rattled. Father Tomasz stood. "How dare you raise your voice to me!" His face trembled with outrage. "You shame me, Karolina, coming here to make threats. You have your papers, now leave the church. The documents may be duplicates," he added bitterly, "but I think they will satisfy the American government."

"Father —"

"May God forgive your sins." Father Tomasz hastily made the sign of the cross, swung open the door and hurried down the darkened passageway that led to the church.

When they were back inside the taxi, Karolina flung herself against the back of her seat.

"You see, the priest knows something!" Father Tomasz was protecting someone or why would he hide information from her? Why would he suddenly bring up Poles who'd helped Jews? Was he alluding to her parents? He had to be! She hugged herself tightly, trying to ease the nausea rising in her throat. *Zhid!* What a word from the mouth of a man of God, a priest who had sat with her father and comforted him as he lay dying of cancer, a priest who must have known that she, the dying man's daughter, was really a Jew. Remembering the disgust in his voice when he said *Zhid* made her tremble with humiliation and fury.

"They both know, but the priest won't tell us more." Philip was glaring at the back of the taxi driver's head. "It's the woman we have to work on."

He was right. After Father Tomasz's dismissal, it was clear that whatever he knew he'd take with him to the grave. "You wish to go back for Basia?" she asked.

"Maybe. Depends on what else we come up with."

Karolina lay back and closed her eyes, taking deep breaths to calm herself. She could sense Philip was sorting through what had happened and she wanted to give him time to think. He was a clever man. She'd seen the way he had studied Father Tomasz and Basia, how he'd scrutinized their moves, assessed their responses as though he could see what they *weren't* saying. She was anxious to hear what he thought.

"Talk to me about the old priest, Demetrius," Philip said at last. "How well did he know your parents?"

"He came to visit often when I was growing up. Once, my father broke his leg fixing roof and could not work for almost a year. My mother told me Father Demetrius helped us."

"How?"

"I do not know."

"Did this happen during the war?"

"I think so."

"If your parents were going through hard times, would they have hidden a Jew for money?"

Would they? Karolina recalled how her mother's face stiffened whenever she heard the word *Zhid* and how her father, quieter with his feelings — sometimes so quiet she wasn't sure what they were — simply stared at the floor until the word dissolved in the stillness of the room. She couldn't imagine them risking their lives to help a Jew — *except* for money. "Maybe, if they were desperate."

"Jake might have gone to this Father Demetrius for help when he heard that the ghetto was being liquidated. Maybe this old priest liked the Jews who helped him out with his delicate feet, and maybe he decided to hook up the two families: one that needed money with one that needed a place to hide a child. Maybe that's what the woman meant when she said Father Demetrius was good, even to the Jews."

Yes, it was possible. Father Demetrius wasn't close with other farmers and his visits always made her feel special. Her mother used to fuss over him, setting out bread or poppy rolls and an old bottle of home-made orange brandy, then she'd hover near the table nervously fingering her rosary while the priest picked at the bread with his tobacco-stained hands and spoke in low, confidential tones. Her father rarely joined them; he'd sit on an upturned bucket next to the stove, whittling or mending the old harness that was always broken. Now that she thought about it, her parents seemed fearful around the soft-spoken Father Demetrius. Why had he singled out the Staszeks? Was he trying to persuade them to return Karolina to her real family? Was he angry they'd taken Jake's money *and* kept his child? Yes, all of it was possible.

"But at Chanukah party your father said your family was poor in Lublin," she said. "How could they pay?"

"My father always wanted us to believe he grew up dirt poor — you know, one pair of shoes at Passover — but his parents owned a business. They must have had some money. Jake would have used every penny he had to save his child."

Karolina turned to gaze through the window at the sweep of brownish black fields in the distance. The sun was going down. The air looked cold. One day, many years earlier, she'd been smuggled down this road to a life not meant for her. She pictured herself curled in terror under a pile of straw on the back of a cart or hidden under a blanket in the back of a car. She tried to imagine a different Karolina, a Jewish child in a Jewish home, but panicked at the thought. How could her parents have loved her if they hated the Jews who bore her? She remembered the feel of Amanda's small hands around her neck, and her thin, vulnerable chest with its faint, birdlike heartbeat against her own. Children were great seducers. Yes, it was easy to imagine decent people committing desperate acts to make a child their own.

She pressed her forehead against the window, suddenly re-minded of the extremes of heat and cold that linked her childhood memories, the icy air whipping her cheeks red, the gusts of heat from the blistering stove where she nestled her numbed feet. When she was sick, her mother would smooth back her hair and give her a bowl of hot water splashed with milk, then watch with worried eyes as she drank. A knot of tears pushed through her. She had known comfort in that poor home. Now she was alone. Even her affair with Jim had the remote, disconnected feeling of an event she'd only heard about. She longed for the touch of her mother's palm against her cheek, her father's rough, sturdy hands lifting her onto their cart. She longed to be a child again, to be loved, to be cherished. "Sometimes I think I am dreaming my life," she murmured and started at the loneliness in her voice.

Philip gently ran the back of his hand across her cheek and then, to her astonishment, kissed her. His lips were soft, tentative. He broke away to look at her with searching eyes, then kissed her again. Her heart sped up, but she moved away until she felt the car door at her back.

"No, please."

He put his hands on her shoulders. "We belong together."

"This will confuse everything," she said, shaking her head.

"I don't care."

"We have a false intimacy," she said. "It is situation. These feelings are not true ones."

He took her face in his hands. "Tell me you're not attracted to me."

"Yes . . ." She leaned away again. This was crazy! "But I do not want this . . . involvement."

Philip's face clouded. He turned away to gaze out the window, his profile stiff.

They moved to opposite ends of the cab and sat in tense silence. He was enthralled by the uncertainty of who she was, she told herself, by the excitement of a foreign adventure. And she by his darkness, his brooding, by the power of his impetuosity, perhaps by the lure of conquering an opponent. But they were both adults. She would ignore this scene and continue as though nothing had happened. So would he. At least he couldn't accuse her of trying to seduce him for his precious inheritance.

She tried to concentrate on the forests that rimmed the horizon, leafless and skeletal against the darkening sky. In the encroaching dusk, a horse-drawn cart slowly made its way down a road through the fields. A farmer sat hunched over his tired animal with his cap visor pulled low on his forehead. What a sad country Poland was. She had never seen it so clearly.

She touched the driver's shoulder. "To the Hotel Victoria."

"Wait", Philip said, grabbing her arm. "Who's that man?"

Turning toward the church, she caught a flicker of movement. A tall figure in a gray overcoat slid along the south wall, then stepped back into the shadows. "I don't know," she said. "It could be anybody . . . oh, please let us go."

The car lurched forward and they sped toward the lights of Lublin glittering in the distance. In the morning, they'd go directly to Zosha's store. It was unlikely she'd know anything about the Landaus, but maybe the man who used to work for her, the man who'd lived on Darius's farm during the war, had spoken of them.

Philip suddenly swung around in his seat and stared at the side of the road. Karolina followed his gaze and saw, receding into the darkness behind them, a simple wooden sign: *Maidenek, 3k.*

Chapter 25

"So how's the vedder?" Ellen asked in a mock Yiddish accent. Philip could hear typewriters clattering in the background. Her Legal Aid office had only two secretaries, but the machines were so old, they sounded like she worked in a factory.

"Cold." She'd gotten through to him just as he was slipping under the down quilt. The sheets felt chilly. He tucked the blanket tighter around his chest.

"The food's okay?"

"We're talkin' Poland, Ellen."

"No Steak Diane on the menu, huh?"

"People here line up for bread."

"That bad?"

"Worse." He couldn't hold back the urge to exaggerate. She'd be hurt if she suspected he was enjoying himself. The night before he left, she'd complained about their cancelled Vermont ski trip, pointing out again that his family could find an English-speaking translator in Poland to accompany Karolina and take down testimony if they found any witnesses. When he'd accused her of being selfish, of not understanding that the trip was a burden he had to shoulder for his family's sake, she'd thrown him a wounded look and left the room. The next morning they acted as though nothing had happened, but he still felt resentful — and guilty.

"And the hotel?" Ellen asked. "Livable?"

The Hotel Victoria in Lublin, with its rose-patterned wallpaper and elaborate moldings, was worn, but its faded elegance was comfortable. When they'd arrived a couple of hours earlier, the hotel staff had surrounded him as though he were visiting royalty, which he quite liked after the non-existent service of Warsaw's Europejeski. Lublin was off the beaten track for Americans and he figured the natives were curious and eager for his dollar tips. Except for his suspicions about the two men in oversized topcoats planted in the lobby who eyed him from behind their newspapers, Philip was beginning to unwind.

"The hotel's not bad by Polish standards." He laughed softly. "And I'm getting a lot of personal attention."

"Oh? Gorgeous Polish women coming on to you?"

A flash of Karolina's face in the car bathed in the last rays of pinkish afternoon sunlight. He shifted uncomfortably. "No, but I think we're being followed."

"Oh, Philip!"

"Karolina says it's routine. The government keeps tabs on all foreigners, especially the Amerikanskis. But it could be someone who doesn't want Jews inquiring about their old property."

"Be careful, please . . . Oh, I almost forgot. Rosalind wants you to call her."

"Tell her I tried from Warsaw. It takes half an hour to get a long distance operator to tell you the lines to the States are down. The same thing happened when I tried you earlier."

He could feel Ellen mulling if she should be the first to break the awkwardness. "How are *you*?" he finally asked.

"Missing you." She'd dropped her voice an octave into the throaty tone she knew he liked.

"Me, too." His own voice sounded unconvincing, which made him feel like a shit.

"We've got a court date for the Gillespie case. I deposed three neighbors who heard the landlord say he'd kill himself before he'd rent to niggers." More clanging in the background. "So what have you two come up with so far?"

What *had* they come up with?: That Karolina's baptism papers were not original; that the Landaus had done business with the former priest of St. Bartolomeo; that the current priest seemed to be hiding something; that everyone bristled when you said the word Jew. He glanced at the dimly lit face of his travel clock: 10 o'clock. He didn't have the energy to tell her.

"Nothing solid. Just innuendos and anti-Semitism. What a

country. They're such bigots they don't even have the decency to try to hide it."

"You expected it, didn't you?"

"I suppose so. Still."

"So, what's next?"

"She wants to track down a guy who worked on the farm next to hers during the time she thinks Jake brought her there. Maybe he'll know something."

"Isn't it strange she doesn't remember anything?"

"She says she was too young."

"How's she taking being back?"

"Hard, I think. Nobody wants to talk. Their eyes start sliding all over the place the minute she says Jew."

"Well, now she knows what it feels like."

"Ellen . . . I saw a sign for Maidenek right on the side of the road."

"What's that?"

"A concentration camp. Jake was there."

"Oh, my God!"

"The camp was right in the middle of town. People here had to know what was going on."

"Oh, honey, this must be so hard for you." They listened to the static for a moment. "Let's go to Stowe when you get back. I can probably take a long weekend."

"I won't have the time. Drottman's going to need me."

He could hear her go still. "I hate it that you left angry," she finally said.

"I'm not anymore."

"I wish you were here."

His body ached with fatigue. He rubbed his eyes with the back of his hand. "I'm really jet lagged. I've got to get some sleep . . ."

There was a pause in her breathing. "I'll see you in a few days," he added.

A cold silence. "Ellen?"

A sharp click, then the line went dead.

Chapter 26

Karolina had booked rooms at the Victoria not only because it was the best hotel in Lublin (which Philip had insisted on), but for its proximity to the store of Mrs. Domanski's cousin, Zosha, as well as to the old Jewish quarter. Since taxis had to be reserved in advance and took forever to arrive, and the trams ran infrequently, it was often faster to walk. If they needed to travel outside the city again, Philip suggested they rent a car.

That first night, Karolina lay awake a long time, thinking about Philip. She tried to understand why she was drawn to him; instead, her thoughts lingered on his contradictions. He seemed by nature guarded, mistrustful, self-centered, the kind of man who looked at life cynically; yet there was a vulnerability to him that fascinated her. She touched her mouth, remembering the feel of his lips on hers, then pushed the thought away. Tomorrow there was Zosha to see.

She'd written Zosha a long letter, explaining why she was coming to Poland, saying she'd visit as soon as she arrived in Lublin. Zosha's daughter, Katya, had been her dearest friend and she and Karolina had spent many happy hours together. Memories arose of two girls rushing after school to the hardware store, where Zosha would always have honey and butter sandwiches waiting for them. Then they would run up the stairs to Katya's room in the flat above the store to dispense with the math and physics they both hated before flinging themselves across Katya's bed to leaf through the stack of old film magazines her friend had swiped from the train station's waiting room. Karolina always made sure to leave before dinner, for although she hated the food at the school where she boarded, it was free, and she'd seen Zosha's cracked leather shoes, seen little Piotr's knobby ankles peeking out from the bottom of his frayed trousers. After Karolina left for Warsaw, the two girls wrote until Katya married and moved to Gdansk where her husband found work in the shipyards. Eight years had gone by since they had seen each other. Five years since they'd stopped writing.

Karolina was feeling more and more uneasy anticipating her visit to Zosha, and now, staring at the shadows deepening in the corners of her hotel room, she could feel dread take hold. Three days in Poland and she'd found nothing but dead ends: her cousin, Pola, had not called back — which meant Pola's parents had no information to relate. The Lublin and Warsaw archives had few pre-war documents; even her baptism papers were not original. What if Zosha had nothing to contribute?

In the distance melancholy church bells chimed. She rolled over and counted them — twelve strokes — then tried to sleep.

They had arranged to get an early start. Philip knocked at seven and when she opened her door, listless from lack of sleep, he was leaning against the wall with his coat and scarf draped across his shoulders and an eager look on his face. His hair was still damp from his bath and fell in dark, glossy curls on his forehead.

"They've got blinis on the menu downstairs," he said. "I've had a look around."

"You like?"

"Sure. They're like pancakes, right?"

"Better, I think."

He pulled her arm playfully, as if signaling there were no hard feelings after yesterday's car episode. "Then you'd better hurry and feed your hungry American."

The restaurant was a spacious, sunlit room filled with the aroma of fresh coffee and warm bread. The only other customers were two men in good suits who sat at a corner table and spoke in hushed tones. Government people, she guessed, the only Poles who could afford this place. It crossed her mind that Philip *had* seen someone at the church, that they were indeed being followed. She felt a fleeting stab of fear, then told herself it was absurd to think that searching archives to substantiate the identity of a Jewish child born before the war could be construed as being against the interests of the state. One of the men glanced in her direction, then looked away. Karolina gazed around at the wood-paneled walls hung with antique, gilt-framed mirrors. No, she tried to assure herself. Neither she nor Philip was important enough to merit the expense of the Victoria for two government functionaries.

A tall, lanky maitre d' in an oversized red jacket with epaulets ushered them to a table near a window on the square. Today was not a market day, and except for a few people on their way to work, the streets were quiet. A flock of pigeons rose up to the seamless, deep blue sky, scattered, then settled down again on the glistening cobblestones.

"Look," Philip said, pointing out the window at the square. A woman emptied a bucket of sudsy water onto the sidewalk, then took up a twig broom and began to sweep. "Amazing," he said. "Even in winter Poles scrub the streets."

"My mother's hands were always cracked from washing," she said, holding up her own hands to demonstrate. "She could not close them completely."

"Were you very poor?"

"Everyone was, but in the country this feels normal."

He fingered the miniature silk irises in the glass vase on the table. "Tell me about yourself. Did you come here when you were a kid?"

"No, our market town was Lubartow, 15 kilometers from here. Every Monday we went there to buy what we could not grow. I do not think you can have such markets in America. It is something left from old Europe: an open square where farmers came with carts of vegetables and sausages and chickens. Dogs and children were everywhere. When I was child, I enjoyed playing with the animals while my parents bargained with farmers. I did not know Lublin until I came here to boarding school."

"Boarding school? You just said you grew up poor."

She didn't understand at first, then remembered that in America only rich people sent their children away to school. "No," she laughed. "Here government pays for school, if you pass examinations. I had teacher who took interest in me and helped with entrance to *gymnasium*. But the school was too far from our farm. It was not

201

possible for my father to take me 20 kilometers to Lublin each day, so I had a room in dormitory. It was terrible day when I left. My mother packed my clothes in a flour sack and when my *tatush* held this out to me in front of other students, I became ashamed." She saw again the big, square man in his soiled sheepskin coat, silently kneading his cap in his hands, waiting for his kiss goodbye. But she had turned away to join the crowd of girls gathering on the school steps that autumn Sunday. "He knew I would never come back to farm. Perhaps he accepted this because I was not his child. I do not know. He was a man who held his sorrow to himself."

There was a scuffling of feet behind her. The waiter set down a basket of seeded rolls, and took out his pencil and pad. Glancing over his shoulder, Karolina noticed that the two questionable men were gone. Relieved, she ordered eggs, something she'd grown to enjoy in America, and pot cheese with vegetables. Philip asked for his blinis and they both turned back to stare at the square as though they'd used up their quota of permissible topics.

The shops on Zosha's street looked exactly the same as the first day Karolina had visited Katya almost fifteen years earlier. The bakery, which she remembered opened for a few hours at dawn, was closed now and would probably reopen at five to catch last-minute customers heading home for supper. As they passed the shoemaker's, she inhaled deeply, testing the air for the smell of glue that always permeated the stretch of sidewalk in front of his shop. There it was, filling her nostrils with the pungent aroma she had loved. She'd walked this street so often that the cracks in the sidewalk and the bend of the curb were as familiar to her as the road to her parents' farm.

She peered through the window of Zosha's hardware store and tapped on the pane. She knocked again, harder this time. The flowered curtains parted and Zosha peeked out. She broke into an astonished smile and quickly unlatched the door.

She threw open her arms. "Karolina!"

"It's so good to see you," Karolina said, hugging her. They linked arms and Zosha glanced at Philip, then smoothed down her turquoise wool dress, the same one she'd worn a year earlier when Karolina had stopped in for Mrs. Domanski's New York address.

Zosha's short ashy-blond hair was arranged in rows of tight cylinders. The curler marks were still visible.

A counter ran the length of the narrow store that was filled with familiar barrels of loose hardware, racks of vegetable and flower seeds, and bolts of burlap. Even the dusty glass lanterns hanging on hooks from the tin ceiling looked as if they were left over from her school days. From the rear, Zosha's grown son, Piotr, paused to gaze at them, then resumed pouring a box of nails into a barrel. The air had a stale, metallic smell.

"Please, please." Zosha motioned toward the wooden stools at the counter. "Your letter arrived just a few days ago, but God knows when you sent it. The mail here — I don't have to tell you." She turned to Philip with a comic smirk: "The Russians are killing us! How can anyone do business? Well, good Communists aren't supposed to do business, are they?" She eyed Philip's cashmere overcoat and the kidskin gloves he held in his hand, and nudged Karolina with her elbow. "Here I've gone on and on and you haven't introduced me to your friend."

"Landau. Philip Landau," he said, shaking her hand.

"He's a friend from New York," Karolina explained.

Zosha looked at him with surprise. "Oh, there were many Landaus in Lublin. So you understand Polish, *tak*?"

"A bit, *tak*," Philip said. "My family came from here."

A shadow passed over her eyes. "They probably left before the war."

"Some," Philip said. "Most died in the camps. In the one just down the road, in fact."

Zosha stared bleakly out the window and gave her head a shake. "Horrible, horrible," she mumbled. "So," she said, recovering a smile. "You've brought a friend along. I hope you're going to show him some of the country while you're here." Before Karolina could answer, Zosha turned back to Philip with a broad smile. "Where are you staying?"

"At the Victoria," Philip answered.

"Oh, that's a nice one. Expensive?"

"Not too bad."

"You were in Warsaw first, *tak*?"

"Yesterday," Karolina replied, growing impatient with the small talk. "Zosha, I came to —"

"Oh, what a beautiful city Warsaw was! The Germans —" She turned and spat on the floor in disgust. "May they slowly roast in hell till their livers are cooked — they burned the whole place down. People say everything is being rebuilt with that Russian concrete that cracks the minute you put it up." She swung around abruptly toward the back of the store. "Piotr!" she shouted. "You remember your sister's friend. Say hello to Karolina."

Piotr had grown into a thick-necked, hulking young man. He put down a burlap sack, nodded sullenly and disappeared behind a curtain at the rear of the store. His boots made a loud scraping sound across the wooden floor. He was as shy as ever.

"I wish Katya were here," Zosha sighed. "She still talks of your school days."

"I'm sorry to stop by unannounced. I tried calling first, but . . ."

"It hasn't worked for months," Zosha said, waving her hand at the telephone perched on the end of the counter. "But it doesn't matter. Piotr's my messenger now. He bicycles all over town with purchase orders. Not that we do so much business." She ran her hand absently across her scalp, breaking apart the coils of blond hair. "Did you know Katya lives in Gdansk? Oh, the families drift, drift." She rose quickly, went to the front door and flipped the store sign to "closed," then hurried back to her stool. "I wrote you back, but of course you haven't received my letter yet. I was shocked. My poor Karolina, you must be mistaken. You a Jewish child! This can't be true! Now I ask you, how could such a thing happen without someone knowing? No one could keep such a secret. And I, well, I never heard anything. When your parents came here they treated you normal, like any parents would. Like their own child. Of course, we never talked much. They were quiet, like most farm people, especially your mother who always waited outside, didn't she? Shy, I thought, and maybe a little embarrassed because . . . you know . . . you used to spend so much time here —"

"What about Josef, who worked for our neighbors, the Hankowskis?" Karolina asked.

"Well, yes, he was on the Hankowskis' farm during the war," Zosha said. "He was related to them, you know."

204

"Related? What do you mean?" Karolina knew the Hankowskis had relatives in Tarnow, but none in the area around Lublin that she could remember.

"He was Darius's cousin, I think," Zosha said.

Philip, who'd been straining to understand, interrupted. "What year was he on the Hankowskis' farm?"

"Till mid 1942. Then he came to town to work for me in the store. Did I ever tell you Darius Hankowski paid me to hire Josef? Yes, he paid Josef's salary and even gave me a little money —"

"Paid you?" Karolina interrupted. That made no sense. Darius's farm was larger than her parents' and he was always short of help. His two older sons had moved to the west of Poland in the 1930s, before Karolina was born, and his wife had lost an arm and couldn't work — which meant that Darius had to farm his ten acres alone. Why would he *pay* Zosha to take on a helper he himself needed?

"Oh, Darius had some story that his wife didn't like having Josef around, and Darius knew I needed someone to help out. The Germans shot my husband the year before, and Piotr and Katya were still small. Strange, isn't it? I can't imagine where Darius got the money to pay me. Oh, it wasn't much — just a few *groshen* left over after I gave Josef his salary — but we were starving and the money helped. The only people who had money then were the Germans. The bastards took the nicest apartments in Lublin and fixed them up like they were going to stay forever. Ha! that's what *they* thought. You know, I never liked Darius after that," Zosha confided. "He never came here to see Josef. The man was a quiet, harmless sort. Kept to himself. I can't imagine what he did to upset Darius's wife so much." She gave her scalp a scratch with her fingernail. "But you never know what goes on between people."

Philip met Karolina's eyes. "How long did Josef work for you?"

"Till about '48. By then my cousin from Stettin moved in with us and I didn't need Josef anymore. Oh, don't think he minded. He hated the city. All he wanted was a corner of a barn and a warm blanket."

"We need to talk with him," Philip said. "Where does he live?"

"He's dead. I heard he got pneumonia a few years ago and went into the hospital and never came out."

Karolina felt her face drain. "Dead?"

"Yes. Sad, isn't it? He wasn't so old."

"Did he have other family? Any close friends?" Philip asked.

"Not as far as I know."

A tremor started in Karolina's legs. Dead, all of them dead. Not a soul left alive who might know about her, the Landaus, anything from the past.

"Oh, I wish I knew more, dear. I'm so sorry I can't help you. I guess you've come for nothing." Zosha's face paled with concern. She ran her hand across Karolina's brow. "You don't look well, dear. You're upset, naturally, but I bet it's that hotel food. Oh, they make it look nice for rich tourists, but it's not fresh, believe me. No wonder you're sick. Maybe you could come for dinner tonight?"

"I think . . . Mr. Landau has other plans."

"What a shame. Remember how you and Katya gobbled up my honey and butter sandwiches? I always packed you a few extra to take back to your room at school, didn't I? Your parents, God rest their souls, they didn't have much to give." Zosha's small, caramel-colored eyes began to water. "Always arm in arm you two, always giggling like there was every reason in the world to be happy. You wouldn't recognize Katya now. She never smiles. Her husband — he works in the shipyards — he beats her. Don't say a word if you speak to her! She's expecting a child in June." She sniffled, rubbing her nose with the back of her hand. "I'm glad the phone is always broken. When it works, I'm afraid she's calling to tell me he kicked the baby out of her."

The room seemed to tilt. Karolina slung her purse over her shoulder, and holding onto Philip's arm, hoisted herself to her feet. "I want to leave quickly," she whispered in English.

He gripped her elbow.

"You'll send my regards to Katya?" Karolina said, moving cautiously toward the front door.

"Of course, of course." Zosha glanced toward the curtained partition. "Piotr. What are you doing back there? I'm opening up now," she shouted, lifting herself off the stool. "Excuse him, will you. Twenty-five years old and still doesn't know how to talk with people." She flipped the store sign to "Open" and shook hands. "It would be nicer if you'd come in spring, of course, but at least there's no snow. Strange, isn't it, for this time of the year?"

"I must go back to the hotel now," Karolina said when they'd reached the street. She touched her forehead. It felt cold and clammy.

Philip held her arm. "What's the matter?"

"I am not well. . . ." The street became a blur, the sound of traffic muffled and distant. People walked brusquely around them. A few threw impatient looks. She took a few tentative steps, reeled, then regained her balance. Looking up, she caught sight of the twin angels of St. Brigittine's spire. The church was around the corner.

"Can you find the way back to the Victoria?" she asked.

"Why? Where are *you* going?"

She nodded in the direction of the spires looming over the rooftops. "To church."

"Why?"

"Why does anyone go to church?" she heard herself say. A sickening sensation filled her stomach. She wanted church, church, the healing peace of church.

"You're white as a sheet. I'm not going to leave you like this," he said.

They climbed St. Brigittine's steps and with all her strength, Karolina pushed open the heavy carved door. Inside, the church was dark. Philip hesitated, then stepped back, as if he'd just looked into an abyss.

"I'll wait for you," he said. "Tell me where."

She pointed toward the end of the street. "There . . . there is cafe."

He descended hesitantly, throwing her a last worried look before heading down the street.

It's over, she said to herself, sliding into a pew, over, over. There is nothing more to find, nothing more to know.

A half-hour later, she found Philip seated at a window table in the cafe across the street from Zosha's store. When he spotted her, he tossed a fistful of crumpled zloty onto the counter, rushed out and took her in his arms. "How do you feel?"

"Better." Her dread and nausea had dissipated, leaving her weak with fatigue. She held on to him. How glad she was that he was there, how good his arms felt. "Take me back, please."

In her hotel room, she yanked off her boots, let her coat drop to the floor and crawled onto the bed, dragging the covers over herself. Philip hesitated at the door, then stalked in and pulled the curtains closed. She heard the scraping of a chair. When she looked, he was sitting beside the bed still in his coat, watching her.

"Do you want some tea?" he asked softly.

She shook her head and wiped her hot neck with a corner of the duvet.

"Tell me what this is about."

In the muted light of the room, Philip's narrow nose and sharp cheekbones looked finely sketched, as though he'd been drawn in the thinnest charcoal. Even in the dim light she could make out his restless eyes. This man was never still. Even now, as he sat helpless and confused, she could feel his attention like a magnet, absorbing her, dragging her toward him. She squeezed her eyes closed. She wanted him stilled. She wanted dreamless sleep.

The room was quiet. There was only the soft rasp of his breathing. She saw that he had removed his coat and was leaning forward, his head bowed over his clasped hands, sitting as he had that Sunday in Noah's living room, listening to her tell her story.

"Did church help?" he asked.

"It was my comfort. When my knees touched the *klęcznik*, my heart opened," she whispered hoarsely. But now . . ."

"Tell me," he said.

All the confusion and anguish that started accumulating the day she had seen Jake's picture rose inside her. "I . . . I don't know where I belong!" she moaned. "And now I never will!" *Belong*. There it was, the word that had haunted her all her life, that had multiplied in her head and pushed until it burst forth like an imprisoned animal. She groped for him blindly, touching his cheeks, his eyes, his mouth. For a moment Philip held on to her wrists, his face suspended in confusion, then he slid his hands across her shoulders until he was cupping her wet, sobbing face in his palms. He kissed her gently and lowered himself onto the bed. She leaned into him as though his very physicality could blot out the world.

Later, she woke briefly and found herself still nestled against him. He was asleep. She breathed in the scent of his damp skin and let herself drift. On the edge of sleep she saw her father's ghostly image, dusty with grain, slowly pulling the nesting box up to the barn rafters. The birds fluttered, filling the air with the pungent smell of their brooding bodies. Their cooing drifted upward, growing fainter and fainter until the sound was lost among the high wooden beams.

She jolted awake. Her arm lay across Philip's chest, her head rested on his shoulder. Her clothes stuck to her. She was covered in cold sweat.

He pressed his face into her hair. "You slept," he murmured. "Better now?"

She nodded.

"I want you," he said, holding her close.

She rolled away, pulling the sheet across her chest. What had she done? She'd gone to him in her pain and let herself be comforted by this Jewish man who had thought she was . . . who still could think she was a scheming Pole. "Forgive me," she said. "I make mistake. Nothing has changed."

He burrowed closer, lightly resting his hand on her arm. "I think it has."

"This cannot be. We cannot be . . ."

"If you don't want me, just come out and say it."

"My God, what a child you are! I cannot know my feelings for you . . . it is too dangerous . . ."

"Don't give me that European 'I'm so wise' crap." He threw off the covers and sat on the edge of the bed. Light filtered through the curtains and she could make out the curved muscles of his back beneath his shirt. How hard and solid they'd felt when she had her arms around him. "I believe you, you know," he said.

"You believe for now. But without proof you will always hold doubts inside. You will always wonder if I am with you because of money."

"Screw the money! I'll give it to charity. We can get past that."

"How can you know such a thing?"

"Because I know how I feel." He faced her, determined. "We'll go back to St. Bartolomeo."

"Why? There is no use. They think you come to take Landau business away from Poles. You are Jew and they still hate you — us." For the first time, she felt the lonely distance she had come from being a child of her parish to an outcast, a member of a despised people. If she were born a Jew, her belief in Christ would not be enough to spare her the contempt of this world.

"Trust me. I can make the woman talk."

"If she speaks with us, she will only tell gossip," she replied. "I want someone who was there, who *saw* the child, Chava, so I will know for sure."

"Then let's pack up and go home."

"Your home, not mine."

"And you stay here?"

"Perhaps."

"No, you're coming back with me."

"I told you, it will not —

He drew her against him once more, kissing her wrist, her eyelids, her nose until his face came to rest in the crook of her neck. What a surprise this man was! She would not have thought him so tender, so open in his wanting.

She eased her body away a bit and smoothed back his hair with her hand. "You are willful man."

"When I want something, yes."

She fixed his particular smells in her mind. His skin was a fragrant mixture of spicy cinnamon and warm soap. A new smell. A strong smell.

"You are right," she said. "We must go back to St. Bartolomeo."

Chapter 27

At breakfast the next morning Karolina and Philip settled into their window seats, casting tentative glances at each other over the bread and cheese that lay untouched on their plates. When Philip took her hand, Karolina held her breath, astonished that she had made herself so vulnerable.

"I don't want you to worry," he said. "When we get to the church, I'll take care of everything."

Ah, her naïve American believed that the mere force of his demanding the truth would reveal it. "Of course, you are strong man, Philip," she said, wryly, "but I did not know you can make the dead speak."

"We don't need Josef. When I get back, there are other places I can check out. I know a guy who can help . . ."

She shook her head hard. "For now, please, let us only enjoy."

He gave her his crooked smile and kissed her hand. "That's easy."

They stopped at the concierge's desk for the address of the closest car rental, then Karolina slipped her arm through his and they strolled along the Wista River, listening to the mournful cry of gulls overhead. She felt his tentativeness, and when he took her by the chin and lightly kissed her, she returned the kiss, letting herself drift with the pleasure of the moment, of the wind on her face and the taste of his mouth.

Once the garage owner saw American dollars, he took them out back to the cars he kept for hire. Philip eyed the three black Ladas lined up in the damp cement enclosure behind the rental office, strolled over to one, and ran his hand over a spot where the fender had been carefully repainted. He peered inside the Lada, then gave Karolina a comical roll of the eyes.

"Is this good enough?" she asked, with raised eyebrows.

"Vintage Soviet is *better* than good," he laughed. "Think of the stories I can tell when I get home."

Philip fiddled with the dials while she filled out the necessary forms, and then they were on their way down ulica Krolewska toward the road they had taken from St. Bartolomeo's two days earlier. It was barely past noon. People on the streets were hurrying home for lunch with food parcels tucked under their arms. A few young women walked by and Karolina noticed their skirts were shorter than she remembered. It was easy to spot the frayed hems repeatedly altered to keep up with the fashion in the European magazines all the woman bought them on the black market.

They were stopped at a traffic light when she spotted the old Medical Academy. She pointed to the large yellow stone building. "There. On top near roof." Philip craned his neck to look. "There is outline. Star of David. This is . . . was once a Jewish school."

He nodded soberly and drove on. She wouldn't tell him about the painted store signs she remembered that still bore the faint shadow of a "berg" or a "stein" beneath the names of the current Polish owners.

The night before, they'd had a meal at a nearby restaurant, then walked to the old Jewish quarter, looking for the Landaus' house. Philip had wanted to see the place as she had, hoping something about the street or the building would fire a memory. But nothing had. The shop at Number 6 ulica Grodska was closed, and she and Philip stood staring for some minutes at the curled and dusty leather samples in the shop window. Now and then, he'd glanced up at the light in the upstairs apartment.

"How did these people get the store?" he'd asked.

"I think government gave this kind of property to people for little money after war."

"'This kind of property . . .'" He'd scanned the row of wooden houses with ground floor shops and enclosed courtyards. "Some day there'll be restitution. Not that anybody needs the pennies these places are worth, but, boy, would I love to try the cases." She'd flinched at the bitterness in his voice, but kept quiet.

Now, looking out at the Lublin streets she thought she knew so well, the sad thought occurred that she could never again walk past these buildings without remembering the people who were torn from their normal lives and so hideously murdered. How often she'd passed the decayed, boarded-up synagogue near her *gymnasium* without giving it a second thought. The overgrown cemetery south of the city's main street with its twisted gate and broken, defaced headstones had always seemed part of the landscape, an archeological ruin. Everyone knew the Jews were gone, slaughtered by Nazis. But Poles had been killed too, millions of them, in the camps and slave factories, murdered in round-ups, often shot down in the street for nothing more than hiding a loaf of bread under their coats. She couldn't say this, of course. Philip would resent her comparing the deaths of Poles and Jews. They'd end up arguing. Who suffered more? Who suffered less? God, did it matter?

"When I was growing up, Jews were like vanished people," she said, instead. "Now I must see everything differently."

"Good. I want you to," Philip said.

She turned to ponder the mauve-streaked clouds on the horizon. Soon, they'd be approaching the turnoff to the main road that would take them back to St. Bartolomeo. Suddenly, she caught sight of a familiar stand of trees and a great ache rose in her. She might never come this way again! "My farm is there. On right. Quickly!"

Though the house was more than a kilometer down a narrow dirt road, she strained to catch a glimpse of the birches that surrounded the pond and the small dell that formed a natural boundary between the Hankowski house and her own. Two years earlier, when her father had died, she tried to sell the property, but even with government subsidy, no one wanted land in this impoverished region. All his life, Jan Staszek had struggled to coax a better living from the rocky, meager soil he'd inherited from his father, planting radishes one year, beets and cabbage the next, once even trying alfalfa before returning to the perennial potatoes that glutted the market. Her *tatush* had not wanted this life, but could never squeeze enough from the stingy, unyielding land to leave. Maybe he'd hoped to buy a better farm with Jake's money, one further north where the soil was richer.

They passed the south pond, now topped with a thin skin of ice. She remembered with absolute clarity the winter she was ten and her cat, Kicia, fell in and drowned. Her father had fished him out with a pitchfork and placed the stiff, elongated body on the dried weeds along the bank. She'd stared at Kicia, struggling to make sense of the bulging eyes and swollen belly. Her *real* cat was somewhere in the pond, she'd convinced herself, and didn't cry. Her father wrapped Kicia in sacking and stored him in the basement until the ground was soft enough to dig a grave. That spring they buried the cat under a tree near the pond and in her best script Karolina went through the motions of engraving a stone and placing it on his grave. *Kicia.* She'd never fully mourned her beloved childhood companion because she refused to believe he was dead. Even now, whenever thoughts of death came to mind, there was a liimit, a wall beyond which she couldn't let her imagination go, and though she disliked this penchant for self-deception, she sensed its rock-like necessity within her.

Her house sat on a small rise a few yards from the road. The windows and door were filled in with cinder blocks that gave the building a ghostly face. To the right stood the barn, its door dangling open on one broken hinge. A rusted pail lay on the ground and nearby, an old enamel pot. She caught sight of a shovel propped against the side of the barn and the rotted leather straps of her father's harness dangling from a nail. There is only this, she thought, all that is left of two lonely lives.

Philip slowed the car to a stop and they stepped into the yard. Karolina righted the pail, then drifted over to the barn. Swinging open the door, she was surrounded by the familiar smell of cow manure and rough grain. The stall partitions had collapsed, leaving the interior of the barn more open and spacious than she remembered. There was a sudden beat of wings. Panic seized her. What? But it was only swallows, fluttering from the rafters. They circled the barn in a brief frenzy, then flew out the loft opening, leaving behind a dusty spiral of air to float slowly to the ground.

Outside, she turned toward the hillock behind the house and searched the horizon for the rim of the forest that bordered their farm. Nowhere were there forests like the ones in Poland. The past autumn, when she'd felt the first pangs of homesickness, Jim had taken her to New England to see the countryside he loved so much. But the landscape was too colorful, too lush to soothe her, not at all like the graceful, haunting woods of her childhood.

Philip stood quietly at her side and waited.

"When I was little girl," she said at last, "I would stand at the edge of our forest and stare for a long time, imagining what was on the other side. And I yearned for this other place that would feel like home even though I had one already."

"Were you unhappy here?"

"No. I do not know why I felt this way. I have always been mystery to myself."

They stood side by side, their breaths misting the air. She inhaled deeply and was conscious of the absence of smells. In spring, especially, the farm was thick with odors, with moss and mud, with chickens and warm milk. Today, there was only vacant, scentless cold.

"If Jake brought you here, it would have been sometime in the spring of '42," he said, squinting at the scrubby fields, "Before the ghetto was liquidated. How old were you then?"

"I thought four, but the date on ID card makes me older." Then why don't I remember? she asked herself, and before she could fully frame the answer, she knew she *did* remember, in half-obscured images that had slid in and out of her life since the beginning of her memory. "I came by car," she said with pounding heart. "A man brought me!" She didn't know how she knew this, but she did. She tried to focus the vision just beyond her reach, just beyond resolution, like an after image from too much sun, but it slid away.

He turned sharply toward the field. "Show me where your neighbors' farm was."

"Darius's property begins a hundred meters past those oak trees," she said, pointing toward a stretch of matted yellow grass.

"Did he farm, also?"

"Yes, he grew horseradishes there, and beets further on, then feed corn."

"He would have worked this area in the spring, right? Around the time the ghetto was liquidated. He would have seen or heard a child next door."

"Yes, yes. That is why I was wanting to speak with Zosha's man, Josef, because he was there." She scanned the ruined landscape. An image flashed: a glint of sunlight bounced off a polished fender; a small suitcase was handed past her. She felt the ghost of a hand pushing her toward the house.

"I want to go now," she said, breathless. "We will make them tell us everything, won't we? The priest, Basia, everyone. And you will help me."

She swung around to face him. Even in the sunlight his face looked shadowed, his dark eyes sharp with determination.

Chapter 28

They sped toward St. Bartolomeo's, 10 kilometers to the north. They'd arrive at the church just after lunchtime. Basia would be finishing up the dishes and Father Tomasz would be in his study. Or maybe he'd be napping. That would be best. Karolina didn't care what the old woman had told him after she and Philip had left the day before, but she didn't want to face the priest again.

Philip turned on the heater and the car filled with the strong smell of mildew. He opened the window a crack. "You'll have to do most of the talking, so let's plan this out. Tell me exactly what the woman said."

"Basia knew the Landaus because Father Demetrius, the priest before Father Tomasz, bought leather from them. She said the Landau son came to the church one night —"

"— which means she knew enough about the family to know there was a father who owned the business."

"Yes. And she heard some of family went to America after the war."

"Were priests allowed to buy directly from Jewish merchants or would they have to meet at night?"

Karolina wrinkled her nose in irritation. "Priests are permitted to do business with anyone they choose. Church is not prison."

"Okay. Just checking out what's customary here."

The engine whined. Philip threw the gear into third and the car lurched forward. "Jake would certainly have gone looking for you right after he was liberated, but you said your family had moved by then. That means he found your farm deserted. If I'm right that Demetrius was the one who connected Jake to your parents, Jake would have gone to him to find out what happened to all of you. But obviously the priest didn't help him."

"How can you know this?"

"Because Jake never found you."

Of course. Father Demetrius knew everything about his parishioners. He would have known her family had left for Koromov. Why hadn't he told this to Jake Landau?

A canvas-covered truck lumbered by, then a horse-drawn cart. Then nothing but flat, straight road and a pale blue sky with puffs of scattered clouds. A moment later, St. Bartolomeo's pitched roof appeared in the distance, gleaming in the afternoon sun.

Philip glanced at his watch. "What usually goes on in a church around two o'clock?"

"Nothing. People are working. If anyone is inside, we will see the carts."

"Is it just the priest and Basia?"

"I think so. Years ago there was a sexton, but I saw no one else last time."

"Can we get in without being seen?"

"The car will be noticed."

"Then we'll park away from the church and walk."

She fidgeted with a strand of her hair. "My God, I feel like criminal."

Philip eased the car onto the shoulder of the road. "We won't waste time talking to the priest. He wasn't here when your parents left. I want to get Basia alone. Tell her I'm working for the Landau family, gathering evidence. Say the Landau business was illegally seized by the Poles, that we're seeking restitution and the Soviets are cooperating with us. Is she likely to believe that?"

"Yes. Country people are not so informed. And of course, they believe anything bad about Russians."

"Then say the assets of the business should have gone to Jake's child, who we have reason to believe is still alive. Would the priest have told her you claim to be Jake's child?"

"I do not think they speak of personal subjects."

"We'll play it by ear. Say if she doesn't tell us what she knows, we'll make trouble with the police. Can you remember that?"

"Yes, but why will this convince her to tell us?"

"Because the woman was devoted to the old priest."

"Yes, but —"

"Tell her we know that Father Demetrius was involved in hiding a Jewish child who wasn't returned to her rightful parents and if the police are brought into the picture they might find something that could damage his reputation. Maybe Demetrius took money for his services. Maybe he lied to Jake after the war about what happened to his child. If she knew anything about this, she'd be an accessory to the crime. She'll know that the Communists won't hesitate to implicate a priest in a case like this. I'm betting she'll want to keep the authorities out of it. We're going to convince her that if she doesn't tells us what she knows, she'll end up in prison and the old priest's name will be in all the papers, even nailed to the church door."

Philip was right again: Basia had adored Father Demetrius. She'd be desperate to protect his good name.

They came upon the woman in the passageway between the vestry and the church. She was crouching in front of a low wooden chest, slipping linens onto a shelf. She must have heard the click of Karolina's heels on the limestone floor because she spun around as they approached.

Karolina held out her hand. "Basia," she said softly.

The woman backed up against the chest, clutching a white napkin in her bony fist. Her pale eyes were bright with fear. "Father Tomasz is in his study. It's the other way." She glanced furtively at Philip who was standing with his arms folded across his chest.

"It's you we want to speak to," Karolina said.

The woman's eyes flitted from Karolina to Philip. "Why?"

In a calm, steady voice, Karolina told her what she and Philip had rehearsed in the car. "Father Demetrius was involved in hiding a Jewish child," she concluded. "Tell me what you know and we'll keep his name out of it."

The woman twisted her puckered mouth from side to side, considering, then glared up at Philip. "You're trying to prove this man was hidden, so he can take back the business, *tak*?" she said to Karolina. "You came all the way from America for a little leather shop?"

"Tell us," Karolina repeated.

219

Basia looked around wildly, then tossed her cloth on top of the chest. "I don't have to talk to you," she spat out and started past Karolina. Philip positioned himself between them, but Karolina pushed him aside. For a moment the two women stood facing each other in the dim vestibule. The smell of onions clung to the woman's clothes.

"Tell me!" Karolina hissed.

The woman staggered back until she was gripping the chest behind her. "I heard a car pull up one night," she whispered. "A man came in with Father Demetrius."

"When was this?" Karolina demanded.

"A few days before the Germans cleared the ghetto."

"Who was he?"

"Father called him *Pan* Landau."

"And?"

Basia pressed her mouth tight. Her silence was furious.

Philip hovered over her. "Do you want me to bring the police?"

The woman tugged at Karolina's coat sleeve. Her hands were trembling. "I only heard a few words," she said. "I was in the vestry when they talked."

"She's going too fast," Philip said in English. "I can't understand her."

As Basia continued, Karolina translated quicker, slipping in Basia's words between deep intakes of air, desperate for Philip to understand every word but afraid to pause and give the woman time to censor herself.

"The Jew talked to Father about hiding," Basia said. "They talked about money. He was looking for a safe place. I thought he wanted to hide himself." Her frantic eyes fell on Philip. "But it was for you, *tak?* You're Landau's son. How did you survive?"

So Father Tomasz had not told her Karolina claimed to be Jake's child. All the better. The less the woman knew, the more likely she was to tell the truth.

"Where was the child hidden?" Philip asked.

The woman's eyes widened with confusion. "Don't you know where they took you?"

Philip's arm shot out, signaling Karolina to remain silent. "Who took the child?" he repeated. "What Pole?"

"I don't know. I couldn't hear."

"Jake Landau survived the war," Karolina said. "He looked for his child afterwards. Father Demetrius didn't help him. Why?"

The old woman made a sign of the cross. "Because . . . because . . . Father Demetrius didn't know anyone was looking for a child, I swear!"

"How do you know that?"

"L-letters came from America. I threw them away," she stammered.

"You what!"

"I thought Landau died in the camps like all of them. I knew he had family in America. I was afraid there would be trouble — or why would he write?"

"Landau wrote because he was trying to find his child!" Karolina cried.

Basia straightened herself and gave her headscarf an indignant tug. "How would I know that? " she said. "I don't read."

Karolina seized Basia's arm. It felt surprisingly fleshy beneath the flimsy cardigan. She wanted to scream in her face, but Philip pulled her away. She shot a look toward the other end of the passageway. Everything was quiet. "Why, in Christ's name, would you do such a thing?" Karolina was weeping now. "Why?"

"There were rumors after the war that the Landau man — I thought it was Landau — was turned over to the Germans," Basia whispered, saliva pooling at the corners of her mouth. "The Russians were after Poles who had betrayed Jews. They held trials. I was afraid someone would find out Father was involved and they would put him in jail. They did that to priests, you know. I thought if no one answered the letters, the Americans would think Father was dead and they would leave us alone." Her eyes brimmed suddenly. "He died a year later." She nodded toward the study door. "That's when that one came here."

Karolina shook her head in disbelief. "You stupid, stupid woman."

"I am stupid? You, who would betray a Pole for a Jew, *Pani* Staszek, calls me names? You who has become a Jew lover like all the Americans?"

Karolina lurched toward the woman, then stopped herself. "What does Father Tomasz know about this!"

"He knows nothing." Basia raised her shoulders in a gesture of helplessness. "He sits in his study all day and plays with his papers."

"Father Tomasz spoke of rumors," Philip said. "What did he mean?"

"Just what I told you: that Father Demetrius helped hide a Jew. He doesn't want to know more. He doesn't take an interest. God, forgive me, I'm grateful he gets up to serve mass." She wiped her running nose with the back of her hand. "Remember how many people used to come here, how they loved Father Demetrius?" she whimpered to Karolina. "Did you see anyone here yesterday? Or today? Nobody comes. Not for that man." The woman groped in her apron pocket, withdrew her rosary and began to mutter the "Our Father." She would not tell them more. Karolina spun toward the church door, Philip in her wake.

"Tell the Russians," Basia called after them. "You think they will help? Ha! They don't care about Jews now. I heard they're throwing them all in jail!"

"The letters . . . she destroyed Jake's letters!" Karolina cried.

Philip slid into the driver's seat.

"She knows nothing about me!" Karolina shouted. "She is only guessing."

"She knows someone was hidden."

"But she thought it was you, that you are child of Jake Landau!"

"It doesn't matter. We've confirmed Jake went to the church to hide someone."

"But who . . . " She stopped to take in gulps of air.

"It's something."

"Not enough!" Karolina groped for a tissue in her shoulder bag and wiped her face. The thin paper dissolved into wet clumps between her fingers and she tossed it aside, cursing herself for not buying proper cloth handkerchiefs the minute she landed.

The sun was low on the horizon. Philip pulled down the visor to break the glare, then stretched his arms across the steering wheel and rested his head on the back of his hands. "Those rumors Basia mentioned about someone turning over a Jew to the Germans. Everyone in your village would have heard them, right? Maybe you overheard your parents talking about this when you were a child and got it mixed up with yourself."

"You think I'm crazy?"

"I didn't say that. I'm just considering other angles."

"My parents never did business with leather people! If they knew Rachel or Chava, if they spoke these names, it was because Jake *told* them." She was shouting at him. He was trying to help her and she was shouting at him.

They sped back to Lublin. Here and there patches of ice dotted the fields where rain had frozen along the edge of irrigation ditches. Without a softening coat of snow, the landscape looked harsh and scrubby. Remorseless.

"I'll put in a call to Rosalind when we get back," Philip said. "Jake might have said something to her about hiding himself with Poles."

"I do not believe it."

"Why?"

"Because she is honest woman who wants to know what is true. She would tell us already if she knew anything."

"It's worth going over it with her. Maybe some memory will surface. That's what lawyers do: Always ask the same question at least three times."

By the time they arrived in Lublin, it was late afternoon. They parked the car on a side street near the car rental and pushed past the crowds milling around the stalls in the main square. Karolina surveyed the goods spread out on the stands and saw the same jars of preserves and pickles, the same wallets and bags tooled in rough patterns from paper thin leather that had always been sold there. Even the sheepskin coats and hats people wore were the same worn, yellow-tan color she had seen all her life. No one had prospered. She was surprised that she should have this strange notion. An American idea. Prosperity was not on anyone's mind in her country, only the struggle to make do.

223

Streetlights had come on, casting shadows on the sidewalk in front of the hotel. Karolina didn't recognize the man until he stepped into the light. He was holding his cap in his hands. His bicycle rested against the wall behind him. It was Zosha's son, Piotr.

"My mother told me to wait for you." He blinked a few times as though the sound of his own voice surprised him.

"Has something happened?" Karolina asked.

"Josef didn't die. I saw him a few months ago when he was in town, buying a shovel." Piotr shuffled his feet from side to side. "My mother didn't know this. She told me to tell you. He works on the Kozlowski farm a few kilometers from the road to Zamosc."

Chapter 29

"Philip, darling, how good to hear your voice."

Rosalind sounded groggy. He looked at his watch. Four P.M. in New York. "Are you okay?"

"Yes, just napping. Please. Tell me, what have you found?"

"Not much."

"Any documents?"

"Only her baptism papers, but they're not originals. They were signed years after she was born."

"What does that mean?"

"That we haven't got anything solid yet." He yanked off his shoes and lay back on the bed. "But listen. I called to ask you something else."

"Yes?" Her voice was suddenly alert.

"Was Jake ever in hiding during the war?"

"No . . . let me think for a minute." Static filled the line. "As far as I know, he was sent to Maidenek right from the ghetto. He said little about that period, just sometimes if he met someone who'd been there, too, or who he knew from the DP camp in Germany afterwards. But that's all. Why do you ask?"

"An old woman who works in the church in Karolina's village says Jake came there one night to ask the priest to help him find a place to hide. But it's not clear whether it was to hide himself or someone else."

"Really! What does the priest say about this?"

"He's dead. He died right after the war."

"Then how can you be sure the woman's telling the truth?"

"Because I scared the hell out of her," he said, remembering Basia cowering against the chest.

"My God, if a woman from Karolina's church knew Jake, then there must be a connection."

"Yes, I think so. The church received letters from America. She thinks from Jake. Did he ever show you letters he wrote to Poland, trying to locate Chava?"

"No, never. I saw official letters that came from Poland, but only by accident. I could never bring myself to ask. He wouldn't talk about them. What else did the woman say?"

"Nothing. She claims she was in another room and that's all she heard."

"You're still suspicious, Philip. I hear it in your voice."

"No, just frustrated about these half-stories we keep getting."

"So, you believe Karolina?"

"Yes."

Rosalind sighed audibly. "I'm glad you feel that way. I think she's honest. It would have been easy for her to lie when I showed her the pictures of Luba and Hinda, but she didn't." There was a pause. "Maybe I *want* to believe she's Jake's child . . . Now she could be *my* child. I don't know, but I like her."

"Me, too." The feeling in his voice surprised him and he realized he was testing her, wanting to signal how he felt about Karolina. Rosalind must have caught his meaning because a silence settled between them. His aunt understood that the family would be all over him for getting involved with a *shiksa* if not a cousin — and for throwing over Ellen, a lawyer, *a real Jew*. Ellen. His stomach sank.

"How's Karolina taking all this?" Rosalind asked.

"Hard."

"What a thing, eh? I suppose she'll want to come back to New York."

"I don't know. We haven't talked about it." Would she? She put him off whenever he brought it up. Maybe he'd overestimated her feelings for him. Hadn't she'd tried to convince him a relationship between them was a hopeless thing? Was that her way of letting him down easy? She'd been emotionally strung out when she'd reached

226

for him. Now that he thought about it, there was no reason to think she cared for him, only that she needed help.

"I'll tell your parents we spoke," Rosalind said. "Unless you think their feelings will be hurt that you didn't call them."

"Don't bother. My father would only yell at me for wasting money on long distance calls."

He heard a short titter.

"I'll be coming back soon," he said. He dreaded leaving. If Karolina went back to New York without any answers, she'd slip out of his life. She'd let in all her objections, all the reasons they shouldn't be together.

"There's one more person to see," he said. "A guy who worked on a neighbor's farm during the war. He lives about 50 kilometers from here. We're driving there in the morning." Could he find a reason for them to stay in Poland a while longer? Had they checked all the places where pre-war records were kept? He still had another week or so before Abe Drottman expected him. He might be able to convince Karolina to visit the cousin her family had lived with after the war in — where did she say — a village called Koromov?

A strange clacking sound came on the line. "I better go," Rosalind said, "I'm beginning to hear the Atlantic. I'll call Noah and tell him what you've found. Keep well, darling."

Philip replaced the phone in its cradle and propped his head against the down bolster. It seemed like a lifetime since Karolina had walked into his office, yet only a month had gone by. He closed his eyes and let himself summon up her strange, loamy smell, the dip of her waist in his hand. She was like a drug. Everything about her — the way she threw back her head when she lit a cigarette, the way she ran her finger along the rim of a glass, her sad, knowing face — everything excited him.

He grabbed the phone.

Karolina picked up on the second ring. "*Tak.*"

She sounded drowsy. He pictured her sleep-softened face, her disheveled hair strewn across the pillow.

"I'm coming to you," he said.

They stood facing each other in the dim light that spilled in from the street lamp outside her window. She moved toward him noiselessly on the cloth slippers he'd seen at the foot of her bed in Greenpoint. He held back, afraid that she would ask him to leave. Instead, she stepped closer and placed her hands on his shoulders. Her robe was long and silky and rustled against her bare legs, her hair swept up in a soft bun. Cautiously, Philip slid out the pins and the waves tumbled onto her shoulders. When he searched her face, he saw that she was smiling at him.

They undressed quickly, letting their clothes slip to the floor. Taking his hand, she led him to the bed, and drew him down. Somewhere in the distance he could hear the tinkling of piano music, then a short burst of laughter. They began to move together, and as he watched her face he saw her shut her eyes, as if retreating into herself. But he wanted more. He drove deeper inside her, afraid he'd hurt her, yet willing her to look at him. To *see* him. To be with him. His face would tell her that he loved her, that Ellen didn't count, that his ex-wife was a memory. She would see how he felt and wouldn't turn away. Gripping her back, he tried to bring her further inside himself. But she kept her eyes closed as if her real world were a torment and only by slipping into another realm could she find pleasure in him.

"Look at me!" he cried, holding her face up. A moment passed before she opened her eyes. Her gaze lingered on him steady and clear, and, as if she had finally discovered that happiness *did* exist, she kissed him deeply and held him so tightly, he hurt.

Philip slowly rolled onto his side with the ease of waking from a blissful dream. She saw him smile to himself and felt his finger tips skim the length of her arm.

"I've wanted you for so long," he whispered, grazing her forehead with his lips.

"Not so long . . ." she sighed, curling against him and resting her head on his chest. Why was this man now easy to love? Could she love him for a lifetime?

Outside, a wind picked up, tearing at the bare branches of the trees in the courtyard. She shivered, thinking of tomorrow, and the possibility of another dead end, of never knowing — or worse, knowing half a story, half her life.

She spoke into the darkness. "Why do you think I cannot remember?"

She realized her mistake immediately. She felt his body tense, his arm fall away from her shoulder.

"No," she said, retrieving his hand. "I am not . . . indifferent . . . I am . . ." She made a churning motion with her arms to illustrate. ". . . full with feeling for you, but I *must* speak of this. Until I know for sure, I will not have a clear heart." She knew she had hurt him by slipping from their intimacy as though making love to him were a casual event. But she couldn't help herself. She desperately needed to go over the details of their conversation with Basia, with Zosha, if only to reassure herself that nothing, not even love, could come before the truth of her past. "Please, tell me what you are thinking."

She saw him struggling with his anger, trying to decide if he should let it go. "All right, then," he said, after a moment. "I suppose a good Freudian would say some things are too painful to remember."

"But what do *you* think?"

"As a lawyer, I would say you know too much for there not to be some truth to your story."

Some truth. How could she trust that his judgment wasn't now clouded by his feelings for her?

Across the room, the gauzy curtains billowed gently out from the window where cold air seeped through the cracks in the frame. She was suddenly exhausted. This possible love would come to nothing, like the registry records, like Father Tomasz, like Zosha's man. Like Jim's confidence in her ability to be happy, and now Philip's confidence he could make everything turn out the way he wanted. Since the day they'd arrived in Poland, she'd been fighting a mounting sense of futility; now it was upon her. She sat up, grabbed her sweater from the chair and yanked it over her head, pulling her hair out from under the neckline with an impatient tug.

"I am afraid that tomorrow may change nothing. I am afraid I will always be outside myself."

She could make out the dark oval of his face framed against the white pillows. He raked at his tousled hair in a gesture that was already familiar and dear.

"Philip," she said, touching his shoulder. "You must understand that without proof —"

"I know, I know," he hushed, and drew her down to the bed.

Chapter 30

A middle-aged woman in a heavy knit sweater and rubber boots was standing in the doorway of the wooden farmhouse when Karolina and Philip pulled up. As they made their way across the gravel path to the front yard, the woman straightened her headscarf, then squinted out from under her shaded eyes. Karolina quickly mounted the two cement stairs. The odor of frying sausage and kerosene lamps drifted out from the open door.

"*Pani* Kozlowski?" she said, smiling into the woman's apprehensive face.

The woman clasped the front of her sweater with her chafed, reddened hands. "*Tak.*"

"Zosha Mazurek sent me. I'm looking for a man named Josef. She said he works for you. He's an old friend of my family."

The woman shook her head. "Mazurek? No, I don't know this person. Maybe my husband, but he's gone to Zamosc. If you want, come back later," she said, stepping back. "Around three."

Karolina put her hand on the door. "Zosha has a hardware store in Lublin," she said kindly. "Josef used to work for her."

Suddenly the woman smiled, exposing chipped, tobacco-stained teeth. "Oh, yes, Piotr's mother, *tak*?"

"That's her."

She pointed toward the barn on the far side of the yard. "Josef is over there."

Karolina and Philip hurried across the yard, sending a few scrawny chickens scrambling out of their way. They saw the man in the stall, pitching dung- and urine-soaked hay onto a wheelbarrow. His brown wool jacket hung loosely from his sharp shoulder blades, and he wore high rubber boots streaked with dried mud. It had rained during the night and the air smelled of wet earth and animal feed.

Josef looked up as they approached and leaned against his shovel. His face was creased and leathery. He pushed back a dusty cap from his forehead.

"Be direct," Philip warned. "Don't give him time to think."

The man's long, impassive face clouded with confusion at the sound of their English.

"May I speak with you a moment?" Karolina called out in Polish.

"You are from around here?" he asked. His voice was barely a whisper.

"Yes, I grew up near Lubartow off the road to Lublin."

He puzzled over this, then paused to study her. An almost imperceptible flinch passed across his face and he moved back into the shadow of the barn door.

"Zosha Mazurek told me you worked in her hardware store," Karolina said.

"*Tak.*"

"She said you were on Darius Hankowski's farm during the war. I wanted to speak with you about that."

The man's eyes widened in fear.

"I was a little girl then," Karolina said. "Maybe you remember seeing me on the Staszeks' farm. It was the next farm over."

The shovel clattered to the barn floor. Josef staggered back, wild-eyed, and fell to his knees. He gazed at Karolina mutely, his eyes roaming her face. "Holy Mother of God, it's a miracle!" he cried, crossing himself. "Oh, Blessed Virgin, you're alive!"

Karolina had the impulse to rush to his side and help him up, but his face was so full of relief, she stayed where she was.

"All these years I thought you were dead . . . and that it was because of me," Josef wept into his clasped hands.

"Dead? I don't understand . . .?"

The man slowly got to his feet. "I thought the Germans killed you! When I told Darius I saw you playing in the Staszeks' barn with their daughter, he went and told *Pani* Staszek. The Staszeks were afraid I would tell the Germans they were hiding a Jew, that's why they betrayed you . . ."

Philip grabbed her arm. "He's going too fast! What's he saying?"

She shook her head, unable to take her eyes off the man. "He says there were *two* girls . . ."

"The Staszeks betrayed you, not me! I wouldn't have told the Germans, as God is my witness."

Karolina's heart began to hammer.

"Ask the Staszek girl yourself," he shouted and broke into a dry hacking cough.

"The Staszek girl?"

"Yes, their daughter. I saw you playing with her by the barn. She was just a little one, but she'll remember. She must have seen the Germans take you away." He shook his head and spoke to the ground. "It was horrible, horrible!"

"What the hell is he saying?" Philip asked. "He looks crazy."

"He says one of the girls was taken away by the Germans. He thinks . . . I am her."

"How do you know this?" Philip grabbed Josef by the collar and pulled him upright.

The man paled. His weathered face was like parchment. "Who is he? The police?"

"No," Philip said. "A friend. From America."

Josef's face calmed. He clasped his hands again and looked up at the sky. "You survived the camps, didn't you? You went to America after the war like all the Jews, *tak*? It is a miracle from God!"

"Please!" Karolina cried, gripping the man's arm. "What are you saying!"

Josef pulled away, rubbing his sleeve across his glistening forehead and sweat-matted hair. "I saw it. I saw it. I was hammering in a fence post on the south side of the property — we had a bad storm that week. I heard dogs barking — no one kept dogs during the war — there wasn't enough food, so I walked up the hill toward the Staszeks' farm and there was a car with a swastika on it and soldiers were running everywhere. I hid behind a tree to watch." He crossed himself again with a trembling hand. "They dragged you out of the barn, you were screaming, the dogs barked and ripped at your arms, your flesh was hanging . . ." He swallowed hard and wiped his mouth with the back of his hand. "You looked dead — there was blood, much blood . . . more screams. I didn't want to look. I have no love of the *Zhidi*, but to hurt a child . . ." He searched her face. "All these years I thought you were dead because of me . . . You remember none of this? Well, you were so young, so frightened . . ."

Karolina was rooted to the ground. The air had stopped moving.

"Afterwards Darius told me the Staszeks had found the girl in their barn, but I knew he was lying. I saw you in your sailor dress playing with the Staszeks' daughter the day before, so I knew they were hiding you. Darius was afraid I would tell the Germans, so he sent me away to work in *Pani* Zosha's store. He gave her money to take me on. It must have been the money the Staszeks got from the Jew to hide you. I didn't want to take the dirty money, but what could I do? We were all starving." Josef pulled himself up indignantly. "As though I would ever betray a Pole to the Germans!"

When Karolina said nothing, Josef pressed his lips together in anger. "If you don't believe me, go ask the Staszeks' daughter. Karolina, Karolina Staszek. They say she lives in Warsaw. She'll remember. It was her mother who betrayed you to the Germans — not me. I saw her talking to the soldiers when they were taking you away."

In the stillness that descended upon her, Karolina became acutely aware of the soft scratching of chickens circling the dusty yard. From the corner of her eye, a cat darted around the side of the barn and disappeared in a blur of orange and white. Time gathered and folded into itself. She sank onto a milking stool by the side of the barn and watched with curious detachment as color leeched from the world around her. Then a stream of images poured out strong, fast, piercing in their clarity, and she remembered.

Chava stumbles and slides on the mud, but Karolina hangs on to the bigger girl, pushing her toward the barn door, then boosts her up the hayloft ladder, one rung at a time. "Chava," she whispers, "don't be afraid." Suddenly, the cows stir in their stalls. Karolina stops in panic, and waits for them to settle before tapping the Jewish girl to continue. When they reach the top rung, Chava hoists herself onto the loft floor and Karolina scram-

bles after. Together they stand motionless for a moment, panting softly in the sharp morning sunlight that shines through the barn window.

"I'll hide first and you try to find me," Karolina whispers, "Like we did yesterday." She motions toward the rafters. "There are lots of places."

Chava squints into the misty light. She has rings under her eyes and her skin is blue-white, like milk. Yesterday was the first time the Jewish girl had gone outside since she arrived, the day it snowed. Karolina had stood in the doorway of the house and watched her step out of a shiny black car, clinging to a man she called her "Papa." The girl wore a sailor dress and glossy shoes and her knees were clean. Karolina was disappointed. No one could play in those clothes, she thought, for although she was told the girl would stay in the cellar during the day and sleep in the kitchen at night and that her parents would beat her if she spoke to anyone, Karolina had plans. She hadn't seen another child for a long time, not since the Germans came, and she was eager to play. And anyway, Chava was a Jew. She had to do whatever Karolina wanted. You didn't have to be nice to Jews because they killed Jesus. Her mother had told her so.

Karolina feels her impatience grow. "Come on, play!"

Chava kicks up a few straws from the loft floor and shakes her head, no. "You have to," Karolina hisses, trying to sound grown-up. "Or do you want to go back to the cellar?"

Chava lowers herself onto a feed bag and puts her head in her hands. "They'll catch us," she whispers.

She thinks the girl is going to cry and that will make her mad. Chava is six, two years older than she is, too big to cry.

Karolina springs down next to Chava and tickles her under the arms. Her ribs are sharp. Chava pushes her hand away. "No, I want to go back. When my father comes for me, I'll tell him you were bad, how you made me go out."

"I said play!" Karolina commands and tickles her harder. This time Chava rolls onto her side and lets out a loud, raspy laugh that startles them both. They sit up abruptly, their heads poised, and listen. The yard is quiet. Karolina is afraid her mother will hear and punish them, but she is tired of Chava whispering stories about Lublin, about her cousins in Yelna, and her father's store, tired of hearing the girl brag about her toys and a doll house so big you could fit your whole body inside. Since the snow started melting, Karolina has been aching to run in the woods. Yesterday morning, when she saw her father get into the wagon, she tiptoed to the bedroom to listen for the rhythmic breathing that meant her mother was still asleep. Today, after he left and her mother slept, Karolina was ready. She'd sneak Chava out to the barn again. They'd play.

Karolina had tried before to play with the girl. When Chava first arrived, Karolina's mother let her bring food to the cellar. Karolina hid one of her cloth dolls under her apron and tried to mime a game with the girl, but Chava only wolfed down the cold potatoes and retreated to a corner where she curled up in her quilt and, shivering, whispered stories about aunts and uncles. She had wanted to stay with them, Chava told her, in Lublin, all of the family hiding together, but her father said she had to go to the country to be safe. Karolina grew bored and shoved the doll at Chava. Suddenly, her mother was towering over them. She crossed herself quickly and dragged Karolina back to her own room on the other side of the kitchen. All that night Karolina lay awake listening to Chava's muffled cries, plotting how, as soon as the snow melted, she'd take the girl to the clearing in the woods and they'd collect stones to build a secret house where Chava would live and she could visit her every day. That's what her mother wanted anyway, for Chava to go, before someone found out and the Germans came to shoot them all. Chava would be safe in her stone house and her family could keep the money Chava's father had given them. Everyone would be safe. And her parents wouldn't fight about Chava ever again.

Now, Karolina rolls over in the hay and tickles Chava again, not so hard this time. Chava smiles and covers her mouth to stifle a giggle. "Close your eyes and count to ten," Karolina whispers, "then try to find me."

Chava does as she is told and begins to count. Jeden, dwa, trzy. Karolina scrambles up the bales of hay along the barn wall, then grabs the rope that hangs from the rafters. Cztery, pięć, sześć, siedem. She lifts herself onto a small platform her father built high up on the beams to hold nesting boxes for pigeons, and steps behind the partition that screens them. Then she slips into one and crouches. The box is full of pigeon droppings and damp hay and smells bad, but it's too late to look for another place to hide. "Osiem, dziewięć, dziesięć," Chava counts below. Karolina presses her nose against the space between the wooden slats and sees Chava open her eyes, turn around several times, and scan the barn.

Outside, a car screeches to a halt. Chava freezes. Doors slam. Heavy boots crunch on the gravel around the house. Men shout. Karolina hears *her mother cry out, "She was in the cellar!" A man yells something Karolina doesn't understand. "A Jew, of course," her mother shouts back. "That's what I told you. We found the Zhid hiding in the woods."*

Dogs yelp. Karolina hears them scamper across the yard toward the barn.

Chava searches the roof beams. Her eyes fix on the rope tucked behind the partition and she waves frantically. "Help me," she whispers.

Karolina is too frightened to get out of the box. She runs her eyes over the rafters for another space that Chava might fit into.

"Help me," Chava moans.

Karolina squeezes her eyes shut, afraid to move, afraid to breathe, feeling her heart pound. The dogs scramble into the barn and then the room explodes with shouts and barks. Men yell. Chava screams, then screams and shrieks over and over until there is a thud and only the sound of dogs panting and whimpering, and boots scraping, growing fainter and fainter as they move from the barn into the yard and finally fade away with the noise of the car.

Karolina lies in the damp box a long time, her eyes sealed, her body trembling, breathing in the sour smell of old pigeon mess and her own hot sweat, ignoring her mother's shouts. Later, when the sunlight streams in through the west window, Karolina lifts herself out of the nesting box and crawls down the bales onto the loft floor. She feels weak and sick and sits down. Patches of straw mixed with dried blood lie scattered across the planks and trail toward the ramp. She stands up quickly, scrambles down the ladder and runs out the door, runs through the muddy puddles and patches of dead grass, through the muck that surrounds the barn, across the endless yard to her house where her mother stands in the doorway, shouting "Karolina, Karolina," crying her name into the cold afternoon light.

Someone was forcing a glass to her mouth. Its hard, cold rim felt good against her lips. She was aware of a strong hand at the back of her neck.

"Drink."

English. Philip. His hand was cradling her head. He tipped the glass to help her sip and vodka seared her tongue and the inside of her mouth. Hands lifted her. There was the scraping sound of the stool falling over.

Pani Kozlowski's face loomed before her. Flecks of green floated in her worried hazel eyes. "*Pani, Pani . . .*" the woman cooed, patting her shoulder.

Philip helped her to her feet. Holding her firmly, he steered her to the car. Just before she lowered herself onto the seat, she turned back toward the barn. Josef stood at the door, holding his shovel upright like a sentry, and when he caught her gaze, their eyes locked for a moment before he retreated into the darkened stall.

Chapter 31

Philip watched Karolina as she slept. Only a glimpse of her cheek and the curled fist that clutched the corner of the quilt were visible. Before she'd fallen asleep she'd been frightening, whispering to him in Polish he couldn't understand. He wondered now if she were really asleep or in some suspended state, wondered if he should call a doctor or Marek, the bookstore owner, someone to help him. He touched Karolina's forehead. Her hair was damp, but at least her breathing had become regular, instead of the hiccupping sobs that choked her on the ride back to the hotel.

When the afternoon light cast long shadows across the hotel room's wooden floor, Karolina stirred. She rolled onto her back and opened her eyes. She didn't seem surprised to see him sitting beside her. He lifted her hand. It looked frail, almost translucent, nestled in his own.

"She has dark hair," Karolina began. Her voice was hoarse, but steady. "She cries often. I remember thinking, she should be ashamed to cry. I never did and I was smaller."

Philip tensed, afraid her sobbing would start again, but she continued in a monotone.

"It is snowing the day she arrives. She comes in a black car." Karolina shivered violently. "Oh, God!" she wailed. "It is my fault! I killed her!"

"No —"

"My parents betrayed her because of me. She would live now if not for me."

He wanted to tell her that none of this mattered because he

loved her, no matter who she was or what she'd done. But she was somewhere else.

"You knew about me from the beginning, that I cannot be Chava."

"Stop it!"

"It was as Basia said: Father Demetrius was good man. He must have wanted my parents to repent, to tell Jake what happened to Chava. I understand this now. This is why Father comes so often to our house after the war when we finally return from Koromov. This is why my mother is frightened when he comes . . ."

She caught her breath.

". . . Jake gave my parents money to hide his child. They would not hide a Jew otherwise. After Josef saw Chava and me together, they give Jake's money to Darius to pay Zosha. She hires him and he is sent away from farm. My parents betrayed Chava because I make her play outside, because Josef sees her and they are afraid he is telling Germans." Her English seemed to disintegrate with each wave of shame.

"Before, I want to know," she moaned. "Now — oh, my God!" She rolled her head back and forth. "Now I know who I am. A murderer."

Car lights moved across the darkened ceiling like search beams, then slid down the walls. The street outside was quiet. He could feel the pulse in her wrist beating against his palm.

"I was sick after. My mother spent much time by my bed. There were candles and soup bowls. I ask about Chava and she says . . . said the girl is gone. The Germans took her because she disobeyed her parents, my mother says, so I must obey mine. My father was angry at her for speaking so. I see how he pulls her to come away. There is a fear in my mother's face that is new and I want to protect her. She sits with me, I think, for days and tells me never to speak of the girl again or soldiers will come back and dogs will chew me up and take me to a place where even Jesus cannot find me."

Her words shocked him, even as he became aware of her pain. "How long was Chava on the farm before she was taken away?"

"I do not know . . ."

"Think! How long?"

"It doesn't matter."

"It does. If she was there for a while, it means your parents meant to keep her and only gave her up because they were in danger."

"Is it then easier to forgive them?"

He took her hand. "You can't blame them," he said and heard the lie in his voice. "If they'd kept Chava after they knew Josef had seen her, there would have been an even greater risk . . . they'd be risking their lives and yours." As he spoke, he pictured Alice's eyes, huge with terror as a drooling muzzle of razor-sharp teeth sank into her flesh. Philip pinched the bridge of his nose hard to erase the image. It wouldn't have been hard for Karolina's parents to give up a *Zhid* to save their own child, and even though he feared he would have done the same, he blamed them for what he knew they'd do again if they had the chance, give up his Alice, who, in this forsaken country would always be a *Zhid*.

A storm broke in the night. She stirred, then slipped out of bed and noiselessly crossed to the window. It was snowing heavily. Philip thought of that first night in her apartment when she stood looking out at the snow and spoke to him of her past. He'd barely known her then, but her willowy silhouette against the street light had stirred him. Now, she pressed her forehead against the glass as if without it, she was afraid she'd fall.

"I will see her all my life," Karolina said. "I can smell the dampness from blanket she wraps around her in cellar — it was an old one my mother used to wash floor. I will hear her child's voice telling me stories of her family, of Lublin." She turned to him, her face a pale oval floating in the dim room. "And I ache for the life I helped to end. How can I face your family — her family?"

"It wasn't your fault."

"I was stubborn. I was told not to go near her. I did not listen."

Philip scrambled for reasons, for something to say that might sway her and knew it was hopeless. The verdict was in. What they'd discovered yesterday was as damning to her as a death sentence.

"But you were just a child. . . ."

She shook her head slowly. "Even if I was a child, I am responsible. We are all victims of chance, no? And we live with the consequences."

They were stretched out on the bed, side by side. Birds chirped in the courtyard. Her breathing was slow and regular, but he knew she was awake.

"All my life I have lived with feeling that in one moment everything could change. Every day I wait for something terrible to happen as though I had done something wrong, but no one came to punish me." She burrowed her face against his chest. "But you will punish me. When you want to hurt me you will say cruel words and later apologize, but there will always be uneasiness between us. You know my words are true. You are a lawyer. You know what people are and what they can do. . . ."

He didn't want to punish her; he didn't want to punish anyone. All he wanted at this moment was to make her pain disappear.

"When I thought I was Jew, I feared that God will no longer hear my prayers, that he will abandon me. Then I thought, no, as long as I do not doubt Him in my heart, he will still love me. I am not Chava, but she has given me Jew's eyes. I am seeing what cruelty was done by my people who say they love Christ so dearly. I fear it is I who will abandon him. And now . . . I am truly alone."

Exhausted, helpless to comfort her, he let her weep.

Sunlight flooded the room. Philip closed the shutters, then slipped out. He would shower and change before returning to her. She would find him at her side when she awoke.

An hour later, as he approached her room, he was stopped by the sight of Karolina's suitcase in the hallway. The door had been left ajar. She was sitting in the armchair, gazing out at the courtyard. The corners of her mouth were ashen. She'd run a wet comb through her hair, but had not pinned it up and it fell in damp strands around her shoulders. Her raincoat and yellow scarf lay next to the neatly folded bedding.

"You'll come back with me."

She shook her head.

Philip fell heavily against the wall opposite her. "Why do you want to stay in this place?"

"I went to America because I think it will free me from past. I am wrong."

He slammed his hand down on the dresser, knocking over a glass ashtray. Three days worth of cigarette butts and ashes tumbled onto the carpet and scattered at her feet. "Come with me!"

"Oh, Philip, you are brave man. You are strong in yourself, but I will always be *shiksa, that Polish woman*. I will always see hatred in your family's eyes when they see me, the Pole who helped to kill . . ." She paused to search his face.

"I don't care about that —"

"Of course you do! You cannot hide these feelings."

"None of this matters anymore . . ."

She stopped him with a smile that broke his heart. "There has always been something between us from the beginning, yes? This thing is strong because there is so much anger in both of us. But when I look at you, it is more than you I see. There is a line of your people behind you and they are all pushing to front so I will see them. And they are all angry. No matter how much you love me, you do not come to me alone."

He shook his head, trying not to hear. "Do you love me?"

Karolina turned away and gazed past the window. "I *do* love you," she murmured, "but here I must stay."

The airport official thumbed through Philip's passport, then opened a file on his desk. "Your stay in Poland went well?" he asked in unhurried Polish. He had a tired face and watery blue eyes.

"*Tak*," Philip said.

"Lubartow does not get many visitors."

So they knew his every move. And Karolina's as well. A flutter of fear passed through Philip. Still, he said nothing, reasoning that he'd not been asked a question.

"But of course Lubartow has churches of historic interest, *Pan . . .*" The man checked the file ". . . Landau."

Next, he'd be asked about the blinis at the Hotel Victoria, Philip thought. He felt his anger mounting, but he held back. They could easily detain him on some technicality, if he wasn't careful. And who knew what trouble they would make for Karolina.

"The church was of interest to my companion," Philip said,

careful to enunciate every word. "She was born near Lubartow. But I think you know this."

The official smirked and returned to his papers. "I see she has chosen to remain here. I suppose America did not agree with her."

"Why should it when she can live in this . . . wonderful country?"

The man fixed him with a malevolent stare, then slid Philip's passport across the desk and nodded curtly toward the boarding area where a small crowd had gathered. Philip pocketed his passport and joined them, relieved to be dismissed before he got into real trouble.

A few moments later, the metal gate swung open. Beyond, the runway lights glowed under the falling dusk and, in the distance, he could make out the cement block apartment houses surrounding the airport. What a hellhole this place was, he thought, fighting the urge to rush back to Karolina, wanting all the while to go home, to go to America, divining with bitter resignation that he was leaving Poland like his father and uncles before him, like all Jews seemed destined to do.

Chapter 32

The bells of St. Agnus chimed. Karolina glanced up from her statue, a piece of sandpaper poised in her hand. She'd stopped going to church several months earlier and would never go again; still, whenever she heard the bells resound in the square she had a vague sense that she'd forgotten something important. The clock over the sink read 1:00 P.M. She'd been up since the first light filled the curtainless studio.

A door slammed downstairs. Marek was back from the market. After unpacking the groceries, he'd carefully arrange sliced radishes and scallions around a mound of the dry farmer cheese she liked. The weather was fine today, so he'd probably walked to the square for grainy black bread instead of buying one of the tasteless loaves from the state-run store down the street. He would have stopped at various kiosks along the way to pick up late-edition newspapers or foreign magazines, if any were to be had. Marek was passionate for the news these days and had developed the habit of calling out the latest events before she sat down with him for the mid-day meal. "Martin Luther King has been assassinated," he had bellowed at the beginning of April as she came down the stairs. A week later, when anti-censorship marches erupted in Warsaw, Lublin and Wroclaw, he had yelled reports up to her studio like a news dispatcher on a deadline. She'd stopped what she was doing to huddle around the radio with him, waiting to hear how far the Soviets could be pushed. The demonstrations had dwindled after a few days, the student leaders jailed; two months had passed and negotiations were still taking place between protest leaders and Gomulka, who threatened to send in Soviet troops to keep down the riots. In early May, when Parisian students tore up their streets, Marek whooped out the news with delight. "See," he had bragged, his plump, moon-shaped face flushed with pride, "Even the French are imitating us." With Czechoslovakia in turmoil and the Russians at the door, it seemed to Karolina that Europe was crying out to be remade; yet each day she returned to her studio, shut the door and let the tumult fall away. Part of her thrilled at the astonishing turns of events, but she was not a rebel. Ironically, for the first time in her life she felt something resembling calm, while the world, it seemed, was exploding.

In the six months she'd been living in the studio above Marek's shop, Karolina had seen no one but him. She sensed that letting people into her daily life would disturb the fragile equilibrium that allowed her to move through her day. The labor of her hands absorbed her completely; when she wasn't working, she slipped into emotional blankness.

She wiped her gritty chin with the back of her hand and gazed at the sculptures lined up against the wall. She'd completed two nudes: one, a statue of a woman walking, the other, a woman sprawled full-length on the ground. She'd placed the pieces near the window so she could see them first thing in the morning, lit by the dappled sunlight that filtered through the leafy branches of the linden tree in the courtyard behind the shop. The unfinished piece she was working on, a third nude lying on her stomach, her legs extended behind her and her arms stretched over her head as if she were flying, would be the last of the grouping. She had a natural affinity for threes, she'd discovered. They made for a pleasing balance, asymmetrical, yet harmonious; simple, yet not stark. An idea brought to completion.

Her statues were still realistic, but sculpted with a new technique. Intrigued by the problem of how to create the impression of movement around a figure, of a body displacing space, she had tried to reduce the nudes to geometric essentials with a simple violin-like contour, like the Greek Cycladic figures she'd always admired.

She stood back to inspect her third woman. Something was still wrong. Perhaps the proportions. She cocked her head. No, it was the slant of the feet. They looked planted, static, simply *there* without a sense of motion. Just a few more days, though, and she felt confident she'd find a way to give life to the legs, to make them move. Then she'd need to make a trip to the quarry for more alabaster and soapstone. With the money Philip had sent her she could afford marble, but she could tell from the feel of the chisel in her hand that she hadn't regained full control of her tools, and it seemed a shame to waste good stone. Five thousand dollars was a lot of money, enough to live on for several years; still, she hadn't lost the old habit of economy.

Philip's check had come at the end of March, almost two months after he returned to New York. He'd written a short letter, urging her to apply for a visa to Paris or even England now that she knew the language. Life was so much better in these countries, he said, and she'd have more opportunities for different kinds of work, in Paris art galleries, for instance, or language schools in London. He'd never forget the lines of people waiting for food in Poland, he wrote, and with the political upheavals taking place in her country, conditions would only get worse. There was no mention of the check.

She'd been stunned by the money. Was he trying to lure her back to New York? Money had been a barrier between them; perhaps he wanted it to become a bond. She'd put the check in a drawer and waited.

A few weeks passed and another letter arrived. If she cared for him at all, Philip wrote this time, she'd accept the money to ease his mind. It was then she began to see his generosity as a gesture of for-giveness. She didn't know why the word came to mind, but it felt right. Still, she wondered: Forgive whom? Her country, her parents, herself? She didn't know, she couldn't begin to guess. What she did know was that she could never forgive herself, and that the emotional detachment she was struggling to maintain was a temporary reprieve that would one day give way to a lifetime of remorse.

And so she wrote to thank him. His kindness was much appre-ciated. She could give dear Marek something for food and lodgings; she could allow herself time simply to be. In this first letter, she was careful to be honest. She told him that she was sculpting again, find-ing her way back to what she loved about her work. She explained that Poland was where she belonged. She had no desire to leave.

247

Afterwards, she felt the need to keep in touch. Although she worried that her letters might give him false hope, she reminded herself that Philip was a perceptive man. He would understand that she was inextricably bound to him and his family. What she didn't write was how often she thought of him, how each time she pictured his fierce eyes on her or the way he cradled her hand in his, trying to comfort her, she felt a stab of longing for the life they might have made together. They'd shared only one dizzying, tragic week together, but she didn't doubt the truth of her feelings, and whenever she caught herself thinking about returning to New York, she'd climb the stairs to her studio and take up her chisel.

Karolina covered the unfinished woman with a drop cloth and brushed the dust from her smock. Suddenly her hands were trembling. Last night's thunderstorm had awakened her from another bad dream, a jumble of dogs and birds and running children. Somehow, she knew these nightmares would never stop unless she faced the farm again. She'd put off the trip for months, waiting for a courage that never came, but this morning, in a fit of irritation at her cowardice, she'd decided to borrow Marek's car. Now though, as she turned onto the familiar dirt road that led to the Staszek farm, her hands on the steering wheel were trembling again.

At the farm, Karolina went immediately to the barn. She stared at the bales of rotting hay piled high, like steps, against the wall leading to the hayloft. There were no nesting boxes, her father having given up keeping pigeons years before. She gazed at the mildew-mottled walls. Shutting her eyes, she sees Chava run across the barn, playing hide and seek. She sees Chava halt suddenly, alert and frightened, paling in the thin morning light, and herself, paralyzed with fear, crouching inside the box. She hears Chava scream and feels the barn shudder with terror. The scene repeats itself over and over, a relentless succession of images racing, unbidden, through her mind, until this vision blurs and she finds herself standing alone again on the decayed, pitted planks of the deserted barn.

Chava's short life had ended in this room, wiped out by fear and hate. Was there no place to honor the child who had once been cherished and dearly loved? Did it not deserve commemoration? A life has meaning as long as others hold its memory within them. Karolina had helped extinguish that life, then betrayed it by forgetting.

She hurried outside and scanned the yard. A large boulder in what had been her mother's vegetable garden caught her eye. Crouching down, she lay her hands upon the rock to let the heat from the spring sun warm her palms. The stone, a perfect size. She looked around. The garden, a perfect place.

She drew out the small chisel she habitually carried in her coat pocket and crouching down, began to cut into the boulder. Using the weight of her body, she pressed against the tool and chipped deeper and deeper into the rock. She wanted more than a superficial scratching that would erode after a few rainstorms and fade in the sun. She wanted depth, breadth, permanence. She chiseled harder, gouging the surface over and over again, working quickly without stopping until she was finished. *Chava Landau, born 1936, killed by the Germans in this place in 1942.*

Karolina paused to run her coat cuff across her moist brow, then made one final effort: a Star of David, its points sharply extended in six directions above the inscription.

She sat back on her heels, spent, and appraised her work. The stone lay half-buried in the eastern end of the garden. Morning light would fall on the marker before the sun circled the sky and dipped behind the great elms that stood on what had been the Hankowskis' farm. The future will bring me here again, she thought. Even years from now, the writing will be sharp and clear and legible, as will my memory, as will my guilt.

She searched the horizon for the row of oaks that formed a sharp, clear boundary between the abandoned fields and the forest. They stood starkly outlined against the steel gray sky. In the distance a horse-drawn cart moved down the road. The face of the farmer came into focus and Karolina wondered if he were the same man she'd seen when she was last here with Philip. As he neared, the farmer gazed at her solemnly, then adjusted his *kapelusz*, snapped his reins, and lurching forward in his seat, continued toward Lubartow where clouds were collecting on the eastern horizon.

Chapter 33

Philip twisted around in his office chair and fussed impatiently with the air conditioner dial that continued to spew out a stream of tepid air. He would have gladly paid for a replacement, but the wiring throughout the suite of offices Drottman had rented since the early 1950s was too ancient to accommodate the newer models. Philip was sure one more BTU would blow the place sky high. Outside, it was one more afternoon in a long string of sweltering days that had enveloped the city. It was almost 4:00 P.M. and the temperature and humidity were soaring again.

"So, should I ask Chuck White or Ed Rosen to handle discovery in the Metropolitan case?" Simon asked, unbuttoning his collar and pulling his tie loose. In the six months since their friendship had ended, he stopped in every few weeks to consult with Philip and more often than that if he needed advice about a case, like the medical malpractice suit against Metropolitan Hospital he'd recently taken on.

"Let Ed do discovery. If you go to trial, Chuck will be great in front of a jury."

"Yeah . . . well . . ." Simon said dismissively. No one expected this high-risk medical malpractice suit ever to get to trial. Simon was after a hefty out-of-court settlement that required serious preliminary work before the hospital would even talk to him about damages.

Philip ran his eyes over his own work piled up on his desk like so much coffee-stained, carbon-smudged flotsam. He should have hustled Simon out an hour earlier, but shooting the breeze with his old partner cheered him — as much as anything could these days.

"Any news on the Groveside Hotel since the Justice Department took over the case?" Simon asked.

"The court slapped them with contempt. They've been ordered to file every three months to prove they're in compliance." He gave Simon a wide, sardonic grin. "I hear Negroes and Jews get the royal treatment now."

"What about damages?

"We're getting attorney fees. It doesn't come to much."

Making a living in civil rights law was almost an impossibility and Philip wasn't surprised when he learned that the four other lawyers in Drottman's firm were independently wealthy. Helping the poor and persecuted turned out to be a rich man's profession. Thanks to Jake's money, Philip was now in the same category, at least for a while.

"So, what's coming up?" Simon asked.

"A case against a Lithuanian living in Queens, a guy named Chechnik. Turns out he was a guard at Bergen-Belsen. Someone recognized him."

"Whoa! The press will be all over that one."

"Let's hope so. Our guy's just the tip of the iceberg. Abe told me the Special Prosecutor's office and the Anti-Defamation League are sifting through archives looking for documents to nail war criminals. My friend Weinstein at the Joint must be in heaven with all the new business."

The door clicked open and Drottman's secretary walked in carrying a bundle of mail. Her slip hung out from beneath the hem of her linen skirt and there were carbon paper stains on the sleeve of her blouse. She plopped down a stack of envelopes and magazines on Philip's desk and, without a glance at either at them, left. She was far from warm and cuddly, but Philip had learned not to take it personally. In the five months he'd been here, she treated him with the same gruff indifference she bestowed on the other lawyers in the office, all of whom had been with Abe for over a decade.

Philip spotted the tip of a blue airmail envelope peeking out from under a copy of *Newsweek*. He discreetly slipped it into his jacket pocket.

"Oops," Simon said, beginning to rise. "I see it's time for me to go."

"No, it's okay."

"That's what you always say when you get one of those letters and okay is what you never are. In fact, you haven't been *okay* since you got back from Poland."

"I don't want to talk about it."

"That's the problem."

"Don't start psychologizing."

"I won't."

"But you're going to give me a lecture anyway, right?"

"You've got to make an end of it one way or another."

Philip gave him an exasperated shake of the head.

"What's it been now? Six months?" Simon's eyes tightened at the corners. "Call her."

Philip pretended to sort through the rest of the mail. "You're going to wear out your welcome if you keep this up."

Simon raised his hand. "Okay, okay." He headed for the door, then turned back for a moment. "Call me if you have any thoughts on the Metropolitan case . . . or if you just feel like talking," he said and left.

Philip pulled out the blue envelope and stared at the squat European handwriting with a sinking feeling. It was perverse of him to keep reading Karolina's letters, knowing all he'd get was a current-events roundup, sprinkled with side bars about her sculptures as though she felt obliged to tell him how much good work his money was supporting.

He tore open the envelope, letting the onion-skin pages flutter onto his desk and skimmed the letter. It was like all the others. He sat for a moment with his face in his hands, hating himself for the power she had over him. For days after receiving a letter, he'd feel raw and edgy. When he'd returned from Poland, he'd felt miserable about deceiving Ellen, and back in February, after they'd spent a hellish weekend arguing over his foul moods, he told her what had happened. She had sat stiffly on his living room chair while he blubbered his lame apologies, saying he was sorry for being such a bastard, but he didn't think their relationship would work out and in all fairness to her, they should end it. She had stomped out of the apartment, leaving him feeling wretched that he'd hurt her. Later that night, she returned, and without saying a word, pulled her clothes from his closet, swept her toiletries into her bag and left. There were times when he missed her, but he'd squelched the urge to make contact with half a tumbler of Jack Daniel's. The week before, when he heard she was dating an ACLU lawyer from Virginia, he'd smarted with jealousy, but listened to his better self and didn't call.

Once his family recovered from its collective shock over what had happened to Chava Landau, Philip and Noah's parents had launched into a litany of "I told you so," then added Karolina's story to their pile of Holocaust horror tales. He'd made a feeble attempt to defend her, pointing out her age at the time of Chava's death and her own personal suffering, but Meyer's combination of fury and loathing had silenced him, and now whenever his parents brought up the Polish woman, he segued to another topic. Noah had sounded stunned on the phone, saying he was sorry for everyone in this awful affair, but mostly for Amanda who'd miss Karolina terribly. Only Rosalind had expressed sympathy for the woman. "What a nightmare to live with," she'd said. Her comment had moved Philip deeply, and on his ride back to Manhattan he'd been tormented with images of Karolina stretched out on the bed next to him, her face tear-swollen and inconsolable.

Simon was right. He needed to stop dragging himself through the day as if he weighed a thousand pounds. Even Alice sensed his misery. She spent her weekends with him and most of the time he wasn't aware how gloomy he came across until he'd find her staring at him with watchful, worried eyes. The Sunday before, on their way to Rumpelmayer's for an ice cream sundae, she took his hand and asked him why he was sad. He was so remorseful at his moodiness that he picked her up in the middle of Fifth Avenue and hugged her like a crazy man.

Philip had been miserable long enough. He had to call Karolina. The sound of her voice would tell him whether he stood any chance of ever seeing her again. During their week together he'd learned to read the shifts in her tone, the small changes in her cadence that signaled whether she was holding something back or telling him what she truly felt. A half year was long enough for her to start healing, to start thinking about a future that included him.

Maybe he could persuade her to come for a visit. Maybe she was ready to be persuaded.

He glanced at the clock: It was almost four o'clock. The six-hour difference would make it 10:00 P.M. in Warsaw. He grabbed the phone and gave the long distance operator the number of Marek's store printed on the top of Karolina's letter.

He heard a click and his heart sped up. "Hello?"

There was a pause. "It is Philip?" Karolina asked. She sounded tentative.

"Yes —"

"Good! I wish to thank you —"

"Don't. You already have, many times."

"If I cannot thank you, I will not enjoy freedom you give me because I cannot give anything back, only thanks." Her tone was eager now, yet formal, as though she'd been waiting for the opportunity to make an official statement.

"Tell me how you are."

"I work much . . . because of you. I finish my statues. They please me. Who knows? If they please others, maybe I will show."

He twisted the telephone cord tightly. "The papers say there's going to be trouble in your part of the world," he said, trying to sound informative, like a good friend doling out advice.

"We have big trouble, but *good* trouble."

Only a half year had gone by and her English was already falling apart. "When tanks start rolling down your street you might not feel that way. You should try to renew your visa."

"No, I wish to stay. Something good comes from this, yes. In your country there is also much . . . confusing."

He pictured her hands cutting the air as she searched for words and felt profoundly depressed. She was lost to him. Now everything was in the present for her, like the only tense in her English.

"How is family?" she asked.

"Fine. That's one of the reasons I called," he lied. "Linda wants a picture of you for Amanda." A picture. That's all he needed!

"Oh, how I miss my Amanda. I ask Marek to take photographie. Tell Linda I will send." Her voice was drowning in a swishing noise. She must have heard it because her tone turned urgent.

"Philip!"

"Yes."

"You forgive me, yes?"

"For what?"

"The pain I give to your family . . . to you."

His face felt flushed and tight. "Don't —"

The line was breaking up. He pressed the phone against his ear, listening to the hollowness on the other end, waiting for a signal, a sound, something to mark the end of the connection. Still clutching the receiver, he gazed at the pages of her letter scattered across his desk. Karolina had written what she always wrote, what she'd always want him to read: she was where she wanted to be, where she belonged.

The line went dead. He stood up heavily, walked to the window and pulled up the blinds. The sun had come out and burned off the haze that had hovered over the city. In the distance, he made out a silvery wedge of the East River. As he turned to get a better view, a sharp ray of light shot from between the two buildings across the street. Philip shut his eyes against the glare and an all-but-vanished memory took shape. He was playing the last baseball game of the season with his Little League team, the Bensonhurst Saxons. Meyer had brought Jake along and both men sat in the bleachers with the other parents.

It had happened during the last inning. The bases were full and the pitcher threw a fastball that Philip hit over the fence, his one and only home run of the season. The game and the championship were theirs. As he rounded home plate, Jake burst from the stands and ran onto the field, scooped him up in his arms and sat him on his shoulders. Philip, a skinny, knob-kneed eleven-year-old, hated being treated like a baby. He squirmed to be let down, but Jake held on, marching past boisterous groups of parents and kids, yelling in Yiddish for Meyer to come down from the stands to join them. Philip hadn't asked Jake to come to the game and now this new uncle was humiliating him with his strange accent and ugly, foreign clothes. He tried to yank free, but Jake held on. "A hero, a Jewish hero," he sang out with jubilation. Philip was furious. He turned in the direction of the setting sun and a spoke of light hit him in the face, making him squeeze his eyes shut in pain. When he looked again, the field seemed to spread out before him like an endless expanse of soft, red earth. "You should be proud, *tataleh,* proud," Jake shouted, his voice carried by the strong afternoon wind. Beneath him, his uncle's shoulders suddenly felt sturdy, and the view from this height made Philip feel tall and strong. He surveyed the ecstatic crowd, then lifted his clenched fists high and let himself be carried triumphantly across the dusty field to where his beaming father waited.

Now, Philip gazed out at the brightening sky. There was a break in the clouds moving across the river from Queens, and the surrounding office buildings had turned a rich copper color under the sun's rays. He opened the window. After a stifling day, a much-wanted breeze was blowing in fresh air from the river.

He spun around to face his desk and pulled out the Chechnik file from beneath the stack of mail Drottman's secretary had unceremoniously dumped there. A survivor of the Bergen-Belsen camp had spotted Anatole Chechnik in an A&P on Steinway Avenue, and after following him to his apartment, called someone at the Anti-Defamation League who got in touch with Abe. Now, other witnesses would have to be found.

Philip tossed the used coffee cups into the trash bin and began clearing his desk. He paused to buzz Abe's secretary.

"Let me know as soon as Abe comes in. I want to talk to him."

"It's almost five o'clock," she said, her voice pitched in alarm.

"That's okay."

"But he's not expected back for at least another hour —"

"I'll be here. Tell him we need to get started on the Chechnik case."

"Tonight?"

He stacked papers along the window ledge, then opened the Chechnik file and scanned the first page, then the next, in a hurry now, stopping only to take note of names and dates, already checking for incongruities and inconsistencies.

"Yes," he said. "Tonight. We've got a lot of work to do if we're going to get that bastard."